THE NIGHT OF RECKONING

THE THIRD GOMER WARS

MICHAEL S. PAULEY

Copyright © 2021 by Michael S. Pauley

Paperback: 978-1-63767-253-2
Hardcover: 978-1-63767-254-9
eBook: 978-1-63767-252-5

All rights reserved. No part of this publication may be reproduced, distributed, or transmitted in any form or by any electronic or mechanical means, without the prior written permission of the publisher, except in the case of brief quotations embodied in critical reviews and certain other noncommercial uses permitted by copyright law.

This is a work of fiction.

Ordering Information:

BookTrail Agency
8838 Sleepy Hollow Rd.
Kansas City, MO 64114

Printed in the United States of America

Dedication

This book would not be possible without the loving support I have received from two people. Therefore, without any further ado, this book is dedicated to both my daughter, Jennifer Pauley LaSovage, who kept the wolves away from my door at work, and my beautiful bride, Elise Bourne Pauley, who is my teacher, lover, and best friend.

Michael S. Pauley

Table of Contents

❧❦❧

Author's Forward vii

SECTION 1: THE TREACHERY BEGINS

Chapter I 3
Chapter II 17
Chapter III 32
Chapter IV 46

SECTION 2: TIMES UP! THEY'RE HERE - AGAIN!

Chapter V 67
Chapter VI 86
Chapter VII 101
Chapter VIII 116

SECTION 3: ON THE RUN! THE TREACHERY IS NOW PERSONAL!

Chapter IX 133
Chapter X 149
Chapter XI 164
Chapter XII 180
Chapter XIII 195
Chapter XIV 211

SECTION 4: THE INITIATIVE SHIFTS - FINALLY

Chapter XV 229
Chapter XVI 244
Chapter XVII 258
Chapter XVIII 273
Chapter XIX 289
Chapter XX 305

APPENDICES

Appendix I: Order of Battle 319
Appendix II: Key Personnel 332

Author's Forward

It seems appropriate to note what this book is about, and what it isn't about. First off, this is a fictional "personal" history of the Third Gomer War. It is written from the perspective of the main character, General of the Army, Michael Patrick, and it follows certain military guidelines in the telling. For example, titles are capitalized, which is standard military language. Even in the most boring Army Field Manual, any reference to rank is going to be capitalized. Otherwise, there is confusion between "in general" and "the General." Another point to consider is purely historical in nature. When General George S. Patton, Jr. wrote his memoirs, (albeit through a shadow writer), it was often using the first person. This wasn't unusual, since this was also done by Admiral William Frederick "Bill" Halsey, Admiral Chester Nimitz, and others when they told of their personal experiences in World War II.

Secondly, there will be mention of technical and logistical considerations. As I've said before in my previous books in this series, there can be no victory without the beans and bullets to make it possible. This means that if you hit an "information dump," then feel free to skip ahead a little. One man's "information dump" is another man's point of "how can this happen" or "how can this be done." As before, the Appendices are offered in a manner consistent with Samuel Eliot Morrison's accounts of the United States Navy in

World War II. Similarly, you may find capitalization as a means of emphasis. This is because FLASH MESSAGES are always written in all capital letters. While stylistic and wholly incorrect in the eyes of English professors the world over, they have specific meaning in the military. After all, the perfect sentence isn't an issue, when survival and fighting the enemy is the issue. As a result, when an order is written or provided to a subordinate, then a capital letter will signify that this is a priority part of the message that should NOT be overlooked.

Finally, the science and engineering considerations contained in this book, just as in the others in the series, are based on actual science and or engineering concepts. As always, my lovely bride is my science and math teacher, but the teacher can only go so far. The adage about teaching the pig to sing is probably applicable here, but in this case, I've done my best in absorbing the concepts. If my absorption is correct, thank my bride, if not, then blame me for not getting it. I hope everyone enjoys this third book. As of the date of my writing this, I can honestly state unequivocally that there is a FOURTH one in the works. [Emphasis added to annoy my Editor!]

March 4, 2021   Michael S. Pauley
                                 Lexington, South Carolina

SECTION 1

THE TREACHERY BEGINS

Chapter I

❧❦❧

Baffin Island, Nunavut Territory, Canada:

The small tramp freighter lumbered her way by Baffin Island at a speed that demonstrated the age and character of the craft. Old, rusty, and noted for rather unscrupulous cargo runs in the past, the *M/V Artamus* slowed to a crawl just off the coast in the darkness. Unseen, except by the small Gomer Fighter Class ship that approached, the Captain of the *Artamus* was taking advantage of proximity to pick up just one more of the many illicit cargo shipments of his career. It had all been arranged by an old friend of his, who was paying him handsomely to transport this 'shipment' from the pickup location to Murmansk, Russia. The Gomer began to hover over the deck, and his hand-picked crew of ruffians began the process of having the cargo passed from the Gomer Fighter ship to the *Artamus*. The crates were heavy, and because they were being manhandled by his limited crew, the Captain was highly concerned that dawn would approach before they would be able to complete the loading.

They sky was turning the deep blue associated with the coming dawn when the Fighter Class ship shot straight up and away from the *Artamus*. Hoping that nobody had spotted the loading process, the *M/V Artamus* continued her extremely slow journey towards northern Russia. The Captain had no idea of the character of the cargo, nor did he care. This was about the profit, not the ideology. So long as he was well paid, he'd decided years ago to leave that political silliness to others. Taking up his new heading, the ship continued her snail-like pace to keep prying eyes from paying too much attention to her movements. He'd also learned years ago as a young smuggler of weapons in the Black Sea, that speed was for suckers, since it was speed that got you noticed. This way there were no questions, no concerns, and no attention. Still, those Gomer things were creepy, and the entire time they were loading the 'whatever' it was he was now carrying, he just couldn't help but be concerned.

American Legion Post, Tybee Island, Georgia:

The older man, a Marine veteran of Vietnam, was making his way through the parking lot when he noticed that there were a lot of people inside the Post. From the raucous sounds, it was clear to him that the bar was open, and the crowd was engaging in their famous card game of "screw your neighbor". Hearing the laughter and noises, he was delighted that the Legion was doing so well, especially since the last two Gomer Wars had done much to reduce the regular population in the area. Sure, they were recovering, and there were even tourists coming back to the Island, but it still wasn't like the old days before the Wars. Thankfully, the Savannah Shipyard and the Port of Savannah were both running at full speed, so the recovery was happening. All of this talk of Gomers, the older man was delighted that he and his wife were lucky enough to be visiting their kids in Ohio when the first War came. As he was about to enter the building, he looked around, and noticed for the first time that there were two men seated in a dark late model Ford sedan. They were definitely out of place, since nobody on Tybee Island ever wore a tie, much less a black tie and the black suit to go with it. Shrugging it off, he assumed that since the War, the veterans were going to come in all sizes, shapes, and weird forms of dress.

As he stepped inside, the smell of the beer and smoke immediately assaulted him, along with the laughter and rib poking at the bar. It was the normal crowd of regulars, and a few folks he hadn't seen in a while. Looking at one such couple, he thought that he knew them from somewhere, but he just couldn't put his finger on it. He'd been active at the Post for a lot of years, and while he knew them, it was nagging him that he couldn't remember who they were or their names. Sitting at his favorite place, which was always semi-reserved for his arrival, he started running through his mental Rolodex. When his favorite beer landed in front of him, it hit him. *"I'll be damned! That couple used to come in here all the time, back before the Wars. Hell, he was even a friend of ol' Bobby. Now what are their names? Oh, yeah. Mike and Leah. Nice couple. Wonder how they avoided the Gomers?"*

Sipping his beer, he made a casual wave at Mike and Leah, who smiled and waved back at him. It was then that he noticed the two suited jokers entering the bar area. They were about as subtle as a hand grenade, and it was obvious that they were 'with the government and here to help you'. Each of them looked like a cookie cutter of the other. Roughly six foot tall, wearing black suits, white shirts, black ties, black shoes, and sporting crew cuts, it was obvious that they were serious. It was so obvious that he was laughing to himself about how these guys were right out of a bad movie. As he watched them, they approached Mike and Leah, and the 'lead joker' stood stiffly as he leaned in and whispered into Mike's ear. Mike didn't appear to be impressed at all, and just waved them away. The 'lead joker' was becoming more insistent, and Mike was equally insistent that he was not going to engage this guy in conversation or move off his stool.

Instead, Mike sipped his beer, and indicated that he was 'standing pat' on the card in front of him. As the conversation was going on in Mike's ear, Leah was passing her card to the next poor slob, who then immediately tried to hand it off down the line. She then leaned into Mike and whispered something, and they both laughed. What was amazing to the older gentleman was the expression on the face of the 'lead joker.' Clearly, he was not happy, but there seemed to be little he could do about it. Finally, he turned on his heel, and the two suited guys stepped outside, where he could see them talking rather animatedly into a radio of some kind in their car. Whatever they were selling, Mike just wasn't buying. As he watched the drama play out, he noticed a copy of the Army Times and decided that since he couldn't get into the game yet, he'd read something while he enjoyed the brew. Looking at the cover, there was a picture of that Allied Guy who, it was reported, was going on leave. Then it hit him like a ton of bricks. Mike was that Allied Guy! *Now I really will be damned.* Looking down at the newspaper and back at Mike, it was that moment of full recognition. Thinking to himself, *Well I'll be, General of the Army hisself is here at this post. Son of a bitch, wait until the guys hear this news.*

Turning in his seat to get up, he felt a hand on his shoulder. "Hey, Bobby, did you know that…"

Cutting him off, his old friend Bobby, another Marine Veteran of Vietnam, looked at him and then down at the Army Times, and said, "Tom. You ain't seen nothin'! You don't know who that is, and you ain't going to figure it out. Got it?"

"What do you mean? He could…"

"Tom. Do *not* make me say it again. The man has been a member a while, and he comes here because all that rank crap stops at the door. Here, he is just some regular guy, and that is the way he wants it."

"But it would be…"

"Seriously, Tom. Where else can a damn General let his hair down, have a beer, and not have anyone screw with him? Besides, if you screw with him, then what do you think happens? I'll tell you, he'll never be back, and we've lost a pretty nice member."

"Okay, but at least we should tell him he done a great job or something."

"Nope, we leave it all at the door. Besides, there are plenty of other things to talk about, like the weather. You see those assholes in here earlier?"

"Yeah, couple of strange looking characters."

"Well, he just told them to hit the road, and that he'd check in when he was damn good and ready."

"So?"

"Dude. Those guys are Secret Service, and he just told them to pound sand. When he says he wants to be left alone to have a good time, he pretty well means it. Seriously, he is a decent guy, so let's just leave him to it."

As he finished this last statement, it was obvious that Mike had just lost his good card to his lovely bride, who passed him a deuce. Getting up from the bar, there was a little newlywed kind of stuff going on, when he put his arm around her and planted a big kiss on her. Standing beside her stool, he told her to get him another beer, and he would be right back. As they both watched, Mike stepped outside to talk to the 'black suits.' After being outside for about 5 minutes, Mike came back inside and sat back down. Leaning into Leah, he whispered something, and she looked almost sad. They sat through the rest of that hand and finished their beers. Then almost like they were being hauled out for an execution, they got up and left. It would be another several years before anyone at the Legion would see either Mike or Leah again.

Coast Guard Station, near Fort Pulaski, Georgia:

Coming through the gate into the National Park area, it hit me just how surreal this entire exchange was becoming. A few minutes ago, I had been enjoying my time being a human again, sipping a beer with my lovely bride, and contemplating my next move in a simple card game. It had been just about perfect, thanks to an old friend of mine who was working hard to let us enjoy our break anonymously. Then these two goons appeared from nowhere, just to say that I needed to talk to their boss. From our brief discussion, it was obvious that they would not take no for an answer, and somebody had really stuffed a rather large burr under their respective saddles. Up to this point, our leave had been pleasant, especially since there wasn't anyone crawling up my ass every two seconds about anything. Now here I was about to have that respite ruined completely, and honestly, I wasn't happy about it. My wife, Leah, was seated beside me, since the Secret Service agents were quick to point out that we BOTH needed to come along as quickly as possible. What I hated was that there was no explanation whatsoever, other than a quick note from my boss indicating that I needed to report to the Coast Guard Station by the fastest means possible. The SOB had promised me he would leave me alone for my leave, but then again, I should be used to this kind of thing. He wouldn't let me retire either.

The salutes of the unmarked car by a flight crew, and the way we were being hustled towards the helipad, also didn't do much for my morale. Obviously, there was a flap of some sort going on, but what? If it were the Gomers, I would have heard something from General Greene. Nope, this was just a little different. This was more cloak and dagger than I cared to think about, and as all the implications finally sank in, I realized that what was happening was decidedly human in origin. The Coast Guard Helicopter lifted from the pad, and we nosed over heading out to sea. As we climbed over the North Channel of the Savannah River, I was finally handed a headset, and I wasted no time putting it on. Adjusting the microphone, I keyed the floor switch, and asked, "Okay, gentlemen, what are we doing here?"

Over the constant beating of the rotor blades, I heard, "Sir. I'm Commander Billings, welcome aboard!"

"Commander, thank you, but before we get all hospitable, would you kindly tell me where the hell you are taking my wife and me?"

"Yessir. We are to rendezvous with the USS Montana."

"The USS Montana? What the hell for?"

"Sir. Something big is up, and we were told to get you to the most secure facility available, and to do it as quickly as possible."

"Commander, we weren't allowed to even pack anything, so exactly what is happening with all that?"

"Sir, I was instructed to advise you that your stuff will have to wait. It seems that your Condo is being targeted, and if you'd returned this evening, it was believed that you would no longer be with us."

"Targeted? Who the hell would be targeting me, Commander?"

"Sir, I have no idea. We got the word from the President through DHS to come get you. So, you have all the dope I know."

"Commander? Can you get me a secure hook up with my Headquarters?"

"Yessir. Standby." As the co-pilot started switching the radio com, the crew chief reached up and flipped my selector switch to an open radio position. Noting which channel was on, I keyed the microphone again.

"Gunslinger Operations, this is Actual, Over."

"Say again?"

"Gunslinger Operations, this is Gunslinger Actual, Over."

"Go, Gunslinger Actual."

"Ops. Is Gunslinger 03 available?"

"Sir! Stand by."

"Gunslinger 06, this is Gunslinger 03, we have you LF, but we are NOT secure."

"Whit. Just what the hell is going on?"

"Sir, we will brief on your arrival. I can tell you that I've spoken with the Grocer, and he says that your dog has fleas, and that you need to get home."

"Roger that, Whit. Okay. Who sent the taxi?"

"Uh, the Big Kahuna decided you might need a ride."

"Gotcha. Okay, Whit. Gunslinger 06 out!" Reaching up, I switched the selector back to intercom and keyed the microphone. "Okay, Commander. What is our ETA?"

"Sir, I've been talking to the Montana, and we're about 10 minutes out for landing."

"Thanks, Commander." Turning back to my wife, I could only give her a sheepish smile, a shrug of the shoulders, and a thumbs up. Her look of icy displeasure was not comforting at all, especially since she was dressed to hang around in our favorite American Legion Post, and not for a flight out over the ocean into the middle of nowhere. Somewhere along the way, a Coastie was kind enough to hand her a blanket for her legs, but it did little to warm the look in her eye. I knew I was in deep, but I had no idea how deep until we touched down on the deck of the USS Montana. Simultaneous with the wheels of the Dauphin Helicopter hitting the deck, I saw my Flag broken out from the Main Mast.

Looking at my bride, I could tell that her mood was even less thrilled than on the flight. I think the real reason might have been the sun dress that she was fighting to keep at a modest altitude around her legs. I know from having flown helicopters, if the right pitch is applied to the rotor system, it is virtually impossible for a young lady to keep her dress down in the high wind generated by the rotor wash. My wife Leah was no exception to these laws of aerodynamics, and I couldn't help admire the fact that after all these years, she still had some pretty awesome looking legs. Unfortunately for me, she was also wearing cute underwear, and it was also being shown to the crew of an entire Battleship. Great! I knew I would be blamed for the way our entire evening turned out and I had a strong feeling that having a pissed off wife would be the least of my problems. I was dead right on both counts.

USS Montana, located 25 nautical miles North East of Tybee Island, Georgia:

Going through the protocol of getting onboard a United States Naval Vessel requires a little knowledge for a ground pounder like me. I'd watched my Dad growing up, so it wasn't completely outside of my scope of knowledge, but I had to remind myself each time I came onboard one of these beasties. You have to pay homage to the tradition, and I made my best effort, despite my civilian clothes, to make it look like I had at least a small clue. After saluting the colors, asking and receiving permission to come aboard, I then asked to be taken to CIC. My wife was in tow and doing her best to remain at least semi-modest as we climbed up the steel ladders leading to the forward part of the ship. I knew I was still in trouble when I heard someone on a lower deck, apparently with a pretty good view, issue forth with a small wolf whistle as we climbed up to the Admiral's Bridge. Once we were on the Admiral's Bridge, I glanced at Leah, and oddly enough, she was grinning at me. I nudged her and said, "See, a cruise! How bad can it be?" Her icy glare told me that I had completely misinterpreted her earlier grin, which must have been more of a grimace. Turning back to the Admiral in Command of the Battlegroup, I asked him, "Admiral, do you have a clue what this is all about?"

"General, I only know what I've been told, which isn't much. Let me get you on a secure line with General Whitney, and let him explain."

"Okay." With that, I was put on another headset and given the microphone. It was going to be a long conversation, so I got comfortable. "Whit?"

"Yessir, General."

"Dammit, Whit, can you at least tell me why my wife is pissed off and I'm sitting on a Battleship 25 miles away from my Condo?"

"Yessir. You were going to have special company tonight at your place. In fact, they were spotted casing you over the last three days. Fortunately, you didn't come out much, so they couldn't get a good handle on you until today."

"Whit, please stop being so damned obtuse. Just exactly WHO are you talking about here?"

"Russians, Sir."

"Russians? I thought I was getting along with Dubronin, and I can't imagine him wanting to have me whacked after all we've been through."

"Sorry, Sir. Not those Russians. The other Russians, you know those dissidents from the eastern parts of the Ukraine?"

"In other words, the bastards that tried to kill me coming out of Romania."

"Exactly, only this time it is with a twist, that I can't explain, even on here."

"So, I'm supposed to come back to Mount Olympus to hear some cockamamie stories about Russian dissidents?"

"General Greene instructed me to advise you that there are fleas on your dog!"

"Okay, so what the hell does that have to do with these alleged dissidents?"

"Sir, the dissidents seem to have the same fleas!"

"You have got to be f... Okay. All right. So, what is the plan?"

"Sir, according to the President, you are to enjoy the next few days onboard the USS Montana while she sails into Norfolk. Once there you will be brought back here via priority air."

"Why do I feel like a FedEx package? Okay, so what do we do in the meantime? All of our clothes and personal stuff are back at our place on Tybee Island."

"Sir, uh, well, ..."

"Whit, you guys think a lot about operations, but if you'd been married as long as I have, then you'd know that wives do NOT move without a logistics package! In fact, I've moved fully loaded Combat Brigades with less crap!"

"I guess we can get General Greene's guys to go pack your stuff."

"That would be nice, but somehow, I'm pretty sure that my wife wouldn't want some strange guy rifling through her 'drawers' drawer. Besides, you know damn well I won't authorize anyone to fly there, pick up our crap, and then fly back out here to the ship! What about those Secret Service assholes that have been watching my every move?"

"Well, sir, it was a move at the direction of the President, so I don't think..."

"Dammit. You're right. Look, we'll manage. I'm pretty sure we can make do with the ship's store, but right now, I would not be offended if someone from the Secret Service would at least pay lip service to packing our crap, and maybe even getting it shipped back to the 'puzzle palace.'"

"Yessir. We'll see you in about three days."

"Whit? One of these days, I just might decide to reassign your sorry ass to Thule!'"

"Hah. Thank you, sir, may I have another..."

Okay, that part was good news, at least Whit still had a sense of humor. Now came the fun part. Explaining this 'minor change in plans' to my lovely bride. When I looked at her, she gave me the same look she gave a 7th grader who wasn't doing what he should be doing in her classroom. Turning to the Admiral, I asked if we could be taken to our quarters, with a small side trip by the Ship's store. He laughed, Leah glared, and I cringed as we headed down four decks to the Ship's store. Fortunately for me, the Admiral was kind enough to clear out of his cabin, and give us the Senior Flag Officer's Quarters. If he hadn't, then Russian Dissidents with Gomer Friends would probably have been the least of my troubles.

When we got to our quarters, Leah looked around at the semi-plush surroundings, and said, "So, this is how you spent all that time at sea?"

"Well, here and in the Combat Information Center. Why?"

"I was feeling sorry for you, but this isn't so bad. Not bad at all. I guess I should not have been worried about you so much. I mean this is a real step up from that damn cave we lived in."

"Gee, thanks. Here put on these jeans, and I'll take you on a tour." Getting dressed in some pants, her mood was already improving. She liked our accommodations, and she felt better just having some clothes that were more suited for going up and down ladders and companionways. She was doing great, right up until we stepped into CIC. Looking around at the maps, communications equipment, cramped space, terminals, and constant movement of the personnel, she made it clear that she was highly uncomfortable. Stepping back out, she looked at me and said, "Sorry, Honey. I was giving you a hard time about the cabin, but that place is scary. It is dark, cramped, and honestly not a nice place to be at all. How much time did you spend in there?"

"I'd say most of the time was spent in there, or on the Admiral's Bridge. Why?"

"Okay, I do take it back from earlier. I guess I was right to be worried."

"Honey, if you really want to be worried, then let me get you a cup of the gawd awful coffee they make in CIC."

The next several days passed in a hurry and despite her wanting to be miserable, I wasn't so sure that Leah didn't enjoy having the attention. One thing I've known, since the day we met, is that Leah is the most adaptable person I've ever met. She is tough enough on the outside to inspire confidence, but yet there is still enough of a curious little girl on the inside to make her the perfect spouse for an old curmudgeon like me. If the last years hadn't been a test of that theory, then there is no such thing. Moving up the coast, I began the process of trying to get my head back in the game. Pouring over the reports and recent observations on the diplomatic front, I could easily see where the Russian dissidents and the Gomers could make for a very dangerous partnership. It was then that feeling in my gut began to churn, and I was very anxious to get back to my headquarters, so I could get the rest of the story.

Robert C. Byrd Medical Clinic, Fort Dawson, West Virginia:

The old Sergeant Major was seated in the hearing booth as part of his annual Airborne Physical. As he peered through the glass, he was doing his level best to guess when the little beep was supposed to come up in his left ear. His right was fine, but now with this new Doctor on board, there wasn't anyone standing outside to give him the thumbs up on when to push the stinking button. He hadn't been able to hear with his left ear since the First Gomer war when a 105 howitzer had gone off near him in Tierra del Fuego. Until now, nobody gave a damn, but all of a sudden, this new guy shows up, and it starts being all by the book. This was bull, he had a Medal of Honor, almost 40 years' experience, and he had made it through another war without being able to hear from that ear. This was crap. Squinting, he was doing his best to discern from the Doctor's actions, just when to push that damn button.

Once the physical was completed, the Doctor called in the old Sergeant Major, to give him the news. "Sergeant Major, I hate to tell you this, but you did not pass your physical."

"What do you mean, Doc?"

"You're deaf as a post in your left ear!"

"Hell, Doc, I've been deaf in that ear since well… Let's say it has been a while. Never stopped me before."

"We can always ask for a waiver, but then there are the blood pressure readings, too."

"Blood Pressure? Hell, I'm fine, Doc, and you know it."

"Sergeant Major, the regulations are the regulations. I'll ask for a waiver, but until we get something back, you're grounded."

"SHIT!"

Chapter II

❧

USS Montana, entering the Chesapeake Bay, near Norfolk Harbor:

Looking out at Fort Story, the ship was rounding the point as the helicopter lifted us off the deck. It turned out to be a fairly enjoyable cruise and Leah wound up having a good time, despite our forced movement from Tybee Island. She still wasn't thrilled at the way we had to leave, but once she got past the thought of someone wanting to kill us, she relaxed enough to feel better about the whole situation. She had worried about the children with these dissidents running around, but when I explained that they were all surrounded by thousands of our finest soldiers, she lightened up enough to enjoy the adventure of it all. The flight into the Naval Air Station didn't take long and, on arrival, we were quickly transferred to another much faster ride back to our mountain home in Southern West Virginia. Such is life in the fast lane.

Supreme Allied Headquarters, (SAHQ):

Stepping out of the VIP aircraft provided by the Navy, we were met on the tarmac by Holly and Chris. Almost as if choreographed, Holly led Leah from the flight line straight to our quarters, while Chris drug me back straight to my office. I threw on a clean uniform, grabbed a quick shave, and was headed to the War Room within about 30 minutes of my arrival. I was met at the door by General Whitney, who then handed me a stack of materials with the Allied Special Operations Report about our "new found" Gomer friends. Flipping through the report, my heart was starting to react, and I could feel the adrenalin starting to course through my system. What I was reading was not good, nor was it going to bode well for any of us. As I got through the materials, I looked at General Whitney and asked, "Whit? Did you read this stuff?"

"Yessir. Scary as hell, isn't it."

"Yeah. Looks like some missing stuff, but yeah. Did General Greene explain how they were starting to get into all this?"

"Yessir, oddly enough he did, and I'll tell you that story later. Suffice it to say, they're into it, and there is new stuff pouring out almost constantly. I think once they cracked the code, it was like an avalanche of alien information."

"So, this was all stuff they withheld from us in the data they transferred on the alleged Tornit?"

"Yep. What is worse, we've also got some movement going on out there, which frankly, is also starting to scare the hell out of me."

"Wow, you're just a cornucopia of good news, aren't you?"

"Last night two Gomer Battleships headed out towards the edge of the Solar System. We tracked them, and they stopped by the planet Neptune, on a moon..." General Whitney shuffled through some papers. "Yeah, here it is, Triton?"

"Okay, so they flew out and stopped at a moon. Where are they now?"

"We don't know. We lost them when they flew around Neptune. They didn't fly away, they aren't in orbit, and they aren't near that moon either."

"So, did they go to Neptune, or did they pass by and we just lost them because of their position in relation to the planet?"

"Not sure, but according to General Greene, well, he has a theory, and now that you're back, he'd like a meeting with you ASAP."

"Okay, set it up."

"Oh, and another thing, which might be nothing but imagination. We've received several reports of visual sightings in the Northern latitudes of the occasional Gomer Fighter Class ship engaged in unauthorized visits."

"Where and when?"

"It is very sporadic, but we got several transient radar hits in the Greenland and Northern Siberian areas over the last several weeks, which might confirm some of the visual sightings."

"Really? Any confirmations with other sources?"

"Not really, sir. We did have someone from a fishing trawler say they saw a Gomer Ship hovering over a ship near Baffin Island, but we weren't able to confirm that sighting by radar."

"Well, keep me posted on any of those sightings, especially if they continue. Right now, tell everyone to keep their eyes open, along with their radar plots running. Now about General Greene, go ahead set up the meeting. I'm obviously not going anywhere soon, so I might as well climb back in the saddle."

"Roger that, Sir."

"So, can you finally tell me how they got into the code?"

"No. I can't, but Chris can." Looking away from me and towards Chris, General Whitney motioned to her and asked, "You want to tell him?"

"Sure. Okay, Dad, first let me say, don't be mad at us for talking about things at home. You know we all have clearances, and..."

"Dammit, Chris, right now, I just want to know the story."

"Okay, well, I know they worked for months trying to get to the bottom of the numbers, and General Greene and ASOC were all going nuts with it. Holly came to visit; I think to visit with John's friend…"

"Chris? Can we get to the punch line?"

"Okay, okay. Well, Holly and I were talking about the code and Holly's algorithms to crack it, and anyway, little man, Michael, asked them how many fingers and toes these Gomers had."

"Wait. You mean, Michael, as in my 7-year-old grandson Michael?"

"Yes. So, Michael asked the question, and all of a sudden you could see the light bulb go off in Holly's head. It was kind of funny. Instead of the base ten numbers she was using in her math to build the algorithm, she realized that the Gomers had to be using a different standard. When Michael asked about the fingers and toes, it hit her. Michael was being all genius on her, and now she has adjusted her computations working off base 12 numbers. These smart Gomers or Glavanna have six fingers on each hand, so she shifted her baseline, and voila! It worked! And now she is getting the information from all sorts of their devices."

"You are kidding me. Michael is the brains behind this?"

"Yep! I'm pretty proud of him."

"You damn well should be, and for whatever it is worth, so am I. Okay, Whit?"

"Sir?"

"Get in touch with General Greene, and tell him I want the latest, and everything else he's got on these bastards as soon as he can get it to me. Also, tell him I want a full rundown on what his plan will be, based on what we're learning, should we need to pull the trigger."

"Yessir. How soon do you want to meet with him?"

"How soon can he get here?"

"Sir, we can have him here in under 12 hours."

"Excellent. Make it happen. And raise our alert level to yellow, increase our monitoring of both near Earth space outward to the edge of the Solar System. I also want you to increase all sea and air patrols at both poles, tell the Russians to step up their Siberian patrols, and while you're at it, put Vandenberg on alert, and have somebody prepare to lock down the Gomers' 'embassy compound' on St. Lawrence Island, just in case. Once you've done that, get me the latest status on how long it will take to close the air space between the Gomers on Mars and us. I mean close it too! This time, I want stuff close enough together that a Carrier Ship can't get through without a bloody nose. I will also need to know what the maximum effort for mining those areas will take, as in what time frame. And... I'll need to know what types and the numbers for the mines we can get in that part of space in any given time frame. Got it?"

"Yes, Sir! What about the dissident part of that last message you have in the folder? Do you want to do anything about them yet?"

"I don't think we can, at least not yet. I tell you what, get our contacts at CIA, MI-6, and over in the Russian Federation's Security Services up to speed and let them keep a close eye on them. Right now, they may be our only real warning system for what I'm afraid is coming next, and besides, if we move too quickly, it might telegraph the wrong message to the Gomers. Then tell the intelligence guys to watch, listen, and report anything they can to us as it happens, otherwise, we might be in for another blind side attack. Finally, pass on the security alert to all the trusted allies, assuming it hasn't been already, and make sure that everyone in the civilian leadership, from the President down to the Secretary of Dog Excrement, has additional security protection. You don't need to explain why necessarily to all our allies, but let Dubronin know as an 'eyes only message,' and then the UK know ALL the details. Got me?"

"Yessir!"

After reading all the reports, evaluating this 'purported dissident group's' relationship with the Gomers' and their Embassy, and then hearing about unusual Gomer ship movement towards Neptune and possibly in our polar regions, the flags and warning bells in my mind were starting to ring all over again. This time, they were ringing even louder than normal, since there was no question in my mind that the "we are not your friend" Gomers were back. This time they were up to something even more sinister than anything we'd ever seen before and, given our history, that was saying a lot.

11th Airborne Division Headquarters, Fort Dawson, West Virginia:

Command Sergeant Major Clagmore wasn't just upset, he was livid to the point that his blood pressure was about to pop something important. Storming into the Division Commander's Office, he brushed past the General's Aide, and launched into a rather colorful tirade about the Army, the Army Medical Department, the doctors, and then most specifically, the parentage of the certain medical officer who clearly couldn't be trusted to pour urine from a boot with the directions on the heel! Listening to the tirade, the young Aide to the General realized very quickly that the Sergeant Major was no longer going to be allowed to jump from a perfectly good airplane. It was quite a blow, since despite the Sergeant Major's somewhat overwhelming personality, Lieutenant Patrick was quite fond of the old soldier. Watching the Sergeant Major storm out of the office to head to his quarters, Lieutenant Patrick turned to the Division Commander whose jaw was still hanging somewhere near his lap. "General?"

"Yeah, Patrick?"

"Sir. What does this mean for Clagmore?"

"Well, Lieutenant, he can either retire, or we will have to find him a new home where he can be useful."

"Sir, unless you know of a hole full of pit vipers that need taming."

"Hah! Nope, Lieutenant, I don't know of ... Wait! Now that I think about it, I know exactly what he would like to do."

"What is that, General?"

"Get your Dad on the line!"

"Yessir." Picking up the phone, he was almost immediately interrupted by a runner who was pounding on the door with a priority message from Allied Headquarters.

"Hold up, Lieutenant." The General threw up a hand while skimming the Priority message.

"Yes, General?"

The Division Commander thrust the paper at the young Lieutenant. "Read this!"

"Well, at least now we know my father is back from his leave. Alert? Wonder what is up. Still want my Dad on the line?" Lt. Patrick reached for the phone.

"Sure, and while I'm at it with him about Clagmore, I'll fish around to see if we have a real problem or not."

USS Inouye, 150 miles Southwest of Iceland, Atlantic Ocean:

The USS Inouye was the last of the Arleigh Burke Class Destroyers to be built before the new Zumwalt/Morton Class destroyers came out, and while she had been retrofit with several "anti-Gomer" weapons, she was still not as sophisticated as the newest Morton Class Destroyer. They looked completely different, but at least they handled the same, and from the crew's perspective, they were better, since they had to do it the 'old school hard way.' This sense of pride carried over to everything she did, especially since she normally worked with the USS Morton in providing escort for the USS Montana. Several days ago, they had even assisted with the escort of the Montana when the 'old man' was on board with his flag. Today, though, she was now bouncing around like a cork in a bottle being shaken by a kid. This hurried rush to patrol at the polar regions was not what she wanted at all, and now she missed having the USS Morton nearby.

"Bridge? ... uh... Radar Plot."

"Bridge, Aye."

"Bridge, we have a very faint surface contact, relative bearing 290° and 180 miles. It appears to be moving away from the shipping lanes towards the north at about 5 knots."

"Radar. Any idea what she could be?"

"No, Sir. Maybe a freighter, but she is definitely a surface contact of small to moderate size."

"Okay, Radar. Keep an eye on it, and keep me posted. Anything else out there?"

"Negative Sir. We thought we had an aerial contact, but it was too transient and too far out to get anything on it. Might be the sea state."

"Roger that! Okay, keep me posted."

"Aye, Aye, Sir."

Turning back to the plot, the young inexperienced Radar operator spotted another transient blip further out. As he was about to call it into the Bridge, it was gone again with the next sweep. Realizing that he might be behind the curve, given his rookie watch, he called over the Chief in the Combat Information Center, to get his opinion. Naturally, the blip never repeated itself, so the question of what might be out there was not to be answered on this watch. Still, it bothered the young sailor, and he vowed to talk to his buddy about it later when he got off watch.

Supreme Allied Headquarters (SAHQ):

The wait for General Greene to get to my headquarters wasn't wasted time. The information from various sources was coming into the War Room at an exponential rate. The picture was coming into focus, and it was highly troubling. Knowing this, I realized that it was time to have a chat with the President. My staff tracked him down easily enough. He was already in his Situation Room, sifting through some of the same information we were receiving, and his stomach was sending him the same signals.

"Mr. President. General Patrick here."

"Hey, Mike, welcome back. Enjoy the cruise?"

"Very funny, Sir. Leah is threatening me, and I might have been better served to take my chances where I was with the alleged 'bad guys' who were hanging around the island. All they could do would be kill me. A pissed off wife, on the other hand, is a lot scarier!"

"I hear you! Toni has had her moments here of late too. So, now that you're back, have you been reading this stuff?"

"Yes, Mr. President. Hard to believe that this all took place in just the 4 months of me being gone. It isn't a pretty picture is it?"

"Hell, no! We've been had, in more ways than one. These jokers have run a scam on us, and have learned enough to make things a little harder for us."

"I know. The crypto guys are going nuts, coming up with a different set of parameters for establishing the new code books for our use. The LF systems will need to be tinkered with, but my Signal Intelligence folks think we're going to be okay."

"That is good news, but can we trust that to work?"

"Mr. President, we will just need to change up and vary our codes as often as possible. I also think we're going to have to use frequency variance within the ULF and ELF bands, to hopefully throw them off, sort of like the old 'have quick' system we used 20 years ago. Somehow, I KNEW that trying to patch them into a common frequency was a mistake, which might be why we specifically held back the ULF and ELF bands from them. Unfortunately, giving them the LF hook up now teaches them to search the lower bands for our transmissions."

"Good thing, I guess. Now then, aside from the communications, can you tell where else we might have been compromised?"

"Well, from what I can see, we may have a problem in the area of metallurgy. The bad news is that some of our Sulphur shells could be lessened in their effectiveness. The good news is that we even hedged our bets there, so we still have a few bolts left in our quiver."

"Do they have anything now that will allow them to see over water?"

"Absolutely not. From what I've been reading, the water is the one thing they can't figure out at all."

"Thank God! Have you pushed for the reconfiguration of the Gomer based weapons systems?"

"Actually, while I was away, General Whitney did a great job in that department."

"Good. Now then, what else do we know?"

"Mr. President, we're working the issue. General Greene is on his way with some of his best information dominance folks, which for us mere mortals is key crypto and cyber staff members. I've asked for an up-to-date briefing, and from what Daniel is telling me, there are things he is not willing to put out except in person."

"When?"

"Sir, I've been told that he should be here in about 8 hours. Would you be interested in coming to listen to what he might have to give us?"

"Damn right! Can you make it a briefing for around 10 am tomorrow morning?"

"Yessir. That will give me a chance to get his feelings and ideas about any future operational plans first. Oh, and Mr. President?"

"Yeah."

"Mr. President. I've taken the liberty to move up our alert level…" I laid our initial actions, which were consistent with the protocol for an impending attack. We continued our discussions related to populations and notices for possible movements, should it become necessary. Finally, we discussed the movement of the Gomers towards Neptune, and the transient Fighter Class Ship sightings here on Earth. Once we covered those areas, the President was as nervous as I was about what might be coming.

11th Airborne Division, Fort Dawson, West Virginia:

The Commanding General was in the process of surreptitiously hunting for a new Command Sergeant Major for the Division. The Commander knew that the last acting Sergeant Major that tried to do the job was not going to work on a permanent basis. Unfortunately, having to wait for the approval of a waiver for Clagmore just didn't fit the needs of the Division. As a result, the search had to be quiet, especially since Command Sergeant Major Clagmore would flip if he knew what was about to happen. Naturally, you weren't going to get anything by Clagmore, since his ability to ferret out details from afar was the stuff of legend throughout the Division. It was incredible, but within 5 minutes of the General hanging up the phone with the Department of the Army Human Resources Command about his replacement, Sergeant Major Clagmore was in the General's office. The visit was neither routine nor pleasant.

"Dammit, Sir. Can't we wait on the fucking waiver?"

"Sergeant Major. I would LOVE to wait on the waiver, but the Division needs somebody now. We've got orders to move, and you know it."

"Shit, shit, shit, shit."

"Look, Sergeant Major, I've got some good news if you are willing to hear it."

"Okay... General."

"Sergeant Major, a job opened up just for you. You are being assigned to the Allied Staff as the Senior Enlisted soldier. In other words, you are the new Allied Command Sergeant Major, with the same rank as the Sergeant Major of the Army! Congratulations!"

"Awwww, fuck that! I want my Division. Those staff guys never get to kill Gomers!"

"Dammit. Clagmore, you have NO idea when to shut up. Now take this fucking gift. I know why I put up with you, but damned if I know why Patrick would have bothered asking for your sorry ass!"

"I'm sorry, Sir. I don't mean no disrespect, you know that. Hell, I love the guy! Shit, he saved my ass and there ain't no forgettin' either."

"Good. Then sew on the new stripes, and get your ass to the Mountain. I've got you out of here in less than 18 hours. I've also got instructions for your wife to check in with General Patrick's wife as soon as you two get there."

"Yessir." Saluting and about to turn around, the Sergeant Major stopped and looked back at the General. "Sir?"

"Yeah?"

"Sir, it has been a real pleasure. Any idea who they're sending to take my place?"

"Actually, he is someone who reminds me a little of you. A guy by the name of Forrester, Command Sergeant Major Carl T. Forrester, formerly the Sergeant Major for the 10th Special Forces Group."

"No kidding! Good choice. At least I'll know you're in good hands. He is a great soldier! He even knows some things about jumping into bad places with nothing but a knife and a grin."

"That is almost exactly what General Patrick said when he made those arrangements."

"Then it is good enough for me. Thanks, General!" Turning, Sergeant Major Clagmore headed out to round up his wife, so they could get on the road. It was only a two-hour drive, so if they hurried, they could be there first thing the next morning. Hell, he would worry about getting their stuff shipped once he reported in. This new "flap" was enough to make him think that his presence just might be needed sooner than later. He was absolutely correct.

Vandenberg Air Force Base, California:

General McDaniel was about to leave his office for the day when his Aide stuck his head in the office. "General?"

"Yea, Captain."

"Sir, we've got something weird you should maybe take a look at."

"Captain. In this day and age, you're going to have to define 'weird'."

"Well, General. The operator recorded this and nobody can make heads or tails of what it might mean. Can you take a minute to see what you think?"

"Okay. Lead the way Captain." Walking out of the office, they headed to the operations center where a number of personnel were at their various stations. Each of these stations was designed to control their assigned satellites and telescopes. One of several such observatory stations around the globe, this was the primary facility to keep track of both Near Earth and Distant Earth items of interest.

"Okay, Gentlemen, what has you puzzled?"

"General. Take a look at this tape." Watching the monitor, the Red Light telescope/satellite system was pulled up on screen. The view of the monitor showed the normal observation areas out in space towards what was euphemistically referred to as "Gomerville," or the Gomers' home planet.

"So? Nothing unusual so far."

"Wait for it, General." Leaning in to the monitor, General McDaniel noticed that the picture blinked for a split second. It wasn't very obvious, but there was no question that the picture appeared to reset itself.

"Wow, that was weird, even by today's standards."

"Exactly, sir. Something weird has happened but we don't know what."

"Okay, have you compared this picture with any of the others, and have you compared this tape with observations of a few hours before?"

"No, we haven't, at least not fully. We did do a cross check, but nothing obvious leaped out at us."

"Do the complete cross check, and check the current observations. This is hinky enough to warrant a report to Patrick and his boys. You might want to copy ASOC with it too. Wait, when was the last known Gomer traffic to earth?"

"Sir, we had an unarmed transport depart from St. Lawrence Island about four hours ago."

"When did this little blip take place?"

"About… I'll be damned. About four hours ago."

"Okay. Get this off to General Patrick and ASOC right now. I don't like it. Then complete your cross checks, and while you're at it, turn the backup Sat system in that direction to cover the same space. Something here isn't right at all!"

"Yes, General! We can move one right now, and it should be in position within the next hour."

"Excellent. Now let them know at the Mountain that we might not have constant coverage for the moment, and while you're at it, make sure that Abramson and Clarkson know that we might have been compromised. I'll be in my office once you have all the date together."

"Yessir."

"Captain, while you're making calls, contact my quarters and let my wife know I'm going to have to be here for a while, and that I'll call her later." Retreating to his office, he started going through the footage that was recorded previously and comparing it to the footage he just saw. It took several hours, but he noticed that the stars and other objects did not appear to be moving the way they should be moving. "I'll be damned. The Gomers have started a loop of pictures on our own damn satellite. I wonder what they could be hiding." Reaching for the phone, he was unable to reach General Greene immediately, since he was in transit to the Mountain, but he did talk with Dr. Abramson, who was going to pass it on to General Greene.

Sitting back in his chair, General McDaniel pulled a cigar from his drawer, and then hit the intercom for his Aide. "Lieutenant, get your ass in here…and tell them to put on a large pot of coffee. We're in for a long night." Turning back to his monitor, now wreathed in the blue smoke, he began running the calculations in his head as to the star movement. He muttered, "Yep, those bastards are up to something, and I really don't like it. Not one damn bit!"

Chapter III

❦

The Moon of Triton, near the Planet Neptune:

The Gomer Battleship disgorged a number of smaller Fighter Class ships that swarmed down to the surface of the moon, Triton. Still outside the observation line of anyone on the Planet Earth, the fighters were merely being transferred for service to their forward base located well inside the surface of Triton. Not wishing to attract any attention, this move was designed to keep the Battleship Class ship well hidden behind Triton itself. Once the Fighters were clear, an incident took place that was not within the Gomer's master plan at all. Three Gomer Fighter Class ships collided, and given their cargo, the effect was almost immediate. A rather high burst of Terahertz radiation was emitted in all directions around the destroyed Fighter Class ships, with the net effect of sparking a massive explosion. The impact of the blast rapidly spread over the surface of Triton and into the area that was only now coming back under observation by Supreme Allied Intelligence and Space Observation personnel. It was guessed by intelligence that the Gomers had to be stunned by the explosion, because the damage to the Battleship Class Gomer was sufficient to accomplish two things. The first was to telegraph her presence near Neptune and Triton, and the second was that she was forced onto an emergency course that was observable and leading directly to the surface of Neptune.

The reports were issued immediately, and the various sections of the Allied Staff were examining the data. Almost before the Battleship Class re-entered the atmosphere of Neptune, this information was streaming into the Supreme Allied Headquarters. It wasn't long before it was also learned that two Carrier Class ships were spotted rising from Neptune to assist the wounded Battleship Class ship back into the planet's atmosphere. This information was also duly catalogued, and passed on to the highest levels. What was surprising to almost everyone, was that it now appeared that the Gomers were already well established on Neptune. The only people not surprised were the Cyber Analysts from ASOC. It would be from them that the rest of the picture would start coming together.

Supreme Allied Headquarters, (SAHQ):

General Greene arrived at my headquarters with his Information Dominance team that consisted of several physicists, crypto analysis experts, and various other more serious cyber warriors. They had a few hours before the arrival of the President, and so Greene's staff members began the task of setting up their dog and pony show. Taking the time to get caught up, General Greene gave me a short version of the information they had amassed from their efforts to crack into the various sources of Gomer information. Our discussion was chilling, to say the very least, and when coupled with the latest information from Neptune, the pieces were all starting to fall into place. There was no question we'd been duped by the Gomers in their alleged peace efforts, and now it would be time to reassess our belief system one more time. When the President arrived, the sense of urgency was monumental, and the room fell to a hush as General Greene began the briefing.

"Mr. President. General Patrick. With your permission, I won't waste any time with the pleasantries."

Neither the President nor I were interested in pleasantries, so we both waved General Greene to continue. Looking the President in the eye, General Greene continued, "Mr. President, we have been had, and now we're about to be the recipients of another more major attack than anything we've ever seen before. The Gomers are massing on Neptune, and will be likely operating from their forward base on Mars once operations begin. Our best guess is that we'll have less than about 42 hours' notice, if we're lucky, that an attack will commence."

The room was stunned, and the President said, "General Greene, one quick question before you continue. Where did you get this information?"

"Mr. President. We cracked their onboard computers from several sources. We hacked into the computer systems from the wrecks around the James River Line, around Antarctica, and from the ship we captured in Antarctica in the first war. We then hacked the data from their systems from the second war wrecks in Greenland, Siberia, and that last Mountain Class or Command ship the USS Alaska took out in the Pacific. Finally, we hacked into their systems during the transfer of some limited building materials to the Gomers at their alleged embassy, on St. Lawrence Island."

"General Greene, you said one source of that information came from a command ship in the Pacific. How'd they do that in such deep water?"

"The Navy was kind enough to put one of their deep-sea research vessels on the job. They drug it back from the new owner, you might remember her as the old *USNS Hughes Glomar Explorer*. You know the one that the CIA used to take a look at the Russian Submarine all those years ago near Hawaii? Anyway, they used it to go down to retrieve what they could from the Gomers' ship. We got lucky that some compartments containing the data systems were accessible enough to allow us to get some stuff out."

"I'll be damned. Okay, I'm sorry to interrupt. Go ahead."

"Thank you, Mr. President. The Gomers have a trend in their planning curve, especially since they had to modify things as they went along. We learned, as you would expect, that they modified their strategy at every turn, based on our actions and reactions to what they were doing. They are smart, and now we know they are also very sneaky. The peace was to take the heat off, and to learn more about us. They wanted to know what we were doing to kill them, and they wanted to know how and who they needed to eliminate to make it easier next time. This entire peace process was a stalling for time to amass more force to throw against us."

"So, they got into bed with the Russian dissidents to learn more about us?"

"Exactly. It didn't take them long to learn about them, and it didn't take them long to learn about who might be in charge in each area. The Russian dissidents themselves filled in the blanks, and the bastard we had on staff here, General Karnaukhov, was passing almost everything to the dissidents. In short, Mr. President, yourself, President Dubronin, King Harold, and most world leaders have been specifically targeted. As for the military, Generals Patrick, Whitney, Davis, Larkin, Petrovsky, Xi Jintao, Sir Harold Manning, Sevitch, Kaminski, Campbell, Thayer, Durham, and myself, along with Admirals Steadman, Lynch, Becker, Pellman, Li Dejiang, Blucher, Tse Hue, Suchkov, Sato, and McDermott have all been identified for elimination. It is believed that they will attempt, with the Russian Dissident's assistance, to assassinate or attack these leaders as the opening move to their attacks. It can also be assumed that all of our headquarters facilities and our LF/ULF/ and ELF communications have either been compromised or identified for immediate attack at the outset of hostilities." Stopping to take a sip of water, it was clear to all in the room that General Greene was more than concerned. He was almost beside himself with real genuine fear.

As he took his sip, he held up his slightly shaking hand and, like a bad commercial where you hear, 'But wait! There's more!' he continued, "Aside from all our headquarters facilities, we're faced with their shift of tactics. We will have little warning once they decide to dive on a target like they did towards the end of the last war. They realized that it worked well, and this time, they will bring their big stuff in and not make the mistake of being led off by a ruse or deception plan. You can expect the opening salvos to be initiated against facilities like this one, from at least 125 miles out, and continuing until the targets are destroyed. Our civil population will also need to find alternate means of shelter, since they can strike at the known locations with relative impunity with these same tactics. We believe they will strike military targets first, then move to the production facilities for military goods, then to the civilian targets of opportunity. We can expect a complete annihilation of our basic infrastructure within the first week, two at the most."

The silence hovered over the room on the last statements, since much of what we learned from the Gomers had been based on our ability to hold the day, and keep ourselves safe within the Sulphur based mountains. Now that they could bring their big stuff to bear, we had little choice but to modify our way of doing business, and this was not going to be an easy task. We also were faced with one other problem, the elephant in the room as it were, how to get millions of citizens to a safe point out of harm's way. Especially when there were no shelters beyond what we were already committed to using. The President broke the silence when he croaked out, "General... How long before they strike?"

"Mr. President. We might have days, weeks, or even years, but my real guess is a few months at most."

"Damn! Anything else we should know?"

"Yessir. You remember the Tornit? Well, they are alive and well, and already here."

"Here?"

"Sir, the smart Gomers are the damned Tornit!"

"Then who in the hell are the Crab guys?"

"Mr. President, we don't know, but Dr. Sylvia Duprey is the biologist who is heading up that question right now. Clearly the Crab Gomers are part of this, but we're not sure yet their place in the hierarchy. We have a lot of theories, but nothing concrete at this point. Dr. Duprey has been pouring over all the lab results, reports, and autopsy information developed by Dr. Abramson and Dr. Clarkson. She is also taking a look at the interaction between the various types of other Gomers, ranging from the 'Dusty' to the alleged 'Smart' varieties. We have also been supplementing her information from all the computer data, so hopefully we can answer your question sooner than later. Right now, all we know for sure is that the data we've found indicates that the Tornit are the 'Smart' Gomers, and they are already around us."

"You mentioned theories. What are some of them?"

"Mr. President, one theory is that the Tornit bred these things for long distance space travel or scouting work, sort of a test tube Gomer. Then they used the neanderthal or 'Meaty' Gomers for a source of energy, thus creating the 'Meaty' and 'Dusty' Gomers we encountered in the First War. I would point out that in the Second War, we only encountered the 'Smart' Gomers. There were no 'Dusty', 'Crab', or 'Meaty' varieties encountered. The second theory is that the Tornit enslaved another race entirely for use as long-range space scouts, but the chemistry doesn't completely explain this theory, although there is some data to indicate that these guys above us have enslaved other planets in their trek across space. Finally, the last theory involves a metamorphous process where the 'Crab' Gomers are a variation of the 'Smart' Gomers, sort of a pupae stage for the 'Smart' Gomer."

"Okay, is it just me, or does that last theory sound especially creepy?"

"That last theory is the one that Dr. Duprey thinks might have the highest chance of being correct."

"Figures. Okay, let's talk damage control?"

"Mr. President, before we get to that, I think you should know some other things first."

"Okay. General Greene, I didn't mean to cut you off. If you have more, then lay it on us."

"Thank you, Mr. President. When our alleged peace process began, General Patrick asked me to keep digging, and we decided that we might have this kind of problem if we weren't really careful."

"Go on."

"I took the liberty to do some things that are very HIGHLY classified, and General Patrick and I are probably the only two people who have a clue of that big picture. For now, I would prefer we discuss these three projects in another setting."

"Okay..."

"Mr. President, aside from those projects, and despite the odds in their favor, there are still several other projects I can mention today. Most notable are Phase II and Phase III of the 'Red Dragon' project that was unveiled during the last war. There we used the Phase I only, so we still have some punches left to us. Fortunately, General McDaniel was not on the list, and Vandenberg, Bozeman, and Site X were so classified that the dissidents couldn't have passed it on to anyone. Phase II is a great upgrade to the Missile Defense system, while Phase III is more defensive in nature, but even more effective than our global minefield. There is also 'Project Fuller' which, if you will recall, was cobbled together during the final actions in Siberia. We have since modified it, added to it, and put it into a phase

II configuration which will offer over twice the power, and four times the striking area from the earlier models. Finally, we have the upgrades to the space mines that should permit us the opportunity to increase the coverage areas for higher altitude attacks over key targets such as New Washington."

"Good to hear some favorable news, but it is the high-altitude attack that scares me. What are your thoughts for those type attacks?"

"Mr. President, we can either do one of two things. If we have time, we can develop alternate locations for shelters for the populations but the crash construction, along with the amount of time available, will be the real problem. The other option is to beef up security, relocate senior staff and the leadership only, which would take far less time, and might be a quicker option should they attack sooner."

"Okay, on the subject of leadership. Where would you relocate me?"

"Sir, I've got a great place in the Rockies, where you'd be more than welcome. Another option, in a pinch, might be on a submarine. Our final option is to move you to another shelter nearer here, but it wouldn't have the same level of amenities, and could take weeks to construct."

"What about Congress, the Court, cabinet, and the rest of the strap hangers. Surely there isn't enough room on a submarine for those folks."

"No, sir, there isn't. In their case, they would have to be relocated to a new shelter near me in the Rockies, and that is just about their only option. I would warn you though, communications will have to be by wire only, and even then, it would have to be kept to scrambled means only."

"That hardly seems workable, General."

"Mr. President, I'm more worried about protection and survivability than workable and political at the moment. I will assure you, if these Tornit decide to attack along the lines of their plans and background, then survival will be a real dicey thing."

"Not an option, General. My cabinet will have to talk to other world leaders, especially my Secretary of State. We can't be relegated to the survival mode. Hell, that isn't what we're paid for, now is it?"

"Then may I suggest that we move Congress, the Court, and other government functions to the Rockies for wire use only, and move yourself and key cabinet members to the USS Seawolf, where you can keep in touch electronically and via ULF/ELF with the rest of the world. We can use other facilities to transfer wire messages from the Rockies to you at sea via ULF, and at least keep that part working. It isn't optimal, but it would at least keep our civilian leadership somewhat more protected than these damn mountains."

"Okay. Start putting the plan together for that contingency. In the meantime, put some effort into trying to scrape out new facilities on this coast. Anything else?"

"Well, this is the stickler, but we probably need to discuss it. How to move our civilian population. If we start to move them too soon, then the bad guys will know we're on to them."

"I can see this..."

"Sir, what we would like to do is maximize the 42 hours for their evacuation, which means we'll have to get some of your cabinet working on a plan to get people out, with minimal military assistance, in that limited time frame. Otherwise, we'll tip off the Gomers sufficiently to make them advance their time table, which in turn gives us even less than the 42 hours."

The President obviously didn't like this option, since he still recalled how there were so many people exposed in the last war. As he was about to jump all over General Greene, I decided it was time to toss in my two cents. "Mr. President, if I may?"

"Certainly, General Patrick!"

"Sir, we've already been pushing people to get out of the current built up areas, so wouldn't it be consistent to begin evacuation through other means?"

"What do you mean?"

"Well, this is just an idea, but maybe your Cabinet can figure out a better way to package it. Say, something along the lines consistent with our ongoing efforts to repopulate certain areas, and at the same time, act to disperse the population. What if we started some sort of incentive program to relocate, and put it all under the guise of economic development. Maybe even get our press involved to make a real noise about moving people around to take the strain off infrastructure, increase work opportunities, and help the economy. You know, the usual media hype over something that might distract the Gomers, and get us where we need to be now, as opposed to cramming millions into a 42-hour window to get to safer ground."

"I like it so far. But what about shelters?"

"Sir, I have no idea how many backhoes there are in this country, but if we started getting people to dig in deep and shelter nearer to their homes, then maybe the Gomers won't be able to get us all with one shot from 125 miles up. Maybe offer them incentives on taxes to dig their own shelters."

"Part of an overall incentive plan?"

"Basically, but we won't make too much noise about that in the press. Instead, we toss that in as an afterthought kind of thing. What we key on is the economics, as opposed to the protection issue. After all, we're at 'peace' with the Gomers, right?"

"Okay. I'll get Transportation, Health and Human Services, Treasury, and the rest of the cabinet working on it. In the meantime, we'll start the slow movement of personnel to their respective places. Oh, and General Patrick?"

"Sir?"

"Where would you be going?"

"Sir, I will take my Headquarters to a place the Gomers have never been."

"Where is that?"

"Sir, we're going to be moving to one of our back-up locations in the Mountains of Honduras."

"Honduras?"

"Yessir. Specifically, on Tiger Island in Honduras, right on the Pacific coast between Nicaragua and El Salvador. We already have the facilities there, which were started decades ago. It is nice and near the equator, lots of sunshine, and best of all, it is well away from the Gomers' beaten paths of the past two wars. The Russians have never heard of it as a facility for the Allied High Command, and best of all, we can leave there easily and quickly by either surface ship or submarine."

"What about your military dependents?"

"Sending most, if not all, of them to the Rockies, and other parts of this same mountain range. Personally, Leah and the rest of my family will be going to a cave I used to run around in as a kid. Not much mountain over it, but it runs very, very, deep. We had someone start building us a spot inside after the First War! Call it my retirement home for any contingency."

"Seriously?"

"Sure. Room for Toni and your Grandkids too if you want. My whole family, with some notable exceptions, will be there bored as hell. It is near Peterstown, West Virginia, and it was used as an underground gun powder factory during the Civil War. Runs miles underground, and it is almost four miles underground where we built up a little family community. We have several structures there with electricity, running water, the whole Megillah. You interested?"

"We'll talk after this, but hell, yes, I'm interested."

"Good. There is no signature above ground, and best of all, Toni would have friends. Whit's wife and Jerry's families will be there, too."

"Okay, that's a deal." Turning back to General Greene, "Now what about other damage control ideas?"

"Mr. President, for the record, I've seen General Patrick's digs there, and frankly, if I still had a family, that would be where I'd put them."

"Thank you, General Greene."

"Mr. President, just my humble opinion, but our other main damage control issues are based on communications and cryptology problems with the compromised LF/ULF/ELF systems. Right now, it would appear that they know of the ULF and ELF, and might be able to register the signal, but we believe they still haven't cracked into the content of the messages. The ULF is still operational, and was likely not provided to them as an option. Frankly, the ELF wouldn't have gotten away from us, if it hadn't been for our Dissident friends in Russia."

"Which reminds me. What are you doing about them?"

"Sir, they are the problem of the CIA, MI-6, and the Russian Security Services. Right now, they are almost completely identified, and under constant surveillance."

"Do we know their deal? What the hell are they trying to do, besides the obvious selling off the entire planet to the Gomers?"

"Mr. President, they are mostly former hard-core communists or anarchists, who believe that the Gomers will give them their utopian society, and then leave them alone, in exchange for telling them all they know about the human race in general, and the rest of us specifically."

"Why not arrest them?"

"We could take them out, but again, we would be sending a signal to the Gomers that we're on to them. We would hate to tip our hand, and trigger them coming at us before we're ready."

With this last statement I had another such statement come to mind from a war many years ago. I couldn't help it, and I just sort of blurted out another one of my history lessons. "General Greene. I can't help but harken back to General MacArthur in the Philippines in early 1941. He thought he had until April of 1942 before the Japanese would attack, so all of his defense planning was based on calling up local Philippine units and getting ready for an attack in April. Unfortunately, if you'll recall, the Japanese weren't working off his time table. Instead, they were on their own schedule, which was about 4 months earlier with the attack in December 1941. I only point this out to remind everyone here, we may not have months, it may come in days, and we need to hustle our plans into actions, with a genuine sense of urgency."

Taking the ball up, the President began, "General Patrick, I agree. When we break up today, I want a maximum effort from you, your staff, and all the players from my own office, down to every player in the field. General Greene, how much of this information can I pass along to the Cabinet?"

"Sir, I discussed this with General Patrick before the briefing. We think you can take all of it back with you, and my deputy at AOSC, General Jones, is prepared to accompany you back to your Situation Room to provide you support and a full briefing on all we've covered to day. We are also prepared to provide them the notes from this meeting, so that they can brain storm as necessary on the suggestions and discussions. Finally, I've got Doctor Abramson on standby at Vandenberg to provide the cabinet a briefing on the special projects we just discussed, although with your permission, I would prefer that we not go into much detail yet."

"That will work, and don't worry. I don't think they need to hear about those projects as of yet. In the meantime, thank you for the briefing, and let's get to work from here. General Patrick, you do what you need to do for force protection, and let's start spreading out as much as possible. Oh, and General Patrick, what are you doing about Allied Liaison Officers right now?"

"Sir, I will take Allied Officers with me, but only the ones who have been fully vetted by General Greene and the CIA's personnel. In other words, only about a third of them will be traveling with me. We've got a cover story for the other two thirds to take leave with their respective governments, until this thing fully develops. I mean face it, until we get a handle on who the bad guys are, and how far they've infiltrated us, then I want to keep my staff small and mobile."

"Excellent. Let's make it happen."

"Thank you, Mr. President." With that he stood up and I walked him out to his waiting security and administrative entourage. Along the way, we discussed more about the family enclave and we made arrangements for our families to start infiltrating that way within the next few days. Fortunately, the Gomers were kind enough to give those days to us, but we didn't have much hope that they would allow us much longer.

Chapter IV

Supreme Allied Headquarters, (SAHQ):

Getting Leah out of the mountain and into our little hideaway took some very serious persuasion. After a number of hours discussing it, she was finally convinced that it was the best thing under the circumstances, especially in light of the extended family that would need to be protected from both the dissidents and the Gomer threats. Assuming that she and the family would be under observation at all times, either by air or by a well-placed dissident, the subterfuge for their movement and relocation took a little planning, a lot of deception, and at least a page or two from the old 'CIA Tradecraft Primer.' Without getting into great detail, the art of getting lost in a crowd takes skill, and the occasional body double, to lead observers down a different path. My family wasn't alone in this operation. General Whitney's wife, General Larkin's wife, and Admiral Lynch's bride, along with President Blanchard's family, were all having to do the same thing. It was probably even more challenging for the President's family, given their overall notoriety, but it was handled with precision. The Secret Service and Military Police were both beside themselves as the operation unfolded, but within 72 hours, everyone that needed to be relocated was now in a new location with plenty of security forces to ensure their safety.

Watching my bride leaving under those circumstances was hard, and it was equally hard having to ship Chris, John, and my grandson to their new quarters hidden away in the new family enclave. The irony of living like a Gomer wasn't lost on me, but it was all we could do under the current tactical circumstances. Chris wasn't happy, because she was not going to be working in my office, and John wasn't happy to be out of the lab. More to the point, the only one who seemed to be happy about the change in circumstances was my grandson, who saw it all as just another adventure. The only family members still out and about would be Holly and Robbie who, because of their military functions, were just going to have to take their chances like their old man. I felt a personal guilt at hiding my family away like this, especially when other people couldn't follow these same steps, but I also recognized that aside from the Gomers, at least other people weren't being targeted specifically by Gomers, terrorists, or dissidents. This latter group would be more likely to take the family hostage, and that was completely unacceptable for any of the key leadership. As a result, our new family enclave was well secured with a number of highly trained ASOC security personnel and their families also in residence.

The Family Facilities, Peterstown, WV:

Leah was not really happy that Mike had offered up the secret family complex to certain members of his staff and their families. Oh, she loved both Toni Blanchard and Martha Clark, and they'd all been friends now for several years, but this was not what she'd had in mind when it came to hiding from the "bad guys." The housing area was originally designed and outfitted to accommodate the family, not a horde of outsiders. There were complete and stocked quarters for Mother Patrick, Chris and John, along with little Michael, and then a space for herself and Mike. They had even taken the time to make sure there were other guest facilities, but all of these rooms were more Spartan, and honestly, were designed to take in other family members, not the First Lady of the United States. Complications only abounded when to the original list, a number of other guests were starting to appear at the main entrance seeking sanctuary, especially since some of these other guests came with their very own entourage of children. The numbers were starting to get out of hand, and it wasn't long before materials were being surreptitiously brought into the cave to permit for the building of other rooms. When the dust settled, Toni Blanchard, along with their two daughters Rhonda Taylor and Hayley Timmons, were now living in what was originally Leah and Michael's quarters.

Rhonda Taylor, wife of Commander Thomas "Tommy" Taylor, USN, is the youngest of the President's children. When she arrived at the invitation of her mother, she came with her three children, four-year-old son, David, five-year-old daughter. Tonya, and her oldest boy, seven-year-old Martin. Toni's oldest daughter, Hayley Timmons, the widow of Lieutenant Colonel James Whitmore Timmons, who was killed in the Second Gomer War, also showed up within a few hours of her sister. She arrived at the facility in less than a normal state of mind. Aside from more shuffling of quarters, it was obvious that Hayley was still grieving and had some rather serious personal issues that would require a lot of attention. She didn't come alone, and it was equally clear that her two children, eight-year-old Heather and sixteen-year-old Daniella, were about the only things holding her together.

Over the following several days, even more families began to arrive. As each new family came to the facility, they were welcomed with open arms, and the living arrangements were modified, at least until other rooms could be constructed. After the end of the first week, it was starting to look more like a trailer park with some very high-class residents, than the simple family shelter originally intended for the cave complex. Leah's frustration was growing, at least until Katie Clagmore arrived. Katie, wife of Command Sergeant

Major Clagmore, was a longtime friend of Leah and, while she was childless, there was no question that she absolutely adored being around children. Given the burgeoning population of children, Katie, along with Martha Clark, were to be a huge help in the days, weeks, and months ahead.

Another arrival was met with much less excitement by both Leah and Mother Patrick. Within seconds of her arrival, the entire mood changed, and not necessarily for the better. Chris made it clear that she loathed this woman, and with her enforced absence from work, she was less than thrilled that she would have to breath the same air as Mrs. Lou Ann Whitney. From the second she hit the cave entrance, Mrs. Whitney had made it abundantly clear that she was a retired Brigadier General who left the Army after the first war, only to please her husband. She didn't have any children to keep her attention, and some would argue that this wouldn't have mattered, since she was far too self-centered to ever raise anything other than a "ruckus." The only thing that might have been a saving grace to either Toni or Leah, was that at least Lou Ann appeared to begrudgingly love her husband, General Edward "Whit" Whitney. Otherwise, she was far too argumentative to ever qualify as "good company."

Finally, there were other, far more pleasant, women to arrive. Each one was not only welcomed with open arms, but it didn't take long at all for them to become vital members of their little impromptu community. Carrie Roberts was extremely sweet, and although a little naive about some things, she was energetically bubbly. Younger than the other wives, at 35, Carrie was soon fast friends with Chris Patrick. They had a lot in common. Aside from being the same age, they were both born in Army Hospitals in Georgia, and they both had little boys roughly the same age. Carrie's two boys were seven-year-old Carter, and nine-year-old Edward. When Alicia Jones, married to General "Deacon" Jones, brought her three children into the facility, the raucous behavior was contagious. Alicia's children, ten-year-old

Marcus, twelve-year-old Samantha, and fifteen-year-old Sonya, were so well behaved that Alicia became the go-to person for many of the younger mothers who were fishing for non-judgmental advice. Finally, there was Irina Dubronin, and their two-year-old son, Yuri. She also had a new surprise for the crowd, when she came straight from the Hospital Facilities in the Mountain with her newborn baby girl, Leah Petra Dubronin. Leah was beside herself over this arrival, since it was obvious that the baby had been named for Leah and for Irina's own mother in Russia.

Over the next few weeks, construction was ongoing in the original "Patrick" facility. The crowd was settling into the cave, and schools were starting up to take care, not only of their own children, but of the several secret service families that were also now moving into the cave. Over the next few weeks, the population had swollen to the point that another cave was now being utilized for the families of the security forces, the billeting of the security forces themselves, and for other more basic services. Leah had worried initially that she would wind up bored, waiting on things to resolve themselves in the world, and now she was doing all she could to keep up with her schedule.

The sheer enormity of the numbers involved, along with their families, can only be understood when you evaluate the size of the protective force that was required. The VIP Family Facility, as it was now becoming known, now included a number of Security Personnel from various sources. The Fourth Army, charged for the main security, contributed a battalion from the 98th Infantry Division. Their job was to man a defensive perimeter around the several cave entrances. Inner security for the two main caves was provided by ASOC, and the men from C/1/75th Ranger Regiment. Located on several nearby ridges were the units charged with the overall Air Defense for the facility. These young and boisterous gentlemen were from the 2nd Battalion, 903rd Gmr Arty Brigade, and when Leah first saw them, she was a little shocked at how young they seemed. Finally, inside the "Patrick" cave, and much nearer the VIP's actual quarters, was located a Secret Service Detachment of 14 Agents and a Special Agent in Charge. They and their families lived in the adjacent cave system, but they worked in the main living area for the VIPS with five agents on duty at any given time.

This wasn't a small operation, and there were contingencies upon contingencies that could be brought to bear in the event of an attempt by any attackers on the facility. The Fourth Army had a quick reaction force, of almost Regimental size, that would be used should the facility ever come under attack. In the meantime, creating an underground infrastructure for these families, without leaving a foot print on the outside, was no small task. Leah couldn't help but feel responsible, since this was her cave and she was the nominal hostess. Naturally, Mother Patrick, Chris, and Holly, shouldered that same feeling. It was obvious to Leah that this would NOT be a simple war, nor would it likely be a short one.

Supreme Allied Headquarters, (SAHQ) - Tiger Island, Honduras:

General Clark stepped off the aircraft and wondered at how this was supposed to be a good idea. The island sat alone in the middle of the water, within sight of the coasts of Nicaragua, Honduras, and El Salvador. Talk about a target! The extinct volcano stood in rather stark contrast to its surroundings, and even the old logistician understood that it was something a Gomer would blast in a heartbeat. He also knew, after his experience watching Diamond Head disappear in Hawaii in the first Gomer War, that the power of the Gomer Mountain or Battleship Class ships, would be more than sufficient to remove Tiger Island completely from the map. Descending into the labyrinth of tunnels, his escort continued to take him downward from the helipad at the top of the Mountain, until he finally arrived at an entrance that led back to the docks of the small Honduran Naval base. Scratching his head, General Clark was then taken to one of the Honduran supply boats that led over to the coast several miles away.

General Clark was not taking this well at all and was about to raise holy hell when the Honduran officer, speaking perfect Oxford English, identified himself as an ASOC operator. One of Greene's officers as a matter of fact, and he made no bones about the General needing to sit down in the cabin and "please don't make a scene." As the boat approached the dock, the General was given a Honduran Naval uniform, and told, "Sir, please, put this on, we can't have anyone spotting you." General Clark wasn't used to this cloak and dagger crap. Turning to the Operator, he said, "Dammit, we're here to fight Gomers, not fricking play spy vs. spy."

"That is quite true, sir. Unfortunately, right now you can't tell them apart, and besides, we have reason to believe that we're being observed by the Gomers."

"You mean right now? All the way down here?"

"Yes, Sir. No question. We know they are tracking all the key players in the Allied Command. That's why you guys are falling off the grid a few at a time."

"Hell, son, I'm just the logistician. 'Box kicker sticker licker,' is what Patrick calls me."

"Sir. General Patrick indicated to my boss, General Greene, that you were absolutely vital, and that you were the best in the business. We are giving *you* the VIP treatment."

"Flattery will get you nowhere, you know."

"With all due respect, flattery isn't why you're here. Besides, if you were being followed or observed, we'd hate for you to lead the bad guys to the good guys, now wouldn't we?"

"Okay. Point made. So how long before I get to where I'm going?"

"Sir, I'd say in about three days, and at least four more changes of clothes. Be patient, and we'll get you there. The good news for you is that some of your peers were taken to your final destination on a leaking old oil tanker, and at least one guy was on a pack mule for several hours."

"Oil tanker? Pack mule? Just where the hell are we going?"

"Can't tell you sir, just in case you don't make it. We can't have you telling anyone else, like the bad guys, now can we?"

"Sheeee-IT! If you were trying to keep me calm, you just failed pretty fucking miserably."

"Sir, if I were you, I'd feel more sympathy for your body double back in the Mountain. I'm pretty sure that the old E-8 from the Truck Company can't be too excited about his chances right now."

"You mean there is somebody back there who is trying to pass themselves off as me?"

"Yessir. He is sick in quarters, but yeah. Nobody really knows for sure whether you are at Tiger Island, or still in the Mountain."

"Okay, now I'm well and for truly not happy. What about my wife?"

"She was going shopping with General Patrick's wife in Washington, wasn't she?"

"Yeah...?"

"Well, she is fine and with the key leaders' wives at an undisclosed location. General Patrick will brief you when he sees you. Just rest assured that she is safe, and should remain that way for quite a while."

"At least that is something. Okay, what next?"

"Next? Well, see that long sleeved shirt and machete'?"

"Yeah. Well, when it is time, you'll be getting dressed again. You're going for a ride on the back of that supply truck after it unloads the fruits and vegetables headed back to the island."

"Fu…"

Supreme Allied Headquarters (SAHQ) - USS Connecticut, SSN 22:

The USS Connecticut is a specially equipped and highly modified submarine of the USS Seawolf class. Converted for special operations use, she was currently operating very silently in the Gulf of Honduras, almost within sight of the Honduran naval facilities at Puerto Cortes. Partially surfacing among the small fishing fleet, several zodiac boats set out to pick up their respective passengers. Among them were Generals Whitney, Roberts, and Clark, who all looked a little worse for the wear. As with most things dealing with the Gomers, this operation was being done almost at high noon, which made conditions even worse. The heat was oppressive, and the water was quite infested with several species of rather menacing sharks. As they climbed on the partially exposed deck, they were not at all happy. Acknowledging each other, they were exhausted after the three days traveling across Honduras. From Tiger Island, to Tegucigalpa, to San Pedro Sulu, and finally to Puerto Cortes, they felt as though they were in a bad Travel Channel special. The Country was beautiful, mountainous, and in some locations, purely breath taking.

The real problem was all the hiding and moving about like they weren't really who they were, not to mention the means of their travel to this destination. General Roberts had drawn the leg of the journey that involved the donkey trip, and while he wouldn't admit it to any of his peers, his thighs and ass were killing him. General Clark had been beaten half to death traveling in the back of a vegetable truck through the mountains, while General Whitney spent a lot of time enclosed in the back of a tourist bus, hiding in the "out of order" rest room. The stench was still heavy in his nostrils, and he was particularly out of sorts about the entire experience. In each case, they'd been flown in like General Clark, and in each case, they'd been smuggled off the island within a short time of their arrival. They each thought that their baggage might never be seen again, although, the ASOC personnel had worked a few miracles to make sure that most of it eventually caught up to them.

Two nights later, the boss finally showed up, on yet another foray of the same fishing fleet to where the USS Connecticut was hiding. Admiral Lynch was the first through the hatch, and they'd never seen anyone look so happy to be on a submarine in their entire lives. Next through the hatch was General Patrick, who was sporting a pair of jodhpurs, brown cavalry boots, and a huge grin. If he'd added a campaign hat and stars to the shirt, he would be wearing the same uniform the Army wore right before World War II. He looked as though he was the only person who had enjoyed his trip. When they compared notes, it was learned that he'd come almost the entire way through Honduras on horseback and, like General Roberts, he was less than comfortable when he tried to sit down. It had taken almost a week, but the entire key staff was now onboard the USS Connecticut, just as the President was now established, along with his key cabinet members, onboard the USS Seawolf. Their only difference was that this was not the Allied Staff's final destination, instead it was merely the penultimate leg of their journey.

Despite their movements, the staff were watching the skies, and monitoring all the movements of both the Gomers and the Russian dissidents. The Gomers were not moving towards Earth just yet, but there were increasing signs of Gomer ship traffic heading to and from the area behind Neptune. There were also more unconfirmed sightings of Gomer Fighter Class ships making brief forays into the remote polar regions. The latest estimates indicated that a total of 123 major or larger Gomer Class ships had transited the areas between

Mars and Neptune over the previous 48-hour period. Some on the staff were seeing this as a good thing, since the traffic seemed to be mostly outbound to Neptune, as opposed to any forces moving towards Mars, thereby bolstering the forces that were capable of a more immediate attack. Others on the staff were reasoning that it was just the shifting of their 'non-combatants' away from the potential war zone. Regardless, General Patrick, General Greene, and the President were all being extremely cautious in their views, and there was no sign to anyone on staff that this drill was going to end any time soon. Instead, the reports from ASOC and General Greene were causing more concern by the day. The outward movement wasn't the problem, instead, it was the movement through the Gomer Embassy on St. Lawrence Island that had them worried the most.

USS Montana, Near the Panama Canal (Atlantic side):

It wasn't my first choice for a flag ship, but that was no reflection on the ship or the crew, it was about the memories of my wife having been onboard. Still, the Montana would be perfect for the next phase, and she would be my home for only the next few weeks. Like some of our enemies from the past, I was now adopting the need to move and shift my position frequently to keep the other side guessing. For now, my staff and I were at least back on the surface, but the USS Connecticut was my back-up, and she was never more than a few miles away from us at any given time. It wasn't optimal, but then again, this time around the dynamic was completely different.

We weren't just dealing with the Gomer threat, we now had to worry about our own kind, and their complicity in selling us down the road. The net was drawing ever closer, and the civilian population was just now starting to disperse. The lack of work in certain areas was starting to be a favorable factor in getting some people to move to more dispersed locations. We were also dispersing all of our manufacturing, but this was the kind of thing that takes a great deal of time. What we could move quickly, we moved, thereby triggering a shift in population. Backhoes around the country were digging virtually 24/7. It was remarkable how many mobile homes, travel trailers, steel containers, and portable buildings were being placed underground, or just outright buried into hillsides. In many instances, people were placing as much lead or Sulphur on top of their new homes as they could find.

News was trickling in that aside from the relocation projects, new shelter projects and munitions production were all increasing as rapidly and as surreptitiously as possible. Similarly, the code breakers and cyber warriors in the Rockies were working overtime to get us the latest in Gomer intercepts. Still, there was no question that we were running out of time. As we watched, the numbers and types of Gomer ships headed back to Mars were increasing to massive proportions. This was no longer regular traffic to another location away from Earth, this was more along the lines of an armada, and it was taking up a position near Mars that indicated that they could be headed our way in relatively short order. The progression was disturbing, and we could only hope that we wouldn't run out of time and ideas at the same time. Meanwhile, the Russian dissidents weren't at rest either. It was clear that something was up, and the reports were that our Intelligence Community was spotting some rather unusual movement of several of the key and known members of this organization.

Stockholm, Sweden:

Standing about 5'5", the old heavyset man could best be described as a rodent or rabid squirrel. His actions were furtive, and everything about him reeked of cheap Vodka and cigarettes. His grey hair was on his ears, and his beard and mustache looked as though he'd eaten a 12-course meal with his mouth open. He was perfect for his role, since most people that saw him, never *really* saw him. Instead, their open disgust at his appearance, smell, and demeanor made them turn away and keep moving. Passing by him on the street, everyone seemed to be hoping beyond hope that they wouldn't have to make eye contact with this creature. What they couldn't know was that there was little danger of his looking anyone in the eye, mainly because he was a former KGB operative, and he was on a mission for 'his' former Soviet Republic. The minor fact that it no longer existed was, for him, beside the point. He was tired of it all, and ready to do what had to be done.

Rounding the corner, he noticed that he had company, but he wasn't worried. These new guys were amateurs, and besides, he'd already set things in motion. At most, he might be looking at a little questioning, or maybe even assassination, but it wouldn't matter. Nothing mattered. Vasili Nemechek had already done the unthinkable, and he along with several other operatives in Europe, were seconds from sending their statement to the world! His friend Numonov was in London, and there were at least a half dozen of his former associates located in Berlin, Oslo, Madrid, Paris, Bern, and Brussels. Their plan would be more than effective when it was finally executed. They were here to pave the way for a new Utopia protected by the Gomers, and for them it would be the opening salvo to a new Soviet Socialist Republic that would span the globe. As the amateurs began encircling his location on the street to make an arrest, Vasili looked down at his watch, and then simply smiled and waved at everyone around him. Anyone who could see Vasili couldn't know that he would be the last person they, and thousands of their neighbors, would ever see.

USS Montana, Near the Panama Canal (Atlantic side):

The ELF/ULF and LF frequencies were going absolutely off the rails, and it was happening virtually all at once. The news coming into the Combat Information Center and the Allied Staff was initially very confusing, and in some cases, down-right misleading. Our initial details were very sketchy, but it was becoming quite clear that time was running out and war with the Gomers was probably imminent. In each of the major capitals of Europe, relatively small but highly effective nuclear explosions had taken place. Ground zero for the London explosion was determined to be the Thames River, right next to Parliament. In Brussels, it was a tractor trailer truck driving by NATO headquarters, while in Berlin, it was another truck driving near the Bundestag. In each of the capital cities targeted by the Russian dissidents, there was little doubt that the explosions were timed for maximum casualties to both civilians and government officials. While it was little comfort to anyone on the planet, at least the dissidents were only able to attack targets in Europe. The only good news was that many of these countries were already quietly dispersing both their populations and their key leadership. The loss of life was still tremendous, and to those of us onboard the USS Montana, we knew that this was merely the first shot. It didn't take long before the CIA, FBI, MI-6, MI-5, and the entire Russian Federation Security Services were making mass arrests and/or taking action as required under the circumstances.

While the remaining Russian dissidents were being identified and located, the urban populations were being evacuated from the rest of the major cities around the world. We were past the economic excuse, and were now quite blunt that there might be a foreign threat that should be taken quite seriously. We were careful not to mention the Gomers, but it wouldn't have mattered. Nobody wanted to be jammed in a location that could be a potential ground zero, especially after what took place in Europe. Taking the appropriate cue from these arguably 'human' activities, the media began to encourage dispersal of the population as a response. Sadly, they did little more than panic an already highly spooked public.

All of this wrangling and media coverage did have one up side - it may have bought us a little time, but only a little. The past several weeks had hosted a number of discussions between our Secretary of State, Timothy Case, and the Gomer's latest version of an "Ambassador." There was nothing in these discussions that would indicate that the Gomers were going to make any moves, but there was little comfort either. Our experiences had already taught us that the Gomers don't give away much in direct communications. Secretary Case was faced with the same dilemma we had from day one with the negotiated 'peace' in the Bering Sea. When talking with a Gomer Ambassador, you cannot pick up on any inflection or tone, and over all, the Gomers would just not show any emotion as we know it. It was also a waste of time to try and evaluate them from their use of body language, since again, it was not something we could evaluate intelligently. In short, there was little to be learned from meeting or talking with them in person, and given their previous lies about their past, there was nothing we could use to indicate anything about their real intentions.

Taking the Gomers and their discussions with us in person out of the equation, we were left with having to read between the lines. We could try and evaluate our communication intercepts of their transmissions, as well as their down-loaded computer data. Otherwise, we were left with examining their actions, such as entertaining the dissidents or shifting a number of their larger Class Ships towards Mars. Predicting their future actions was only a little better than a crap shoot, but at least it was an educated crap shoot. Consequently, it was our collective assessment, after reading all the information we had available against the actions of the Russian dissidents, that we were running out of time.

What really tipped the scales were their actions after the blasts in Europe. On the second day after the blasts, there was very little detectable movement from any of the known Gomer locations. On the third day, it began extremely slowly at first, and while fairly imperceptible, it wouldn't take long before a steady stream of the more major classed Gomer Ships was moving in formations of twos and threes from Neptune towards Mars. The ASOC and USAF personnel charged with watching and observing their movements were getting the count together and watching as the Gomer fleet began building up in strength near their colonies on Mars. This time there were no Moon or Mountain Class ships visible, but the numbers of Battleship and Carrier Class ships near or behind Mars was starting to grow exponentially.

On the fourth day, the estimates of Gomer strength were becoming such an astronomical number, it was triggering a very real concern that the fleet could well be greater than double or triple the size of any fleet we had previously encountered. This time, they could well overwhelm us between the sheer numbers and with their anticipated shift in tactics. Watching the buildup of forces, we contacted the President about the criteria and rules of engagement. Most of us knew that, like it or not, we were going to have to give serious consideration to a preemptive strike on the buildup of forces, or run the very real risk of not being able to stem the tide. Then again, their intentions were just as foggy now as they were three weeks ago.

At my direction, we were able to get the USS Seawolf on the ULF, and ask for instructions. It was then I learned that the USS Seawolf was now cruising within an extremely short distance of our location. Setting up a rendezvous, we made arrangements to meet with the President and his staff to discuss our options, and what the rules of engagement might dictate as the time began rapidly towards running out.

The Family Facilities, Peterstown, WV:

The Special Agent in charge of the First Lady's security detail, along with the Commanders responsible for the facility, were crammed into the small makeshift office near the VIP quarters. Each of them read the latest messages and were wondering how much to disseminate to their charges, when the First Lady herself knocked on the door. Looking up, Agent Snellgrove leaped to his feet, and invited Mrs. Blanchard into the small space. Looking around, Mrs. Blanchard waved back behind her, and both she and Leah stepped inside. Stepping in the room, Leah closed the door behind her, and motioned the First Lady to begin.

"Agent Snellgrove? We know what happened, and we think it is high time we started getting the ladies ready to go in a hurry, should something happen around here."

"Ma'am. How did you know what…"

"Mr. Snellgrove, I've been an Army wife for over 36 years, and a first Lady for the last 4 years. I happen to know things that you can only guess at. Now, we want to talk about the 'back door' to this place, and we want to work out a plan for getting out if we need to get out."

"Well, Mrs. Blanchard, we don't…" Leah, cut him off, and jumped into the conversation. "Agent Snellgrove, the First Lady isn't kidding. When General Patrick and I put this place together, we made sure it had a back door. It is marked, and right now, I'm the only one that knows the way. I'm sharing this now, since it would appear that the paradigm has changed out there."

"Mrs. Patrick, I have no idea what you're…"

Toni Blanchard seldom suffered fools, and she knew when she was being sandbagged on something. Face it, she'd raised enough children to know when someone was full of it. Before Agent Snellgrove could finish his sentence, he saw what few men had ever seen. Toni Blanchard was now officially pissed, and when he saw the look on Mrs. Patrick's face, he knew it was contagious. "Agent Snellgrove, as the First Lady of the United States, I'm telling you, not asking! You are to put together a plan, you are to consult with us, and you will make sure that we've run a few practice drills, so that we can get out of here."

"Ma'am. With all due respect, I honestly do not think there is a need. The Gomers won't..."

Leah jumped in this time, and she did it with a glare that would have frozen water at 250 yards. Turning to the Lieutenant Colonel in command of the infantry battalion, she simply said, "Colonel, if this jerk won't do it, then I'm counting on you. I want protective masks, you know, gas masks for everyone. Oh, and included in that needs to be at least five gas masks or suits for infants. Next, I want at least five pair of Night Vision Goggles, one starlight scope with IR emitter, two IR strobes, and two dozen IR emitting chem sticks. We seem to be good on weapons, so I think we have everything else we need, but assigning us four soldiers to assist in the movement of the children would probably be a good idea."

Without skipping a beat, the Colonel responded with a "Yes, Ma'am. You'll have it by this evening. Anything else?"

Now it was the Secret Services' chance to chime in, "Ma'am. The Gomers, ..."

"Agent Snellgrove. Sorry to interrupt, but I wasn't talking to you. I was talking to the Colonel. Now then, for your information, the Gomers are no longer our main problem. If you're too slow to see it, then that is between you and your bosses. The Colonel here knows what I know. The real threat is now the same human element that committed these acts of terror inside the cities of Europe. Agent Snellgrove, you can't fool me, I'm not that damn stupid."

The silence was deafening, and the Secret Service Agent in charge just discovered that he was not "baby sitting ladies." Some of them knew their business, and while he had never met Mrs. Patrick, it was obvious that either her husband rubbed off on her, or she rubbed off on him. In either case, her request was pretty damned specific, and her knowledge of what was going on was frankly unnerving. Once the ladies left, he turned to both the Lieutenant Colonel and the young Ranger Captain, and asked, "How do they know so much?"

Without skipping a beat as he turned to leave, the Colonel looked over his shoulder and said, "Dude. One is an Army wife with over 36 years' experience on shooting ranges, and the other is former CIA, and a graduate of the 'Farm.' You'll figure out which is which, but both of them can outshoot most of your agents in this damn facility. If I were you, I'd stop pissing them off, since I happen to know for a fact that they both could kill you in your sleep, and then make it look like a bat from Romania did it."

SECTION 2

TIMES UP! THEY'RE HERE - AGAIN!

Chapter V

❦

USS Seawolf, 100 yards away from the USS Montana, 65 miles off the eastern coast of the Florida Keys:

Standing on the bridge wings of the USS Montana, the lookouts had spotted the USS Seawolf almost the instant she broached the surface. Once the USS Seawolf was close enough, the signal lights between the ships were constant until the USS Seawolf was finally within actual hailing distance of the USS Montana. Several members of my key staff and I were preparing to leave the USS Montana, when we were instructed by signal light from the USS Seawolf to hold fast. Looking towards the submarine, we watched as a zodiac was launched with a number of personnel on board. The small boat pulled up to the gangway of the USS Montana, and the President rather unceremoniously began the long climb up the ladder to the deck. After stopping twice to catch his breath, the President saluted aft, and then requested permission to come aboard. There were no "side boys" and no "honors" as befitting a President, it was just business as usual, even if it was hurried business. After the Officer of the Deck gave permission for him to come aboard, I went forward and saluted the President. Smiling at me, or maybe it was more of a grimace, we immediately made our way to the Admiral's cabin, where I was now maintaining my quarters. Neither of us said much, at least until the bulkhead hatch was secured, and then we got down to business.

"General Patrick, how the hell are you?"

"I'm fine, Mr. President. How about you?"

"I have to tell you, Mouse. Submarine living is horse shit! I have to get off that damned sardine can, otherwise I'm going to hurt somebody."

"Mr. President. You were a tanker, so I didn't think that a small steel space would be a problem for you."

"In a tank, you can at least stick your head out of the top hatch. From what I've seen, that practice is just a little impractical on a submarine."

With that, I burst out laughing, and the President continued, "Dammit. I mean it!"

"Sir, I never thought of it that way, but now that you mention it…"

"Okay. Mike, we have to find other arrangements. Safety be damned!"

"Marty, we may have just the deal for you. Daniel Greene advised me this morning that the new alternate command center is in place near his location. He says it is deep, has remote and cabled relays for all radios, regardless of frequency, and that it can accommodate you and your key staff."

"Why wasn't I told of this sooner?"

"Sir, you know the drill. Security, security, and security. Besides, it wasn't finished and ready to be opened until about three hours ago."

"Good. How long to get me there?"

"Admiral Lynch and General Whitney have worked on the deception plan, and we should have you there in about 32 hours or less. No direct routing, but it can be done, assuming you decide to head there."

"DONE! I'll tell my boys to pack!"

"Sir, if you don't mind, I'll get General Whitney to handle that for you. In the meantime, we need to chat, and we'll be sending you and Secretary Todd separate from the rest of your staff."

"Okay." With the President's approval, I got on the line and told General Whitney to make the arrangements and set up the staff transportation.

"Now, Mr. President, you're all set and when you leave here, it will be to head to your next destination. We've got a cargo flight headed to Kings Bay in about 30 minutes, and you'll be on it. General Greene will personally meet you, to escort you to your new Situation Facility."

"Excellent."

"What I need from you, sir, is some guidance on the Rules of Engagement."

"What do you mean?" With his question, we began our explanation and discussion about our concerns over the fleet that was gathering overhead around Mars. After 15 minutes of discussion about the situation, and 5 minutes of thought, the President offered the best guidance I ever received. "Clearly, if the bastards move towards the Moon, kill as many of them as you can. As for anything else, use your common sense and I'll back your decision." When those latter words came from his mouth, I reminded him of where they'd been spoken once before.

"Mr. President. You do know that the 'use your common sense' Order was given by Admiral Kimmel to Admiral Halsey a few days before the attack on Pearl Harbor?"

"I did know it, which is precisely why I'm giving it to you. This time, we have to avoid the 'Pearl Harbor' type attack that we both know is coming. Hell, no! Not on my watch."

"Yessir. We will continue to disperse as much as possible, but near points from where we can move quickly to strike back. Fortunately, our end strength, despite Congress not being happy about it, is still large enough to field our two main Army Groups, along with several of our Allied Army Groups. We just need to lay it low, since we don't want to lose what we've lost before in the last two opening bids as the war started."

"Good. Now, how the hell do I get back to dry land. I'm Army, dammit!"

"Mr. President, talk about history! I had almost this same conversation with a certain Sergeant Major we both know. Not once, but now twice"

"Ha! That old bastard! Where is Sergeant Major Clagmore?"

"He is two decks down, and he is the brains behind the operations to get all of our families to their new secure homes. Officially, he is my new Allied Headquarters Sergeant Major, and despite his kicking and screaming the whole way, he is doing one excellent job. He also handpicked all of the troopers that are the outer and inner rings of security around that facility."

"How'd you manage that?"

"Well, I had a little help. He flunked his last Airborne physical, because of a ruptured ear drum, so I snatched him up." The President howled and we parted with a handshake as I accompanied him to the aft helipad for departure back to dry land. When he stepped on board the helicopter, it was without a doubt the happiest I'd seen him in quite a while. I wasn't so sure he'd look that happy if he'd known the path he was about to take to get to his new home, but then again, at least his trip wouldn't involve a horse.

After the President departed the ship, and the rest of the President's staff were being processed and sent in their various directions to rendezvous with the President at their new location, we then began the daily process of verifying that our units were where we wanted them, and that there was a viable and secure means of communicating with them. Initially, this situation created more problems, but believe it or not, the use of very old school technology was making it at least workable. Teletype systems were coming back into vogue, as were the old telegraph lines throughout the world. Cable systems were employed where possible, and anytime we could talk through a wire, that was the procedure followed. Needless to say, we were starting to discover that being at sea on the USS Montana, with our communications limited to VLF/ELF burst transmissions, was becoming somewhat of a problem in the coordination of our ground units.

Over the next several days, we were constantly updating the information related to both the Gomer force and our own. I had Generals Whitney and Roberts begin their daily briefings by identifying the locations and dispersion plans for most of the Allied Army. We were still relying on mountainous locations, but they were at least a little more spread out and well defended. Admiral Lynch then would give me a similar update on the dispersion of our Naval Forces around the world. General Kaminski, Allied Air Force Operations, would launch into his dissertation regarding the dispersion of the Strategic, Tactical, Strategic Mobility, and related Missile forces. What wasn't ever covered was the status of Site X, but otherwise, both Vandenberg and Bozeman facilities were briefed in full. Finally, General Clark, my Logistics expert, would provide me an updated briefing on the latest version of the dispersion plan and on the locations of the critical supplies we would need to sustain our forces. Only time would tell if we were on the money with the dispersion plan, but there was no question that we had already accomplished a great deal in a very short period of time.

With each briefing, I felt more confident that we had accomplished these Herculean feats without tipping our hand to the Gomers or the Russian dissidents. The only hole in our diversion and deception plan was in the area of Russian Forces, where it could be assumed that there was a higher potential for the infiltration of dissidents among their ranks. As a result, Major Dubronin, my aide and son to President Dubronin, of the Russian Federation, was very careful but specific in talking with his father. They too were painfully aware of the situation, and they accepted that they would have to employ deception within even their own forces. The solution for them was an exercise of record proportions within the Russian Army, Air, and Naval forces. In fact, it was the largest exercise ever mounted by their country, and it was justified within the parameters of the recent devastation of the various Capital cities within Europe. President Dubronin himself was in the field to observe these exercises, and was fairly confident that they had done what they could to be away and hard to find. One thing was sure, President Dubronin had a high incentive to engage in this process, since there was no question that the dissidents had made him a priority target for their plots to eliminate him as the legitimate government.

Supreme Allied Headquarters, (SAHQ) on board the USS Montana, now located 75 miles Southeast of Maine:

The next intelligence report broke within a day of the President's return to his new Situation Facility in the Rocky Mountains. Coming over the wire from General Greene's Headquarters, it was learned that a large cache of hand-held "Gomer" weapons was intercepted in transit from the Gomer Embassy to a location in Russia. The freighter, the *M/V Artamus*, was found to be containing these weapons. A frequent sight in the northern latitudes, the *Artamus* had left northern Canada, taking the Northern Route, only a few days before being intercepted. The interception was simply a matter of pure luck, but sometimes luck is all you have working for you. In this case, the old freighter developed engine problems, and was encountering some bad weather near Iceland. The USS Inouye intercepted the ship to render aid, and it was discovered that there was a shipment of Gomer hand-held weapons on board.

What tipped off the crew of the USS Inouye? When the naval ship arrived to render assistance, the crew of the freighter refused any help, despite the obvious need for all the assistance they could receive. This was not the normal actions of a ship that was obviously disabled and transmitting that it needed assistance on the high seas. Given the heightened tensions, the Captain of the USS Inouye was immediately suspicious and, following my guidance to all commanders to 'use their common sense,' he sent over an armed boarding party. It didn't take long before almost 200 cases of weapons were discovered hidden among the rest of the cargo. It was also learned that this wasn't the first trip made by the M/V *Artamus* with possible Gomer contraband on board, and the crew and her Captain were still being interrogated at length by representatives of the intelligence community.

This was just one more sign that either the Gomers were going to attack us directly or, at the very least, were arming any human they felt would assist them with the elimination of their own kind. In either instance, we were looking at a *Casus Belli*, which was sufficient for whatever steps we would need to take as the overall picture developed. Simultaneous to our seizure of these weapons, the Gomers were continuing to build up their combat strength near their Mars colonies.

A new trend was developing concurrent with the addition of the Major Combat Class ships; the Gomers were sending almost 5 times the number of normal transport traffic towards Mars. In almost all cases, these unarmed transport vessels were being escorted by several Carrier Class Ships as they transited from Neptune, and its moon Triton, to Mars. These ships were not landing, but instead, were in a holding pattern that kept them mostly obscured by the Martian planet. The clear inference was that this time their attacks could well be accompanied by Gomer ground forces, as well as partisan action from the Russian dissidents. We did not relish this potential combination, and several of our Special Operators within ASOC were working on various contingencies to counter the problem. Unlike the sabotage of my aircraft in the Second Gomer War, this time around, we could expect more open support from the dissidents, especially if they were being equipped by the Gomers with any of their weapons.

The final part of our preparations involved the controlled proliferation and deployment of additional Gomer Guns, of both large and smaller varieties, to many of our allied nations. This time, the Chinese, all of our NATO allies, the Japanese, and certain trusted Russian Units were deployed with the Gomer technology. These Russian units were supposedly very elite, having been hand-picked by President Dubronin himself, and we could only hope that he was good at filtering out the dissidents. We were even prepared on a more global scale by modifying the technology to extend the range of some of our key weapon systems to an excess of 150 miles into space. This was a huge help, especially where we were concerned about the standoff range of both the Battleship Class and Mountain Class Gomer ships. The down side for this new Gomer weapon system involved the immobility of the weapon itself, the costs in production, and the limited numbers available for use around the world. As a result, we could only place these monsters in very limited, but highly vital areas, such as Vandenberg, Bozeman, around key installations, and at two different ports with ship yards. The replacement of Sulphur based munitions, expended in the previous war, was almost complete, and we also had a few new surprises based on at least one newly discovered weakness. While we were ready as we could be, at least under the circumstances, none of us deluded ourselves into believing that we were really ready. As Command Sergeant Major Clagmore was often fond of saying, "Nobody is ready for a fucking Gomer!"

On our last full day of peace, we had finally moved into our new defense complex in a secure location that was carved out of a Mountain in the heart of New Hampshire. We were still in the process of transferring some of the staff into our new home from our transient location in Maine, but we were at least online and operational. Not to put too fine a point on it, we were barely online and operational, but we were up and running nonetheless. We didn't know it at the time, but we only had a few hours before the Gomers and the Russian dissidents would finally tip their hands. It was pure luck that allowed our Headquarters to be back online with a full array of communications when the attacks began, and by the end of the first day, this would make a huge difference for all of us.

Seward Peninsula, Alaska:

The twilight line was just passing over the town of Seward, in the State of Alaska, and heading for St. Lawrence Island, when several Gomer Fighter Class ships were spotted by ground observers in the Seward area. It wasn't a huge flight of them, but there were approximately eight ships flying to the Southeast towards St. Lawrence Island and the Gomer's "Embassy" compound. They had not received permission, nor would it have been granted, since they were armed ships.

What scared us the most is that they were not identified until they were already entering the atmosphere of the Earth. This raised a number of alarm bells, since it was quite apparent that these craft should have been detected earlier in their travel from Mars. This led to the immediate re-booting of the observation system, and an increase in the surveillance posture, that would now include the incorporation of more visual observation personnel using high powered telescopes. It was one of these telescope stations that spotted the initial attack fleet, and it was one of these stations that identified the large quantity of Fighter Class ships that were even then moving into the atmosphere over various key targets. Three of the original flight of eight Gomer Fighter Class ships made an abrupt landing inside the Gomer compound area, and our observers were able to verify fairly quickly that the "Ambassador" and his Gomer staff were all airlifted out within minutes of the first Fighter's touchdown. All of this information was quickly processed, and the War Warning was dispatched around the globe within seconds.

The last of these first three Gomer Fighter ships was lifting off from the Embassy compound, when the first of the remaining flight of five ships was touching down in several remote areas around Kamchatka. They did not remain on the ground long, but it was long enough to either deliver or pick up something from that area. Each of the five remaining Fighters continued to sweep along right behind the Twilight line, while the three dispatched to retrieve the Ambassador immediately left Earth Space continuing onward to Mars. In fact, it was the tracking of these three ships heading outbound that led our observers to identify the massive oncoming fleet of more Gomer Fighter Class ships that appeared now to be on a path that would take them inbound towards Northern Russia.

Continuing to follow the Twilight Line, the original five remaining Fighter Class ships made a number of stops. They were not absorbing energy but, instead, were either continuing the pattern of dropping something off or picking something up. It didn't take us long to determine that these stops were not random, but were more likely the exchange of supplies or materials from the dissidents. Each of these stops was at a location we believed to be the location for several key Russian dissidents scattered around that part of the world. A brief consultation with our own CIA Liaison Officer confirmed that each of the spots where a Gomer had stopped was an area that was suspected to be a location where the dissident's leadership was hiding.

The initial wave of these Gomer Fighters continued along behind the Twilight line until they reached a location near Greenland and the Denmark Straits, where they made an abrupt departure from Earth. The observers all watched as these last five ships raced outwards, and on direct courses straight for Mars. The speculation was long on what they may have been doing in their trip around the world, but it was clear that they had ceased any pretense of a diplomatic presence with the departure of their "Embassy" staff. It was also highly suspected that they were either extracting key dissidents, or they were providing them direct assistance. In either instance, this had to be verified, and the CIA, MI-6, and Russian Federation Secret Services, were all moving in on the last of these locations shortly after the departure of the Gomer Fighters.

At the same time, several police type raids were conducted ahead of the Twilight line, in Canada and the United States, to eliminate any home-grown potential threats. It was here that we learned, for the first time, that each of the cells of dissidents had a Gomer advisor. We didn't learn this until a second raid in Quebec was completed, and a Gomer in a hazmat suit was found dead among the dissidents when their "safe house" was struck before night fall. A rather large cache of Gomer hand held weapons was also recovered, and unfortunately, there were more weapons found than we had as a total count of known dissidents. This led us to believe that the cancer might still be a threat, simply because we didn't get it all.

Ural'sk (Oral), Kazakhstan:

The General in command of the Russian Army Group, Vladimir Petrofsky, was engaged in the exercises that were being observed by President Yuri Dubronin. All ten of his Field Armies were now scattered from the Ural Mountains to the Caucus Mountains, and into the region around the Carpathian Mountains. Along with the Russian President, he was summoned into his headquarters bunker where he was met with an extremely worried staff. The information that they were receiving from the Supreme Allied Headquarters was not good, and the War Warning message, coupled with the overflights by several of the Gomer Fighter Class ships, was sufficient for him to put everyone on high alert. The staff immediately set about contacting each of the Field Armies to advise everyone of the situation and to put their operations plans into action. These calls were all acknowledged, except by the two Army Headquarters located in or around the Caucus Mountains. For some reason, these units were not responding, and more to the point, reconnaissance reports were indicating that these Armies may well be moving northward towards Moscow.

At various check points along the route from Groznyy, it was being reported that the advance units of the 8th Russian Army were attacking and eliminating anyone along their path. What made this even more alarming was that they were using Gomer Weapons in their attack. From what President Dubronin was getting from General Petrofsky, these weren't just the larger artillery type weapons, but hand-held weapons were also being employed. Within an hour, it was determined that one more Russian Field Army was now also "offline" and moving from the Carpathian Mountains towards Kiev, Ukraine. It was apparent to both General Petrofsky and President Dubronin that they weren't just facing the Gomers anymore. Now they were up against a civil war, being supported by the Gomers.

Supreme Allied Headquarters, (SAHQ - Main):

Our operations staff was continuing to monitor the movement of the Gomers and the massing of their Fighter Class Ships, when a number of strange messages began to arrive from the Russian Army Groups monitoring the Siberian areas. While the picture was not particularly clear, it gelled quickly when my Aide, Major Dubronin, Russian Federation, came rushing towards me. "General!!"

"Alexander, you look like you've seen a ghost. You okay?"

"Sir, there is a revolt in my homeland. According to my father, three full field armies are now on the side of the dissidents, and fighting is breaking out to the south and west of Moscow."

"DAMN! Like we don't have enough problems with the Gomers. Okay, show me what you know." Major Dubronin wasted no time in pointing out the situation on our maps, and he briefed me fully on what he knew about the events in his homeland. This information came to him directly as an urgent message from his Father and, from assessing the picture, it was quite apparent to me that we would need to elevate this to the President, and make arrangements to get President Dubronin somewhere safe as quickly as possible. Whatever happened, we couldn't let Murmansk or Archangel fall into the hands of anyone in bed with the Gomers, or a dissident to become the leader of the entire Russian country. If either of those things happened, there would be the devil to pay to get our troops there to defend against the Gomers, or to prevent them from moving back into Siberia.

Once I was fully briefed by Major Dubronin, I called over the rest of the staff to hear what I just heard, and while Major Dubronin was getting them caught up, I contacted the President via the land line. "Mr. President. We have a very delicate situation with a rather sizable contingent of our foreign forces."

"What?"

"Almost a third of the Russian Army Group has flipped over and is now supporting the new Communist dissidents. As of a few minutes ago, three full Russian Field Armies are marching either towards Moscow or towards Kiev. My guess is that the Russian forces headed to Kiev will then also turn towards Moscow. Regardless, the kicker is that some of these forces are reportedly now using hand-held Gomer weapons in their advance. No word on casualties, and no word on President Dubronin's current status."

"Son of a bitch! You mean the Gomers have been outfitting an entire human ground force?"

"Yessir. It sure looks that way, but what I can't figure out is how they hid it as well as they did."

"Damn. Nobody at CIA had a whiff, and nobody in the Federation. Dammit! They must have people there, too."

"That would be my guess, too. Mr. President? I need your permission to do two things. The first is to get some Naval support and General Larkin's forces headed to Archangel and Murmansk to secure those ports. The second is to get President Dubronin to a safe point, where he can continue to be the legitimate government, otherwise the dissidents take over and open the door completely to the Gomers."

"I concur, and you have my authority. I'll want all you've got on this possible coup business to Doctor Khelm and our boys at the CIA as soon as possible. In the meantime, you do what you have to do to keep those ports open and to keep Dubronin safe, assuming that is possible."

"Mr. President, I would propose getting General Greene's people on it, since I feel fairly confident that his Russian personnel were vetted sufficiently to weed out any possible dissidents. Of course, having said this, the bastards did a great job hiding the fact that almost a third of their damned Army is now equipped with hand-held Gomer guns."

"I understand completely. Do what you have to do. In the meantime, any word on the Gomers and their Fighter Class ships?"

"Sir, we are still watching them, but other than a few Fighter Class entries into the atmosphere, most of them are still staged beyond the moon. NONE, I say again, NONE of their big stuff is headed our way yet."

"So, why not activate the mine field and take out the little guys?"

"Sir, if we do, then we'll be expending ordinance on the little stuff, which will allow the big stuff free range later. I don't think we can replace the weapons we have fast enough to justify using them yet."

"I see your point. I just hate to let them on the planet."

"Mr. President, I agree with the notion, and if I had more of the stuff to use, I would be very inclined to use it."

"Nope, you can't. I agree. Okay, I'll let you go deal with this Russian problem. I would hate to see them turn on the rest of the human race, but then there is no understanding their thinking. Surely to God they have to know they're being duped or used as pawns by the Gomers."

"Sir? I wonder if the Gomers are holding off long enough to see how we're going to handle these jokers. I mean, what if the Gomers won't attack until they think the dissidents have sufficient control of the areas in Siberia to allow them to retake that real estate?"

"Makes sense. What would you like to do about it?"

"What if we used the Chinese to hedge our bets in Eastern Russia, and then hit the Russian Dissident's forces on their way to Moscow?"

"Hit them? Hit them with what?"

"It is just a germ of an idea, but I think we might have something devastating to use that just might back them off, or at least hold them off, from getting too far north."

"Dammit. What is the germ of an idea?"

"What if we hit them with a phase II weapon like we used in the last war?"

"Red Dragon?"

"Yessir. The inverse Gomer Bubble would likely have the impact it did on the Gomer fleet, and it would be especially devastating to troops in the open. If we lured them out, and then popped one, then they would be like those kids on the USS New Jersey a couple of years ago."

"Geez... I don't know. What about civilians?"

"Sir, I said it was a germ of an idea. Let me staff it first, and we'll see what else we might have as an option. If the germ gets to be our only alternative, we'll do a full assessment and then ask for your approval."

"Okay. Do the assessment, and check for other options. I would hate to unleash that, but if you have no choice, then we should at least consider it as an option. Go ahead, but do your best to see if it can be avoided."

"Yes, sir, Mr. President."

I hung up the line just in time for the next series of reports coming out of Russia. The picture was developing, and the Russian dissidents were definitely fighting their way towards Moscow, with President Dubronin having been cut off and now headed into the Ural Mountains with the rest of their Army. An Army that we could only hope would remain loyal to the Federation. My next phone stop was going to be General Greene, but I had to get Generals Whitney, Larkin, and Davis headed in the right direction first. Passing on the mission to secure the northern ports, I then turned my attention to the rescue of President Dubronin. The call to General Greene was quick and to the point.

"General Greene?"

"Yessir."

"You monitoring the situation in Russia?"

"Yessir. I've been closely following it, and we've got some people there trying to get us a full evaluation. No question that the Gomers are driving the train from a distance."

"I agree. Daniel, I need your guys to get President Dubronin somewhere highly secure, and we need to keep him in touch as the legitimate government. Can you do that?"

"I think we can, General. We've got a planning cell working on it already, and we've got an idea of where to take him and secure him, so he can stay on Russian soil."

"Excellent."

"Sir, is General Larkin's 21st Army Group going to pick up the slack and reinforce the ports?"

"As a matter of fact, Whit is sending those Orders out even as we speak."

"Roger that, sir. Okay, just warn him about the Gomer Weapons packages that may have been passed on to the dissidents. We've got a report that the hand-held ones are particularly nasty at close range."

"I'll make sure Whit passes that intelligence on to General Larkin. Anything else?"

"Not now, sir. I've got our people monitoring the frequencies to see just how much direction the dissidents are getting from the Gomers. Right now, we don't have much visible contact. I think given what we've found out already, and with the Gomers having advisors with the various dissident cells, it all supports the idea that they will be with those Russian Armies too."

"I'm ahead of you, Daniel. Your coding boys should have received a directive already that tells them to shift code key assignments for all operations. We're taking the Russians off the net, and we're stepping up Electronic Warfare efforts with those units that are now moving towards Moscow."

"Great."

"One other thing, Daniel. Get your people to give me an assessment for the use of a Phase II of the Red Dragon over or near those advancing Russian units, and then give me any other options your whiz kids can come up with to stop those units in their tracks."

"On it, sir. We've had a team on that problem for the last several days."

"Several days? How in the hell…? Crap. Never mind, it was one of your hunches, wasn't it?"

"Yessir. I've never trusted them, you know."

"Which ones, the Gomers or the Russians?"

"Yessir..."

"I know, and for the record, like you, I've never been a fan of either group."

"Yessir, I've heard such rumors."

"Okay, Daniel, get your ass to work. Your priority is to get Dubronin safe, and then help us with some ideas on how to stop the Russian dissidents and their part of the Army."

I heard his quick, "Roger that, sir" as I hung up the line. Now it was time to get the full staff together, and start making this happen.

The Family Facilities, Peterstown, WV:

The family drills were coming together, and everyone knew what they needed to accomplish should anything happen around the facility. The only problem through the entire process was Lou Ann Whitney. Agent Snellgrove and his personnel were now embracing the concept of needing, and then exercising, a plan to facilitate a rapid egress of the various families. The children loved the drills, and some were getting rather adept at watching over the other children. The Commander of the Ranger Company was also into the spirit of it, and he even went beyond the number of personnel requested by Leah to help with the protection of the group. The four soldiers assigned by the Infantry Battalion were augmented by four Rangers, whose orienteering, rope, and cave skills were extremely helpful.

Lou Ann, on the other hand, was constantly reminding everyone of her status as a Retired General officer. Her constant shots at Leah were now coming to the point where Toni Blanchard finally pulled Lou Ann to the side.

"Lou Ann? Would you say that being the First Lady trumps being a Retired General?"

"Uh, yes, Ma'am. I guess it does."

"Good, I'm glad you see it that way. So, let me be brief. I have no idea why you feel compelled to mouth off all the time, and I sure don't care about your past with General Patrick. Instead, I care about keeping good order and discipline among the families that are here. Are you with me so far?"

"I think so, Ma'am."

"Good. I will be very clear on this point. Your past doesn't mean a thing to me, but the present attitude is about to get your ass tossed out of this facility. You read me?"

"Ma'am. I'm far more qualified and have combat training, so why should Mrs. Patrick, a civilian, be accorded such deference in our planning?"

"Lordie, you're thick. Honey, she has more combat training and experience than you've ever even thought about having. She was trained by a civilian agency, and she has the same skill set as someone with years of Ranger and Special Operations training. Do YOU have any of that skill set?"

"No, Ma'am, I don't."

"Good. Now shut the hell up, and let her do what she knows how to do. And for the record, if you mention any of what I just told you, I'll make sure that you're not only out of here, but that your husband will retire as the Officer in Charge of latrines. Is that clear?"

"Yes, ma'am. I'm clear..."

Leah never knew why, but Lou Ann Whitney no longer sniped at her at every opportunity. In fact, her cooperation and input were helping advance the evacuation plan. It was all their collective hopes that it would never be required, but one thing they all knew deep inside was the dreaded corollary of Murphy's Law. "If you don't have a plan, then whatever 'IT' is will most assuredly happen."

Chapter VI

USS Massachusetts, Battlegroup in the North Sea, near Norway:

The Admiral in command of the USS Massachusetts Battlegroup was reviewing the latest message traffic regarding the movement of both the Gomers and the rogue elements of the Russian Army. His Orders were to proceed to Archangel and take up a position to the east of the USS Iowa Battlegroup, which was now off the coast near Murmansk, Russia. The latest turn of events was very disconcerting, and he decided to raise the condition level for his entire Task Force. He thought to himself that if the Russian Army had rogue elements, then why not the Russian Navy. Without hesitation, he advised the destroyers escorting his Battleship to increase their search for any underwater targets in the vicinity, then after a little more thought, he passed this message on to the three submarines that were also operating with his Battlegroup. Normally, everyone was looking skyward for a Gomer attack, but this time around, there might be some eyes that would direct the Gomers more specifically towards a target. It turns out that he was right to worry, and absolutely correct on the shift in tactics.

Two hours after stepping up the alert and setting the appropriate condition for possible submarine attack, one of the escorting destroyers, the USS Stout, radioed that she had a sonar contact. Startled at first, the Massachusetts Battlegroup Commander immediately began the process of setting the appropriate defensive posture for his fleet. The tracking of the target continued, and it was soon apparent to the Anti-Submarine patrols (ASW aircraft and escorts), that this was a Russian made Akula II type submarine. The Akula II was the Russian Federations more recent nuclear submarine type, and this one appeared to have a rather odd pattern to its movements around the Battlegroup. At no point did the Russian make a move to approach any closer that roughly 20 miles distance to the USS Massachusetts. Instead, the Russian submarine was following a semi-circular path, while maintaining that relative distance and speed, as it traveled around the entire Battlegroup. Clearly, the Russian submarine was tracking the Battlegroup, and she was staying just far enough outside the exclusion zone to appear non-threatening, at least on paper. The tracking of the contact continued for almost 6 continuous hours, and nightfall was rapidly approaching when the Admiral was advised that the contact appeared to be surfacing 21 miles to the South of the formation.

Unknown to the Akula II Russian Submarine, the USS Hampton was 4,000 yards away and directly behind and below her position. The tense standoff was causing the entire Battlegroup a great deal of nervousness, and it was especially concerning when the twilight line began to cross over the fleet. It was exactly one hour after the darkness had surrounded the USS Massachusetts, that the Battlegroup got their first warning of the events that were coming. As the crew in the Command Information Center listened, a burst transmission was sent from the Russian Submarine on the VHF and UHF frequencies. Seconds later, a large formation of Gomer Fighter Class ships appeared directly overhead, and began descending onto the fleet at over 4,000 feet per second. With little time to react, the USS Massachusetts was hit almost immediately around the aft portion of the ship, with numerous other hits throughout the ship following rapidly. As the damage reports began pouring into the Bridge, it was apparent that despite their best efforts, there would be little they could do except fight back long enough to report the attack, and the tactics being used by the Gomers.

With the first hit, the USS Hampton unleashed her attack on the Akula II, which was immediately blown from the water with a direct hit astern. Unfortunately, this would be too little, and far too late, to help anyone onboard the USS Massachusetts or on several of her escorts. Within a minute of the transmission of her report to the Task Force Commander, and a rather vain attempt to deploy the "Gomer Bubble" air defense weapon, the USS Massachusetts violently exploded and sank almost instantly. The loss of life was virtually complete, and with the Gomer attack continuing on the escort ships, the entire Massachusetts Battlegroup was rendered completely ineffective within minutes. The crew of the USS Hampton looked on in horror at the destruction of the surface portion of the Task Force, and as they continued to watch, the Gomer Fighter Class ships rapidly departed the area following the same path heading straight upwards and then dispersing back into space.

Supreme Allied Headquarters, (SAHQ):

The bow of the USS Massachusetts was pointed skyward as she slipped below the waves when her final message was re-transmitted from the Fourth Fleet Command to the New Hampshire location of our Supreme Allied Headquarters. It only took moments before the reality of what took place quickly shifted to complete horror at the change in the overall picture. Admiral Lynch re-read the report, and then immediately turned and searched around the room for General Patrick. This was serious, and now that it was confirmed by the report from the USS Hampton, there was no doubt that anything Russian could no longer be trusted at face value.

"General? I've got a report here that you have to hear."

"Admiral, you look like it's the end of the world as we know it. What happened?"

"Sir, the USS Massachusetts Battlegroup, Task Force 40.1, has basically been wiped out by the Gomers in an air attack AT SEA!"

"At sea? As in 'the middle of damned ocean' kind of sea?"

"Yessir!"

"How in the hell did that happen? Have they finally learned how to spot us in the ocean?"

"You could say that, sir. There was a Russian submarine, likely under the control of the dissidents, that acted as a spotter and forward air controller for the Gomers' Fighter Class ships."

"So, where the hell were our observers watching the damn Gomer fleet? You mean to tell me that the Gomers got an air attack going, and we didn't see them coming?"

"Sir, they only used their Fighter Class ships, which are hard to see when they come in without massing first. From what we can tell, they all converged over the USS Massachusetts by infiltrating into the airspace directly above the Battlegroup. In other words, while we did see some movement, it was all in space and in very small groups. Apparently, once they were in the troposphere or a little lower, they converged from different directions to strike at one time."

"Son of a bitch. That shows a great deal of coordination on a lot of levels. Okay, get the rest of the staff back in here and get Major Dubronin. In the meantime, get your guys working on a warning to send to the rest of our Task Forces and Battlegroups."

"Aye, Sir!" Admiral Lynch rushed off and left me to my thoughts. The more I pondered this development, the more I could feel the bowling ball growing in my stomach. This was a nasty turn of events. Most of our ability to fight the Gomers' larger stuff revolved around our larger caliber weapons systems, like our big gun ships. The "hole in the water" concept was a key piece of our strategy at sea, and if we had to worry about the dissidents acting as spotters, then we had a serious problem on our hands. Then there was the issue of them sneaking in their Fighter Class ships, to hit us in mass. I already had visions of the dissidents following in their fishing trawlers, just like the Soviets had done during the Cold War, and passing all the information on to the Gomers who would hit us at will. Picking up the line, I advised the President of the sinking of the USS Massachusetts and her escorts, and of what I thought might be the implications.

"Mike, any ideas?"

"Yes, Mr. President. Let me get someone in touch with Dubronin, and advise him to get a message out to all Russian shipping, both military and civilian, that proximity to any formation of our naval ships, will get them promptly sunk. In other words, let's extend the exclusion zones from each of the Task Forces operating at sea to 250 miles."

"Damn. I don't think we can do that, can we?"

"Mr. President, I don't know what else to do, since the attack by the Gomers happened only moments after the burst transmission from the Russian submarine. Sir, it isn't like we can tell them, 'you can come close, so long as you don't transmit.' Their transmission and the attack happened so close together, there wasn't a damn thing the crews in the Battlegroup could do to stop it, or even maneuver to avoid it. Hell, the Russian was over 20 miles away and was still calling in the air strike. If this happened to more of our fleet units, we'd lose the capability to defend our coast lines, and it could set us back to having to fight like we did before the first war."

"Let me get back to you, but go ahead and issue a warning order, and see if Dubronin can shed any light on this. Hell, maybe he can tell us honestly how much of his military is out of his control."

"Sir, I hate to rain on that parade, but you know President Yuri Dubronin as well as I do. When is the last time he came completely clean?"

"How many times have we saved his ass, General?"

"I don't know how many times total, but the last time I personally saved it, he still lied to me."

"Point taken. Still, it can't hurt to ask him. If nothing else, it might put him on notice that we're about to eliminate them from active involvement in any global defense outside Siberia."

"I'll get his son on the horn with him, and we'll see what he can or will tell us. Mr. President, do you have any objections to my at least advising him of the step I'm considering as to all of his warships, civilian ships, right on down to the stray fishing trawler?"

"Nope. Go ahead, but don't order it until I get back to you. I don't mind you scaring him into telling you the deal, but it would be a different matter entirely if you actually ordered it. That would be my call, and I'm not making it yet, at least until I know more."

"Mr. President, I'll also get General Greene's folks to sniff around. Right now, the dissidents could pull this crap anywhere, so we'll need guidance pretty soon. They are staffing my other idea too, the one with the Phase II weapon."

"I understand completely, and I'll get back to you within the next two hours. For now, you may extend the exclusion zone, but only as to warning. There will be no firing unless they clearly appear to be hostile. As for the Red Dragon, Phase II, I'd say once they get an operable plan on line, do it!"

"Mr. President, I sincerely hope that the other Battlegroups will still be here in two hours. As for Red Dragon, thanks, we'll make it work the best we can to minimize civilian casualties."

"General, advise the groups to defend themselves as required, but before starting a campaign against random shipping or extending the exclusion zones, I want confirmation that the entire Russian fleet is either out of control, or that a group of them have been identified as hostile."

"Yes, sir, Mr. President. In the meantime, we'll see about other options to counter the threat. Right now, it wouldn't take much more than a lifeboat with a radio to sell us down the road!"

"I'll get on my end of it, and you let me know what Dubronin says. I'll also get Secretary Chase to ask the same questions, and then we can compare answers."

"Roger that, Mr. President."

Hanging up the line, I turned to see the staff and Major Dubronin gathering in the conference room. I grabbed a cup of coffee, and walked into the room. The largest issue, which would impact more than the war at sea, was the simple question of how do we stop them from infiltrating their Fighter Ships onto our planet. This question was made a top priority, along with the second question, which was finding ways to keep the Russian dissidents from compromising our assets. After we laid out the situation, and left the staff to work on alternatives, Major Dubronin and I headed to the Communications Center. We had a phone call to make, but first, we had to determine where General Greene's personnel were hiding the Russian President.

"Daniel? Patrick here. Where is President Dubronin, and how can we reach him?"

"Hey, General. I've got him secured at their older facilities outside Saint Petersburg. We can get him on a secure line in about 10 minutes. Why?"

"Huge issues, Daniel, mostly Navy issues, but it is also something you'll need to work on, along with your crypto guys. We will also need to warn him about the possible Red Dragon use. Get him moving to a secure line, and then listen in as a party to the conversation. When I brief Dubronin, you will be as up to date as we are on the subject."

"Sir? Does this have anything to do with the USS Massachusetts?"

"Yeah, what do you know about it?"

"Not much, except that it must have gotten ugly quick. We intercepted some Gomer communications that we thought MIGHT be about the USS Massachusetts. Honestly, we weren't sure it was about the Massachusetts until we saw the message from the USS Hampton. This might help us decipher their current code with the dissidents, which we haven't really been able to get into at this point. We are also working on the locations where most of their messages are originating."

"Excellent. Look, Daniel, get me what you have on that subject, get me what you have on the dissident defections from the Russian Federal forces, and get President Dubronin on the line. It's time for us all to have a little chat! Oh, and Daniel, when we chat, take my lead but be completely candid with what you know. I think Dubronin needs to know that we're not the bad guys, nor do we think he is a bad guy, but somebody around him is maybe not telling him everything, and we have to get to the bottom damn quick."

Secure Location, near Saint Petersburg, Russian Federation:

President Yuri Dubronin, surrounded by security personnel from both ASOC and his own Federation Security Services, had only arrived a few hours ago. His journey was painful, to say the least, and it involved several hours of hiding in a ditch from several Gomer Fighter Class ships that joined the search for his movements northward. Nothing was secure, and his reliance on the radio nets had almost been his downfall. The last time he tried to communicate, even via ELF, he was perilously close to revealing his location to the wrong people and the Gomers. His security officers were loyal, and so were most of his soldiers, but the element of dissidents that had infiltrated a number of key positions throughout his military forces was now a very real threat. The Armies that had been marching towards Moscow and Kiev were being held somewhat in check, thanks in part to various assets provided by the 21st Army Group and his old friend General Jerry Larkin. This was done despite the dissident's air support coming from the Gomers.

The Gomer Guns received from the Americans, and the select forces arriving from the 21st Army Group, all made it tough for the Gomer Fighter Class ships in their efforts to attack targets that would help the dissident forces in their advance. That was the good news. The bad news was that now he had rogue elements in all of his services that were providing tons of information on all movements to the Gomers lurking overhead. His reports coming in from the Air Force and Navy were not comforting at all, since it was obvious that the rogues were also hiding in these services.

Learning of these events forced Dubronin to turn to General Vasily Orlov, Chief of the Federation Security Services, and even now the process was well underway to identify the key personnel who were subverted by the dissident movement, and to assess the damage. President Dubronin was the classic former communist. His background in the old KGB made him far less likely to either suffer fools, or to cling to the hopeless concept that things would ever go back to the way they were before the "wall came down." He had a certain nostalgia for it, but he knew that, thanks to the Gomers overhead, things like economic and social ideology were no longer as meaningful in today's new world. Even most of the nations in the Middle East were no longer quite as concerned about their former ideological passions, so why were these dissidents so sold on the Gomers? That question was haunting him the most, and he simply had no answer.

Reading through the information he'd already received from General Orlov, he could see that the damage was extensive to his own internal military organizations. Few could be completely trusted, but many of the dissidents were readily identifiable. The most common element among them was a background connection to either Romania, parts of Georgia, Chechnya, or the Ukraine. This confused him, since these nations couldn't wait to leave the old U.S.S.R., and in some cases, throw in with NATO forces at the end of the Cold War. Many of them hated Russia, this is true, but now they were turning on anyone who was allied against the Gomers. This fact alone was enough to make Dubronin wonder what deal must have been made? Unfortunately, after the First Gomer War, his military had opened up and started taking many people from these regions to fill out their manpower needs. Still, they all volunteered, so what was their real incentive? What was the motive? "Der'mo" Yuri Dubronin quickly looked around at the staff surrounding him, and realized that his expletive had been uttered rather loudly to no one in particular. Seconds later, he was summoned to the secure land line. Now he would have to deal with General Patrick, and this time he knew it would not be a friendly call.

Supreme Allied Headquarters, (SAHQ):

The phone connections, and getting through on a secure line to President Dubronin, was becoming a real serious problem. The physical routing issues were minor compared to the more pressing problem. Regardless of route, all of these lines appeared to be compromised at some point as they entered Russia. Without the secure capability, then whatever was said would be overheard by dissidents, and then passed on to the Gomers. This forced the ASOC personnel in St. Petersburg to try and obtain the appropriate secure radio equipment that would be compatible with the ELF/ULF systems. While these too were compromised by the enemy, the use of the coded transmission was going to be the only viable alternative. As a result, it would take a couple of hours before any sort of meaningful conversation could take place on the Russian's "unsecure" phone line.

"Yuri?"

"Ge..."

"Uh, Yuri, just use names."

"Da! Moose!"

"Did you hear about the problem with the boat, the one carrying the bean crops?"

"Da!"

"Yuri, I have to know, what is the quality of your bean farmers?"

"Is okay. Not good, but okay. We have bug problems."

"I may have to spray some serious insecticide in a much wider arc around the crops. So, keep your pets far away from the field."

"Da. How far?"

"At least two and a half miles."

"That far?!"

"Yep. Otherwise, they can expect to get sprayed before the bugs infest the crop."

"Da. I understand, and agree. Consider-ed it done. We will move dogs, but cats could be issue."

"We will do our best to avoid the cats, but if they get into the field, then so be it. So, how many cats do you have?"

"Okay. Always can replace cats, especially since we have so many. Right now, I think we only have 5 cats. Now a good dog on the other hand... Still, we have more dogs than cats. Always hated cats anyway."

"Thanks. I'll talk to you later, Yuri!"

"Da. You too, Moose. Good luck with bug problem."

Hanging up I turned to see a completely confused staff. General Whitney smiled and turned to the staff. "Let me translate on behalf of the General."

"Go ahead, Whit. Explain it to them."

"Okay, the boat carrying the bean crop refers to the Boston Baked Bean, and Boston is in Massachusetts. Right, sir?"

"Correct. I just hope it was a little more obtuse to the dissidents."

"Oh, whether it is or not, the 'two and a half miles line' will be tough for them."

"Bingo. Yuri knows that if it were really two and a half miles, I'd have said '2.5 miles' as opposed to spelling it all out. Now he knows that two and a half means two hundred fifty miles."

"Which means that the dissidents will think they can come inside the ring to a distance of 2.5 miles?"

"Again, you win the prize. Admiral Lynch?"

"Yes, sir?"

"Get that out on the secure teletype to your Allied, NON-RUSSIAN, Senior commanders at sea. If a ship comes inside the 250-mile exclusion zone, be highly suspicious. If one starts to wander all the way up to 2.5 miles, consider it hostile."

"Kind of close, isn't it?"

"I said up to, and depending on when night fall is coming, then the local commander will have to make that call at sea. And for the record, while we were waiting to get through to President Dubronin, President Blanchard called back and verified the authorization to expand the exclusion zone to the maximum range of 250 miles, and we have a green light for using Red Dragon Phase II around the advancing dissident forces if necessary. He did caution that the exclusion zone itself wasn't a free fire zone, and that we were to take all steps to turn them back first. He also said for local commanders to exercise their judgment in the protection of their force. Any questions?"

General Whitney spoke up and asked, "What about President Dubronin's folks on land? Is there a change in the rules of engagement there too?"

"No! Whit, our guidance to the forces in the field is unchanged. We are only to fire on a Russian force, IF, and only IF, they show hostile intentions. Fortunately, we can tell that on the ground a whole lot easier than this 'one - two punch tactic' at sea. Any other questions?" There were none, and I then broke up the impromptu meeting to get back to the other remaining question. Just exactly how were we going to identify and prevent the Gomers from massing their Gomer Fighter Class ships over their target?

The USS Missouri Battlegroup, 440 miles Southeast of the Kamchatka Peninsula:

Admiral Becker was reviewing the same reports, and now he was struggling with the last report from the USS Massachusetts. He knew there was an answer to this, but he just couldn't quite put his finger on it. Meanwhile, his Chief of Staff, a young Rear Admiral, was doing his level best to coordinate the Anti-Submarine Warfare or ASW search pattern with the air staff onboard the USS John C. Stennis, located 150 miles to their south. Then there were the three submarines attached to their Battlegroup, who were conducting their underwater searches to determine if there were any approaching submarines. The latest intelligence report from Admiral Lynch indicated that there were at least another 5 rogue Russians submarines, which meant that each Big Gun Battlegroup had to be under observation. Unfortunately, while the air search was great during the day at keeping the bad guys away, after dark it would be a completely different problem. Given the Gomers' flight patterns, any night flying would be high risk for anyone not in the correct aircraft. The new F-35, even the new naval variation, was a great fighter to fly at night, but it had very limited ASW usage. No, for that they needed more helicopter support, which just wasn't a good option at this stage.

While Admiral Becker's staff struggled with these issues, the Akula II trailing their formation was finally discovered by a helicopter from the USS Fuller. This time, it was only 5 miles away, and it was approaching slowly and very quietly towards the heart of the group's formation. "Damn. How in the hell did he get that close before somebody picked him up?"

"Admiral. Some of the boys are a little rusty, and this guy is still pretty good at his trade."

"No fricking excuse. We've been looking up too damn long, and forgot how to keep track of the SOBs under the sea."

"Admiral? What are our orders?

"Sink the bastard! If she surfaces, or you catch any sort of transmission, then advise the Captain, and the Captain of the USS Fuller, to fire the Gomer Bubble immediately. Do NOT wait on an Order. Just do it!"

"Sir? Won't that..."

"Look, I've read the reports from the USS Massachusetts. Once they send out a transmission, we have mere seconds to respond. The only way we even have a shot at defending ourselves against those kinds of numbers is the bubble! Got it? They are not to hesitate. They hear transmissions, then they are to cook it!"

"What about the aircraft within the vicinity?"

"If we get hit by the Gomers, they are screwed anyway. Sorry, but I'm not going to risk this fleet for a flight crew. In the meantime, sink that damn Russian!"

"Aye, Aye, Sir."

Unfortunately, as was pointed out earlier by his Chief of Staff, the training in such things as Anti-Submarine Warfare (ASW), had fallen considerably over the last several years, especially since there hadn't been much need with everyone playing nice. No, the real problem had been from the air, and it was the two wars that had sucked away their attention. Now it was hurting them. The only good submarine hunter in the group was the brand-new USS Fuller and her crew. A Morton/Zumwalt Class Destroyer, she had the latest in ASW capabilities, but the least amount of experience in ASW. The young crew, fresh from the school environment, might still have been a little green at seamanship, but they understood how the equipment should work. Having said this, there was sufficient green with the crew to keep them from getting the quick kill. As darkness began to fall over the fleet, a series events came together almost simultaneously.

Chapter VII

❦

Vandenberg Air Force Base, California:

The operator of the latest in near-space observation technology was making adjustments in the resolution and focus in the newest satellite system. At first, he thought it was some sort of bug in the system, and then he saw it with greater clarity. There, next to one of the older observation satellites, was a Gomer ship. It was not of the normally observed type. Instead, it was smaller than a Transport Class, but slightly larger than the Fighter Class. He started the process of recording the observation on tape, and then continued his observations in and around this portion of the Pacific sky. This satellite was more passive than its predecessors, and was coated in lead shielding to hopefully preclude detection. So far it was working, because there on the monitor the operator could see almost 100 Gomer Fighter Class ships, forming up. Knowing that this was a serious threat, he hit the alert button that sent an electronic burst to his higher headquarters. Shortly thereafter, this information was being routed to the Supreme Allied Headquarters staff. The operator was updating his information when the formation of Gomer Ships began a dive straight down into the airspace over the Pacific.

The USS Missouri Battlegroup, Task Force (TF 71.1), located approximately 440 miles Southeast of the Kamchatka Peninsula:

The crews throughout the Battlegroup were at their battle stations, and even though the Russian Akula II submarine was still evading the USS Fuller, she was at least identified to within a few thousand yards. The USS Fuller was lining up for a kill shot when the submarine surfaced and emitted a short burst signal. At this moment, two things took place. The USS Fuller got off her kill shot, and the USS Missouri unleashed her Gomer Bubble technology. Once the RUM-139 VL-ASROC, anti-submarine missile left the rails, the USS Fuller fired off her Gomer Bubble, and everyone throughout the Task Force held their breath.

Within a few seconds, the impact of the Gomer Bubble weapon system could be felt throughout the entire group. The expanding electromagnetic and Terahertz charge coursed through the air around the ships, and into the onrushing Gomer Fighter Class ships that were now in an almost vertical dive from out of the troposphere. This high burst of energy completely destroyed the attacking Gomer Fighters, with many of them disintegrating and falling as wreckage into the sea. The one or two who managed to break off their dives were then tossed into a flight envelope that exceeded the capability of their craft. In short order, these handful of surviving Gomer Fighters were destroyed on impact with the surface of the ocean.

The Russian Akula II submarine managed to evade the efforts of the first shot by the USS Fuller, but she could not evade the next one. The impact of the Gomer Bubble on the first RUM-139 VL-ASROC missile was to throw it significantly off course, where it wound up harmlessly on the bottom of the sea. The Captain of the USS Fuller realized this immediately, and watched the static levels drop sufficiently to allow a second missile to be launched. Thanks to the violent maneuvers of the Russian in an attempt to evade the first missile, and the effects of the Gomer Bubble, the Russian Submarine was no longer difficult to track by the crew of the USS Fuller. This time around, the second shot was more than successful. In his report back to the Allied Headquarters, Admiral Becker was kind enough to point out that the number of cats out of the bag was now down to four. He also pointed out that the message from Vandenberg arrived at his location a full two minutes after the attack.

Vandenberg Air Force Base, California:

General McDaniel was anything but a happy camper. Striding into his main operations area, it was patently obvious to anyone but an idiot that the 'Old Man' was four plus pissed. Gathering his key personnel around him, they headed over to the hapless Sergeant who was manning the terminal that led to the alert. Thus, the inquiry began. "Sergeant! Do you have a clue why I'm pissed?"

"Uh, no... sir?"

"Son, you took too long to send out an alert, and a lot of guys could have died out there!"

"Uh. Sir, once I saw them, I hit the button."

"Dammit son, you should have noticed them sooner, why the hell didn't you?"

Gathering a little more confidence, the young Sergeant replied, "Sir. I was refocusing the new system when I spotted them. With all due respect, General, that system wasn't even supposed to officially come on line until tomorrow."

"Son, you have a point, but we almost lost another Naval Task Force..."

"General? Sir. There is something else I need to show you. I sent it up the line, but well, this is bothering me."

"Okay. Show me." The Sergeant turned in his seat, and hit the replay button on the footage of the new type of Gomer Ship that was 'parked' near the main long-range satellite. As they watched the footage, this latest in Gomer Ship type 'un-docked' from the satellite, and sped off back in the direction of the moon. Turning back to General McDaniel to hear what he thought, the Sergeant was surprised to see the General running back towards his office. The Colonel who was his supervisor, said, "get that video into the General's office ASAP!" Then he too was running after the General. The Sergeant then went back to dealing with his near-Earth adjustments, when the overall alert was sounded. It wasn't until then that he fully realized what he'd seen earlier.

Supreme Allied Headquarters, (SAHQ):

The Allied Staff was in the process of sifting through the messages and reports coming out of the Pacific about the recent attempted raid on the USS Missouri Battlegroup, TF-71.1. The news was heartening, and given the preceding raid and destruction of the USS Massachusetts, it was the first good news in days. Certainly, there were problems that needed to be addressed, such as the ASW capability of the fleet as a whole, and the rather slow process of getting the Vandenberg reports to the end users, but all in all, it was at least a guide on what to do in the future. No question that Admiral Becker had saved his forces to fight again another day, and he had demonstrated, yet again, that he was a premier naval commander at sea. A victory at this point was a good thing, and the lessons learned would be invaluable. The adjustments and tactics were being passed on to the other commanders in the field, when the message from Vandenberg came into the operations room.

"General Patrick?" It was General Kaminski, the Allied Air Force Officer, and he had the same sick look I'd see already on Admiral Lynch the day the USS Massachusetts was sunk.

"General Kaminski?"

"Sir. I've got General McDaniel on the line, and he needs to show you something on the monitor. I mean ASAP, sir!"

"Right. I'm coming." Getting to the monitor near General Kaminski, I picked up the line, and told General McDaniel, "Whatcha got, Randy?"

"General, look at the monitor, and you'll see what we have been seeing for the last 36 hours around the moon."

"Randy, I don't see anything at all."

"Right, General. Now look at the Near-Earth system pictures we're getting from the new satellites we launched."

Looking at the monitor, the picture shifted to a new angle, and there they were. It appeared to be close to 5,000 ships of all types, massing near the moon. "Dammit, Randy, when were these taken?"

"General Patrick, those are real time pictures, but that fleet has been hiding because of this shit." Flipping a switch, the monitor was now showing me the same footage that General McDaniel had obtained from the young Sergeant in his operations center. "General McDaniel! Get on standby for the Red Dragon system, and I'll get right back to you."

"Roger that, sir!" Hanging up the phone, I immediately got on the line to the President's Situation Facility. "Mr. President. Patrick here, and we've got a real problem. The Gomers have been tampering with our telescope and satellite systems. The bastards have amassed an invasion fleet right next to the moon, and I need your permission to put Red Dragon into play."

"Show me!"

"Yessir. Watch the monitor, and I'll get Whit to give you the same show we saw from General McDaniel not even a minute ago."

"All right. Let me see." The last word was barely out of his mouth when we showed the same footage to the President. When the real time footage popped up, you could hear the President's audible intake of breath over the line. "Okay. General Patrick, you are cleared to engage with the Red Dragon. How many will you need?"

"With your permission, I'd like to let General McDaniel structure and lead that strike. I just need to give him your authorization."

"Okay, Mike. You're a go."

"Thank you, sir. I'll be right back to you. We also have some news out of the Pacific we need to share."

"Yeah. I know. Admiral Becker did a helluva job!"

"Yessir, he did, but no, we have something else. Let me get word to McDaniel, and I'll call you right back." Hanging up the line, I immediately got General McDaniel back on the phone. "General McDaniel. It is official. You are to employ, at your discretion, a Red Dragon strike on the Gomer fleet. You have authorization to engage with the number and types or phases of the weapons you feel will be necessary to eliminate the threat. My only caution is that you use only what you think is necessary, so as not to completely exhaust our ability to engage with that weapons system. You are also cleared, on my authority, to engage the Capital or Mountain and Battleship Class targets that might enter the area between Moon and the Earth. Any questions?"

"No, Sir. I don't think so, at least none at this point."

"Good. Go do what you have to do to nail these Gomers, just don't fire up the entire supply if you can help it. Oh, I do have a question for you. What is going on between Mars and Neptune?"

"Well, I was going to say nothing, but we now know that isn't accurate. Those Sumbitches have messed with our equipment, and we're reconfiguring the new stealthy stuff to look in that direction. Right now, we're kind of limited in what we can see, but we're working on it."

"Good. Do we have their new ship classified yet?"

"Not really. I would call it like a tug boat, but that's me. It looks like a service ship of some kind, and from we can tell from looking at the video, it doesn't appear to be armed, or at least armed heavily."

"Okay. Well, let somebody else name it, but service ship sounds close from what I just saw. Good luck, sir!"

"Thank you, General. I'll do my best to not let you down."

"I know, Randy. Just keep me abreast of the score!"

"Not a problem, Sir!" When he hung up, I knew that we'd just handed him the biggest assignment he'd ever held in his hands before. This time, we had too much to deal with to micro-manage this operation. Besides, he was the expert, he knew the logistics behind it all, and most of all, he wouldn't lose time waiting on the teletype or phone line system to belch information. Right now, aside from the dissidents, our crappy communications systems might be our greatest weakness.

Gathering the staff, we began the issuance of warning orders throughout most of our forces. We also contacted the Russian Forces, through their General Staff co-located with President Dubronin. The information we provided was all in special code, and only explained that a massive Gomer force was observed approaching Earth. The guidance around the world was simple, "Invasion appears imminent, target site unknown, but believed to be in Russia or at the poles. Deploy accordingly, and protect your forces as necessary." This meant different things to different units. The Army began the process of digging in, while the Navies of the world did their level best to become our classic "holes in the water." Once these orders were sent out, Admiral Lynch approached me to advise that he had Admiral Steadman on the line. Admiral Steadman, the Chief of Naval Operations, was an old submarine man, and I had a feeling that he must have an appreciation for the latest dissident threat. I wasn't wrong. Picking up the line, I began, "Admiral Steadman, what can I do for you?"

"General. It is what I can do for you. I've heard from several of my submarines, and it would seem that we have found the four cats!"

"No kidding. I thought we were down to three, but go ahead."

"Sir. I read the report and transcript of the conversation with President Dubronin, and I thought the same way you did, I thought that he was not aware of that first kill when he said they only had 5 left. Instead, he was aware of the first one when he spoke, and we were looking at 6 total submarines on the prowl. The USS Hampton got one, Admiral Becker got one, and that left us four more to go. We have one now near the USS Iowa, one near the USS Montana, and one near the USS Alaska, that were all spotted and are even now being tracked. Five minutes ago, I heard that they located the last one near the USS New Jersey. I am calling about this last one."

"Okay, first of all, who has them located?" I was starting to get a headache from trying to keep mental track of all the new information.

"Sir, the best way to hunt and kill a submarine is with another submarine. The toughest one is the bastard on the USS New Jersey. She is not an Akula I or II, but instead what some would argue is that Akula III. I'm not going to get into all that controversy, since that is some crap to be argued in *Proceedings Magazine*. What I'm saying is that it is the newest Russian technology for their submarines, and for our purposes, I'll use the proper name. It is a relatively brand new 'Yasen Class submarine.' Regardless of what you call the damn thing, it is quiet and it can fire at targets on the surface with the Onyx missile. The Onyx missile cruises at supersonic speeds, and it is designed to hit a surface target up to 186 nautical miles away."

"Whoa! How far is that thing from the USS New Jersey?"

"Sir, she is right at 200 nautical miles and closing."

"Okay, what do you need? Authorization to sink the bastard?"

"Yessir. Right now, the USS Virginia is lined up on her, but we need to let them know she can take the shot."

"Hell, yes! I assume she is headed towards the New Jersey?"

"Yessir. She is headed directly towards her, and from a quick check with my counterpart, there would be no reason for her to be in that area of the Pacific."

"How long before dawn?"

"About another hour, which means she might either guide them in tomorrow night, or she could be ready to just put a missile of her own into the USS New Jersey." Admiral Steadman seemed to have all his ducks in a row as far as information went.

"Admiral, I'm not sure we can risk it getting into range. I'd say lay her ass out, and I'll worry about the fallout later. Right now, we can't afford to lose another Big Gun platform, especially of the Iowa Class!"

"Aye, Aye, Sir. We're passing the word on to the skipper of the USS Virginia. On another topic, I'm going to try and rebuild the lost Battlegroup around the USS North Carolina. Any objections?"

"No, none at all. I do have a question though. How long before the new Montana Class is ready to sail? I'd hate to lose the big gun support for an invasion capability. I have a feeling we're going to need it before this one is done."

"Sir, The USS South Carolina should be ready in about two more months, less if we keep the fires lit under the builder."

"Okay. Do what you have to do, and gird yourself, I assume you've seen our worldwide message about what is over us right now?"

"Yessir. I've seen it, and we're rechecking our deployments now. That is one of the main reasons I want to detach the USS North Carolina, along with the USS Thomas Gates, USS Porter, and USS The Sullivans."

"Admiral, I don't want to tell you how to do your business, but you might want to put another Destroyer with them, mainly because the North Carolina doesn't have the 'Gomer Bubble' installed.'"

"I hate it when you do that. Okay, you're right. I'll see about getting the USS Halsey to join them. She is a new Morton/Zumwalt Class destroyer, with all the latest bells and whistles, and the cruiser USS Thomas Gates was just retro fitted with the Bubble too, so that should cover them."

"Speaking of which, do you have any more of the Morton/Zumwalt Class destroyers on the way?"

"General, you're being coy, and you know damn well we have three more. One in Savannah, one in Norfolk, and one in Bremerton. Each of them will be out and on their feet within the month."

"Thanks, Admiral. Get them up and running as quickly as possible. I have a feeling they could be invaluable in the very near future." When I hung up, I realized that I was now relegated to fighting a damn war by telephone. What a way to do business. GOD, I hated it! What was interesting was watching Sergeant Major Clagmore. If there was anyone who hated this more than me, it was him. Sitting on the sidelines was driving him a little nuts, and I decided that doctor or no doctor, Waiver or no Waiver, this man had to be unleashed somewhere besides on my headquarters staff. The only real question was where to turn him loose.

Supreme Allied Headquarters, (SAHQ):

I owed the President a phone call and now that I finally had the chance. I got him up to speed on the latest out in the Pacific, and about the ideas advanced by Admiral Steadman for dealing with the shadows that each of our main Battlegroups had picked up. Then we discussed the exclusion zone and the reason for the distances based on this new type submarine that the dissidents had put into play against the USS New Jersey. Once we were done, we had all the authorization we needed, and we got guidance from the President I didn't expect. This one was very specific. We were not to show any quarter as to the Gomers. This time there would be no peace discussion. It would end either with their deaths or complete capitulation and departure from our solar system. There was the other option, which would be our own deaths, but nobody was ready to ever say that one out loud. This time around, we were doing things just like we had done in the first Gomer War. This time it was for all the marbles.

Armed with this guidance, I contacted both General McDaniel at Vandenberg and General Greene at ASOC. My Orders were very simple; while we would not pursue that "no quarter" policy with the dissidents, if it was within our power, the Gomers were going to become an extinct or, at the very least, an endangered species. General McDaniel was about to have his hands full, and we kept it short. General Greene, on the other hand, reminded me of something we'd kept very close to the vest during those short months of "peace" with the Gomers.

"General, you do recall that we passed on some metallurgical technology to assist the Gomers in their building efforts on Mars?"

"Yeah. Daniel, you don't mean to rub... Wait a minute. While I was out, did you go forward with your idea about some 'planned obsolescence?'"

"It wasn't my idea. You can thank your son-in-law for that concept for the plan which, for the record, was a plan endorsed by both Dr. Abramson and Dr. Clarkson."

"I remember the discussion early on, when neither of us trusted the bastards, but it wasn't anything concrete when I left for leave."

"Yes sir. I know, but John sat down with some of our guys, and came up with a compound in the alloy we provided them. It was designed to be activated on order, and it was a wonderful mix of nano-technology and chemical interactions."

"Seriously? John is a great son-in-law, but I had no idea he was working with nano tech stuff."

"He wasn't working with it, but in collaboration with Dr. Turner who was doing some things in that area, the two of them put it in place before we passed on the metal sheeting to the Gomers."

"Okay. What do we need to do to kick that game into play?"

"Nothing, sir. We can make it happen with a long burst of Terahertz radiation, say, like a burst that might come from the use of a Red Dragon at a distance, for example, around our Moon."

"Wow. Fail safe then, unless we had to cook one of those, it wouldn't have been an issue for them, but the minute we had to defend ourselves, it would start the process. Hell, that is genius!"

"Yessir. No question. John came up with that idea, and if you don't mind, I'd like to retrieve him, along with Dr. Patrick, from that family location you have…"

"Shit! Okay, get them back. While you're at it, snag up Chris and Michael too. No sense in splitting them up. Can you keep them with your folks?"

"Yessir. I think we can manage it."

"Okay. No matter how much Leah kicks and screams, make her stay put. I'll try to get word to them to be prepared to go when you guys move to get them."

"No need, sir. My guys are already in place, and will have them within the next hour. Besides, if you send them a message it could be tracked. Better it should come out of my folks."

"You're right. Okay. Make it happen, and let me know how long the degradation process will take, once we cook the first Red Dragon."

"Roger that. Oh, and boss? We'll take care of Chris and Michael, I promise!"

"You'd damned well better, Daniel. Otherwise, you're going to spend the rest of your life with my foot up your ass, and my hand on your throat!"

"Yessir! I would expect no less!"

Vandenberg Air Force Base, California:

General McDaniel hung up from his conversation with General Patrick about "no quarter for Gomers," and turned back to the latest tactical display of the area around the Moon. Double checking the figures, he told his staff to run the numbers one more time. This attack would require precision, and it would take careful placement of the weapon systems. Currently, the bad guys were just out of a comfortable range of the Red Dragon system, so he was going to have to anticipate when they would start moving. Then it hit him. There is all this going on at sea with the Russians, I wonder if this was part of a coordinated attack plan. Checking with his intelligence folks, he was now putting into the equation the factors related to the positions of the Russian Submarines tracking the main Battlegroups, the timing of sun down at these locations, and whether the initial strike could be in hours as opposed to days. Once the data came in, it was clear. The massive fleet overhead would be moving sooner than later. If he waited any longer, he would lose his best chance to maximize the damage to the Gomers.

General Patrick left it up to him, so he took it by the horns. Looking at his own command staff checking the numbers, he then turned to his Chief of Staff, and said, "Paul, take the first three Red Dragons, Phase II, I say again, Phase II, and begin the countdown process. Firing time should be optimal at 10 minutes. If we wait, we're screwed, and if they don't move like we think, we're equally screwed. I hate it, but cut them loose."

"Sir? Three won't do it."

"I know, but we can follow it with another three and hope for results closer to home plate. If we wait, we at least can be a little more precise with the second hit, and if necessary, we can supplement with the Phase I system for a more direct fire attack."

"I hope you're, right sir. I'd hate to miss."

"Paul, just do it! Oh, and put Bozeman's Phase I and III people on standby as well."

"Yessir."

Just like in the last conflict, the three Red Dragons were fired at their appropriate intervals, in fairly rapid succession. The "shot out" message was transmitted to SAHQ, and Admiral Lynch advised the task forces scattered around the globe to be prepared. Now it was a matter of waiting, since it would take some time for these weapons to reach their target. While they had been upgraded with stronger propulsion systems, it still was the kind of weapon that would ultimately "coast" into the detonation position. This is what caused all of General McDaniel's grief, since he was having to anticipate where the Gomer Fleet would be located at the moment in time when the missiles would reach their target point. Without a crystal ball, there was only so much the computer could do to make this work. The most critical component now would be good old-fashioned luck and a little "Kentucky windage".

USS Virginia, located in the Pacific Ocean near the Philippines:

Silent as a tomb, the USS Virginia had been stalking the dissidents in their Akula III as it made several approaches towards the USS New Jersey Battlegroup. Several factors made this a pretty remarkable feat. The Akula III wasn't like her predecessors, and detecting her had been tough. As the Akula III maneuvered, it was apparent to the Captain of the USS Virginia that this new submarine was not going to be an easy target. Compounding his challenges, this entire experience was becoming a very tedious process. Over the last several hours, the Akula III would break off the approach to the Battlegroup at roughly 200 miles distance, and then repeat the process with each new pass. Just as the USS Virginia would line up for a shot at the 190-mile range, the Akula III would turn and continue to maneuver around the USS New Jersey Battlegroup.

There was no question about the intent of the Akula III, but even knowing this, there was enough ambiguity to make the Skipper of the USS Virginia hold his fire. The tracking had been problematic, but the good news was that the one part of the fleet that was still quite adept at antisubmarine warfare was still the attack submarine. The course throughout the day had dealt with variations in depth, through water currents and convergences that were as unpredictable as any in the Pacific Ocean. Finally, with only an hour left before sunset, the Akula III made the mistake of getting up to that magic 190-mile line. As the Akula III began a slow rise to a depth of 75 feet, it was struck amidships by the torpedo fired a short distance away by the USS Virginia. Within seconds it was finally over, as the hulk of the state-of-the-art Russian submarine, completed and launched less than a year before, broke up and headed towards the bottom. Honestly, there was some small satisfaction onboard the USS Virginia, as both the Captain and his crew listened to the implosion sounds emanating from the dying Akula III, since they knew they had done their bit in a war that was only now taking shape.

Chapter VIII

❦

Supreme Allied Headquarters, SAHQ:

News of General McDaniel launching the first Red Dragons reached the staff almost at the exact same moment that Admiral Lynch was advised of the USS Virginia's actions against the Akula III. The other news filtering into the War Room was that the initial portion of the Gomer fleet was now beginning to make a formation movement from the area around the Moon. The Carrier and Battleship Class ships were approaching the initial minefield, and it was apparent that they had done their homework. The Fighter Class ships were preceding the larger ships, with the express mission of locating and destroying the outer ring of mines. During the months of peace, the Gomers took advantage of their passages to and from Earth to map out the limits of the mine field. It was also obvious that they had no qualms about using their Fighter Class ships to ram a mine to get it to detonate.

Our monitors revealed that when the Gomer attack fleet began to advance, the smaller Transport Class ships were falling into line in the middle of the huge formation. At the same time, the advance guard of Fighter Class Ships included a slightly smaller force of ships that were headed to various strategic locations around the globe. An analysis of this movement indicated that they had a very extensive target list, to include several major cities, our more strategic military formations, several of our command-and-control centers, and finally, our Big Gun Naval Battlegroups around the world. The plan to disperse had been a good one, since it was glaringly obvious that New Washington, our Mountain Allied Headquarters facilities, the new Pentagon, and Tiger Island, Honduras, were all on the target list. It was clear, too, that several of our more critical ports around the world were in the cross hairs, places such as Murmansk, Anadyr, Vladivostok, and Archangel, Russia; Dutch Harbor, Alaska; Norfolk, Virginia; New York Harbor; Boston Harbor, and finally, at Scapa Flow, in Scotland. Other Gomer forces seemed to be set to attack our Russian allies near the Ural Mountains, and one force was already lined up with a number of transports heading towards the same areas as their original enclaves located in Siberia during the last war. Thule Greenland was also in their sights, and we were anticipating another run at Greenland, but this force did not appear to have transports in any great numbers.

The down side to the Red Dragon weapons system was the very thing that made it so effective. The slower speed and stealth that allowed it to get on target meant that a lot of guess work was involved. In this case, General McDaniel had done a pretty solid job of getting the timing right, although, the results were not perfect. The first Red Dragon, the one that didn't have as far to go, detonated as the Twilight Line was starting to pass over the Kamchatka Peninsula. The success was mixed, since it did stop the lead elements from entering Siberian air space, but it did little to the more distant transport ships, or the Ships heading for other Pacific locations. Observers at or near the southern coast of Honduras reported that Tiger Island was no longer a feature to be found on the map of the globe. Instead, it was eliminated with a single strike by a Gomer Class Battleship that was part of the more lead elements that had infiltrated through our outer ring of defenses. Several other of these lead Gomer ships were also wreaking havoc in the Pacific Region, with several strikes in Hawaii,

Dutch Harbor, and in Japan. Casualties, thanks to the dispersion of both population and military forces, were relatively minimal.

As the first Red Dragon detonated, the surviving Gomer ships, many of which were of the Transport Class, began to turn and head back towards the Moon. This allowed the second Red Dragon to reach a mark much closer to the Moon where it too detonated. This one had the effect of being devastating to many of the transports, which now had begun to cluster in the space between the initial and second blasts. It was here that the third Red Dragon found the target. As it detonated it, too, released the Terahertz radiation that the Gomers were finding so devastating. Our ground monitors were reporting that the destruction of the "invasion" or Gomers' Transport Ships, was essentially total. The few survivors that were monitored were mostly dead without any apparent power or ability to move. For these last survivors, the controllers of the mobile mines systems were flying them into the sides of the last remaining Gomer ships still located in the space around the Earth.

Our best estimates, despite our clear successes on the bulk of the Gomer Fleet, still indicated that the remains of a sizable fleet of Gomer Ships had broken through and were even now prowling our skies. Ground and Naval forces around the Pacific soon got a fairly good indication of where these survivors were going, and about their numbers.

"General Patrick?"

"Yeah, Whit, whatcha got?"

"Sir, even though we got the majority of the bad guys still lining up, you are definitely NOT going to like the numbers we're getting in from our reporting stations."

"Go ahead, give it to me."

"Sir, the Gomers have what appear to be 6 Mountain Class ships, around two dozen Battleship Class ships, and our best guess is around 8,000 to 8,200 Carrier Class ships, and approximately

480,000 Fighter Class ships, that have broken through are even now trolling the Pacific region."

"Damn! What about Transport and Service type ships?"

"Uh... Okay, we are looking at approximately 550 Transports, and maybe three of their Service types."

"Hell, Whit, the total numbers of surviving ships is larger than what we had during the First Gomer War, in both the Northern and Southern fleets. Just for my own edification, just exactly what are the estimates of kills with the Red Dragon strikes?"

"Sir, we think, based on the computer data and real time observations, that we took out 55 Mountain Class ships, 350 Battleship Class ships, and upwards of 18,000 Carrier Class ships. We can add to that total approximately 550,000 Fighter class ships, 18,000 Transport Class ships, and best guess, around 520 of that newer Service type ship."

"Get a message to General McDaniel that I'm impressed with his shooting skills. So, we're anything but out of the woods. Where are these survivors headed?"

"Not back into space, and from what we can tell, the remains of their fleet are headed back towards Romanian and Southern Siberian airspace. If I had to guess, I think we are looking at their attempt to consolidate with the dissidents that are boxed into that area."

"Makes sense."

"It looks like once they get over dry land, they are back into the 'slash and burn' tactic of shooting anything suspicious. Unfortunately, they're doing it with their big stuff."

"Roger that! Okay, Whit, get the Air Forces online to use their stuff at maximum standoff range, let's see if we can whittle them down some more before they hook up with the other bad guys."

"Yessir!"

Vandenberg, Air Force Base, CA:

General McDaniel was proud of himself and his staff. They had taken an equation with one too many variables, and made it mostly work. The results were beyond what he had even wildly hoped, but it was still a crap shoot. When he got the call from the President, with General Patrick on the line, he wasn't surprised. He wasn't wild about it, but he wasn't surprised.

"General McDaniel, President Blanchard here. I don't want there to be any misunderstandings, so I've got General Patrick on the line too."

"Yessir."

"General Patrick, you on the line?"

"Yessir, Mr. President."

"Okay. First of all, General McDaniel, that was some damn fine shooting, and I want to commend you and your staff for pulling it off."

"Thank you, sir."

"Now here comes the fun part. General McDaniel, as the President, I am authorizing you to initiate the sequence for the release of the 'Phoenix IV' weapon system."

With that pronouncement, both General McDaniel and myself were more than a little stunned. I broke in for the first time and asked, "Mr. President, what do you know that we don't, that would make you want to show that hold card at this stage."

"General Patrick, that is a fair question, and one that we will address when we're done here. Just let me say that General Greene will provide you something that I got just a few minutes ago from our civilian intelligence."

"Okay, sir, I'm sorry to interrupt." Knowing that something monumental must have taken place, I stepped back into my role of listener, and the President continued.

"General McDaniel, you may release the weapons' codes for the Phoenix IV, and may fire only the prototype and Warbird 1, is that clear?"

"Yes, Mr. President."

"Good, you will fire the weapon as soon as the system can be brought online, which I'm assured will take all of 35 minutes. Is that estimate correct?"

"Yessir."

"Excellent. The Target is pretty far away, can you give me an estimate of flight time?"

"Yessir. Well, the target is approximately 4.5 billion km from Earth, and the speed of Phoenix IV is about 20 km/second. So, I would anticipate that it will take approximately 7 years and 3 months, give or take. Assuming time for maneuver to be precise in our targeting, and a couple of other variables, give it about 7.5 years."

"Great. Now then, I'm not done."

"Yes, Mr. President?"

"I am also authorizing the release of a second Phoenix IV to the secondary target."

"Sir? I don't have that one on my scree... Okay, I've got it. Uh... Damn!"

"General McDaniel, the commentary won't be necessary." When the target ID hit my screen, I broke into the conversation. "Uh, Mr. President?"

"Yes, General Patrick."

"Sir, I hate to interrupt, but we may have an alternative to that one, which might save us that additional Phoenix IV for something else. When we get updated by General Greene, I'll pass on what I've got as an alternative. Please delay this one until I've had a chance to brief you on it."

After a considerable pause, the President replied, "Okay Mike, but only reluctantly. Right now, I will hold off on that order. In the meantime, what is the time frame for that second strike, General McDaniel?"

"Mr. President, thanks to some Gomer technology, we can get a Phoenix IV on that target in about 45 days."

"Okay. General Patrick, you have your temporary reprieve, but your idea had better be a good one, and in either case, I want the ball rolling in the next two days. Got it?"

With his last question, General McDaniel and I both responded, "Yes, sir, Mr. President."

Within two hours, the large Phoenix IV missile, which looked very similar to the launch vehicle known as the Titan Rocket on which it was based, roared out of the silo and into the California sky. Increasing speed, the missile left our atmosphere and broke free of Earth's gravitation to begin its secret mission half way across our Solar System. It would be years before we knew the success or failure of this mission, and General McDaniel couldn't help but wonder if any of the Earth's population would be around to see whether it had worked or not.

Supreme Allied Headquarters, SAHQ:

When the connection was broken with the President and General McDaniel, I directed General Whitney to get General Greene on the line. It took only a few minutes, and I got to it in a hurry. "Daniel! What the hell is going on with the President and his urgency to release the big stuff?"

"Sir, sorry we didn't get you the word right away, but honestly, we couldn't get through to your headquarters."

"What do you mean you couldn't get through?"

"Sir, for some reason, we were cut off from you, and we have yet to figure out the glitch. Not real sure it isn't a viru... OH SHIT!"

"Yeah. 'Oh, shit' seems to cover it. Okay, scramble the backup lines, and I'll meet you on there when you can come up for air. In the meantime, get your people the hell out of there, and move to your alternate headquarters."

"Yessir." We hung up, and I immediately looked at General Whitney. "Okay, Whit. Scramble the land lines, and all of our communications codes. We need to activate our movement plan. Also, get a message via courier to the President's people, tell them that we've been compromised, and it can be assumed that each headquarters will be hit within the next few hours, or after dark depending on location! Move all personnel via fastest transportation to alternate locations!'"

"Yessir. How in the ..."

"Dammit, Whit. Right now, we just need to move. We'll worry about how later."

"Roger that, sir."

My best impression of the next several hours was the classic line, "assholes and elbows." The movement itself wasn't a major problem, since we had a contingency plan already in place for just such an incident, and a strong alternate location to utilize. The real problem was going to be re-establishing communications with all the players. General Greene's main headquarters wasn't moving, but his forward command post had been compromised, and I knew that his people were already in the process of getting out the door. I was equally sure that the Gomers knew where we were now, and we too had to bug out. Given our recent conversation with the President, it was just as likely that his hide location was in jeopardy, and the logistics of re-establishing him in a safe place would take a little more effort. Presidents have far more entourage than my key personnel, and they weren't designed to jump to another location in a hurry. The good news is that President Blanchard, especially during this more recent onset of Gomers, remembered how to be a General. His staff had been trimmed, and he could travel far lighter than just about any President in our history, but it was still going to take more time than for any of the rest of us.

Within an hour, my staff was packed and moving. We had various means of transportation from our location that ranged from small private aircraft, to commercial looking trucks, to privately owned vehicles of all types that were commandeered for just such an escape. The key to a safe movement under these conditions is to leave and arrive at a new location as innocuously as possible. We felt that any mass movements from a target area would be tracked from space, and the Gomers would be pretty stupid if they didn't pick up on the fact that all they had to do to adjust their target would be to watch the "ants leave the one hill, and then move to another hill." As a consequence, we had to dry clean our route.

Dry cleaning requires you to shake off anyone who might be observing a movement either by air or on the ground. The easiest way to do this is to head to an urban area that allows for egress in multiple directions. You arrive in the city, disappear to a point, such as a subway station, and then disperse in all directions from there. Eventually, following various circuitous routes, you can reassemble at various times, based on the route, at a new safe location. Every member of the key staff had to have the skill to verify that they were not being observed along their route, and it was just as important to recognize that if you were followed, then you would go anywhere but the new safe location.

Our troopers at the Allied Special Operations Command or ASOC were experts in this little bit of tradecraft or as some laymen call it, 'spy craft.' My headquarters key personnel were also fairly well versed in it, especially since many of us were all former special operators at some point in our career. The real challenge was for the

Presidential staff, who frankly, had no clue. I never thought I would say this in my entire life, but 'thank goodness for the operatives of the Central Intelligence Agency' and the Secret Service, who all worked several minor miracles getting the civilians on the President's staff to their new locations. Unfortunately, we weren't quite as lucky with the President himself. His movement would cause us all more than a little grief over the next few days. Reading the reports done after the move, it was apparent to me that while the President had been a General officer, he was a tanker, and face it, tankers are not very adept at hiding in a sewer.

During this major shift of locations, General Walter G. Crouse, the Commander of the Fourth Army, was forced to 'hold the head of the goat.' His headquarters location in the mountains of Southern West Virginia was not optimal, but it was fully equipped and it allowed us the time we needed to get back up and running without any loss of command and control for our forces in the field. Similarly, the command-and-control elements for our allied forces were still up and running, which were vital to our continued tracking of the enemy and for our overall defense of Earth. It was to his headquarters that the next Gomer move was becoming apparent. Several hours later, once General Greene's forward headquarters was established at his new location, this news was duly passed on for his evaluation. In light of the other information that had prompted the President's earlier Orders for the employment of the Phoenix IV system, this latest trend was extremely unsettling.

New Pentagon located in the Mountains of Southern West Virginia:

General Crouse was not in the habit of being patient, especially when the entire leadership was in a huge state of flux. The President and most of the Cabinet were now scattered all over the northeast, trying to get down to a new secure location near Smith Mountain

Lake in Virginia. This was only going to be an interim movement, since a new area was being built near there. With the latest need to scramble all of the key players, the construction schedule at several key locations was being rushed, along with the need to get communications secured and running again. He himself was currently underground and underwater, at his new secure location underneath the dredged and deepest part of Bluestone Reservoir. The dredging to extend the lake's deepest part to over 200 feet took a year, and the lateral tunnels were another effort that took almost a second year. This was the originally planned facility that was begun during the First Gomer war to house the "new Pentagon," and it would be the model for the other facilities that were being built in the area. Unfortunately, despite the need to scramble the bosses, none of these projects were fully completed.

These logistical concerns aside, General Crouse was now looking at a number of intelligence reports and observer reports coming from the field, and they were all giving him a case of serious heartburn. The first series of these reports were simple enough, a group of the larger Gomer ships were transiting around the globe, and diving down on several of the major locations and headquarters scattered around the planet. Tiger Island, Honduras, was a memory, as were the older Headquarters facilities in Hawaii, Japan, and Kamchatka. The Ural Mountains were hit, but again, it was largely an empty gesture, since all of these locations were now evacuated. Romania was a headquarters already overrun by the Russian dissidents, and was therefore spared the large strike package from space. The various key Russian Ports were hit, but not with the same devastating effects as first feared. These latter strikes were relatively ineffective, not because of any great defensive effort, but because the Gomers treated them like a diversionary strike.

It was the diversionary character of these hits that bothered General Crouse considerably, and it was at this moment that he really missed having someone to contact to discuss the issue. Going through the reports again, he recognized something he'd missed earlier. The large Gomer Ships were not operating with many of the Carrier or Fighter Class ships. Instead, the Battleship Class ships were marauding around striking what they believed to be key locations around the globe. A few hours previously, the recently evacuated SAHQ, located in the mountains of New Hampshire, was destroyed. The ASOC forward Headquarters suffered the same fate only a few minutes before the SAHQ was hit, as did the location from where the President was operating. The only bright spot was that none of the Second Gomer War facilities were struck, but there was no question that they could only be used as a means of last resort. Right now, the Gomers were hitting hard and fast from an altitude that was definitely out of effective range for most of the defensive weapons systems.

When the next observation reports filtered in from Russia from General Larkin, General Crouse immediately recognized what was happening. The diversion was hiding the main movement of the Gomers, who had taken most of the Carrier and Transport Class ships into the areas where the Russian dissidents and the defected Russian units were being contained by the Allied forces. The observers were all reporting that the Gomers were picking up and moving these Russian dissidents to act as a ground force at other locations. Within a few hours the picture became crystal clear. The dissidents and their defected military forces were going to be used as human strike forces for the Gomers, and to provide security at the Gomer enclaves now being established in Greenland, points in northern Siberia, and in Northern Alaska/Canada.

There was no question that General Larkin had his hands full with the 21st Allied Army Group, and the orders coming from his headquarters weren't always being met with cooperation. General Larkin and General Davis, with the 42nd Army Group, were both discovering that several of the Allied Nations, thinking that the Allied Command and the Government of the United States had lost their key leadership, were operating solely with their self interest in mind. The Russians were still as focused as ever and, fortunately, Major Dubronin had been in contact with his father during the "bug out." The Chinese, Japanese, and Indian forces, on the other hand, were now taking a different approach. Absent guidance from the Allied Headquarters, as opposed to a Deputy Commander, they were now pulling their forces into positions where they could only assist in very limited fashion, and only on their own turf. In other words, despite being the Acting Deputy Commander speaking for General Patrick, General Crouse was not getting what he needed from some of our allies. They believed the worst had overtaken the Allied Command, and now they were no longer inclined to completely cooperate in presenting a joint front.

The Family Facilities, Peterstown, WV:

Leah was missing her children. Holly, Chris, John, and her grandson had left for the big ASOC facility in the Rockies about a week ago, and their absence was truly bothering her. Especially since she wasn't even sure they were in the Rocky Mountains anymore. Feeling a little sorry for herself, she was going through the motions of making a meal for herself and Mother Patrick. Lost in her thoughts, she must have jumped a foot when the Alarm suddenly sounded throughout the facility. It did not help either that with each clang of the alarm bells, the tension inside her began building to a new level. Somehow, she knew that this was the real thing. As she gathered Mother Patrick up, snatched her "go to hell bag" and shouldered her weapon, all she could think about was giving Toni some help getting her brood moving. Jumping out of the door to her quarters, she could see Toni, her daughters, and their children all grabbing their pre-packed escape bags. Within another minute they all began their trek to the assembly area.

Over the last several months, Leah had made sure that everyone had adopted her earlier version of the "go to hell bag" so that, in the event of an emergency, the families would at least have a minimal means of sustaining themselves. For the children, this entailed back packs containing flashlights, water, and sufficient pre-packaged food and snacks to hold them until rescue. There had also been repeated drills, just to get everyone used to the notion of having to make a run for it. They even trained some of the moms on basic combat skills and issued weapons. Most of the time these drills took on a holiday spirit, especially for the younger children, but not this time. This time it was markedly different. This time, Leah was glad that her own children were miles away in a different location. This time, when her eyes met Toni's, it was clear that they both knew that this was no drill.

When Mrs. Blanchard and Leah stepped out of their quarters, they were immediately surrounded by the security details assigned to them, who took up a defensive posture as the children were guided away from their rooms. To even the most casual observer, this was new and different, and as the other families began their movement to the assembly area the addition to the drill was immediately noticed. Another thing that got everyone's attention was that the security forces Leah had requested were also now taking up their defensive positions around the family assembly area. Lou Ann Whitney was the last to arrive and, like some of the other moms, she was carrying her assigned weapon. For the first time since the drilling began, the children were not making jokes or laughing. Instead, except for the occasional guiding hand or admonition to keep moving, the entire group was stone silent.

Once assembled, the families waited, and watched as the young Ranger Captain strode up in front of the group. When he faced everyone, he was met with silence and the worried faces of more than one of the mothers. "Ladies. There is an ongoing attack on several of our facilities around the east coast, and we have alerted you to take up your positions near the rear of this facility. We don't have any definite information as to the present threat. I can say that for right now, nothing appears to be headed in our direction. Still..." Before he could complete his sentence, Mrs. Blanchard nodded at Leah, who then had all the families start lining up to head back along the narrow pathway to the alternate position behind another layer of rock. Within another five minutes, the entire group was in their new position, silent, seated, and waiting for any new developments. Several of the mothers, to include Leah, were armed and in firing positions in both directions. The young Ranger Captain was so impressed, he vowed to himself that these ladies, and all their children, would be protected with his last breath. With each ticking of the clock the tension grew. Still, the Captain imagined that like many pioneer mothers over 150 years ago, these ladies were ready for anything. Then he thought to himself, "God help the bastard that comes after these women, since I have a feeling that they will be hard to get around." What he couldn't know was that he had just predicted the future with far more accuracy than he would have ever thought possible.

The hours passed, and finally an all clear was sounded. Once they returned to their quarters, they each knew that things had changed on the surface. What they didn't know was exactly how. For the first time, perhaps in recorded history, these military wives, with their normally perfect system for "knowing things," did not have a clue. Unfortunately, this lack of information was going to last for a few days.

SECTION 3

ON THE RUN! THE TREACHERY IS NOW PERSONAL!

Chapter IX

Near Mount Washington, New Hampshire:

While General Crouse was wrestling with the events around the globe, some of us were struggling to get from our old home to a new one. Once the Order to "bug out" was given, the preset plan went into effect to begin moving the key staff and other personnel to alternate locations. I was teamed up with General Whitney, Command Sergeant Major Clagmore, and Major Dubronin. We were satisfied that everyone was headed in the right direction, so we too finally began the process of moving to our new home. We had never rehearsed this particular plan, but some of us had been there before in other parts of the world, so we weren't lost either. We knew where we were going, and we knew when we had to be there, but otherwise, the plan was very simple. Make your way, using whatever assets you can beg, borrow, steal, or scrounge that won't leave a trail or mark your movement. We were going to have to exfiltrate our way out of New Hampshire and get to West Virginia, moving both day and night, without leaving a noticeable trail to anyone watching from the sky or on the ground. From experience, I already knew when we set out that this might be an adventure from which none of us would ever recover.

Heading down the Mountain on several All-Terrain Vehicles, we got to the location where we had an older pickup truck hidden along a trail. Once we got the branches off, we set out to get down to the highway, New Hampshire Route 16. At this point along the route, the highway was referred to as the White Mountain Highway, and we moved along as quickly as we could with darkness approaching. We were about 20 miles away from our old Headquarters when twilight arrived, and it was only 15 minutes later that the blast could be both felt and heard as we were driving down the darkened roadway.

The shockwave rolled over us as we were speeding down the road. Sergeant Major Clagmore, who was driving the old pick up, turned to me. "Christ, General! Was that what I think it was?

"Sergeant Major, our old haunts just got zapped."

"Shit. Should I pull over?"

"Yeah, go ahead and pull into the next wooded driveway over there." After we turned in and stopped, we got out to check on General Whitney and Major Dubronin. They had a ring side seat for the event, since they were riding in the bed of the truck with their backs up against the cab. No question, they'd already had the ride of their life with our bouncing around the roadway, but what they had seen was worth talking about.

"General Whitney? Could you see anything?"

"I didn't see much, but Major Dubronin here saw it all. Unfortunately, the flash I think has temporarily blinded him a little. God, it was bright!"

"Alex? You okay?"

"Yes, sir. Flash was very bright, and the time from then until we felt it on the road, was perfect for hit on our mountain."

"Did you see how they did it?"

"No, General. It must have been from far up."

"Okay, Whit? Do you think the Fighters will be here soon?"

"Yessir. I figure if it was a maximum range shot, then the Fighters should be down in the area within the next few minutes."

"Okay. Do we sit or go? What are your recommendations?" I looked around at the entire group, and to a man, it was clear that they wanted more distance between us and the mountain. Finally, the Sergeant Major spoke up and simply said, "Sir, I'd rather get hit on the move than just sitting here. Hell, we can't fight back, as long as we're hiding."

"All righty then. Let's hit the road."

The Sergeant Major and I climbed back into the truck, and we pulled back out onto the highway. Sergeant Major Clagmore had the foresight to bring some night vision goggles with him, so we were making pretty good time without any lights on. As a passenger without night vision, it was more than unsettling hurtling down the dark road, trying to put that important distance between us and our former headquarters. Within a few minutes of our pulling out, we saw a second bright flash behind us, and we all recognized in that instant that our decision to keep moving was the correct one. This time it was quite apparent that the force of the blast was greater, and probably delivered at a much closer range. It would be about an hour before our concern for any marauding Fighter Class ships finally forced us to park in a wooded area, just to make sure that nothing in the sky was stalking us. Finally, with only a few hours left before dawn, we decided to risk moving forward on our race to the south.

It had been some very hard driving, when we finally arrived at the little town of Rochester, New Hampshire, and pulled into the Skyhaven Airport. It was the first airport along our route, and Sergeant Major Clagmore and I decided that it was time to switch our ride. Relying on our other skills, developed as much younger special operators, we managed to locate and then "liberate" a Cessna 172, four place light aircraft. In other words, we hot-wired an airplane. I won't get into it too deeply, but stealing an airplane isn't as hard as it sounds. The hard part is making sure that somebody remembers how to fly the damn thing.

"General Patrick? When is the last time you flew one of these things?"

"What? a Cessna?"

"No, well, yeah. When is the last time you flew *anything*?"

"Hmmmm, let's see, my last flight as a pilot in command in a helicopter was probably sometime in 1999. Why?"

"Geez, Sir. This ain't no chopper. You sure you can fly one of these things?"

"Ah, don't worry about it, Sergeant Major. I think I remember how it works."

"General, I am not feeling a lot of confidence when you say remember."

"Relax, Sergeant Major! What is the worst that can happen?"

"Sir, do you honestly have to ask?"

"Not a problem. I think I can remember how to turn the damn thing on, and besides, we aren't going to get to Boston in time if we don't cheat a little."

"Yessir. In that case, fuck it. Drive on!"

With those happy words, I tossed Major Dubronin the check list, and we began the process of getting the engine started. Once we got the older Cessna showing green on all the engine instruments, I released the brakes, and we started towards the runway. Checking the old wind sock, we did a rather hasty and fairly sloppy take off. What I hadn't told the Sergeant Major was that the last time I'd touched a fixed wing aircraft was in 1988, and even then, it was to fly as a co-pilot. Honestly, I hadn't checked out in a Cessna 172 since the late 1970s, and there was much I didn't remember. I got Major

Dubronin to drag out a VFR Sectional, and we began the process of trying to fly south. Finally, I wound up doing the classic IFR flight, only this time IFR didn't mean Instrument Flight Rules. Instead, it meant "I Follow Roads."

After about an hour, I had Logan International Airport in Boston spotted. For once, this wasn't as bad as it sounds, simply because we were the only air traffic, and the airport was officially closed and virtually deserted. This alone made us nervous, so we made the conscious decision to dump the plane after landing, and "borrow" a car. I won't discuss the landing, since pride demands that we don't discuss the repeated bouncing down the runway. I guess technically, I could claim four landings off the one for my log book. The real joy was seeing the look of relief on Sergeant Major Clagmore's face as we bounced the last time and finally came skidding to a stop near a taxiway leading to the general aviation area. We got even luckier when we discovered that near this ramp was a rental car facility.

Our best moment in Boston came when we realized that Hertz was kind enough to lock their keys in a safe that Sergeant Major Clagmore could crack in his sleep. It was equally fortunate that I had developed those similar skills when it was necessary to unlock a fuel pump near the parking area for the rental car company. I was very proud of my efforts, right up until Sergeant Major Clagmore opined, "Sir. You know a crow bar would have popped it far quicker than you with a lock pick!"

"Thanks, Sergeant Major. You know, of course, that you could suck the air out of most things that are fun!"

"Sorry, Sir. I just thought you were in a hurry."

"Sergeant Major. You're absolutely correct, now do me a favor."

"Yessir?"

"Piss off!"

"Yessir. Glad to help."

It was mid-afternoon when we began making our way from Boston towards the Massachusetts Turnpike, headed west. This time we were in a slightly more comfortable ride, and General Whitney was taking his four-hour shift behind the wheel. It should be noted that each time we made a transition in vehicles, we would use as large a built-up area as we could find, and then switch to a different means of transportation. We were also forced to use rather circuitous routing to get from where we were to where we needed to be going. The journey was constant, and tracked from Interstate 90, to Interstate 88, until we finally got on Interstate 81 in Binghamton, New York. Again, darkness was forcing us to make several risky choices. When there is little traffic in the open, it is obvious that you must be someone moving with a purpose. We knew that such movement had to attract the wrong kind of attention, so we opted to use frontage roads, and frequent stops in areas covered with trees.

It was along one of these frontage roads where we spotted a Fighter Class ship coming along behind us. General Whitney was on the wheel wearing Sergeant Major Clagmore's goggles, and the Sergeant Major and I were being bounced around in the back. It would be a toss-up as to whether Clagmore or I noticed it first, but we could see a brief flash of light behind us reflected off the mirror of the car. Sergeant Major Clagmore simply said, "General, pull off now, and stop."

General Whitney asked, "Why?"

"Sir. There is a Gomer coming along behind us, I am guessing about a half mile or so back. I think he is sweeping those cars that were bunched up along that truck stop parking lot."

"Crap. Okay, hang on."

Whipping the wheel sharply, we screeched to a stop along the side of the road near some woods. Without any hesitation, we all scrambled out of the car and into the woods. Taking up positions with weapons ready, we watched as the Fighter Class ship approached our position. It was moving along and scanning all vehicles and buildings along the highway. We watched as a second, and then a third, Fighter Class ship appeared. They joined into a formation with the first Fighter Class ship, and they began to assist in the sweep over all the parked cars. When they got up to our car, the beam of light traveled over the car, and then around the immediate area. Fortunately, they didn't waste their time scanning towards us over in the woods, but they did accomplish something that set us back. They completely drained the battery in the car, and because of the proximity of their scanning, they also drained the special batteries in our night vision device. Command Sergeant Major Clagmore was able to rectify the battery problem for the Night Vision Goggles. Contained in his pockets were several replacement batteries, and our distance coupled with the shielding provided by his lying in a mud puddle, kept them charged and working. The car on the other hand, was a bigger problem.

After trying the car again, we headed over land to a road not too far from the frontage road where the Gomers had scanned everything. On this more secluded back road, we found a slightly used, but serviceable utility vehicle. The tool bins had been ransacked, but it ran, which made it our first choice. Moving along with four of us crammed into the cab, we were able to at least get far enough down the road to find another ride. Throughout the rest of our trip, there were several other instances where we could see Fighter Class ships diving on areas along the road way, and there were at least two more close calls where we were only barely able to duck under cover at the last second. Add to this the use of back roads, all of which were quite unfamiliar to us, and I can assure you that traveling was both tedious and more than a little nerve wracking.

Shortly after the sun rose on that second day, we were still moving and headed south on Interstate 76. It would be about an hour later when we picked up US Highway 220/US50 that eventually took us into Clarksburg, West Virginia. From there we took Interstate 79 until we exited onto US Highway 19, or the Mountaineer Expressway. This was our final major roadway, which would eventually lead to Summersville, West Virginia, the site of our new home. It was almost dark when we left the roadway and pulled onto Aldredge Avenue, near Summersville. It was here that we picked up a Military Police Escort at a check point. Once we all checked credentials, on both sides of the check point, they guided us down Long Point Access Road to our new home under the lake. This was perhaps the longest and toughest 48 hours any of us had seen in quite a few years.

Overall, our party held up quite well, and Sergeant Major Clagmore and I had definitely put our skills to the test. Aside from a number of locks, and at least two key safes at rental car companies, we'd also managed to liberate no fewer than 8 cars, 5 trucks, and one small airplane over the previous two days. At the end of our journey, Sergeant Major Clagmore and I agreed that we didn't too badly for a couple of old "has-beens." Most soldiers our age would have retired years ago, but here we were running around like a couple of thieves on the run. Exhausted from our ordeal, we were finally escorted into the entrance of our new facility that, from the outside, looked like dilapidated old farm house. While the entire facility was not quite finished, it was at least to the point where we could work around the construction, and open it as a headquarters. There was no question that at this point, we were far more concerned that we make it functional than we were about the aesthetics. After all, how pretty can concrete and rebar really be to anyone other than perhaps an engineer? Unless of course it is a soldier that sees all that concrete and rebar as a haven from the bad guys. We were so damn glad to see the place, that whether it looked like an office or a concrete room, just didn't seem so important. If I were being completely honest with myself, I may have opted for the concrete look as my first choice in living quarters.

Supreme Allied Headquarters, (SAHQ) - near Summersville, WV:

The most significant problem from our being in transit wasn't our new semi-completed surroundings. Instead, it was that we'd missed a lot over the two days we were incommunicado. Despite our exhaustion, we were now dealing with getting up to speed and making the entire Allied Command operational again from an entirely new location. Sleep being for sissies, our first challenge was to begin the process of stepping back into the fray and assuming control back from General Crouse at his headquarters. In order to accomplish this, we had to have the rest of our key personnel located and returned to our location. This is where Sergeant Major Clagmore was invaluable. His efforts to track down and recover many of our staff was vital to getting all the key players rounded up and settled into our new home.

Along with finding all our personnel, we also had to reestablish secure communications around the globe, and thankfully, within three hours of our arrival we had at least managed to re-establish contact with most of our forces. Generals Larkin, Davis, and Crouse were all delighted to hear from us since, up to that point, only General Greene had resurfaced on the command network a mere four hours earlier. General Crouse also advised us that the President was still out of touch, and that he didn't even know if the President was still alive. We wouldn't get an answer to that question for several more hours, since the one serious problem with our having to "bug out" like we did, was that communications had to stop to the key leadership elements that were even now seeking safety from the Gomers.

While we waited to see where the President might be located, or when he would surface, we worked to get our Chinese, Japanese, and Indian forces back into the fold. This too was no easy task, especially given our enforced disappearance for over 48 hours. It took a while to verify that we were back in the saddle, and that we weren't some imposters put into place to keep everyone in line. The resulting video conferences and code words made this process more secure, but a damn sight longer to accomplish. General Greene had been working along these same lines, and he'd had a several hour head start to our efforts. Based on the significant ground work General Greene accomplished, we were finally able to get most of these forces back into the mood to cooperate by the end of the third day. It also didn't hurt that the Chinese had been dealt a rather significant black eye by the Gomers during the time we were in transit. After being hit hard, their initially brazen view of "we got this" was no longer an issue for them. They sounded genuinely happy to hear that the Allied Staff was not only alive and well, but up and running again.

During this same period, we also officially learned that our original locations for both ASOC and SAHQ had been completely destroyed with direct hits from above. Conversely, the President's facilities were not hit on the first night, but were attacked and destroyed on the second night. This told us that the Gomers did not base their attacks on signal intelligence but, instead, on a leak from a dissident hiding within either our staff or on the ASOC staff. My bet was that it was on our staff, and we again began the process of vetting all personnel, not just foreign officers, to make sure they were not "feeding the animals" any critical information. This was especially important, since we had no intentions of leaving this latest facility for any reasons, and insider information was only going to make life harder for all concerned.

The most significant change between our former headquarters in all prior wars, and in this war, was that for once we were in more Gomer-proof facilities. Taking a page from the "submarine headquarters" book, our new headquarters would be more permanent with each of them established under a body of water. General Clark, our capable Allied Logistician had designed each of these new facilities using multiple lateral tunnels, and other more innovative entry systems, to get our facilities located both deep underground and underwater. As luck would have it, General Clark was already at our new facility doing an inspection when the "bug out" took place, and it was work along with the scientists that made the facility even possible. More to the point, our scientists were positive that the use of water features as shielding had the potential of negating the impact of any Gomer weapons, regardless of their power levels. The eggheads were equally convinced that the deeper the water, the better. Since this was irrefutable logic, we began the process even before the last war was ended. Where necessary we also added both dredging as required, and then tunneling even further below the deepest parts of these lakes. We wanted to make sure that each of the new facilities would be down deeper than the deepest points of the overhead water feature, which gave them all added protection. The upside was the protection from Gomer Weapons fired from space, the down side was that you were now living in a damp basement with tons of water overhead. It was not a place for the faint of heart or the claustrophobic, but it was secure and safe.

Our new SAHQ facilities were now located underneath Summersville Lake, WV. The large earthen dam that creates the lake is located on the Gauley River, near the town of Summersville, and the lake covers a drainage area of roughly 803 square miles. I found it interesting that they named the dam, not after the closest town of Gad, but a town that was just a little further away. I remembered as a kid, my Dad took me there while they were building the place, and I could recall the stories about the original idea of naming it the "Gad Dam." Since that wouldn't go over really well, the planners opted out of that notion, and just named it after Summersville. Either way, what makes it work for us was that the dam itself is a rock-fill type, thus appearing as a natural structure, as opposed to being man made. The dam is 390 feet high and 2,280 feet long, and it creates a wonderfully deep-water feature. The depth of the lake, which in places is up to 327 feet deep, was perfect for our security and needs.

In short, our new Headquarters facility is under a lake with sufficient depth to preclude the need to dredge the lake to an appropriate depth to avoid Gomer Weapons fire. Despite this, we still didn't hesitate to move forward by digging an additional 100 or so feet below the deepest point. Now we would be well over 400 feet below the surface of the lake and earth, which we were assured from our testing would be completely shielded from any Terahertz weapon attacks that might be mounted by the Gomers. Dr. Abramson and Dr. Clarkson were in complete accord that our new headquarters would be completely untouchable even if the Gomers were using their largest ships and weapons, and regardless of their altitude at the time of firing. I'd watched what their weapons could do, and watched as Diamond Head was turned into gravel during the First War, so I wasn't quite as confident. Still, it was far better than anything we'd been in before, so it would be here that we would plan on making our final stand as a Headquarters.

The other new facilities included places like our newer Pentagon Operations facility, where General Crouse was trying to hold things together. This headquarters was now established underneath the Bluestone Reservoir, or Bluestone Lake, WV. Here the lake is nearly eleven miles long, with an area of 2,040 acres during summer pool, though the water level does change frequently. Normally, maximum depth for the lake is around 90 feet, which meant that this was going to require more dredge work. The facility was the first one we constructed, and it took a lot longer to build than any of the others. The deepest part of the lake had to be dredged to a classified depth of over 200 feet, with tunneling required below this deepest part to add another 150 feet in depth. The Dam itself was more obvious, which made this the most vulnerable location for all of the Government facilities, should the Gomers ever decide to destroy the obviously man-made structure. Knowing this, we designated Claytor Lake, VA, as the alternate and future location for the Pentagon Operations personnel to use as a war time headquarters. Claytor Lake was a good choice because it backs water up a distance of 21.67 miles. Here the reservoir has a surface area of 4,472 acres at the normal full pool elevation of 1846.0 feet with approximately 100 miles of shoreline. The storage capacity of the reservoir is estimated to be 225,000-acre feet, with a maximum depth of 115 feet. Again, the classified depth, after dredging, was 200 feet, with an additional 100 foot drop below the deepest part where the headquarters facilities were under construction. Unfortunately, construction on this facility was only begun shortly before the war, and it would be months before it would be ready for any sort of occupancy.

The Allied Special Operations Command was now established below Lake Moomaw, Virginia, which is located in a canyon once called Kincaid Gorge. Similar to Lake Summersville, there is a massive earthen structure that backs up the Jackson River for over 12 miles, forming Lake Moomaw. Lake Moomaw was originally constructed for downstream flow augmentation (water quality), flood control, and recreation. Now it was to be the home for a large part of the displaced government and the Allied Special Operations Command. Lake Moomaw is the second largest impoundment in western Virginia, and it covers 2,530 surface acres with a maximum depth of 152 feet. What made this an appealing location for ASOC was that there are 43 miles of undeveloped, wooded shoreline. Here dredging wasn't necessary, since there were two distinct layers of water, one of which acted as an excellent barrier for detection by the Gomers. The distance for effective shielding from Gomer Weapon's fire only required the digging of an additional 100 feet below the bottom of the lake at the deepest part.

Using the same lateral tunneling system for entry as in our other lake facilities, the space below Lake Moomaw was able to accommodate the ASOC Headquarters staff, and the President with his staff, until their own facilities could be completed. The least expensive of each of the facilities to build, after Bluestone Lake, it was the first new command facility completed and operational. The proximity to the New Washington facility also made it the prime location for the President and his staff during the massive transition. Once the bug out began, this was the place the President was to go, and while the Vice President and Secretary of State were already present at this facility, the main staff and the President himself were still in transit.

Finally, the facility designated as the NEW Washington was being built underneath Smith Mountain Lake, VA. The surface area of Smith Mountain lake is roughly 32 square miles with an average depth of 55 feet, and a maximum depth of 250 feet. Again, there was no need to dredge the lake deeper at the construction location, but when the tunnel was completed, it would be 150 foot deeper than the deepest part of the lake. This fact alone made it more of an engineering challenge, based on the soil types presented in and around the lake. Compounding the problem was the fact that this lake was far more developed, and hence far less remote than the location at Lake Moomaw, VA. The price for this fact was that the subterfuge required to complete construction unnoticed was considerable.

Alternate locations were also developed below Lake Moultrie, Lake Murray, and Lake Wateree in South Carolina as locations for our Marine and Naval personnel. The US Navy also moved their main HQ to a location in the Chesapeake Bay, near the Bay Bridge Tunnel, while the USAF maintained a main headquarters near the Hampton Roads Bridge Tunnel outside Norfolk, Virginia. The key in selection for all of these facilities was to look for the deepest bodies of water, with more remote access, so that personnel could be hidden as they came or went from the underground facilities. Wiring, power, and communications for each of these facilities also dictated that the sites be selected to accommodate the use of power from nearby nuclear facilities. These considerations, coupled with extensive backup systems for power and communications, made each of these newer facilities virtually undetectable for the Gomers, and mostly impregnable for their weapons. In fact, our only real threats were from humans who might stumble into the facilities nearer the surface, or from a lucky shot by either a Gomer or a dissident that might close off an exit.

The Family Facilities, Peterstown, WV:

While the families were settled back into their quarters, it was still a very restless arrangement. The last "drill" had not been a drill, and everyone knew it, which gave everything they now did a real sense of urgency. This time the news filtering back into the facility impacted almost everyone personally, and some of it wasn't good news. Everyone had a loved one that was either on the run, or had been on the run, since that first night. What was killing most of them was the lack of knowing what was happening. The security staff did their best to keep people informed, and as each missing individual surfaced, the news was passed on to their families. Still with each passing hour, many of the families were on the verge of panic. Sensing this, Leah did all she could to keep people focused. While they didn't drill their escape plan, they did discuss how to make it better, or what new things they should consider for their various "escape bags" or emergency backpacks. Then, on the second day, the chemical protective equipment finally arrived.

Leah, Katie Clagmore, Martha Clark, and Lou Ann Whitney made it a point to drill everyone on the proper wearing of the gas masks. Katie made sure that all the mothers with younger children and infants were well instructed on putting on the masks. Where possible, older children were assigned to help the younger ones, and by the end of the fourth day, there wasn't a single child or parent that couldn't get their mask on, or a suit over an infant, in under a minute. Katie and Leah were both rabid on the subject, especially after Katie Clagmore had mentioned one evening that her "biggest fear was that someone would just toss a 'bug bomb' into the hole with them." Leah immediately shared this idea with Toni, and so the request had been made some time ago for this chemical safety equipment. Fortunately, after the last alert, there wasn't any discussion, argument, or resistance to everyone participating and learning. The military detail also participated in the training, and even went so far as to issue antidote pens, and train all the parents on the medical treatment for exposure to the potential chemical agents.

The last idea also came from Katie Clagmore, when she said, "we might need more ammunition, and another day on the range." Again, nobody wasted time putting her idea into action. All of the moms, and a few of the older children, took their turns firing, loading, and adding ammunition to their back packs. Mrs. Jones, her son, and two daughters were becoming expert marksmen, and along with the moms who were already assigned weapons, this "Mom Brigade," as they were calling themselves, were all getting prepared for the worst. Now school work included the training of defensive skills, orienteering, and basic survival. Granted, this was not the way anyone ever wants to raise a child but, given the alternatives, it was the smartest way of doing it under these conditions. The best side benefit was that it kept everyone's minds occupied and off what might be happening to their loved ones. The best direct benefit was that within days, it would save a lot of young lives.

Chapter X

❦

ASOC Headquarters, now established below Lake Moomaw, VA:

The check point was located almost three miles away, along an access road, that would lead eventually to the back entrance of the new ASOC facility. The security team manning the post were not at all surprised to see the old school bus pull up to the first barrier. Over the last two days, they had seen several older converted campers, pickup trucks, beat up cars, and even a John Deere Tractor pull up with refugees from the President's last bunker location. This bus looked absolutely horrible, and it even had tinted windows. Still, something told the security team leader that this didn't look right. Going immediately on alert, all of the team were deploying into their fighting positions, as the bus pulled up to the stop point. The bus almost came to a stop, and then several things happened at once. The bus began pulling rapidly forward and turned around the first barrier. Despite having been ordered to stop, the bus continued to pick up speed, and there was no question in the Team Leader's mind that it was going to attempt to ram through the gate on the road leading to the back entrance. Thinking quickly, he triggered a trap device, and a large steel and reinforced concrete barrier quickly shot up from the ground right in front of the bus, as it increased to "ramming" speed. The crash was horrendous, and the firefight that followed was both swift and deadly to anyone on the bus.

A group of Russian dissidents, likely deposited by a Gomer transport, were on a recon mission around the area of the first Presidential bunker. From our best guess later, we believed that these dissidents had captured several prisoners who were trying to make their way out of the area. It was from these prisoners that they learned where the President might be heading, and it was for this reason they were trying their best to find and capture or kill the President. General Greene was inspecting the aftermath of the fire fight when another vehicle approached this carnage. Moving forward slowly the bread truck stopped at the first barrier, where the driver exited the vehicle with his hands up. Moving in quickly, the security team put the man face down on the ground and placed him in flex cuffs, while several of the soldiers searched the truck. Inside they found a wounded secret service agent, and a woman who had been wounded and was unconscious. She was in a tattered uniform, and General Greene was summoned to see if he could identify her, since the uniform seemed to be that of a General Officer.

Before General Greene could reach her, the man on the ground moaned out something that made General Greene stop and take a closer look. It was then he realized that the man on the ground, covered in mud and blood, was the President of the United States.

"Holy hell! Mr. President! Are you okay?"

"Uh, yeah, I guess…"

General Greene signaled one of his men to cut off the flex cuffs, and as they were lifting the President from the ground, he passed out. General Greene and the Security Team leader lifted the President, along with the other wounded, including the President's military advisor, Lieutenant General Maria Hookman, into General Greene's vehicle. Once everyone was loaded and secured, General

Greene immediately headed back down the road towards his facility, and the hospital that was located there. A later search of the bus revealed almost 25 dissidents, and the identity of two of their prisoners, who were now all dead in the wreckage of the bus. The first of the two prisoners was the Secretary of Defense, Secretary Richard Todd, and the second was Dr. Henrich Khelm, the President's National Security Advisor. These two gentlemen were high value targets by anyone's standards, but the Gomers would never know just how close they had come to capturing one of their highest value targets. If this attack had taken place later, or if the President had just come along only an hour earlier, the result could have been truly devastating.

Supreme Allied Headquarters, (SAHQ):

Sometimes the sheer enormity of events can lead you to overlook the basics. In our case, we were now trying to survive, as opposed to identifying the tactics and strategy being employed by the Gomers. The near miss with the President was just such distraction, and if it were the plan of the Gomers to keep us off balance, then they did one very excellent job. Everyone, from myself down to the individual soldiers manning a perimeter, was hyper focused on operational and physical security. Normally, this is a good thing, but in the process, we were losing sight of what the enemy might have up their sleeve on a more global scale. Even as we were reeling from the first attack on the ASOC headquarters at Lake Moomaw, the Gomer Battleship Class ships were massing for attacks at each of our known and suspected positions. Fortunately, the only actual location that was hit was the ASOC facilities at Lake Moomaw. The older facilities, which were abandoned at the onset of these latest hostilities, were now coming into the Gomers' crosshairs.

The following evening, just as the darkness began to settle in over the East Coast of the United States, a coordinated attack was initiated by the Gomers on each of these older sites. There was no significant loss of life, but there was considerable property destruction. Several older mountains in and around Southern West Virginia were devastated, and it was very apparent that someone had provided the Gomers with the exact coordinates for several of our former fuel and equipment depots. The only active location struck during the attack was at Lake Moomaw, in Virginia. This attack was anticipated, and it did much to destroy a portion of the back entrance area where the dissidents had attacked earlier in the day. ASOC itself, along with the President and his remaining staff, were not injured or impaired in any fashion. The best news from the entire incident was that it confirmed the findings of Dr. Abramson and Dr. Clarkson, that the water would attenuate the effectiveness of the Gomers' main weaponry.

The attack was raging overhead at ASOC before the President was finally sufficiently conscious to provide any information about their journey. His Military Advisor, General Hookman, was also conscious, but her injuries forced the doctors to keep her heavily medicated. The Secret Service detail originally consisted of four agents, and only one was still with the President when they arrived in the Lake Moomaw area. The other three were killed during an earlier attempt by several dissidents to attack the President. The last one died shortly after his arrival at the ASOC facility, leaving the only survivors of the President's party as the President and his Military Advisor. We also lost our Secretary of Defense, National Security Advisor, and the 15 soldiers that were detailed to provide security for the President's senior staff. Someone on the President's staff, someone that knew their evacuation plan, route, and timing, was not to be trusted. The entire party was ambushed on the evening of the first day by a group of dissidents that were dropped off by Gomer Fighters along the President's route of egress. It was a well-planned ambush, and it was only luck and the hard fighting of the security detail that allowed Marty Blanchard the chance to escape. Over the next several days, they were pursued relentlessly, with it culminating in the attack at the ASOC back entrance. I read the report forwarded to me by General Greene, and it caused a chill to run up my spine. It wasn't us that had the leak, it was the President's own staff. Someone there had betrayed the trust of the world and the nation, and for all we knew, he or she could still be with the President.

Even though he'd regained consciousness, President Blanchard would remain mostly out of it for another 48 hours. Dehydrated, he'd only had minimal food or water for almost their entire trip to the ASOC location. It was only his mental and physical toughness that made him the "last man standing" on their arrival at ASOC. The bread truck they'd "borrowed" was the Secret Service Agent's last act. He commandeered the vehicle and had loaded everyone up when they were shot at by the same dissidents that were in the school bus. In the resulting firefight, General Hookman took a round for the President, while the Secret Service Agent was injured driving away. Before the vehicle crashed, the President took over the wheel and continued their escape. It was a miracle that they were able to elude the attackers by hiding in the open at a location along their route. He noticed a grocery store, and pulled into the back, alongside several other delivery vehicles, until the school bus had passed their location. Then they had to wait a while longer, while a number of Fighter Class ships appeared to be searching for them on the roadway. It was finally a consensus conclusion that the dissidents had extracted a lot of route information either from Secretary Todd or Doctor Khelm. Some even argued that maybe some other prisoners may have given up the information, and that there were no leaks from the inside. I didn't buy this theory, mainly because the ambush was in place, ready to pounce, before the order was issued for everyone to bug out. Any way I looked at it, the pieces still didn't fit together in my mind. Consequently, my orders were simple; increase the security around the President, and assign outsider personnel that could be trusted to conduct another vetting process for all of the President's staff.

ASOC Headquarters, underneath Lake Moomaw, Virginia:

On the morning after the first attack on ASOC, General Greene put into place a brilliant scheme to throw off our Gomer invaders, and maybe even a few of the dissidents. The first step was to reposition a number of the Gomer Gun batteries in his area. The reposition of these weapons was normal procedure after an attack, and that in itself wouldn't raise any suspicion. The only difference was that now they were all repositioned around a fictitious location a relatively short distance away. The next step to his plan was even more simple. General Greene created a false area, now ringed by defensive weaponry, that was chocked full of explosives and available combustible materials. It was close enough to the lake to fit the profile of the information already known to both the dissidents and their Gomer friends. Finally, when the plan was underway, he purposefully planted misleading information into the hands of several members of the President's staff that he suspected might have mixed loyalties. From there he simply waited to see it all come together.

The advantage to General Greene's plans were that the traitor, assuming there was one on the President's staff, wouldn't have much idea of exactly how to judge exactly where the headquarters was located in relation to the above ground back entrance. It was a series of tunnels and cross tunnels that would eventually lead you to the main part of the facility located well under the lake. Unless you were a true expert in engineering, or orienteering, or perhaps had the correct set of blue prints, you would have no idea that this rabbit warren of tunnels led you to a location further to the west under the lake. The above ground observers, and even some of the Gomer Battery's gun crews, had no idea that they were not in position to defend the main facility. This part of the deception was complete, and General Greene was quite confident that it would lead them to a traitor, and throw the bad guys off the scent.

Twilight was already approaching when the rat finally decided to leave the hole. Noting the comings and goings from the facility, General Greene already had a team in position and ready to follow the traitor when and if he decided to leave the facility. The blue was already starting to spread a little over the eastern sky when the President's Press Secretary, Frank Lombardi, decided that he needed to head out for some fresh air. Telling the entire staff that he was claustrophobic, he made the right noises to defer any suspicion from those who worked with him. He made his way up and out of the tunnel system, and was departing through the only entrance he knew existed. Seeing the scene of the previous day's encounter with the burnt-out bus, he shuddered to himself, and then continued to walk further and further away from the facility and towards the back gate. He flashed his Presidential credentials, knowing that nobody in the security staff would question his authority to come or go as he pleased. The guards admonished him that he didn't have long before sundown, but he made the same excuse about needing to walk in the fresh air to help with his "closed in feeling." He said he'd be right back, as he passed on out towards the access road leading away from Lake Moomaw. The team assigned to follow anyone leaving moved along at a discrete distance, completely unseen and undetected by Lombardi.

Darkness was settling in when the Team noticed that Lombardi was now holding something in his hands. At first, they couldn't see what it might be, but then they realized he was on a small hand-held radio. He wasn't talking, but instead, he was just keying the microphone. The Team deployed around him in the immediate area and were watching as a Gomer Fighter Class ship edged its way over the tree line to the open area where Lombardi was now standing. The Fighter Class ship pulled up and stopped, and then slowly descended into the clearing where it sat down beside the traitor. Lombardi began moving towards the ship when, from the darkness a hand was placed over his mouth, and he was thrown face down to the ground. At the same moment, the Team leader and two operators moved to the entrance of the Fighter Class, that had just opened its access door. The Team leader didn't hesitate. Taking a flash bang grenade from his web gear, he tossed it inside where it exploded with a very loud flash of light and sound. Immediately after the little explosion, he and the other two Team members rushed inside firing as they went. Within a few seconds, they had caught both the traitor and a Gomer Fighter Class ship.

The rest of General Greene's trap worked equally well that evening. Within a few seconds of the assault on the Fighter Class ship, two Battleship Class ships began their attack from a very high altitude on what they believed was the new ASOC headquarters location. Throughout their descent to a lower altitude, the Gomer Gun Batteries put up a vigorous defense, thus convincing the Gomers that they were now focused on the correct location. In short order, the Gomer Battleship Class Ships were convinced that they had found their mark, when a number of intense explosions with secondary explosions convinced them that their mission was successful. Concurrent with these explosions, the entire area went completely dark with the only visible emissions of anything coming from the resulting fires. The Gomer Gun Batteries had been instructed to cease all firing and shut down all power sources as soon as the explosions took place and, to a man, that is exactly what they did. The net effect was to further convince the Gomers that the complex no longer existed. The ruse was effective, and this was to be the last Gomer or dissident attack on the ASOC facility. After all, why waste time when you know it was destroyed. Naturally, nothing could be further from the truth, and it would later come back and bite both the Gomers and the dissidents.

At the conclusion of the operation, Mr. Frank Lombardi, now the *former* Press Secretary to President Marty Blanchard, was remanded to the custody of General Greene's more creative interrogators. The entire process took exactly 10 minutes of discussion before Mr. Lombardi began cooperating and revealing the extent of the dissidents' network within our various headquarters. The web didn't stretch as far as I thought it might, but it went a darn sight further than it should. My hunch that outside personnel needed to be used to conduct the vetting process also paid off. Especially when we learned from Mr. Lombardi that one of the other well-placed "rats" happened to be the very person assigned to lead the vetting process. Mr. Eric Adams was with the CIA, and had been since he graduated from college. But the real Eric Adams died as a child in grade school, and *this* Mr. Adams was a well-placed mole left over from the KGB's Cold War program of infiltration. For their part in these traitorous activities, and for their acts of espionage for the enemy committed during a time of war, Mr. Lombardi and Mr. Adams were both tried by a military tribunal and sentenced to death. My only hope was it would be a slow painful one.

Supreme Allied Headquarters, (SAHQ):

We firmly believed that we had now solved our insider problem, but to verify it, one more effort was made to suck out the bad guys. It was also being used as an operation to make sure that there were no more dissidents hiding out in the local population around our facilities. Over a period of several days, "Operation Presidential Visit" was put together, where the President's entourage and the President were impersonated by several Special Operators from the ASOC staff. This specialized unit would bait a number of traps in and around their movements in order to ferret out any insiders that might have been missed. The mission was simple, find and eliminate any potential local threat. The use of the Gomer Fighter Class Ship was also on the table, but for the present, the craft was moved to another location where it was being outfitted for yet another of General Greene's potential operations. For now, we were just trying to get a handle on the moment, and make sure that our own houses were clean of any more traitors.

Operationally, our allied forces were now engaging in defensive operations with our offense limited to mostly hit and run tactics. The HARM missile systems were now coming into play, but not just on Terahertz transmissions. We were also using them in their original design to track down and strike any Radar and other Radio waves that the dissidents were sending out. While this campaign escalated with the use of other more conventional weapons systems, so did the Gomers' attacks on various targets around the world. The full picture had not developed when, as luck would have it, a new wrinkle was to present itself.

Presidential Situation Room, ASOC, Lake Moomaw, VA:

President Blanchard had been out of circulation for almost a week. Between the bug out adventure, which took almost four days, and then his recovering from the concussion, things were just a little disjointed for him. The initial briefings, provided by General Greene, got him partially back up to speed, but he was still unsettled about something. He knew it was on the "tip of his brain," but he just couldn't come up with it. Finally, during a conference with General Patrick on the line, it seeped through the cobwebs inside his mind.

"General Patrick, you were going to tell me something. Something about Phoenix and Mars."

"Yessir. Mr. President, we need to save the Phoenix IV, and instead, all we need is one more Red Dragon hit somewhere on the back side of the Moon."

"How will that help?"

"Sir, General Greene has the exact details, but we have a way of sabotaging the Gomers on Mars with just one good defensive burst on the dark side of the Moon. It basically will cause all of the technology from us to fail."

"All of it?"

"Yes, Mr. President. ALL of it. The metal sheeting, the building materials, their communications links from us, all of it."

"Communications links? Then why didn't we hit them with it already?"

"Sir, no excuse. That last part just got to me a few hours ago, when one of the eggheads developing it called me."

"Who?"

"My son-in-law. He's been sequestered and only now back in the saddle. If we time it right, we can play hob with their communications with the dissident forces. It won't solve the problem, but it is one heck of a start."

"Then do it!"

"Yessir. I'll get General McDaniel on it right away. The other thing you were going to tell me sir?"

"Uh..."

"Mr. President. You were going to tell me something about why we launched the Phoenix IV towards Neptune."

"Oh! I'd forgotten. Okay, our analysts here and with ASOC said that Neptune was their main base, and has been for at least the last 500 years."

"You have to be kidding me. The last 500 years? How in the hell do they know that?"

"Mostly from their own computers, and from Man's own observations of that planet."

"Doctor whatshername... Sylvia somebody. Oh crap. Anyway, that doctor who is studying the background for the various Gomer types."

"You mean Dr. Duprey?"

"Yeah, that's her. Anyway, she thinks that Neptune might have been colonized several thousand years ago, which is where some of Man's legends about Tornit came from."

"Okay. Sir, I hate to ask, but are you okay?"

"Yeah. I'm sore as hell, and my head is throbbing, but otherwise I'm fine."

"Mr. President. Please take care of yourself. Nothing against the Vice President, but face it, you're the only one up there that can handle this crap. Something happens to you, then we're all screwed. Not to mention that I'd lose a pretty damn good friend."

"Thanks, General. I'll do my best. The doctor said I'd have some memory issues for a few more days, but otherwise I'm fine. I'll get the details from Greene about the Red Dragon strike, but you're clear to go. I trust you."

"Thank you, Mr. President."

Vandenberg, Air Force Base, CA:

General McDaniel was sitting hunched over in his office peering at a number of photographs taken from the areas approaching Earth. There were no new concentrations of Gomer Ships visible near the Moon, but there was a steady stream of traffic moving between Neptune's moon Triton, and Mars. Pondering how to strike these locations was foremost in his mind, when his Chief of Staff started knocking on the door with a TWX or teletype message form. "General?"

"Yeah, what is it Colonel?"

"Sir, we've got a fire mission for a Red Dragon III. Target 1,250 miles behind the Moon."

"What the hell for?"

"Sir, I haven't a clue."

"Okay, Colonel. Get General Patrick on the horn. I want to confirm this crap. Maybe someone there has either lost their mind, or they know something we don't."

The Colonel stepped out, and picked up the line to SAHQ. When he finally got through to General Patrick, he knew something was up. "Colonel, I was expecting General McDaniel's call. Tell him to get his sorry ass on the line."

"Sir. Hang on, I'll get him." Sticking his head through General McDaniel's door, the Colonel waved for the General to pick up the line. "General Patrick? General McDaniel here, I've got a quest..."

"General McDaniel, let me guess. You think we've lost our minds or we know something, right?"

"Well, uh, yessir. That sums it up."

"Okay, this is your official verification. Fire the Red Dragon in accordance with the message."

"Sir. That doesn't really answer my question."

"Sure, it does. Now fire that missile. Understand?"

"Yessir."

"Oh, and ask Dr. Clarkson. He can explain it to you personally, but not over the phone. Got it?"

"Yessir. Fire in accordance with the message. Any other instructions?"

"Yep. Keep an eye out on the traffic headed in and out of Mars. Not that you wouldn't do it anyway, but keep me apprised of ANY movement. I want to know immediately if so much as a rock moves off that planet."

"Yessir." Hanging up the phone, General McDaniel turned to the Colonel and said, "Okie Dokie, Bob. Get Dr. Clarkson in here, and get me the fire control officer on duty. We will be firing in accordance with the message's instructions. All settings will be verified one more time, but plan on doing the fire mission. Oh, and Bob?

"Sir?"

"For some reason, General Patrick wants us watching Mars. Get our best guys on it, and tell them to notify me of any movement onto or away from there." The Colonel nodded, but said nothing as he scrambled from the room to find Dr. Clarkson. Whatever was going on, would at least make things interesting over the next couple hours. If nothing else, he thought, it is more target practice.

At a location near Bozeman, Montana:

The teletype machine was going nuts, and everyone in the fire control center knew that this was another fire mission. They'd done several of these over the last weeks, so it was becoming something of a routine process. Noting the coordinates, there was much head scratching, but despite their confusion, the Red Dragon III missile was fired at precisely 1800 hours local. Noting that it would be several hours before anything came from it, the missile crews followed the procedure to button up their facilities and wait. Unlike firing most things at an enemy, their business often did not yield immediate or at least immediately measurable results. As missilemen, they were becoming kind of used to it, and after the missile left the silo, it wouldn't be long before they were back to the routine tasks that would often fill their days and nights. To a man, they all thought the same thing, "this is a helluva way to fight a war."

The Family Facilities, Peterstown, WV:

Leah burst through Toni's door to her quarters waving a message form in her hand. "Toni?"

Toni's daughter, Hayley, looked up from the book she was reading. "Hi, Leah. Mom's in the bed. I think Dad's being missing is really working on her."

"Hayley, go get your Mom! I've got some good news for once." Leah barely finished the sentence when Toni stuck her head around the corner. "Did I hear good news?"

"Yes, Toni. Good news. Marty is back, and while he doesn't appear to be in the best of health, he is alive and kicking."

"Is he hurt?"

"According to Mike, he is dehydrated, exhausted, and will be in need of some minor treatment, but otherwise, he is fine!"

"Great! What else did Mike say?"

"He said to tell you that… Well, hell, read it yourself." With that Leah handed Toni the message form from the President. It simply said, "Tell Toni that I'm fine, and I love her!"

Toni turned to towards Leah, and then grabbed her in a long hug. Hayley, who watched the entire exchange unfold, let out a sigh of relief, and then joined into the hug. There were many tears, and even though the message form didn't have a lot on it, they all read it over and over until Toni slipped it into the side pocket of her "go to hell bag."

Chapter XI

※

Supreme Allied Headquarters, (SAHQ), near Summersville Lake, WV:

Now that we were not dealing with the more personal issues of being slammed by the Gomers and our own survival, we were starting to think more in terms of the overall situation. We knew that we had to cut the dissidents off from their Gomer allies, and come to grips with a fleet roughly the same size as what we'd seen before in the First Gomer War. We also were going to have to adjust based on their changes in tactics, and keep them from being reinforced from Mars and Neptune. Unfortunately, the Phoenix IV was going to take too long, and we were still having to deal with the more immediate issue of a potential influx of Gomers from their forward base on Mars. It was against this problem that an idea hit me. Picking up the phone to General Greene, I only had one serious question. Granted it had more than a few sub-parts, but it was a germ of an idea.

"Daniel? How many Gomer Fighters do we have our hands on right now?"

"We have the newest one we took a few nights ago, and four older ones that are half torn apart in Dr. Clarkson's lab. Why?"

"Daniel, how hard would it be to get our hands on about six of them?"

"Flyable?"

"Yes, flyable."

"Well. We do have a few more stashed away from our exploits in Greenland in the last war, but flyable is another question."

"Okay, get with Dr. Abramson and Dr. Clarkson. See what it would take to get them flyable. Then get Dr. Abramson to give me an estimate on how long it would take for the damn things to fly from Earth to Mars, and then another estimate on how long from Earth to Neptune."

"Who in the heck is going to fly them?"

"Don't know yet. Ask the eggheads to see if they can get them to fly, and then, can they fly via remote control or some other means without anyone on board."

"What are you thinking... Sir?"

"I'm thinking, what if we can get a Phoenix IV punch on target sooner, faster, and with more bite?"

"Well, I'll start the ball rolling. I like it, in fact, I like it a lot."

"Great. Now, one other thing. If we can't fly it, think about snatching a few prisoners that we can turn loose, or let escape, who might decide to fly it home. Which means, we'll have to give them the weapon, without them knowing it is a weapon. Then let them fly it home. It would have to be something they think is important enough to get back to their home planet or at least as far as their bases on Mars."

"Damn, sir. No tall orders here."

"Just an idea, and I realize it might be a little 'Guns of Navarrone.'"

"Sir, if I recall correctly, you're the one that reserved that expression as meaning something that was too harebrained, with too many steps, to ever work."

"Glad to see you remember your training. Just give it some thought. I just think we might need to cut off the supply of reinforcements at the source, sooner than later. I'm just not sure we have seven years to wait for the Phoenix to save us."

"Roger that, sir. I'm on it."

"Excellent! And Daniel, keep this amongst us girls for now."

"Yessir." As I put down the phone, General Whitney handed me another message from our forces in Northern Europe.

Reading through General Larkins' assessment of the latest situation, it wasn't a pretty picture. The Gomer Fleet was pounding everyone's positions at random and hard. Our casualties were mounting, and the dissidents were now on the move again, this time employing airmobile tactics similar to our own. The larger Gomer Carrier ships were able to handle a fairly sizeable number of the dissident forces, and they were air lifting them to positions in both Siberia and Greenland. They were obviously headed back to their old haunts and, this time, their defenses were going to rely on an outer ring of well-armed humans, then an inner ring of their own Gomer forces. In both locations, there was solid evidence of the Gomers building bases from which their smaller and largest ships could operate. This time, they were making a foothold that would be much harder to crack. To this point of the war, we'd mainly been on the defensive. Other than the major strike at their much larger fleet as it came inbound to Earth, and our other more recent projections of several weapons into space, the Gomers were relatively untouched in their marauding around our planet.

I was in my Headquarters thinking of the old Yogi Berra quote, about "deja vu all over again," when word of their next attempted strikes reached us. The Russian facility near Saint Petersburg, Russia, where President Dubronin was now in seclusion, was attacked by a relatively large force of dissidents. They were airlifted in by their Gomer friends, and the strike was about as productive for the Gomers as the strike on our ASOC facilities at Lake Moomaw. Fortunately, the forces defending the Russian Headquarters was comprised of a number of both conventional and ASOC forces. The dissidents were driven off and, while it was not destroyed, the Large Gomer Weapons did a great deal of damage to the facility. The command structure in Russia was now doing what we'd done the previous week. Running for their lives, President Dubronin and his Generals were dealing with a far greater enemy concentration than we'd seen in their efforts to take out our leadership. Such was the price for having a much greater proximity to the dissidents and the ground the Gomers wanted so badly. It would be several more days before President Dubronin would surface again, and when he did, he was in far worse condition than President Blanchard had been the week before.

It was now time to start using part of our heavier weaponry on our own planet, and it was not an easy decision. The impact of a Gomer Weapon does not discriminate between friend or foe, and this is an even harder issue, when you have no idea who you can trust to warn of its coming. Sadly, we were starting to look at a situation where we had to do something to shift the tide back to the offensive. Given the present condition of the forces scattered around the world, we were not only feeling the losses from the high casualties, but it was obvious to all of us that we were losing this war of attrition. While we were putting together our next strategy, the unthinkable was unfolding almost right under our noses.

Ridgeline directly adjacent to the Family Facilities, Peterstown, WV:

Peering through the Night Vision sighting system, the young Sergeant on duty saw something that obscured his vision for only a few seconds. Not very clearly defined, he realized that he was seeing the approach of a Gomer Carrier Class ship. Reaching down, he hit the alarm system for his headquarters. Unfortunately, it was the last thing he would ever do. After hitting the button, and turning back to peer through the scope, he noticed a flash of dull metal right before it crossed his throat. The foreign soldier wielding the knife was well trained and efficient, but his timing had been just a little off. It was this mistake that allowed the young Sergeant to alert the rest of the Gomer Gun Air Defense Battery. Sadly, this alarm was too late to help stave off the attack, but it did buy the people inside some very valuable time.

The Gomer Gun's firing was short lived. Sadly, they were overwhelmed and destroyed by the small force on the ground that was also directing the fire of several Gomer Fighter Class Ships. Within a minute, two Gomer Carrier Class Ships were discharging a landing force a short distance from the entrance to the Family Facilities. The guard forces near the entrance were taken off balance, but the lower level immediately went to a higher alert level the second that the shots were fired from the upper ridge. When the first Russian Dissident forces began their charge towards the entrance, the volume of defensive fires increased to a deafening level.

Inside the Family Facilities, Peterstown, WV:

Inside the VIP area within the cave, the distant firing could be heard just a few seconds before the Alarm sounded. There was no question this time that this was the real thing, and everyone moved accordingly. Each of the armed mothers went to their positions around the group, while the mothers who were to herd the children began checking their back packs and lining them up to move. This time at the assembly area there were no speeches, no discussions, and most of all, no noise. It was well rehearsed and, as it turned out, this would be critical to their very survival.

Three minutes after the initial Alarm sounded, Leah and the Ranger Captain were starting for the next defensive position, with all the families lined up and following. The rear guard was already deploying, as the four troopers and three assigned Rangers set up a defensive line to allow the last of the families to move into the next cavern chamber. This time, the group did not stop at the next level of defenses, but instead, kept heading towards their next position further under the mountain. At each point, they would only rest for a few minutes, check their bags, and then move on. The mothers to the rear, under Lou Ann Whitney's guidance, did all they could to eliminate any trail that they might be leaving behind. This, too, had been rehearsed.

After the families were clear of the main chamber, their rear guard collapsed their positions, and then followed along behind the retreating civilians into the cavern system. It wasn't long before the outer defenses began to crumble under the onslaught of the attacking force, but at least they had bought time and sent the alarm to all of their supporting units. Now it would fall to the inner security forces to make sure the families had even more time to get away. Before moving into the main chamber, the Rangers who were manning the inner perimeter detonated the explosives that closed off this portion of the cave to anyone from the outside. The idea behind the blast was to eliminate anyone who might be following too closely, and to make it appear as though there was no back door. If they looked as though they were now defending in place, it would force the attackers to deploy and fight their way inside. At first, the deception plan worked, but then almost three hours later, the Gomers' dissident attackers used sufficient Gomer weaponry to blast a perfectly round hole through the debris blocking the chamber.

When the smoke cleared, dozens of Russian dissidents, all of whom were former Russian Commandos, came pouring into the chamber. This time the fire fight was brutal to both sides, and it would last for almost four hours, before the main chamber was secured by the enemy. Thankfully, this gave the families a solid six-and-a-half-hour head start, and it would be time that they did not waste. More time was bought when the attackers took their time making sure that there were no family members present, before attempting to figure out which way to move to find the back door. There were several tunnels leading out of the chamber that could afford an escape route, and since none were marked, the attackers were depleting their numbers by splitting up to move out searching. The last nasty surprise to the attackers came when they entered these potential passageways out of the mountain. Each one was booby trapped, in a different way and location, and each one exploded creating more debris and attacker casualties. It would be even more hours before the attackers could bore their way into the correct tunnel. During that time, the families were several miles away, traveling as fast as they could through the darkness.

Supreme Allied Headquarters, (SAHQ), near Summersville Lake, WV:

The code words shot through the headquarters like a lightning bolt. General Whitney and General Clark were discussing the Moon strike that was about to happen, when the single phrase "Prairie Fire" came into the communications center. It would only take seconds before I was informed that the Family Facilities were under attack, and the range of emotions that shot through me were beyond any terror I had ever experienced. We quickly had eyes on the forces that were attacking, but for the moment, we had very little way of hitting them without creating a real danger to the adjacent facilities. We knew that the bulk of the defending Battalion, and their dependents, were all still alive inside the neighboring cave system. They were completely cut off, since a Battleship Class Gomer had blasted the mountain top directly above their facility. The resulting rock slides blocked the entrance, and from all accounts, also did some damage inside. Our immediate problem was that if we used any heavier weapons to eliminate the Gomers, then everyone in both cave systems would be in jeopardy.

Our best intelligence indicated that the attacking force consisted of at least a Battalion-sized element of Russian Commando-type forces, former Spetsnatz, along with another Battalion size group of "meaty" and "smart" Gomers that were supporting the attack. The Gomers were using a Battleship Class Ship and two smaller Carrier Class Ships in direct support of the attackers. The Battleship Class was being used almost exclusively for suppressive fire on neighboring ridge lines, and to block any approach by reinforcements. Fortunately for us, by maintaining this covering position, the Gomers made the Battleship Class a little more of an inviting target. We also learned that the Carrier Class ships were used mainly to insert the enemy forces, and to keep up any fire as required to support the attackers on the ground. At the same time, at least a dozen or more fighter class ships were involved in the attack, and they were cruising the area looking for anyone who might escape anywhere along the mountain range.

I had one advantage. I knew where the families were going to be coming out and, so far, the Gomers were not near that location. The down side was that the nearest LZ, or landing zone, we could use to recover these families was far enough away from the back exit that some overland travel was going to be required. Naturally this would leave them exposed, unless the timing was right.

When Command Sergeant Major Clagmore appeared in Operations, several ideas hit me at once. Turning to him, I advised him of the situation, briefed him on the map locations for the exit and potential LZ, and then gave him a blank check to assemble a special force. He knew exactly what I had in mind, and within an hour, he was already making arrangements to get himself and his 14 troopers to the back entrance at first light. He also had enough explosives with him to do two things. Create a new landing zone, and to seal the cave. I knew we would have to make it count, but if anyone could carve a trap for the Gomers and the dissidents, it would be Clagmore. Besides, I knew that if I didn't give him something constructive to do, while his wife was running for her life, then he would never be able to stand it. It took all I had in me not to be going with him.

The second idea was much simpler. It was risky, but a flight of three F-35s, equipped with the X-51A missile system, were ordered into position to hit the Battleship Class Gomer. Four hours after the attack began, and before the remaining security force inside the main chamber of the cavern was defeated, the Battleship Class Gomer was hit hard from three different directions. As it crashed into the mountains, on the Virginia side of the border away from Peterstown, our remaining Gomer Gun Batteries were finally able to unmask and start firing on the Carrier Class Ships. This turned into a running battle, but by dawn, there was only one remaining Carrier Class Ship, and it was forced to leave the area with a lot of damage. The remaining Fighter Class ships also left with the arrival of the Sun, which bought Command Sergeant Major Clagmore the time he needed to get on the ground and start moving into the back door to reach the retreating families.

Deep within the caves near Peterstown, WV:

The explosion inside the main living chamber could be heard in the distance, and Leah and the Rangers knew exactly where they stood. The situation, while not hopeless, was becoming dire. The column could only move as quickly as the slowest person, which everyone had thought would be Mother Patrick. The combination of age, poor eyesight, and a weak ankle would make her journey especially difficult. What nobody, except Leah, realized was that Mother Patrick was not a shy retiring flower. The ankle was well taped at the first stop, and eyesight doesn't mean much in a completely dark cave. Age wasn't that much of a factor either, since she was a whole lot more desirous of living than Hayley Timmons. When the group would start moving after a short rest, it was Mrs.

Timmons that would start lagging behind. After an hour, with the party covering only about three quarters of a mile underground, it was clear that regardless of the head start, something had to be done. Leah and the Ranger Captain were making their way back to see what was causing the delay, when they overheard the following whispered conversation.

"Hayley?"

"Yes, Mrs. Patrick."

"Hayley, honey. I'm old and broken. What is your excuse?"

"What do you mean?"

"Honey. You are moving slower than molasses. I am almost 90, and if I am passing you on the trail, then you are either dead or about to be. So, what the hell is your problem?"

"Ma'am? I don't have a problem."

"You're about to have one. If you don't speed up, then I am going to knock your ass silly with my cane. You have those beautiful babies to look after."

"I'm sorry, but without James…"

"GOD, you are thick and whiney. My husband died years ago, but you don't see me crying about it. I don't drink like a fish either. Now remember those babies, and get your butt moving."

"Yes, Ma'am."

Leah, listening in the dark, couldn't help but smile. There was no question that Hayley needed to hear that speech, it was just that Leah never expected her Mother-in-Law to be the one to give it. For the rest of their escape, Mother Patrick dogged Hayley Timmons almost every step of the way. There were even times when Hayley helped Mother Patrick get over various obstacles. No longer were they the problem moving the column forward. Now it was just about time, distance, and exhaustion. Their motivation was simple, every little bit, they would hear an explosion behind them, as the covering force of Rangers would seal off a chamber or blast a tunnel full of bad guys as they pursued them through the mountain. Their head start, which you would think was a big one, only amounted to about a mile or so in distance. Once this was conveyed to the crowd, making people move wasn't really an issue anymore.

Near the back entrance to the Family Facilities, Peterstown, WV:

The skies were clear of any Gomers, and there did not appear to be any dissidents on this side of the mountain top. The extraction team had selected a small field, only large enough for one UH-60, and started from there. Moving toward the back entrance, they were setting up a perimeter a mere 2 hours after sunrise. Placing explosives around the back entrance, they then began the process of setting up a makeshift landing zone. Using even more explosives, they wrapped trees with a cord explosive. Once the families had been located, they would detonate these to expand the field they had landed in earlier. The plan was to eliminate any overland travel for the families, and get them in the air as quickly as possible. Given the time limitations and numbers of people involved, they would need to make enough space for at least two CH-47 helicopters. They could do it with enough space for one, with the aircraft using the LZ one at a time, but this took time, especially in the loading process. Time was the key, and they weren't about to waste any of it.

The plan was simple. Get the families loaded and gone towards the facilities near Bluestone. The loading should be no more than 5 minutes, with a direct route flight time of under 15 minutes. If the military personnel couldn't be extracted before sundown, then they would move tactically to the lower landing zone for pick up the following morning. They didn't bring in a massive group of reinforcements to the upper side of the mountain, since those forces were all headed to the main entrance to come at the bad guys from behind. It was also important to keep the main force focused on getting to the other mountain facility where a lot of people were trapped. They had the bigger job of mopping up bad guys, digging out the survivors, and then clearing the civilians out of the adjoining cave system. Then they had to get them to a safe zone as quickly as possible. The fear was that the Gomers would return and just blast everything, before these people could be moved. The only reason they hadn't earlier was they were minimizing the damage while they got what they were really after. They wanted to kidnap hostages, and who better than the families of the very leadership they couldn't get to directly.

Command Sergeant Major Clagmore, after making sure that the initial tasks were all completed, took several troopers and entered the back entrance of the cave. They got about 100 yards when they realized that they had no idea of where they were going. Here the cave branched off into three different directions, and so he positioned a man at each, and they sat and listened. Heading back to the surface, Clagmore now was forced to do something he hated more than anything. He had to wait.

ASOC Headquarters, underneath Lake Moomaw, Virginia:

News travels fast, and bad news travels even faster. Chris and Holly were both huddled together near the communications center, and they were beside themselves. They had been nomads since they left the Family Facility, having gone to the Rocky Mountains, and now to this God forsaken place, and they were already feeling homesick for the old Facility. This just made it worse. Leah and Mother Patrick were in harm's way, and there wasn't a darn thing they could do about it. At least if they had been at the facility, they could have been doing something. Now, like Sergeant Major Clagmore, their lot was to sit and wait. The more the clock ticked, the sicker they felt about it all. Holly was so worried that when the message from Vandenberg, AFB, came in, she completely ignored it as it passed out the door on its way to General Greene. Chris noticed it, but only because John was smiling, which for some reason really pissed her off.

General Greene on the other hand, was delighted. From where he was sitting, this meant that John's idea would now start taking effect. The blast behind the Moon, while not readily visible to the naked eye, had been one of splendor to view remotely. The debris was apparent as it drifted from behind the cover of the Moon, and from their best estimates, there must have been a sizable force lurking there. Dr. Abramson was equally thrilled, since the Moon had not shifted from the blast, nor did there appear to be any geological changes that would be significant. What most people wouldn't know was that this blast was going to be the trigger to a series of bad things that would happen to the Gomers in their Martian bases. Now it was General Greene's turn to wait and watch.

Supreme Allied Headquarters, (SAHQ), Lake Summersville, WV:

Trying to be a good soldier, while also being a loving husband, son, and father, are not always consistent. I was so distracted by the situation around the facilities in Peterstown that, like Holly, I almost missed the message from General McDaniel. I wasn't the only one either. General Whitney and General Clark also missed it, or no longer cared. Just a day before, they were both intently watching all the data, movement, and disposition of the Gomers around the potential impact area, but today, they were almost useless. Fortunately, the rest of my staff didn't miss it. I knew that regardless of my personal feelings, I had a war to run, and I wasn't going to do my family a damn bit of good if I got distracted from the big picture. Shaking the personal feelings to the back burner, I knew it was time to get my guys back on task.

"General Whitney? General Clark?"

"Sir?"

"Gentlemen. I have had an epiphany, which I will now share with you."

They both responded by just looking at me. Once I knew I had their attention, I continued. "Gentlemen, we are not doing our families any favors by sitting here moping and watching the clock. If you want to help, then let's get back to it. You want to help, then let's kill us some Gomers and get this damn war over with… Got it?"

Looking sheepishly at the ground, they both nodded, and Whit spoke up with a "Yessir. I get your point, but…"

"NO buts! Listen Whit, my bride and mother are there too, but we can't sit here with our thumbs up our ass. Now start getting me an evaluation of the impact of the blast behind the Moon. Get with General Greene, and get me his estimates. Next, General Clark, I want you to start putting together the logistics numbers, location, and condition for an offensive. Those bastards are making camp in Greenland and Siberia again, and it is high time we went from ducking to punching. You reading me?"

They both responded by coming to attention, and saying "Yes, Sir!"

"Look, guys, the only way to keep them from pulling crap like this is to take back the night! So, get focused. If there are any changes, then I am positive that Clagmore will fill us in. Now move!"

Deep within the caves near Peterstown, WV:

Leah was right behind the Ranger Captain as they made their way into what they hoped would be their final rest stop. Looking at his watch, the Ranger Captain turned and whispered to Leah that they should go ahead and take a break. Turning around, Leah used her flashlight to motion for the families to take a break.

"Mrs. Patrick?"

"Yes, Captain?"

"Ma'am. I would like to move out ahead to see how far we are from the surface. I'm concerned since, if my watch is right, it is getting dark again up there."

"I know what you mean. Do we have a clue how far behind us the bad guys are?"

"Not far enough to make it through the night."

"I somehow knew you'd say that…"

"Ma'am. I would like to scout ahead, and see if there is somewhere we can hold up for the night either at or near the surface. My guys are about out of explosives, and I want to see if maybe we can get out of here, or at least nearly out, and then try to block off the whole cave with what I have left."

"Sounds like a plan. I'll let you get about a 10-minute head start, and then we'll start moving the families."

"Thanks, Ma'am. Now, let me get Sergeant Knowles up here, and he can help guide you."

"Jesus! Captain, who taught you guys how to get out? I got this. Keep Sergeant Knowles back there to keep the rear guard together. Instead, send Katie, and Lou Ann up here. If I need security in the front, the three of us can handle it."

"Yes, Ma'am. Just don't shoot me in the butt, okay?"

"Just use the safe word, and we won't bust your ass. Now go. I've got this."

"Yes, Ma'am." With that he moved back down the column, and sent Lou Ann and Katie Clagmore forward. He also briefed his men on what they were going to try and do, and for good measure, he also made sure that he had a good count on their remaining explosives. While he was at the rear, the scout he had back down the tunnels arrived back at the column. "Captain. They are about an hour behind us, and they are picking up speed in that last chamber. Sir, they ain't stopping, and I'm thinking maybe we shouldn't either."

Nodding his head, the Captain went forward and briefed Leah quickly about what was behind them. Without any further discussion, the entire group was on their feet and now moving with a slightly more serious sense of urgency. The Captain picked up his pace, and moved on ahead of the group, hoping to find somewhere defensible. His concerns about nightfall, and the closeness of the bad guys, almost got him killed.

Chapter XII

❧

Near the back entrance to the Family Facilities, Peterstown, WV:

Sunset was rapidly approaching, and Command Sergeant Major Clagmore realized that they had to make arrangements to protect themselves and keep an eye on the cave. Knowing that there wasn't much he could do after dark, he gathered his team, and they entered the cave complex through the back door. Before moving inside, they went about their business of making sure that they didn't leave anything that could be spotted from the air, and they advised SAHQ that they were going to be moving under cover.

Once inside, he relieved the men watching the three possible passages into this last fairly open cave chamber and then put together a quick reaction force, should they be needed to either help get out the families or knock the bad guys on their ass. Each of the troopers goggled up with their night vision equipment, and were on a high state of vigilance. After getting them organized, they finally ate their first MRE, and then began the improvement of their various positions.

Darkness was settling in when Clagmore got the message from his men on the back entrance. "Sergeant Major, we have a Gomer Fighter Class ship right outside."

"What's he doing?"

"Sir, he was moving in a pattern, but he is now sitting right on top of the field where we came in this morning."

"Think he sees something?"

"Hmmmm. Maybe. Where is the detonator for the tree explosives?"

"Sergeant Major, I've got it." One of the men spoke quietly from the darkness.

"Okay, Donaldson. Keep an eye on him, and if he gets over the trees there on the left side, let her rip. Oh, and let me know if he gets low enough to drop anyone off. It would be a hell of a note if he were to put forces on the ground. So, like I said, if he lands, or gets over the trees, detonate the explosives. If nothing else, it will attract their attention and it might also take the bastard out."

"Roger that, Sergeant Major!"

Turning back to the center of the chamber, he saw the IR signal from the men covering the tunnel on the far right. Moving as quickly as he could, he got into position behind his men. One of them turned and whispered, "Sergeant Major, I've got movement about 30 yards out, and it looks like one guy."

"Check. Okay, Stephens. Line him up with your Scope."

"Sergeant Major, he has an IR emitter and he's wearing goggles."

"Okay, Stephens. Standby. Can you see anyone behind him?"

"No. Nothing."

"Okay, line up the shot, and wait for him to get a little closer."

The explosion behind the Sergeant Major was completely unexpected, but in an instant, Clagmore knew exactly what happened. The Gomer got too close and was either trying to land or over the right part of the woods. Either way it didn't matter, since the approaching man immediately dropped to the ground. This probably saved his life, since he dropped just as the sniper on Clagmore's team was about to "fire him up." Now that the element of surprise was gone, Clagmore did something unique. He issued a challenge to the approaching man.

"Halt, Asshole!"

"Asshole?!? Who the hell are you?"

"Nunya fucking business. Now who the hell are you?"

"I'm Captain Jackson, US Army. Unless you want me to kill your sorry ass, you'll now tell me who you are!"

"Captain Jackson. I'm Command Sergeant Major Clagmore, and unless you know the fucking password, the odds of you killing me are slim and none."

"Shit. Okay. Apples!"

"Farmer... Now Captain, move slowly, and advance to be recognized."

"Fine." Once they got through the ritual of making sure the others were who they were supposed to be, it was learned rather quickly that the families were about a quarter of a mile behind him. Knowing now which tunnel to use, the Sergeant Major sent the Captain and three of his men back down the tunnel to help move them along. Heading back towards the entrance, it was then that the Sergeant Major learned that the Gomer had indeed landed, and that there just might be some survivors out on the ground.

"Sergeant Major. That Gomer Ship ain't going nowhere, but I've counted at least a ten to twelve guys setting up a perimeter around the crash site."

"Dammit! Okay. Well, now the LZ is big enough, but it is also occupied. That sucks. From what I've just learned, we have another force coming on the heels of the families. Alright. We will beef up the perimeter here, and on the tunnels behind us. Hey, Marks. Got any more explosives?"

"Yes, Sergeant Major."

"Okay. Wire up all three of the tunnels leading into here. I want to close them all after we get the families in here with us, just in case."

"Roger that."

Quarter of a mile from the back entrance to the Family Facilities, Peterstown, WV:

Leah was walking point, when she heard the approach of several men coming back down the tunnel towards them. Motioning for the ladies to halt behind her, Lou Ann stepped into position beside Leah, and aimed her weapon back up the tunnel. Leah whispered, "Lou Ann, we have one man out there, not several. See if you can confirm how many are coming this way?"

"It looks like four men, and they are all wearing NVGs. Look armed to the teeth, too."

"Okay, keep watching, and if they get too close, don't be afraid to pop them. Once you fire, I'll move up to that point to the left, and see if I can't use Mike's old trench gun to clear us a path."

"Okay."

"Katie. Tell the others to get down, and pass the word back to the Rangers that we might have company coming up front."

Turning back forward, Leah was inching her way back towards Lou Ann, when she heard the voice of Captain Jackson. "Apples!"

For the second time in one night, Captain Jackson came perilously close to being hit by a sniper. Lou Ann would later admit that she had been seconds from pulling the trigger. Instead, the young Ranger

Captain issued the magic word, just in time, and then said, "I've come with friends."

Leah stood up and moved cautiously forward. Getting closer, she realized that the men around the Ranger Captain were very familiar to her. It hit her in flash, "I'll be! These guys are all from Mikes' personal security detail." There was some very real comfort knowing that each one had either been a Delta Operator or a Navy Seal, and they definitely knew their business. For the first time in almost 24 hours, Leah breathed a sigh of relief. Unfortunately, it was way too soon to be relieved.

"Mrs. Patrick. We have a security force near the surface, but we're going to need to move quickly. I'll let the Sergeant Major brief you when we get there. Now let's get them moving. We're not far."

"Okay, but Captain, we have a few folks that appear to have hit the end of their endurance. Can we get some help moving them?"

"Yes, Ma'am, but it won't be much."

"Anything at this point is better than nothing." As she finished her statement, the operators moved through the families and took up positions to take over for the Ranger covering force. As the Rangers moved forward, two of them picked up Mother Patrick in a classic fireman's carry, and they began moving rapidly forward up the last tunnel. Similarly, two more Rangers were also herding Toni Blanchard and her family along at a much faster pace. Yes, they were all exhausted, but the group was now putting on that last push towards the finish line. At least they hoped it was towards the finish line.

ASOC Headquarters, underneath Lake Moomaw, Virginia:

General Greene entered the President's quarters, where the President was still dealing with his recovery from his own ordeal. Over the last 24 hours, the President had been kept blissfully unaware of the outside situation near Peterstown, because he'd been sedated following surgery to repair a blood vessel that had been causing some swelling and minor memory lapses. During this time, unknown to the world, the Vice President was holding the reigns, but now that the President was awake and alert, it was time to read him into the picture.

"Mr. President. How are you feeling?"

"General Greene, I've got a pretty nasty headache, but otherwise, I'm feeling the best I've felt since we got here."

"Mr. President, I need to brief you on something."

"Okay, go ahead." General Greene briefed the President on the entire situation, at least as he knew it. He described the attack on the Family Facility, Sergeant Major Clagmore's relief operation, and the Brigade operation to open the other facility back up and get those families out. Then he briefed on the Moon strike out of Vandenberg. The President took it all in, and then asked, "General. How do we know they're alive, and assuming they are, how long have they been running inside that damn cave?"

"Mr. President, we know they're alive because the Gomers are still working the area, without hitting things with their big stuff."

"Okay, fair enough, but how long have they been running?"

"Sir, a little better than 24 hours now."

Letting out a huge sigh, the President covered his eyes and sat extremely still for almost a full minute. Finally, looking back towards General Greene he said, "General. Please keep me posted, and if you get a chance, send a message to the Mouse. I have a feeling he is every bit as upset as I am."

"Sir. General Patrick is holding it together. I'm not sure how, since I can remember when I first met him and Leah. There is no question in my military mind that she is just about the whole world to him."

"Yeah, I know. They've spent their whole marriage looking after each other, hell, even before."

"What do you mean before?"

"You do know she was with the Company, and they met the first time several years before they got married."

"I didn't know that, sir."

"Yep. Great story, but no question, she saved his ass once, and he never forgot it. He didn't know it was her, but he never forgot."

"I'll be damned. How many people know that story?"

"Right now, maybe you, me, and only a few old school special operators, like Clagmore."

"Good to know. Is there anything I can get you, Mr. President?"

"No, son. Right now, I just need to get out of this fucking bed, and get back into the business of running what is left of this country. Tell my aide, General... wait. She's dead, isn't she?"

"Yessir. She passed away."

"I knew it. My memory is coming back with a vengeance. Okay. Get me a new aide, and tell my Chief of Staff to get his ass in here."

"Yessir." With that, General Greene stepped out of the room, and got the Chief of Staff for the President. Heading back to his operations, General Greene felt for the first time in days that maybe the President was finally back in the saddle.

Vandenberg, AFB, CA:

General McDaniel was reviewing the information coming in from various observation posts. The blast did ferret out Gomers, but it still didn't have the immediate impact he expected. Instead, aside from some debris that indicated a modest fleet of bad guys behind the

Moon, this strike appeared for all intents and purposes to be a waste of missile assets. Contemplating this waste made him mad, since he above all people knew how little they could just toss out there for the hell of it. They had to make every shot count, and this was not what he felt would be a worthy use of assets. Reaching into his sideboard, his hands passed over the good scotch, and landed on a good old bottle of Jameson Irish Whiskey. Now this was what you drank when you were pissed, not the good stuff. While pouring the whiskey into his well-worn tumbler, his Chief of Staff entered his office.

"General, I hate to interrupt, but I've got something you should see."

"Colonel, you are not interrupting. Would you care for one?"

"Sir! Yes, I wouldn't mind one at all."

"Okay, here you go. Should be another glass in there somewhere."

"Thank you, sir."

"Okay, Colonel. What's up?"

"Sir, you are aware of the attack on the family facility back east, right?"

"Yes."

"Well, sir. There are no large units moving anywhere near the east coast tonight. Instead, there are only a very few Fighter Class Ships, and that is it."

"Good news. Have you passed that on?"

"Yessir. We did, but that isn't the big news."

"Okay, Colonel. You going to just keep me in suspense, or is there a point to this aside from you drinking my whiskey?"

"Well, sir. It might mean nothing, or it might be significant. About an hour ago, we tracked several Gomer Ships of various types, headed back towards Neptune."

"Seriously?"

"Yessir. At first it was only a trickle. Looked like the normal courier kind of stuff, but now it is growing into a steady stream."

"What kind of stream?"

"It started with one or two ships, and then the numbers kind of grew. So far, we've seen almost a half dozen Mountain Class ships, at least a dozen of their Battleship Class ships, and one Moon Class we didn't know about, all headed back towards Neptune. The stream of Carrier, Transport, and Service class ships is also growing the same way. Not sure why, but they appear to be backing off for some reason."

"Okay, get that off to SAHQ and ASOC right away. Oh, and while you're up, hand me that bottle of scotch. Might be time to change horses here."

"Yes, Sir!"

ASOC Headquarters, underneath Lake Moomaw, Virginia:

Dr. Abramson started tallying the numbers, and it was clear to him that John's plan was working perfectly. They weren't really backing off, instead these rats were deserting their sinking ship. What he didn't know was how rapidly the metal was disintegrating, but given the fact that they were now being fed the Sulphur, they couldn't stay where they were any longer. When John was summoned into Operations, he was like a kid at Christmas. He hadn't had the heart to tell Chris about any of it, since she was so worried about her family, but this was a major triumph. Dr. Abramson was telling him about the shift in numbers headed back to Neptune, and then asked him how long things would take to completely degrade. It was then that Dr. Abramson and General Greene fully realized that John not only designed it to degrade rapidly after a Terahertz burst, but the speed of degradation was tied to the amount of Terahertz radiation that was absorbed. Adding insult to this injury, John had convinced his nano-tech partners to include a layer of Sulphur gas that would be released as the material degraded to a certain level. In other words, his plan was to gas them in their holes. This is why he was so adamant about the coordinates being used for the Phoenix IV, since he knew that this would provide for the most rapid rate of disintegration.

Staying in Operations, John was gratified to see that the rate of ship departures peaked, and then completely stopped. What was even more gratifying was that some of the later departures all crashed as they tried to leave Martian airspace. This was hard evidence that the project had been a smashing success. Excited beyond words, he finally left Operations to tell Chris. He'd hoped that it might cheer her up a little. Instead, when he saw the look on her face when he came up to her, he decided to keep it to himself for just a little while longer. He reached out, and hugged her. She settled into his shoulder and held him as tightly as possible, then she said, "John. Please just go sit with Michael. See if you can keep him occupied right now, I know I ..."

"Sure, honey. I'll head there now. Love you."

"Love you, too."

Supreme Allied Headquarters, (SAHQ), Lake Summersville, WV:

The teletype was running at full speed as a number of messages poured into the headquarters almost all at once. Sorting through it all, General Roberts saw the Vandenberg Message, to include the intelligence dealing with incoming traffic to the east coast. Passing it off to General Whitney and I, he had no idea how happy he'd just made me. Not having to worry about more big stuff or reinforcements for the dissidents hopping around on our turf, I knew we were catching a break for once. Without wasting a second, I ordered the Air Operations people to, "get four A-10s, and four AH-64s, on station near the back door over in Peterstown. Tell them to kill anything in the air, and to keep at least one aircraft of each type on station until after sunrise. Nothing big is coming, so give them a full release, and make sure they know about Clagmore and his mission. Brief them on his frequencies, and if he gets back above ground tonight, he will want to know they're there."

Knowing that was all I could do in support of the Families for the moment, I shifted my attention to the rest of the messages that were coming in. The collapse of the Martian bases was great news, and there was no way we could wait to exploit that either. On my order, we unleashed a series of Missile attacks, using Sulphur based weapons, on all of the newer enclaves being established jointly between the Gomers and the dissidents. For once, the momentum was going our way, and I sure wasn't going to waste the opportunities. Getting in touch with my Army Group Commanders, they were both Ordered to commence offensive operations where possible on all fronts. We now needed to shift things to keep up the pressure.

Back entrance to the Family Facilities, Peterstown, WV:

Leah was the last civilian into the chamber near the back exit. As the group passed through, she made it a point to count off in her mind the passage of each person. They hadn't lost any civilians, and she was delighted that they were now in the company of Sergeant Major Clagmore's team. Along the way, they had lost the remaining Secret Service Agents, and one of the Rangers, who had remained behind to establish an ambush to buy the group more time to get out. Captain Jackson already knew that these men had given their lives to help get them out, since his rear-guard scout had watched as the Russian dissidents had overwhelmed them in the last seconds before that tunnel was blown. She was relieved that they were this close to extraction, but that relief didn't last long. Sergeant Major Clagmore, who was delighted to see his wife, was also quite candid about their situation.

Behind them, a force of unknown size was still in pursuit, and likely only an hour or so away from reaching their position. Ahead were at least another dozen Russian dissidents on the ground who were now blocking them from the closest landing zone. Finally, it would be another 8 hours before sunrise, and the skies were full of Gomer Fighter Class ships that were still searching for them. The next closest landing zone for pick-up was at least four miles away, down a mountain, and next to the New River itself. This was the original pickup or emergency extraction point. An open field surrounded by heavier trees, this landing zone was on the banks of the New River. Not accessible by road, the closest roadway ends several meters to the north. The only good news was that it could accommodate up to four UH-60s, or two CH-47s.

Leah could only think of the old expression that they were now trapped between the devil and the deep blue sea. Taking stock of the situation, there were 15 members of Clagmore's team, counting the Sergeant Major, and there were now only 7 other soldiers left from their original force trying to get them out. Captain Jackson made the total 8, so she could count on 22 soldiers. Well trained killers, but without knowing how many were to their rear, there was only one solution in her mind. If they tried to take back the closest LZ, it wouldn't matter, since nobody could land before dawn and the Gomers left. If they stayed, then they would have to fight for upwards of 8 hours, against a force of unknown size, in a confined space. She looked at the Sergeant Major and Captain Jackson, and said, "Well, I guess we'll have to head out of here, and see if we can't lose them on the way overland to the old LZ."

Captain Jackson responded first, "Ma'am. That would be my best plan too, but these ladies have been moving without much rest for the last 28 hours. I'm not sure they'll make it if we push through tonight."

"Captain. They will have to move. We all will. We can't stay here, and if we attack the LZ that is closest to us, then nobody could get us out anyway. Now could they?"

Sergeant Major Clagmore remained silent through it all, and then after some thought said, "well, I might have another option." Motioning over one of his team, he asked about the status of the available explosives, and then he asked what Captain Jackson had left. Finally, he spoke up again. "Leah? I think I have an idea."

"I'm listening."

"Okay. I will have six of my guys attack the bastards on the LZ, while the rest of this party starts down the mountain towards the LZ by the river. Call it a diversion. Meanwhile, Captain, if you'll get your Rangers to finish closing the hole here, we have just enough explosive to do two things. The incoming tunnel with the bad guys can be wired to create a kill zone, and then collapse on top of whatever is left. We have four claymore mines we can put into place in a classic ambush then, once the tunnel fills with Russians, we can flip the switch. This will take out a portion of the force, and give us more time while they start digging a huge hole to get out. Next, with the LZ forces distracted, hopefully they won't be able to give pursuit to anyone headed off the mountain. Finally, Leah, this is where your ladies with skills come in."

"Huh?"

"You know. Half these broads... Excuse me, ladies, know how to shoot and shoot well. Hell, my Katie can shoot a gnat's ass off at 100 yards, and I notice they're all packin.' Anyway, you take everyone down the mountain about 100 yards or so, and then circle out due west for another 100 yards. Don't go too far down the ridge. Stay under heavy tree cover, set up a perimeter around the families, just dig in and wait. You know what I'm talking about cause you've done it before with your husband. Now then, we can maybe buy enough time till daylight, if we're free to move around and stir them up. If we can keep the heat off you guys, then we have a real shot. If we don't come and get you in the morning, then take everyone down the mountain at first light and activate your light strobe. Okay with you?"

"Sounds as good as anything. Do we get to keep at least two guys to protect Toni?"

"You mean the First Lady?"

"Yes, I do."

"Leah, take two of the security team troopers over there. I'm sorry, but I'm going to hang on to these Rangers. They will be my force to trip the ambush, and once they come out, then I'm going to blow the whole mess. In the meantime, the rest of my guys will be giving those bastards over there a bloody nose."

"Alright. When do we start?"

"Give me five minutes."

As luck would have it, five minutes was about all they had left. When the Rangers crossed back into the cavern closest to the exit and set their detonators, the opposing forces were starting up the tunnel.

It was a near thing, but it just might work. Leah got her ladies lined up around the families and waited. Finally, she heard the distant firing, directed against the perimeter around what looked like a crashed Gomer Fighter Class ship. Not wanting to waste time, she immediately left the cave entrance and did exactly what the Sergeant Major told her to do. Moving as quickly as they could into the opposite tree line, she headed down the mountain roughly 100 yards, and turned west along the ridge for another 100 yards or so. The entire time she was keeping one eye on the sky, and one on the ground. She knew what the Gomers could do, and she wanted to stay under the thick cover as much as possible.

Finally, once she found a spot she liked, she got her "broads" into position around the families. She thought about what Mike had said during the first war when they'd had to flee the house, and she made sure that they could defend themselves from anything or anyone that might be on their trail. Placing the two remaining solders into positions close to Mrs. Blanchard, all they could do now was watch, listen, and wait. It would be at least another 6 or 7 hours until sunrise, so silence and sleep would be a good thing. Taking shifts, they did their best to ignore the not very distant explosions and gunfire, while trying to cat nap and keep the little ones quiet.

Chapter XIII

❦

Ridgeline 6.4 miles north and west of the Family Facility, Peterstown, WV:

The two AH-64 helicopters unmasked from the trees overlooking the adjacent open area to their east. Side by side, the two aircraft immediately got "eyes on" the LZ that was blown into the trees by Clagmore's men. Scanning the terrain before masking again, the crews noted both the crashed Gomer Fighter and the three Gomer Fighter Class ships that were approaching from the southeast. Using a short burst transmission, and then shifting position to their south, they unmasked again, just in time to see the missiles from the A-10's strike their targets. The resulting explosions lit up the night sky, even as the two Apaches moved forward towards the LZ.

Sergeant Major Clagmore immediately keyed his microphone and sent his recognition signal to the aircrews. Now it was going to be a fair fight, and the Sergeant Major was beyond excited. He was downright ecstatic. Sending a runner forward, they immediately marked the limits of the enemy perimeter with IR strobe lights, and then told their new found Apache friends to "have a ball." When the Apaches unleashed their 30-millimeter chain guns, the sound mimicked that of a large heavy zipper being torn open. What they didn't know was that the brass being ejected from their weapons was now falling among the civilians huddled in the woods below. Leah was amazed at the display, but less than impressed when a piece of very hot brass bounced off her leg as she was prone in the treeline. "Damn, now that is going to leave a mark. GOD, that's hot! Even through my jeans, that is hot." Realizing she had said it out loud, she wasn't too worried about giving away their position, since the noise from the Apaches was deafening.

Within a minute, the Apaches were shifting their positions again and, as quickly as they had appeared overhead, they were gone. In the relative silence, they heard the explosions coming from around the cave's rear entrance. She could only guess at the carnage, but they remained in place, staying as quiet as they could. Several of the children could be heard sobbing, but they, too, became quiet as their mothers held them tightly, admonishing them to be quiet. Suddenly, to their front, there was a crashing through the woods. Several men were running towards them, and Lou Ann fired her rifle dropping the first one to the ground. Within seconds the running men started firing towards their direction. Moving away and forward to a better position, Leah was able to see that these men were running away from the Apache Aircraft and from Sergeant Major Clagmore's men.

The first shots from the ladies were deadly for the men trying to escape, and as they tried to take advantage of their speed and position to burst through Leah's lines, they began to drop like flies. Nobody kept score, but there is little doubt that the ladies ran up a pretty impressive total. None of the dissident attackers survived their attack, and when Clagmore's team entered the fray from their rear, the rest of the night's battle went very quickly. When the firing finally ended, the ladies were alone. Their casualties had been light, but they did have them. Lou Ann was hit in the arm, and even though it was just a grazing wound, it still was impressive. Katie Clagmore wasn't shot, but she had a piece of the hot brass from the Apache go down the back of her shirt. To her credit, she had kept up a vicious volume of fire on the bad guys, despite (or as some would argue later, maybe because of...), the burn to her lower back. Otherwise, aside from a few bruises, near misses, and splinter wounds from trees that were struck with bullets, everyone else seemed to come through okay. Even the youngest combatants, twelve-year-old Samantha and fifteen-year-old Sonya Jones, had done their bit to keep weapons loaded and the fight going. Leah was pretty proud of the old "broads," since they had done better than hold their own. Not a single child was hurt, the First Lady was fine, and from Leah's perspective, that was what it was all about.

Hayley Timmons had even had her own epiphany when it was crunch time at the height of the battle. Picking up an extra weapon from one of the guards, she had joined the fight with a vicious volume of fire that killed several of the attackers as they neared her children and Mother Patrick. Something inside finally came together for her and she decided, then and there, on the side of a forgotten mountain, that these bastards weren't going to take anything else from her. At one point, Mother Patrick even had to pull her back down as she was about to charge forward yelling at the top of her lungs. When it was over, she put her hand on Mother Patrick's shoulder, smiled, and simply said, "I'm fine now."

Sergeant Major Clagmore approached the ladies' positions very gingerly, calling "Apples" on a pretty regular basis. After thinking he was about to be shot, he finally made contact with Katie and Leah. Taking a few minutes to assess the situation, they began the movement of all the families back to the closest landing zone. Dawn was coming, and already there were two CH-47s, being escorted by the Apaches and A-10s, on the way to pick them up. Finally, they were going somewhere safe, and in some cases, to be reunited with their loved ones.

ASOC Headquarters, underneath Lake Moomaw, Virginia:

Chris and Holly finally got the news they had been waiting to hear. It was a personal message from General Patrick that simply said, "Mom and Mother are fine, and on their way to my location. Will advise of arrival." The sense of joy was overwhelming for them, and the tension of the past several days flowed from them leaving them both more than a little drained. Stumbling back to their quarters, Chris finally learned about John's triumph over the Gomers on Mars. Holly, who had followed Chris, was overjoyed to hear the plan had worked, but despite the exhaustion, and joy from the recent events, she looked at Chris and simply asked, "How did those bastards know where the Family Facility was located?"

"I don't know, I mean nobody knew about the facility that wasn't living there. We knew, but I couldn't tell you how to get there, much less where exactly it was located."

"I know. We only went in the one time, came out the one time, and each time it was such a convoluted trip, I ..."

Chris snapped up and said, "That sorry bastard Lombardi!"

Picking up the phone, Chris took advantage of her position and got General Greene on the line. "General, this is Chris Patrick. Did Lombardi have knowledge of where the Family Facility was located?" After listening several minutes, Chris hung up the phone and looked at Holly shaking her head. "Daniel just told me that he suspected that Lombardi or Adams gave away the exact location for the VIP cave. Because Lombardi was the press secretary, he was part of the cover operation to get the family of the President relocated."

"You mean, he ratted out Aunt Toni and the other moms and kids?" Holly was incredulous.

Chris continued, "Precisely! he knew exactly where the first family was being housed and when the attack on the President failed, their plan B was to take and hold Leah, Grandmother, the first family, and hopefully any other VIP families, like Irina and the babies. They wanted hostages for leverage against Dad and the President."

"You reckon Dad knows?"

"I'll bet he knows, and I'll assure you that if he does, then despite what a trial court does, I already KNOW what will happen to Lombardi and his ass clown buddy, Adams. Nothing personal, but I've known him longer than you, and I still remember his old days as an Operator."

"Yikes. Nothing like making it personal."

"No kidding. Dad doesn't care for personal, not one little bit. I wouldn't give you 5 cents for what is about to happen to Lombardi, and I know Dad well enough to know it will look to the world like one helluva accident!"

Supreme Allied Headquarters, (SAHQ), Lake Summersville, WV:

The reunion was fantastic, even if the quarters weren't much more than barely livable. Leah was almost sad to see Toni and her family headed to Lake Moomaw, VA, but she was far happier to be back with Mike. Mother Patrick was exhausted, and the wounded Lou Ann was also with them. Carrie Roberts, Alicia Jones, and Irina Dubronin, along with their children, were at the Summersville facility. Martha Clark, and Katie Clagmore were now with them, too. Leah was happy, since all of the real shooting "broads" were still together, and still quite the team. Poor Katie, with her burned back, was in a great deal of pain, so when Sergeant Major Clagmore began to pick at her about getting a "tramp stamp" to cover the burn, she was anything but amused. Lou Ann was also dealing with the stitches on her arm, but one thing was clear from their ordeal. None of these women would ever be the same. They had forged a real bond, and anything from the past that might have been an issue was simply buried and forgotten. Now, they were like a real sisterhood, a sisterhood that would make a Mafia Don jealous.

I was just glad to have them all safe, and to have my bride back near me. Now it was back to the war, and this time, I knew that we'd either win it or die together. No more safe places for any of us, to include our loved ones. We had been lucky to get most of the families out of the adjacent facilities with as few civilian casualties as were suffered, and thank God there were no children killed in the melee. Now that relocation was complete, it was time to get back to the business at hand, and to start moving towards the original play book for "killing Gomers." The current situation wasn't a good one. The Gomers and Dissidents were still hitting us hard in places, and we were suffering more casualties in our forces globally. Still, it could have been worse.

Thanks to the combination of Gomer and Dissident assault forces, most of the losses we were suffering were on the Pacific side of Siberia and in the immediate vicinity of the Ural Mountain areas. Thule, Greenland was also devastated, with bad guys pouring into the more desolate areas of Greenland, but at least there were fewer troop losses. The rest of that story was that Greenland again was becoming the location where the Gomers were setting up a major Base for their few remaining Mountain and Battleship Class ships. Their fleet appeared to be relatively Earth bound, since the Gomer bases on Mars and behind the Moon were no longer viable for them to use. We weren't seeing much additional traffic coming from Neptune, which was our other saving grace. At least now we had an idea of the numbers and types of ships and forces that the Gomers could put against us. We also had one or two more tricks up our sleeves and, with a few phone calls, we were getting a handle on how to put them into action.

12th Army Group, near the Ural Mountains, Russia:

General Larkin was not in the least bit pleased. The guidance from higher headquarters had been interesting over the last month. During the "bug out," General Crouse wasn't much help. While they were able to see the bigger picture at Bluestone, General Crouse and his staff were simply out of their league when it came to providing any meaningful guidance for operational planning. General Greene was equally pre-occupied with God knows what, which left the big local decisions up to him, and to General Davis on the Pacific side. Their attempts at coordination were made more difficult with the constant harassing raids being made by the Russian dissidents and the Gomers on the lines of communication running east and west. All of his forces were waging both a conventional, and very human war, alongside the twists of fighting a well-equipped and determined alien force. When General Patrick was finally back in the loop, General Larkin was still little comforted. The missing President, and then the Gomer Raid on Petrstown, were enough to keep anyone distracted, and General Patrick was no exception.

General Larkin's current situation was starting to approach grim. Supply lines were being constantly interdicted at night by the Gomers and, by day, by the threat of the Dissident's own air force. Ship traffic and convoys were getting through, but defending the ports was a monumental problem. Missile supplies, reinforcements, fuel, and other ammunition requirements were being stretched to the outer limits. The troop losses over his entire force were becoming a real problem, and he still couldn't get the release of any airborne forces to supplement his already beleaguered units. What made it especially bad was the order to return all airborne forces, regardless of nationality, to CONUS. Between the Pacific and Atlantic theaters, this took two British Airborne Divisions, two French Airborne Divisions, two German Airborne Divisions, a Belgium Airborne Division, two Norwegian Airborne Divisions, and several middle eastern based Airborne Divisions, all out of the available troop mix. The hardest of these forces to lose came from Egypt, Israel, and Saudi Arabia. The insult was that the two complete American Airborne Corps were also taken to an undisclosed location in the United States. General Larkin knew that these would eventually be the striking force, but why pull them all out for training? Hell, he needed these forces now, and not later when they could only be used to clean up after the dead and wounded.

Having reached his boiling point, he picked up the direct line to General Patrick. It was time to raise hell, and lay it on the line. "General Patrick. Larkin here!"

"Hey, Giant, what can I do for you?"

"Dammit, Mouse. What's the idea of pulling everyone with jump wings back to the States? Have you lost your damn mind?"

"Nope."

"Can you at least explain it to me?"

"Nope."

"Have you got something in mind?"

"Yep."

"Dammit! Mouse, tell me…tell me why I've got guys pulling double duty, and dying because there aren't enough guys to step up and plug the holes!"

"General Larkin, I'd love to tell you, and here in the near future you'll be told, but right now, on this line, it ain't going to happen."

"Sir. With all due respect, I think I have a need to know."

"Well, General. You WILL have a need to know, but not yet, and not until we're ready. I will say that it won't be much longer. I'll also say I will need you and General Davis back here within the week for a consultation. Once we get face to face, then you'll not only be told, but you'll be read into the whole picture. In the meantime, not that it will help much, just hold with what you have. If anything, at your discretion, pull in your horns, consolidate your positions, and protect your supply lines. I promise that help is coming, and I'll see you in a few days."

"Sir? When will we be summoned?"

"You just were, and a telex will arrive with details in less than 24 hours. Be prepared to move, and move quickly. Got it?"

"Yessir. I don't like it, but I've got it!"

"Glad to hear it. Now then, you'll be glad to know that Mrs. Larkin sends her best, and she is now relocated with Leah."

"Thank you, sir." Breaking the connection, General Larkin was happy to hear about his wife, but still madder than hell about what was happening to his force. Consolidate positions? Just how the hell was he supposed to do that, when every time they moved, they were being dogged day and night, either by the Alien assholes or the Russian assholes. The only good news he heard was that there was at least a plan in the works. He just hoped it was worth this war of attrition that he was now fighting.

Supreme Allied Headquarters, (SAHQ), Lake Summersville, WV:

After hanging up with General Larkin, I was digging my way through the morning message traffic. Three things jumped out at me, and all three were messages I'd been dying to receive. The first was personal. Chris, John, and Holly were all okay and at Lake Moomaw with General Greene and the President. Holly was working feverishly with John and the other eggheads on a solution that was explained in far greater detail in the next message. I'd waited a while on this one, and couldn't wait to get the full briefing about how it was going to come together. The third message came from my ace in the hole, hidden on the other side of the Rocky Mountains. This message was also directly related to what General Larkin was upset about, and merely confirmed what I had hoped was the case. The new Global Strike Group, which was the equivalent to an Army

Group, was now 98% deployable, and would be ready to move with their new equipment and tactics, within a week.

After sorting through the rest of the messages, I called together the staff and put them on notice. "Gentlemen. We are now about to turn this sucker around. General Roberts, I want you to drag out the plans for Operation Sparta, get your staff up to speed, and then be prepared to brief it to the President in two days. General Whitney, you will cut orders for Generals Larkin and Davis to join us at Lake Moomaw in three days. Fastest transportation, secure, and all the rest. Make sure there is a deception plan in place to get them to ASOC. Admiral Lynch, your job is to keep the supply lines open and keep the fleet ready. You're a big player in Sparta, so get with Roberts, and update what you need. Finally... Whit. I want you, General Roberts, Admiral Lynch, and General Kaminski, all ready to move with me in two days to Lake Moomaw. Finally, cut orders adding Admiral Steadman, General Mahan, General Crouse, and General Thayer to the same list as Generals Davis and Larkin. I want a conference at Lake Moomaw in three days. It is high time we were all singing off the same sheet, and it is high time we taught the song to the bad guys. Now then, are there any questions?"

"Sir? I've got a bunch, but I assume you're not going to tell us yet?"

"General Roberts, when you read Sparta again, I think it will come to you. I just got a message from our guys at Site X, and from the Rocky Mountain training areas, and they are all telling me that we have a green light now."

"Excellent! Thank you, sir."

"Anybody else?" The room was silent, and after scanning the room and looking everyone in the eye, I finished, "Well then. Time to grab, root, and growl! Get on it." Turning from the crowd, I headed back to my quarters to pass on the personal news to Leah, and to make sure that Jerry's wife knew that he'd be home for a day or two.

ASOC Headquarters, underneath Lake Moomaw, Virginia:

Travel between facilities was always an exercise in deception, and this was no exception. Now that the Gomers were ignoring it, the process was a little easier, but only marginally. We did not want to give them any evidence that the place still existed, so the process was still full of cloak and dagger. After finally getting into the place, it was obvious that it was quite the new underground city. Not nearly as basic as our own headquarters facility, there was no question that ASOC knew how to live. The first briefing was to get the President up to speed, and the briefing scheduled for the following day was to get our operational commanders going on the same subject. Naturally, this didn't quite happen the way we thought, since the first briefing went far better than I had ever hoped possible.

After taking our seats around a large conference table, General Greene acted as our host. Stepping up to the podium at the opposite end of the table he began by introducing Dr. Clarkson, who got right down to it.

"Mr. President. General Patrick. We have solved the problem you gave us some weeks ago about using the Gomer Fighter Class ships we'd captured." With this statement, a real hush fell over the room. No longer was anyone shifting in a seat, or shuffling a document. Now the room was completely riveted. Continuing, Dr. Clarkson explained, "We have written a computer program, with the help of Doctor Patrick, that will allow us to fly any Gomer craft to and from target areas without any significant emissions of any radio waves, regardless of wave length or band. After consultation with General Greene, we believe that the applications are significant. We can now deliver a weapon to Neptune within a matter of days, and we can even send one up and back, to gather intelligence information. We currently have at our disposal 10 Fighter Class Ships that are flyable this way, and the process has been tested successfully. I must admit we had 16 such ships, and lost one in our earlier testing. Fortunately, we found the bug, fixed it, and have done over a hundred test flights since that one loss. Now then, if you'll turn to the screen, you will see that we've even tested the equipment in space."

Looking towards the screen at the end of the room, we were treated to some rather dynamic video footage through the front of the Fighter Class ship as it conducted a survey of the Moon surface. After about 10 minutes of watching, and seeing for ourselves the amount of debris now scattered over the dark side of the Moon, Dr. Clarkson dropped the real bombshell. "Gentlemen and Ladies, this footage is not delayed, but happening as we speak. We have sent this same fighter on this same mission three times now."

"Excuse me. Doctor Clarkson?"

"Yes, General Patrick."

"Doctor, when you've sent this ship to the Moon, has it encountered any 'live' traffic that might challenge it?"

"General, we have passed several of their Fighter Class ships, and at least one Transport Class ship, without any challenges that we're able to monitor. It has come and gone unmolested now on three separate occasions."

"Now you said it could be flown to and from Neptune, but how much of a Phoenix IV type system can the one Fighter Class ship carry?"

"I know where you're going, and the answer is, not enough."

"How much would be enough?"

"One Carrier Class ship or bigger would probably do it, while it might take ten to twenty Fighter Class ships to accomplish the same thing. We've done the calculations, and you've anticipated what we were going to bring up today."

"Good. Then I'll shut up."

"No, General, it was perfect timing. We think that if we can get one Gomer Battleship Class or even better, a Mountain Class ship, we can destroy the Gomers on Neptune in less than a week, as opposed to the seven years it will now take."

The President was still not quite himself, but for the first time since our arrival, it was obvious that he was given a huge shot in the arm. Looking up and around the room, he asked, "Okay, then. What do we have to do to get a Mountain Class ship? Hell, seems like we had one, didn't we?"

Dr. Clarkson looked around the room, and then directly at the President, "Sir, we dismantled it to get all the information."

"Damn silly thing to do, but okay. What do we need to put it together again?"

General Greene took up the gauntlet, and trying his best to disguise his surprised look at the President's obvious lack of memory on the subject, he said, "Mr. President. We've used the computers, propulsion, and weapons to develop our own responses. Besides, a new one shouldn't be impossible to find, and it is less likely to draw attention during the transit back to Neptune."

"Okay."

"Mr. President. If I may?" I knew the President might not recall everything that had happened before his ordeal and, frankly, could not remember myself what the President may have been told about certain operations.

"Go ahead, Mike."

"Sir. Greenland is crawling with them, and I might have a force that could not only get us one, but maybe even a couple before it is said and done."

"Excellent. Then make it happen."

"Uh… Yes. Mr. President." The President smiled at me, and then fell forward face first into the table top. General Greene and a nurse were at his side almost immediately, and as we watched, they rushed in the emergency medical team. Thankfully, he was alive, but the rest of the story would take another week to unfold. For now, it was obvious that we were on our own again. When the Vice President took over the reins, despite his own personal shock, he was briefed up to speed as quickly as possible. After almost a four-hour briefing, he gave us our guidance. "Do what you have to do, and do so with my authorization, if there is a problem, then I'll back you up. Right now, you are the experts on the Gomers, so just keep me informed." On the subject of the dissidents, he was a little more circumspect. "Do not allow any American Forces to violate the Geneva Convention, as to the human combatants, but if the Russians take a different position, then it won't be our place to judge."

Medical Facility, at ASOC Headquarters, underneath Lake Moomaw, Virginia:

Toni was rushed into the waiting area, along with her family. The minutes drug into hours, until the surgeons were able to find the source and stop the bleeding. When the doctor stepped into the waiting area, he found an extremely distraught family, and a very worried General Officer. Taking a deep breath, he finally said, "So far we're okay, but we're not out of the woods. We've induced a coma to keep him comfortable for the present, so he will be out of things for several more days at least. We got all the bleeding stopped, and we hope there will be no loss of cognitive function. We won't know about any other problems until we get things under control and can awaken him. Only then will we be able to fully assess the damage, if there is any, he might awaken and be fine, it is just too early to tell. I can tell you that the swelling was significant, and we had to remove a portion of his skull to take off the pressure. I did not see any permanent issues with the brain tissue, but again, we will have to wait until the swelling subsides to know what we're dealing with."

Toni could only nod her head weakly, as Hayley held her closely. The Doctor had held out a thin thread of hope, and they were taking it. This was a good thing for them, and I made a mental note to try and get Leah and Mrs. Larkin on a flight to ASOC right away. This was no time for Toni to be without her friends. I leaned over and gave them both a hug, before turning to leave. Stepping towards the door, the doctor motioned to me, and we stepped out of the room.

"General? I want you to know that I am not real sure he will be back for a while."

"I somehow knew that, and I'll make sure that the Vice President knows that he could be holding the head for a while."

"Thank you, sir, and I'll send him my official report. I guess my real concern is that he might not ever be back."

"I kind of guessed that too, but since you held out some hope for the family, ..."

"General. That was for the family. I'm telling you in your official capacity, that the President has a less than 45% chance of ever returning to a semblance of cognitive normal."

"Thank you, Doctor. I'll advise the Vice President, and you keep me posted. I prefer the unvarnished truth, and not the family version."

"I thought so, which is why I got you out here."

"Doctor, as of now, you will keep me informed if there are any changes, improvements, or setbacks, and I want to hear from you at least once a day."

"Yessir."

"Oh, and Doctor. Thanks. He is my friend, in fact, he might be my best friend on this godforsaken planet..." Doing my best to fight back the emotions, I stepped out only to bump into Chris. She took one look at my face, and knew that it wasn't a good thing. I pulled her to the side, and told her both versions of the President's condition. I then told her to do all she could for Toni, Hayley, and Rhonda, and to keep it light. She smiled and patted me on the arm "Dad. He'll be okay, and so will you." With that simple gesture, all was right in my world again, and I went to face the rest of the story. We had a war to fight, and I was going to win this thing if it killed me.

ASOC Headquarters, underneath Lake Moomaw, Virginia:

The following day, the rest of the key players arrived at Lake Moomaw, and for the first time they learned that the President was in a medically induced coma, and that the Vice President was now the acting Commander in Chief. This was shocking news enough, but it was becoming quite apparent that the Vice President wasn't that well versed on the situation on the ground. With each new revelation of secured and classified information, his jaw was sinking just a little lower. By the end of the day, he now knew about Site X, the Global Strike Group, the potential mission to Greenland, as a test for the Strike Group, the Neptune Mission, and all of the Phoenix missile variants and the Red Dragon systems. He also knew that in Europe and Pacific areas, we were barely holding on, while the Gomers were making life miserable using our very own human race as combatants.

The entire process of getting him up to speed took hours, and we were now a day behind in my hoped plan. The Vice President gave us a green light on everything, and made it clear that his policy regarding Gomers was the same as the Presidents. We weren't to give them any quarter this time. After the last several months, there wasn't a soul in the room that would ever disagree with that statement.

Chapter XIV

❦

ASOC Headquarters, underneath Lake Moomaw, Virginia:

The Vice President traveled light, both literally and figuratively. He wasn't married, having divorced almost three years before the first Gomer War, and there were few personal attachments that needed to be relocated. He was a career politician who, during the First Gomer War, served briefly as a reserve Major assigned to a non-deployed Infantry Brigade that was defending New Washington. When that war was over, he returned to a life of politics, and was quite content to build up his resume, in hopes of someday finding his way into the Presidency. Most of whatever he had learned in his brief stint with the military he had promptly "flushed" the second he was able to get out of the service, but he wasn't completely incompetent either. He did feel confident that he could get compromises done with congressional leaders, but when it came to understanding the military, his own experience was of little or no help. Now he was afraid he was in over his head, and he was terrified that his next move might be the last of a political career. His reticence did little to help anyone, since the strong leadership of President Blanchard was crucial to winning a war. Initially, I was convinced that unless the boss got back on his feet, we'd be well and for truly screwed. Then I realized that the Vice President wasn't just an empty suit. He was more than willing to leave us largely alone to do what we needed to accomplish. This was a mixed bag, since for the moment, at least until he got his feet under him, we really were on our own without any significant guidance or direction.

Over the next several weeks, as we moved our offensive plans towards a point where we could take action, the President's condition went back and forth. There were at least two times we thought we were going to lose him, but each time he came back and was showing some signs of real strength. For me personally, this was almost as low a point in my life as when Leah was on the run in the family cave system. Leah and Chris were with Toni and her family throughout the ordeal, and from them I learned what real strength was all about. Finally, on the eve of some serious decisions we had to make regarding our operations, the President awakened from his coma. The news from both the Doctor and the family indicated that President Blanchard was responding physically and mentally quite well. The Doctor admitted that his mental recovery was coming along far better than expected, and while he wasn't fit to return to duty, he was making sufficient recovery for us to hold out very real hope that eventually he would be back on the job. The one down side to the President's recovery was that the Vice President suddenly realized that he wouldn't be on the hot seat much longer. This meant that when it came to any serious strategic decisions, he was dragging his feet since he was afraid that his decision might be contrary to that of the President. In other words, as the President improved, the Vice President became a little more intransigent and less helpful or supportive of any strategy or plan.

General Larkin, on the other hand, was very helpful, and after some discussions and in-depth explanations, he agreed to take over my pet project. General Crouse replaced him as the 12th Army Group Commander in Europe, and General Larkin was faced with his new command. The Global Strike Force was something new, different, and more to the point, audacious. As a result, I needed

Jerry's penchant for being that "gutsy whacko" to lead them. He took to the role immediately, and left for his personal training in the Mountains, and then on to assume command at Site X of what would eventually become the "Global Strike Force" or 1st Allied Airborne Army Group. While he didn't have as much time with the equipment, he was given some wonderful tools to help him learn. One of them was my own son, the recently promoted Captain Robert Patrick, USA. No longer the aide to the 11th Airborne Division Commander, Robbie was now a resident expert on both exoskeleton technology and Gomer weaponry. These skills made him a prime choice for Jerry Larkin who, on taking command of the Group, made Robbie his aide. Despite upsetting the 11th Airborne Division Commander, Jerry knew it was his best choice, since it never hurt to have the boss's kid around. Especially where the project itself was years in the making, and complex to the extreme.

The Global Strike Force was something completely different. It was comprised of forces from around the world, and manning and training was a challenge. There were new tactics to be employed, and the shortages of equipment, coupled with the development of new technology, required someone who hated red tape. In General Larkin, we had finally found the right fit. As weeks turned into a month, things were shaping up far better than expected. The troopers were finding that the exoskeleton technology increased their stamina, range, and fighting power exponentially. The only limits now were the delivery of sufficient quantities of this new equipment, and an overall training goal for consolidation of these forces at the right time. Of course, for General Larkin, the real question was always how best to train and employ these new forces once they were fully equipped? This took all the skill and experience he could muster, but he finally was able to field almost a complete Army Group sized element of international forces.

The exoskeleton, or Exo-suit, had been in development for decades. The uses originally ran from the simple step-in system that augmented limb movement, up to medical uses, where they were applied to assist in the replacement of lost limbs. This technology developed as part of the Wounded Warrior efforts for those injured by Improvised Exploding Devices, or IEDs in both Iraq and Afghanistan, and included a great deal of advancements into the integration or interface between human nerve endings and the replacement limb. The combination of these things was cutting edge. The biggest drawback to the Exo-suit was the limited power source technology. Now, thanks to the Gomers and the research we were able to pull from their ships and computers, we had that problem solved. The suits themselves were extremely dynamic but, while bullet resistant, they were not bullet proof. Still, they allowed the average fighting man the ability to fight and travel faster and further. They also had the added advantage of a built-in climate control feature that made fighting in the harshest environments a lot easier. Make no mistake, these were not space suits, since they carried no independent oxygen supply, but they could handle radiation and chemical warfare scenarios with their filtration systems. In simplest terms, they were individual Exo-suits that increased the fighting efficiency of the average soldier by a good 95% in a cold arctic type climate.

Simple to operate, the scientists were able to take one version of the Exo-suit and add an aerial capability. This, too, was older technology that was in development as far back as the pre-Vietnam era in the United States military. In that case, power sources were again a real problem. The original flying ability was limited to roughly 21 seconds of fuel for a rocket burn. Not very efficient, eventually the system could fly a man for upwards of 4 to 5 minutes. Now, again thanks to our Gomer enemies, we had that problem solved. The power cells utilized by our scientists, all reversed engineered from the Gomers, allowed for the Exo-suit and the Aerial or Exo-Suit A, to be used by our strike force. Just like every other war in mankind's history, this one was leading to some remarkable advances in technology.

Starting with the application of this new technology, it was decided that a new Allied Force was needed, and who better than our Airborne Forces to make it work. They were well trained, and common threads ran throughout the world in both that training and in their application. Face it, even though the language was different, there were only so many ways to "stand up, hook up, shuffle to the door, jump right out, and count to four." Thus, the creation of this force was the forging out of the fire of war, a brand-new kind of fighting force. From the outset, the concept for this force was speed, surprise, and overwhelming fire power. It was necessary to utilize the exoskeleton technology to give each individual soldier both individual protection and a decided advantage in speed on the ground, or in some cases the air. From speed came surprise, and as for fire power, the reversed engineered Gomer hand held weapons were superior to those provided to the Dissidents by the Gomers themselves. This combination was hopefully going to give us an edge over the enemy forces that we would be attacking. Given the deployments around the northern latitudes by the Gomers and their Dissident minions, we were also looking at technology that would increase our capabilities to operate in that hostile Arctic environment. In short, we now had a strike force that could not only operate in hostile environmental conditions, but one that would hopefully exceed what the bad guys could put together for defense.

The only real problem we had now was time and the need for decisive leadership. Naturally, the Gomers were not operating with the same constraints, and they were making some very good use of their time. Our offensive operations were more about trying to get forces into sound tactical positions for a later attack than they were about inflicting harm on the Gomers. Finally, after almost another six weeks, things were coming together. The President's mental recovery was excellent, and he was finally more or less back in the saddle. His physical condition was still an issue, and he was using a wheel chair to get around, but finally the Vice President truly stepped up and did all he could to help in the process. It was believed that he would be able to walk again, but it would take a while, and a lot of therapy. Regardless, when he was able to reassume the reins, he did so with a vengeance, and our planning curve got very short, and our offensives started to have more meaning. Finally able to disseminate the plans for Operation Sparta, the next challenge was getting our allies to cooperate in the short term, while we got all the pieces in place.

Russian Command Bunker, outside Saint Petersburg, Russia:

General Vlad Korsikav, the Russian President's Military Advisor, stepped out of the Operations section for a breath of fresh air, and to carry a message to the Russian President. The message from General Patrick had only come over the wire a few moments earlier, and it was marked "Special Attention" for President Dubronin. General Korsikav laughed to himself when he read the message, since it was a simple and brief statement. Turning the corner to enter the President's office, he first felt, and then heard, a massive explosion from somewhere near their bunker location. Concrete dust filtered to the floor, and as he entered the office, he was almost bowled over by President Dubronin, who was rushing to the door to find out what happened.

"General? What was that?"

"Sir. I have no idea. I was bringing you a message from General Patrick."

"Let me see it."

"Yes, Sir."

After reading the brief message, President Dubronin couldn't contain his grin or his laughter. "Well, General! I am to be a Grandfather, yet again."

"Congratul..."

Before General Korsikav could complete the sentence, an aide rushed up with news.

"Mr. President! General! Someone has exploded a nuclear device in Saint Petersburg!"

"Colonel, what do we know?"

"Mr. President, someone used a missile, and it appears to have been launched from somewhere near the northern Urals."

"Why wasn't there a warning?"

"Sir, we believe that the Gomers jammed the system."

Turning to President Dubronin, General Korsikav said, "Sounds like a coordinated attack with Gomers and Traitors. We need to advise General Crouse and General Patrick."

"Da! Get it done." General Korsikav gestured with a brief hand salute, and then ran back towards operations. Dismissing the aide as well, President Dubronin stepped back into his office and asked his secretary to see if she could get General Patrick on the line. This was something they half way expected, but despite that expectation, the chill running up and down his spine was unavoidable. Was this a game changer for Patrick's Strike Force? Would this be a problem for their troops now defending the Ural Mountains? Was there something else that the Gomers were doing? Was this a diversion? Maybe Patrick would know something, but even if he didn't, President Dubronin simply felt a compelling need to talk to someone who might understand. One thing was clear, this was the first time the Dissidents utilized a nuclear warhead on actual Russian soil. Prior to this, they were doing all they could to preserve the Motherland and the infrastructure. Certainly, they didn't want to displace the government and reinstall the Soviet Union on charred ground. So, why now are they destroying it?

Supreme Allied Headquarters, (SAHQ), Lake Summersville, WV:

Initially, I was as puzzled as President Dubronin about the dissidents using tactical nuclear weapons on their own city, until I realized that all they were doing was feeding the Gomers. Most of the targets in Europe were cleaned up by the passing Gomers as they raided, and now St. Petersburg would be included on their route. It also was a chance for the dissidents to clear away the vestiges of the "New" Russian Federation, and its ties to the pre-Soviet history of Russia. This wasn't anything more than the Dissidents taking a political shot, while at the same time providing a new feeding spot nearer the ports. It was probably a long shot hope at cutting our supply lines from the northern ports to the troops that had the dissidents boxed into the terrain against the Ural Mountains. The good news for us was that we still held the high ground. Naturally, President Dubronin didn't see it this way, and within a few days, the weaponry being used on the dissidents was becoming far more indiscrete. If our President wasn't still under the weather, this would have ended sooner. Unfortunately, it now fell to me to talk some sense into President Dubronin, and it was a conversation quite typical of our "love/hate" relationship.

"President Dubronin."

"Da. General Patrick. What can I do for you?"

"Mr. President, I would really appreciate you not unleashing the tactical nuclear weapons so close to our forces. It is not helping us hold the ground, and instead, it is providing the Gomers several new places to recharge."

"Patrick, these dissidents must be stopped, and since it is taking too long to do anything, we are taking it into our own hands."

"Yuri! Dammit! You're killing and wounding some of the good guys in the process. This crap has to stop! If it doesn't, then I'm going to stuff one in your ear, and I know where you live."

"General, why you talk this way to me?"

"Because I need to get your attention, and because you're killing the wrong damn people with this crap. You may not realize it, but right now you're aiding the enemy, and you're not making it easy for us to ever be able to counter attack over that ground. You have got to stop. Besides, they have pulled this same thing on the Chinese side of your border, and they aren't buying into it. Believe me, it isn't because they don't want to do it, but they have enough respect for your sovereignty not to do it. Now if you keep nuking yourself, how long before the Chinese start cooking them off in your back yard?"

"This is your reason? To let them take me out of office, you are now siding with them?"

"Geez. Yuri, you can be about the thickest bastard I've ever known. Stop thinking like a Cossack, and start thinking like a Russian! You have got to stop screwing with your land. If you continue, the Chinese will render the entire western part of your country completely unusable for the next thousand years. I've got help on the way, and they will be arriving sooner than later, so you need to hold off. Hell, less than an hour ago, you cooked a Nuke off at a location that forced us to stop an attack in that same area near the Urals."

"You serious? Why you no tell me this beforehand."

"Yuri, we did! I sent you a coded message two days ago about the operation, and your son's wife being pregnant. Aren't you reading your fricking mail?"

"Two days ago? You send this to me? Same message as son and Irina having baby?"

"Yes. Two days ago." On hearing these words, President Dubronin looked at his aide, and then picked up the message that was on his desk where he had thrown it after the nuclear strike near his bunker complex. For the first time, he realized that he hadn't read anything past the initial part of the message, about Alexi and the new baby on the way. In all fairness, he was distracted when the first nuke went off outside his bunker. Looking sheepishly at no one in particular, he paused and then said, "General, I will look into it. If I did get message, I will be careful to refrain from any more attacks for now. Still, I need to know details of plan."

"I thought you might, and I also thought you might have been a little distracted in reading your mail, especially with a missile hitting so near your bunker. So, General Crouse will be coming to your location in about 4 hours' time to give you a personal and full briefing. Please meet him and listen closely. He is there for me, and he is a friend."

"Da. Okay. How is son and Irina?"

"He is fine, Yuri, and Irina is not only fine, but she is glowing, and definitely pregnant. You have my entire family's congratulations on what looks to be a third grandchild."

"Thank you, old friend. I will take care of problem with mail system, and I promise it will not happen again."

"Just sit tight for a while, Yuri, you have my word that we have something up our sleeve, and it is something YOU will personally love."

"This I will do."

"Excellent. Mr. President, please have a good evening, and General Crouse will be there in a few hours to fill you in on the details." Breaking the connection, I turned to Admiral Lynch, and asked, "Are your units in position?"

"Yes, Sir. We've got two battlegroups running the first part of Sparta, and it should bring some results around night fall tomorrow."

"Excellent. What about the submarine decoys?"

"Right where you wanted them, along with the USS Morton and the USS Fuller, which are both positioned next to the coast line."

"Excellent. Now we wait for them to take the bait. General Whitney?"

"Yessir?"

"Is Larkins' crowd in position yet near Thule?"

"Yessir. Waiting on the green light from the Navy." In anticipation of my next question, General Whitney then continued, "The Ural Air Strike package is also in position, and prepared to release the Phoenix Ground variant, as soon as the trap is sprung over the Denmark Straits."

"Okay, so what haven't we done? Anybody?" The silence around the room was a positive sign, either that or we were all too afraid of what was coming to speak. After looking every man in the eye, I then asked the communications officer to "Get me the President on the secure line. But first, make sure that General Crouse has finished briefing President Dubronin. I do not want any more surprises!"

Presidential Situation Room, underneath Lake Moomaw, Virginia:

The President was feeling some better, but he was a far cry from his old self. Hearing that General Patrick needed a video conference, the President had Toni wheel him into the Situation Room where, along with the Vice President and General Greene from ASOC, they took their seats. When General Patrick came on the line, there was the usual brief greetings from everyone, and then they leaped into the heart of it. General Patrick began first, "Mr. President. Our forces are set up for the first phase of Operation Sparta. I just spoke with President Dubronin and verified that he was fully briefed by General Crouse about their portion of the plan. We were very careful NOT to reveal any of the details of Operation Troy, since we still don't know if everyone in Dubronin's headquarters can be trusted."

Looking at the monitor, President Blanchard spoke up, "General Patrick, I not only agree with that decision, but right now, I don't think Operation Troy should ever be mentioned to the Russians, at least until this is all over. Can I assume that his knowledge of Operation Sparta is limited to that part where it is our attempt to test the new Global Strike Force and their technology, in an operation to retake Greenland?"

"Yessir. With one exception. He is also aware, by necessity, that the rest of Sparta is to suppress the Gomers, and to destroy as many dissidents as possible in Russia. I had General Crouse explain this part in detail, mainly to let Dubronin know that we understand his problems, and that we will use this opportunity to destroy those people that are threatening the rest of his country with their use of stolen tactical nuclear weapons."

"Good point, General. I should have recognized that one, too."

The Vice President spoke up, and said "Mr. President, I will take responsibility for approving General Patrick's release of that information to Dubronin. When this first came up, I made the call to limit information on Troy, while releasing most of the Sparta information."

I was gratified to hear the Vice President stepping up, and more than impressed that he would take that kind of responsibility for a decision that we recommended. While it might seem silly to most, this meant that if anything went sideways, the Vice President was willing to assume that responsibility. I just hoped that Dubronin's headquarters was finally tightened up enough to keep the news from spreading to the dissidents. I think we all felt that way, but now the Vice President was willing to take the hit if they blabbed. In this circle, that was the political version of jumping on a hand grenade, hoping it wouldn't go off.

From here the briefing continued with General Greene going over the plans for both Sparta and Troy. Operation Sparta was strategically risky and complex, while Operation Troy was all about technological risk and complexity. In both cases, we were going to be firing our best shots. Needless to say, questions were many, and speculation about the things that could go wrong was equal to the questions. The short version of each plan sounded simple, but only at first. In Operation Sparta, we were going to be using a Battleship Task force to lure two Gomer Carrier Class ships and a Battleship Class Ship out of Siberia and into the area around the Greenland side of the Denmark straits. Once these forces were on the way, we would then send our Battleship task force to the south. While clearing the area to the south, submarines would take over the electronic traffic. Concurrently, the USS Morton, USS Gregg, and USS Stephens (all destroyers of the new Morton/Zumwalt class with integrated 'bubble systems'), would take up position to the west of the Submarine Position just to the east coast of Iceland.

Once the Gomers took the bait, we would have nine Gomer Fighter Class ships pre-positioned on the ground in Iceland, loaded with light/special ops assault forces. Their job was simple, once the Gomer Fighters that were launched by the Carrier and Battleship Class ships were destroyed, they would approach from behind, dock, and then launch individual raids inside to capture these large units. Once the Fighters landed, then Phase II would begin. This would consist of simultaneous integrated air strike, using Gomer Phoenix Technology, to eliminate any dissident forces in the open around the launching sites of their tactical nuclear weapons, and an insertion of the Global Strike Force to take over the bases in Greenland that were being used by the Gomers as supply and maintenance facilities for their Carrier Class and larger sized Ships. Once the strike was complete, the conventional forces arrayed in defensive positions around the dissident outer ring in Siberia would advance and engage the dissident enemy.

Operation Troy was a completely different animal, and sadly, until Operation Sparta was completed successfully, the final details would still remain up in the air. Technological and scientific staffs were prepared, and had sufficient information to make it work, but in the meantime, it wouldn't mean a thing unless or until we had Operation Sparta well in hand. This was a matter of timing and, frankly, was the largest reason for launching the first operation. The inception, success or failure, of Troy all turned on what happened in and around Greenland. This was where we had to roll the big dice, and everyone at the table and in my headquarters knew it. At the conclusion of this briefing, the President gave his official authorization, and the Vice President confirmed that our allies were also providing us the official "go ahead" to begin the first phase of Sparta.

Denmark Straits, aboard the USS Montana Battlegroup Flagship:

The task force was comprised of the USS Montana. To her starboard was another member of her class, the USS Iowa, who had come up on loan from the 4th Fleet. To their south and west, by 100 miles, was the scratch Battlegroup built around the USS Wisconsin and USS North Carolina. Directly to their east, near the coast of Iceland, sat the Destroyer Flotilla made up of the USS Morton, USS Gregg, and USS Stephens. Finally, submerged beneath the Montana Battlegroup, were seven attack submarines, the USS Dallas, USS Rickover, USS Oklahoma City, USS Newport News, USS Charlotte, USS Hampton, and USS Toledo. Each poised to surface and assume the noise being emitted by the USS Montana and her consorts. Everyone aboard knew the risks, and everyone aboard was waiting with baited breath as the clock ticked nearer sundown. There were still several hours to go, but this didn't make for a comforting moment. These ships had learned not to emit any sort of electronic signature, and given the weapons range of the bad guys there was a great deal of concern that at the right moment, they might not be able to get away fast enough.

The tension built, and the discussions throughout the group were all focused on shutting down the noise as quickly as possible. Finally, the clock ticked over and at precisely two hours before sundown, the entire Battlegroup stopped emitting the signals. These signals had all been designed to make it appear as though the entire group was having maintenance breaks and issues in movement. In other words, the deception was that they were having serious problems with a search and rescue type operation. The hope was that the bait would indicate that there was an ongoing problem, and that a fat sweet target would be there when the bad guys showed up. Thankfully, it seemed that the Gomers were taking the bait. Just prior to shutting down and hauling it south, intelligence indicated that the Gomers were sending three Carrier Class Ships and a Battleship Class Ship. Now the concern was there was one too many ships, but as events unfolded, this picture would change two more times as the Montana and her group sped away, and the submarines surfaced and took their place.

The transmissions continued, almost unbroken, and the enemy came on towards their position. Now that the ball was in motion, tension in a lot of places was moving beyond palpable.

Near Grindavik, Iceland:

Colonel Basham, the Commander of the ASOC forces scattered around the several captured, but quite flyable Gomer Fighter Class Ships, was concerned as he monitored the intelligence reports. His force was put together knowing that the Gomers normally responded to these type targets with two Carrier and one Battleship Class Ship. The addition of a third Carrier Class Ship was unnerving, since now he would have to modify his attack plan. This wasn't good, since three teams per ship seemed to be the best way to attack, and if there was a fourth ship, then this would reduce his capabilities with each target. Still, there was a contingency for it, and while not optimal, it was still quite possible to pull it off. When the Gomers crossed the UK, the final shore-based report was coming in, and now it seemed that the initial reports were off by both size and type. Now, instead of facing three Gomer Carrier Class and one Battleship Class ship, the types were further identified. The game just changed considerably.

Briefing his team leaders, Colonel Basham advised them of the latest information. Reading from the message form, he related, "FLASH MESSAGE. GOMERS SHIPS ARE AS FOLLOWS: ONE CARRIER CLASS, WITH DAMAGE FROM LONDON BARRAGE. ONE BATTLESHIP CLASS, NO DISCERNABLE DAMAGE; ONE MOUNTAIN CLASS SHIP, RESPONSIBLE FOR DESTRUCTION OF AIR DEFENSES AT AND AROUND HEATHROW AREA." Damn, now this was something serious. The Teams were trained on Carrier and Battleship Classes, but Mountain?

Within seconds of the first message, the radioman handed Colonel Basham the second message, "TO STRIKE TEAM ALPHA. FROM ASOC/SAHQ. ATTACK STILL A GO. UTILIZE BATTLESHIP TEAM ON MOUNTAIN. SAME PLAN, REFER TO INFO PACKET DELTA FOR SOFTWARE FIX. ALL ELSE STANDS AS ORDERED. GOOD LUCK."

Colonel Basham was no rookie, and he had anticipated this problem. Addressing his team leaders, he passed on the relevant information, and each team leader headed out to get their people briefed and advised of the new issues involved with the new target scheme. Knowing that this could get ugly, the only other change Colonel Basham made was to move the scientific staff with them around. Dr. Holly Patrick, (whose presence was completely unknown to her father, General Patrick), would be riding on the Fighter run by Colonel Basham's team. She was about to have a front row seat in their attempt to take on the Mountain Class Ship.

SECTION 4

THE INITIATIVE SHIFTS - FINALLY

Chapter XV

❦

Far Eastern Edge of the Denmark Straits, aboard the USS Morton:

"Radar to Bridge. Three Bogies passing to the North on a relative bearing of 010 degrees, Range 38 Miles and closing."

The Captain of the Morton turned to the Executive Officer, "Ted, signal the other two Destroyers that targets are on Radar and should be in sight within another few minutes. Use the signal light, and tell them to standby to execute the turn to follow on my order."

"Aye, Aye, sir!"

The tension was mounting, as the three large Gomer ships began their turn back towards the west headed for Greenland. In the twilight, the lookouts sounded off, "Bridge, we have targets in sight, relative bearing 358 degrees, range …7 miles."

"Exec. Standby to send the execute order."

"Bridge. Radar. The bogies are turning almost due east"

"Roger that. Okay, Exec. Send the signal to execute. Helmsman. Begin the slow turn to a heading of 275 degrees, and make speed to stay behind and at a range of 3 miles."

"Aye, Aye, Sir."

The three-ship formation of Gomers had bypassed Iceland and its rugged sulphuric landscape, and was now on a course directly towards where the Submarines were keeping up the Montana Battlegroup transmissions. Dropping behind and maintaining a range that would allow for closing in behind the ships, the USS Morton and her destroyer flotilla, were lined up and keeping their distance.

Near Grindavik, Iceland:

The flight crews, assault forces, and the accompanying technical personnel were waiting. Lined up and camouflaged from aerial observation, these captured Gomer Fighter Class ships were not wanting to lift off too soon. The Mission Commander, Colonel Basham, waited by the communications equipment on the lead captured Fighter Class ship. He was maintaining a close listening watch on the communications from the USS Morton, while the assault forces in the rear of each Fighter Class ship engaged in the "talk through" of their respective missions. Holly Patrick was especially busy, since she was rapidly modifying the software package to accommodate the changes necessary to control a Mountain Class ship. Fortunately, they had started the process by modifying Mountain Class software for use for the other class ships, so the changes were not unfamiliar to her. The down side was trying to get some of her settings back to "default," and then to process the code for the modifications in the ship's course that would follow later. (She hoped.) Regardless, as busy as she was, the Colonel Basham assigned her two "assault soldiers" as her personal escort, and one of them just wouldn't shut up.

"Ma'am. Is there a chance that this will work?"

"Uh, huh."

"Ma'am. What codes are different?"

"Shit. Sergeant, they are all different, so please shut up so I can work."

"Sorry, Ma'am. I just wondered..."

"Sergeant. I don't mean to be rude, but I've got too much to do to chat!"

"Yes, Ma'am. Still, I need to brief you on the mi..."

"Dammit! If I don't get this done, the mission won't happen, so PLEASE shut the hell up!"

"Yes, Ma'am."

Finally, the soldier got the hint, and left her to the business at hand. She was too busy to feel very nervous, which was probably a good thing. Before the mission changes came through, she was wondering how the heck her Dad had done this sort of thing as a younger man. Now she understood. Sometimes, you're just too busy to be scared, and way too focused to think about the worst things that could happen. Now that she thought about it, she realized that it was probably a good thing that she was too busy to notice these things.

USS Dallas, located in the Denmark Straits, to the west of the USS Morton Destroyer Flotilla:

Transmissions continued as the sleek attack submarine, USS Dallas, continued to present as much of an electronic target as possible. Her sister ships were scattered around the same piece of sea, doing the exact same thing. The plan was simple. With decks awash and an ability to get under quickly, they would continue to send the radio traffic associated with a Search and Rescue operation for a damaged battlegroup. The radiomen had worked overtime, and eventually, it devolved into a lot of meaningless radio chatter. Still the Gomers came on and were now lining up for a strike on their position. Noting that discretion was the better plan, it took all the Captain of the USS Dallas had in the way of moral courage to simply stay this close to the surface. It was a long wait, but he finally got the transmission he wanted to hear through his sonar gear.

"All ships from Hampton. Gomers now launching Fighters. Execute dive and scatter pattern as briefed!"

This was the message they'd all wanted to hear, and the Captain of the Dallas wasted no time to get things moving. "COB, pull the plug! Make depth 2 - 5 - 0 feet, heading 180 degrees, all ahead flank. We're outta here!"

"Dive, Dive, Dive! Helm, standard left Rudder, steady up on 1 - 8 - 0 degrees, level at 2 - 5 - 0 feet!" It didn't take long, and the Dallas was a very serious hole in the water. Now she would head off to the south, and wait.

Denmark Straits, aboard the USS Morton:

Moving along in complete radio silence, the crew of the USS Morton were as anxious as her Skipper. The three Gomer Ships were overhead, and it was clear they were launching a number of fighters. Allowing his speed to drop just a little behind the monsters overhead, the Captain realized that this was going to be a game of timing. All of a sudden, he felt his stomach knot up, and his mind screaming at him that this was suicide if they popped the bubbles too soon. Then again, pop too late, and it all falls apart too. Out loud he simply said, "Dammit. Okay, Bubble Crews, standby. Exec. Signal the rest of them to form up and maintain speed with their Gomer Targets, and await my signal to execute."

"Yessir. Signal from the Gregg, sir."

"Okay, what is it?"

"Sir. Gregg signals that her 'Carrier' Class is NOT, say again NOT, launching any fighters."

"Crap. Okay, make sure to send that signal out, in the clear, as soon as the Bubble static clears!"

"Aye, Aye, Sir."

"Radar. Captain."

"Aye, Captain."

"Radar. What is the Carrier Class position relative to the other Gomers?"

"Sir, she is in the van."

"Exec? Advise Gregg to release her Bubble with the rest of us."

"Aye, Sir."

"Captain. Radar reports 'many bogies' coming from the lead and trail Gomer Ships."

"Roger, standby."

"Captain? They are forming up a strike on the Subs."

"Roger, standby."

"Sir, we have over a hundred Fighter Class ships, directly overhead and heading to the west."

"Roger, Exec. Signal all ships, EXECUTE, EXECUTE!" Within a matter of seconds, each of the destroyers released their Gomer "Bubble" weapons, which spread upward and outward from the flotilla. The energy released was wreaking havoc on all of the fighters, and each of the destroyers then activated their secondary batteries to engage any stragglers. The timing appeared to be just about perfect, since the larger ships were still moving to the west, and the fighters were no longer moving towards their targets.

The static was dissipating, and the energy levels around each of the destroyers was reducing to the point where the next transmissions could go out. "FROM USS MORTON TO SPARTA. TARGETS MOVING 275 FROM MY POSITION. FIGHTERS NEUTRALIZED. CARRIER CLASS DID NOT LAUNCH, SAY AGAIN, DID NOT LAUNCH. YOU ARE CLEAR FOR FOLLOW-ON PHASE."

Near Grindavik, Iceland:

Colonel Basham read the message from the USS Morton in the lead Fighter Class, and immediately advised his mission group to "Get these beasties in the air! Form up on your lead, and follow me. Stick Three Leader, be advised, your target did not launch and may be full. Stick to plan, but if necessary, you are cleared to destroy the target." Each of the captured Fighter Class ships acknowledge the latest change, and then lifted off to form into three groups of Fighters. The Mountain Class ship strike group had four of the captured Fighter Class ships, while the Battleship Class strike group had three ships. Finally, the captured Fighter Class ships destined to strike the Carrier Class was comprised of two of the captured Fighter Class ships.

The plan required that they remain on the ground when the bubbles were fired. They absolutely couldn't afford to take any chances that their ships might be impaired, and it had to appear to the Gomers that they were either reinforcement craft, or that they were returning from an earlier strike somewhere. In either instance, it was important that the large Gomers accepted them at face value. This part of the plan was a real long shot, and everyone on this mission knew it. As they broke ground, they advanced their speed to enter a parabolic arc that would make it appear that they too had transited Iceland to the northern side. Their journey wasn't more than 8 minutes, but now they were lined up behind their respective targets.

Stick One, Chalk One, behind the Mountain Class Ship:

Stick one was lined up with her four other Fighters in a line formation approaching from below and behind the behemoth Mountain Class Gomer. The hanger doors appeared to be open, and the lead ship slowed and then entered into the hanger bay. Each in their turn followed the same way until the three other ships were also inside and landing on the deck. Each ship set down, and within seconds, a number of "meaty" Gomers were attaching lanyard type devices to tie down each of the Fighters. Busy in their tasks, nobody noticed as the back ramps were extended, and the assault troops exited the ships at almost the same instant. Recalling the detailed schematics they'd studied about the Gomer Mountain Class ship, thanks to Dr. Clarkson's early studies of the craft, the teams immediately began their various tasks to move from the hanger area to key locations around the craft. Colonel Basham's first thought, as the assault teams moved rapidly down their ramps, was that this might be the first time in years that anyone could honestly give the command, "Boarders Away."

One team took complete control over the Hanger area and had it secured in less than two minutes. The "meaty" Gomers that were present were either neutralized, captured, or killed, and then the other three teams moved off in their assigned directions. Colonel Basham, his team, along with Dr. Holly Patrick and her escorts, were headed to the control room. Passing several lateral passages that converged into one junction, they left two soldiers to secure that junction from anyone trying to move towards the Control Room to interfere with the operation. Nearing the main entrance to the control room, Colonel Basham waited and then like General Greene during the first Gomer War, he keyed a small hand-held VHF radio. Within seconds the Control Room Door sprang to life, and the assault force rapidly entered with a flash bang grenade followed by a lot of shooting.

Even knowing what they were going to find inside, Dr. Holly Patrick was not ready for the carnage, or the sight of her first real live "Crab Gomer." It took all of her effort to keep from losing her lunch, which was telling, since she'd skipped lunch, being too nervous and busy to eat before the mission. Suppressing her gag reflex, Holly waited until Colonel Basham's men cleared the rest of the control room, and disconnected the "Crab Gomers" from the control systems of the Mountain Class ship. Moving with her case of electronic equipment towards the main control panel, she was able to attach her computer adapter to the Gomer equipment, all despite her violently shaking hands. Flipping open her laptop, she began the process of entering the codes necessary to change the Mountain Class ship's approach to a brand-new location. During the process, she had to stop at least three times just to calm herself down. Her armed escorts were now surrounding her and maintaining watch, as she did her best to keep from being too scared to get her job done.

Finally, after several fits and starts, the Mountain Class Gomer Ship was under her control. The computers were "talking" and the ship was accepting the commands from the program she'd written. Unfortunately, the fight for the ship was far from over. The team headed to the Propulsion compartment, was having a real battle on their hands. From the outset, it was felt vital that this position be taken to ensure that they Gomers couldn't override any commands from the control room. Similarly, the weapons systems had to be shut down, and this was also a source of more combat. The plan for the Battleship and Carrier Class ships weren't quite as complex. In both of those targets, the Control Room was also the control point for the weapons systems, but in the Mountain Class, the size made this an issue. On this monster, it was a whole different arrangement. This is why the fourth team was necessary, even if it left them one team short for the Carrier Class ship.

The original plan had each of the assaults broken down to one assault team for one objective. One team was to take down the Hanger Deck and keep it secure, while the other teams would fan out to take over the Control and Propulsion sections. Now that the Mountain Class was in play, the two remaining teams for the Carrier Class were either going to have to form a third team from their already limited numbers to handle the last section, or they had the option of not securing the hanger deck. This decision was left to the discretion of the team leader, since there was no way of knowing what they might find in the damaged Carrier Class once they were onboard.

Colonel Basham was monitoring the entire operation via his hand-held VHF, and from all reports the Battleship Class was almost completely under control. The only exceptions were some small pockets of resistance that could be handled once that ship landed at the new destination. Their strike went like clockwork, and the plans were absolutely correct, thus allowing the team that rehearsed the operation to find very little different once their assault began. The Carrier Class assault was altogether different. Shorthanded, they had opted to kill everything in sight on entry at the Hanger, and then only leave three men behind to keep their two ships secure. The flight crews also remained on the Hanger Deck, and kept the ships powered up with their main weapons prepared to fire at the entries onto the deck. Gutsy call, but one that allowed them to form three assault teams for the rest of the ship. Their attack went very smoothly, right up until the software was being loaded. Then the glitches began to mount, until it became a very near thing that anyone was able to leave the ship. The already damaged Carrier was hit at or near the computer control banks, and the Sulphur weapon used was eating away at the materials containing the command control sequences. Seeing this, a decision had to be made quickly, and the assault team began fighting their way back out to escape.

The story on the Mountain Class ship was slightly better, but the numbers were much larger. The control systems were not a problem, but the sheer numbers of various types of Gomers onboard made the operation more of a real battle than a skirmish. Upon hearing that the Carrier's two teams were fighting a retrograde operation back to the Hanger Deck, Colonel Basham decided that the thing to do would be for them to move to the Mountain Class Ship as reinforcements. When the last Fighter Class pulled off the Carrier, it fired a Sulphur-tipped Cruise Missile inside, along with a blast from the Fighter Class ship's main Gomer weapon. Pulling away towards the Mountain Class Ship, the Carrier exploded and descended into the Greenland coastline. The force of the blast almost destroyed the two Fighters, but after the shock wave passed, the flight crews were able to bring them back around and onto the Mountain Class ship. Seconds after landing, the Fighters were secured, and their two assault teams were on the way to the propulsion section to reinforce the men already engaged in a fire fight to gain entry. These added forces were vital, and after another 15 minutes, they had the propulsion section secured. Unfortunately, this still wasn't the end of the battle.

Thule, AFB, Greenland:

The drama overhead and in the Denmark Straits was just unfolding when the first of the C-17s began their airborne operation. This time, it wasn't your typical parachute operation but, instead, the first ever combat insertion of the new Aero-Exo-Suit equipped Airborne Division. As the aircraft passed overhead at lower altitude and faster airspeed, the lead elements of the 11th Airborne Division (US) began leaving the aircraft and steering themselves directly onto the Gomer positions around the airfield. The second flight came overhead, and the identically equipped lead elements of the 1st Airborne Division (UK), began their assault on the opposite side of the airfield. General Larkin and Captain Patrick followed in the third flight of aircraft, coming in with the lead elements of the XVIII Corps Headquarters assault personnel. Their target was the Gomer facilities on the south end of the old Thule Air Force Base that was overrun on the second day of this latest Gomer War.

The Gomers had no idea what had hit them and, thanks to the new equipment, their confusion led to their immediate demise. When the aircraft came in with their fourth, fifth, and subsequent waves, the XVIII Corps was in complete control of the facility and all of the areas in and around the airfield. The offloading of the rest of the 11th Airborne Division (US), the 1st Airborne Division (UK), and Corps Headquarters, went without incident. Only a few firefights of any consequence took place, since the Gomers were completely surprised by the sheer force that was applied to their position. The Gomers were not heavily entrenched, and were using the facility as an emergency area for any of the ships that were too wounded to continue. In short, the Gomers had been using Thule as a "stripping" facility, to put as many spare parts back into their system for use on the other side of Greenland at the main Greenland Gomer Base. The fact that the base was so limited in Gomers made the target perfect as a "live fire" exercise, and the first combat test for the new tactics. So far, they had worked like a charm.

Throughout the rest of the day, the 101st Airborne Division (US) (Air Assault), was inserted and began offloading their equipment and helicopters. Thanks to the newer technology and the Gomers' weapons, the assault was completed with only three casualties, and all in under 8 hours. General Larkin was more than ready to receive his new guests, and as twilight approached, he knew he wouldn't have long to wait. His chief concern was to get the Gomer ships under cover and to set up a defense, just in case the Gomers on the other side of Greenland decided to come calling.

South of the Denmark Straits on the USS Montana:

The battle was well underway when the USS Montana left her holding pattern and began making her way up towards the western approaches to Greenland. In the company of her escorts and the USS Iowa, they were to rendezvous with the USS Morton, USS Gregg, and the USS Stephens to close the door to any Gomers that might decide to leave Europe and head to Greenland. Knifing through the waters headed back north, the Commander got the Coded Signal from Colonel Basham. "PHASE ONE COMPLETE!"

"Captain, make this message to the Battlegroup."

"Yessir. Admiral?"

"Group set formation Zulu, expect Morton flotilla to join to starboard. Go to Condition one, and settle into positions as previously assigned. Weapons Tight."

"Aye, Aye, Sir. Oh, Admiral?"

"Yeah, Bob?"

"Sir, does this mean we're not clear to fire on all overhead targets?"

"Yes, it does. Anything that might even remotely be considered friendly is now clear the area, but I still want to make sure we don't tip our hand too early."

"Excellent. Should I pass that on?"

"You bet your ass! I DO NOT want any confusion."

"Aye, Aye, Sir."

"Once the Morton has joined us, let me know. I want to get a message to her skipper the minute she is within light range."

"Yessir."

SAHQ, Lake Summerville, West Virginia:

The most difficult part of any operation is watching it unfold, while you have a complete inability to influence the outcome. I'd been down this road before, but it never got any easier. I know exactly how Eisenhower felt on D-Day, or how MacArthur felt when the invasion of Leyte or Inchon took place. All you can do is watch from a distance, and I wasn't even afforded the opportunity to be on the deck of a ship or in an airplane to personally see it unfold. Throughout the entire ordeal, we were relegated to eavesdropping on the transmissions going back and forth between and among the various commanders making it all fall together. Without a doubt, this was a day for lots of coffee, cigarettes, and pacing. I have little doubt that I drove General Whitney and Admiral Lynch virtually insane with my pacing and peering over their shoulders as each new message came into the Operations Center. General Kaminski was the only one who finally looked at me and said, "Sir. You're going to wear out those shoes if you don't sit down!"

Operation Sparta was moving forward with greater speed now, but the one weak link was still an open issue. General Larkin and the Global Strike Force were well on the way to controlling Thule, the USS Morton had done her bit, and now it was up to the assault teams on the Gomer ships to come through and deliver. Sadly, the information coming from them was far more difficult to obtain. A few transmissions were all that were monitored, right up until the "PHASE ONE COMPLETE" message. For the first time in almost 18 hours, I was able to take a deep breath, at least right up until the next message arrived.

Onboard the Mountain Class Ship, on final approach to Thule Greenland:

Holly was finally sure that the system was going to work, and looked up at her escort and smiled. He had returned her smile with a thumbs up, and then disintegrated before her very eyes. Neither of them saw or heard the first shot but, thankfully, the second Gomer shot missed both her and the remaining escort. This second shot was immediately followed by a huge din of firing erupting all around her. A small contingent of "Meaty" Gomers had entered the Control Room from a panel on the opposite side of the room, and were firing on the command personnel. Colonel Basham rallied his forces, but not before a number of casualties were suffered. Holly was almost in shock, until she realized that the firing had knocked her control system offline. While she didn't know it, the ship was beginning a descent towards the ground.

General Larkin's staff duty officer saw it first, and contacted Colonel Basham to advise him that he was in about a 2000 foot per minute rate of descent. Turning to Holly, Colonel Basham screamed that they were crashing, and she saw that her connection had been broken. It was a very near thing, but at the last second, she was able to regain control. Flaring the Mountain Class Ship after the near crash, the ship landed rather abruptly near the far end of the longest runway. It would be almost a full half hour before the forces on the ground were able to get to them, but the reinforcements were highly welcome. This particular Mountain Class ship was crawling with Gomers, and the fight was rather intense to finally secure the craft. Thankfully, the Battleship Class made a normal landing, and the reinforcements designated for this target had the entire ship clean of any Gomers within an hour.

Thule Greenland, Headquarters of the Global Strike Force:

Colonel Basham reported to General Larkin, and gave him the formal after-action report. When General Larkin read that Dr. Holly Patrick had been on board and had saved them at the last second, he couldn't wait to pass on the message. Sending it coded to SAHQ, he then grinned and waited for what he was sure would be the explosion heard round the world. General Larkin then picked up the field phone to his aide, and advised him to "get your ass down to the Mountain Class Ship, and pick up the Technician. I want her here ASAP. Got it?"

"Yessir. Who is it?"

"Your sister, and I would highly recommend that you bring her back here without a lecture. I have a feeling she will get one far worse than you could ever deliver when her Dad gets her on the line."

"Yessir." Robbie just shook his head, and did as instructed. He knew that somebody's ass was in trouble, but he sure didn't want it to be him. After all, it wasn't him that volunteered, and it sure as hell wasn't something he knew anything about. Shaking his head as he headed down the runway, he remarked to nobody in particular, "Nope, little sis. This time you're on your own!"

Chapter XVI

❧

Supreme Allied Headquarters, (SAHQ), Lake Summersville, WV:

I love my family, but sometimes they drive me more than just a little insane. As word filtered back that we now had possession of a Mountain Class Gomer Ship, I was ecstatic. After all, Dr. Abramson and Dr. Clarkson agreed that this monster would handle sufficient Phoenix material to take the war to Neptune, within a much shorter time line than our current 7 plus years. Moving into our next phase of the operation, General Whitney sidled up to me and whispered into my ear.

"General, you wanted to know who the techie was that saved the Mountain Class?"

"Damn right! I want to decorate them! That was a real lifesaver, and according to Basham's folks, and General Larken, if it wasn't for that person, we'd be on our butts right now."

"Well... Uh..."

"Geez, Whit, what's the problem?"

"Sir, it was Doctor Patrick."

I guess the shock must have shown on my face, because I was literally speechless. With my jaw hanging to my knees, General Whitney continued.

"Sir, I had no idea she was going, and from what I was just told, nobody else knew either."

"Bull shit!"

"Seriously, General Greene swears he didn't have a clue, and didn't find out until Colonel Basham told him a few minutes ago."

"Dammit, Whit, there isn't a thing we can do about it now, but I seriously don't much care for the fact that neither of them had a damn clue beforehand. Especially Basham! His ass lead the mission and the team that took the Mountain Class. Do you expect me to believe he didn't have any idea that she was a stowaway?"

"Colonel Basham said that Holly... excuse me, Doctor Patrick, insisted, and he wasn't going to argue with her."

"Damn. I know where she gets it from, and I am a man of my word. Decorate her ass when she gets back, and trust me, I want her back. She is to report to me personally on arrival, and as soon as they are finished with the reprogram and launch of that big bastard, I want her skinny little ass on a plane to our location."

"Yessir. Oh, and the message from General Larkin, indicates that Doctor Patrick is in Captain Patrick's custody. Any other instructions back to him?"

"Yeah, tell him to leave her alone. She's earned it. Despite being so damn hard headed, she truly did save our asses here."

"Yessir." With that General Whitney smiled at me, and wandered back to the Communications Center.

Not trusting myself to speak, I turned back to the problem at hand. We still had an ongoing operation, and the timing was becoming rather hair-splitting. General Larkin needed to get his forces reorganized to hit the Gomer facilities on the other side of Greenland. This meant that he had his Airmobile and Airborne forces to get ready for the next push that would be just hours away. Then there was the problem with our cyber warriors, scientists, and the ASOC personnel in getting what available ships back flyable, packed with Phoenix materials, and ready to launch.

General Larkin's problems were compounded by having to prepare for the assault while providing security for the scientists who were programming the two captured large units. The Battleship Class and Mountain Class ships were loaded with Phoenix weapon systems, nuclear explosives, and basically turned into giant cruise missiles. This was going to leave us one ship short for Operation Troy, which was a problem, but not an insurmountable problem. General Greene had anticipated this once he got word of the number of ships that were in flight that were captured. Knowing he was one short, he started the process of organizing another capture team to insert with General Larkin's assault on the Gomer's maintenance and supply area in Greenland.

I was summoned to the phone by General Whitney, who advised that Greene was on the line asking for permission to insert this additional team.

"General Greene, Patrick here. Go ahead."

"Sir, as you know we're one bird short. I need your permission to send Colonel Basham's team in with Larkin's forces to get us one more big ship."

"I can approve that with one proviso. I want Doctor Patrick back here ASAP. This time she is NOT to stowaway. Bad enough that she did it once, damned if I'm going to let her tempt fate twice."

"Sir, I think she wants to talk with you."

"Dammit, Daniel, the answer is NO. Listen, it is more than her being my daughter. If this thing goes sideways, then just who the hell is going to be able to accomplish the code breaking she's done to date?

"Well, I can say that we have a few people that are good, but none of them are as adept at reading this crap off like she does."

"My point exactly. Tell her I'm not being sexist, or a parent. I'm being practical. The knowledge she has is vital to the overall war, and not just to some pirate mission to get us another Gomer ship."

"I'll tell her sir, but wouldn't it sound better coming from you?"

"Actually, Daniel, I don't think it would. She needs to hear it from someone else that her ass is more important in cracking code, computing her damn algorithms, and helping us with the big picture. Otherwise, she'll always believe it was because her Dad didn't want her in danger. Besides, it is way the hell too late for that, since we're all already in danger. Now get her ass back here!"

"Yessir."

Hanging up the phone, I realized that she would probably never believe me, and might even hate me for pushing the issue, but she really was the one to get the math right. She was also the only one after her mentor was killed in the last war, to understand what these Gomer bastards were thinking. Nope, it was time to get her back to OUR headquarters.

Thule Greenland, Headquarters of the Global Strike Force:

Holly Patrick was not a very happy camper. She was already consulting with Colonel Basham about the capture of another ship, all while helping with the loading of the Phoenix materials, and keeping her brother Robbie at arm's length. Robbie was strangely quiet about everything, and this scared her. The moment she saw him she was expecting the lecture, and when it didn't come, it was well... unnerving. Instead, she only stopped what she was doing when Colonel Basham sprang to his feet and saluted someone behind her. Turning, she saw General Greene, who looked at her like she had two heads.

"Doctor Patrick, you have orders to get back to SAHQ, so grab your gear, and get your ass moving."

"Sir, does this have to do with my Dad?"

"Nope. You were a stowaway on the last mission, and according to everyone that knows anything about warfare, you should be there and not here."

"That is so much bull, General! I know these things as well as, if not better than, anyone else. I saved this one, didn't I?"

"Yes, you did, and that is exactly why your services here are no longer required. Now get your crap ready to go. Your flight leaves in 5 minutes."

"General. This IS my Dad, and that is definitely bullshit. He's hung himself out my whole life, so he sure doesn't need to worry about me now."

"Dammit, Holly. This isn't a request, and this isn't about your Dad. You have specialized knowledge that is vital to the folks in the rear. All of them. Your Dad being only one. There is also Dr. Clarkson and Dr. Abramson, who both contacted me directly to raise tons of hell. Besides, your knowledge, your security classifications, and your personal involvement with our most senior commanders, makes you an asset that we cannot, by any standard, leave on the front lines."

"But, Sir..."

"God almighty! You are thick headed." Turning from Holly, General Greene looked directly at Captain Patrick. "Captain!"

"Sir?"

"Place Doctor Patrick under arrest, and cuff her ass if you have to. I want her on MY plane out of this place in..." Glancing at his watch, he looked back up and finished, "3 minutes."

"Yes, Sir." Almost before the yes sir got out of his mouth, General Greene was already striding away towards his aide and Colonel Basham. Robbie looked at his sister, and smiled.

"You know, Holly? I've been waiting years to hear someone tell you the deal, and I've waited even longer for the chance to put your butt in handcuffs."

"Oh, screw you Robbie!" Turning away to hide her true feelings from her brother, she gathered up her laptop computer, and started towards General Greene's airplane. She only stopped once, as if to say something, but Robbie held her arm, and whispered.

"Sis, this is a good thing. You know too much, and despite what you might think, we honestly can't afford to lose you."

"Shit. I know it, but sometimes I feel so left out."

"Sis, you're lucky to be alive, and you've earned this ride home. Now go tell Dad how to beat these guys. Okay?"

"Yeah, okay."

Five minutes later, Robbie and General Larkin were standing on the tarmac watching the loading of the initial assault teams for the next part of the operation. Looking behind them, they were just in time to see General Greene's aircraft leave the runway and turn for home. Robbie looked up and for a brief moment felt wistful about his sister and his family. Then realizing that this wasn't the time for such things, he turned back to his General and asked for instructions.

Holly was safely in her seat next to General Greene as the aircraft reached altitude and turned southward. Not having too much time before things would start to pop, they were making their best speed back to AOSC Headquarters at Lake Moomaw, Virginia. After reaching altitude, General Greene handed Holly a disk of the latest intercepts from the Gomers, and then headed in to his in-flight communications center to monitor the events that would transpire during their journey. At the same time as these events, Holly's brother, along with General Larkin, were finishing their final loading and beginning their flight towards the other side of Greenland. As the twilight line advanced, the timing was going to be critical. They wanted to take the occupants of the Gomer Maintenance and Supply base by surprise but, to do that, they needed to hit them at or just before the twilight line reached their location.

On board the last transports to leave Thule were the scientists and cyber warriors belonging to ASOC. Like their boss an hour or so earlier, they were heading back west ahead of the twilight line. Their job was done, and the Mountain Class Ship and her consort, the Battleship Class Ship, were now programed, loaded, and waiting the onset of darkness. Only a handful of security personnel were surrounding these monstrous craft, but the area itself was highly secured with at least two divisions of Airborne troops and a number of Gomer Gun Batteries. The stage was set for Operation Troy, at least the first part of it. Now it would be up to General Larkin's Airborne Army to deliver the last part of the triad.

Denmark Straits on the USS Montana:

The Admiral's bridge on the Montana Class Battleship is an impressive location, but not nearly as impressive as the adjacent Combat Information Center that is available for his use. Before the Gomers, or back in the old days, this place was sterile as possible. There was no smoking and little coffee drinking. Now, thanks to people like General Patrick, this wasn't the case. In fact, the General took the position that men who are about to be harm's way shouldn't have some politically correct crap shoved in their face. Stress is handled by everyone in lots of different ways, and for some the smoke and/or coffee kept others alive.

The Admiral chuckled at Patrick's last remark on the subject as he lit a cigar the last time on board. "Admiral, I can't see the concern over my second-hand smoke. If I don't have one, then I'd just kill them outright now, which means I smoke so others may live just a little while longer!" Knowing the General's reputation, the Admiral had to laugh, since he knew it was probably a quite true statement. Breaking his musing was the approach of his Chief of Staff. Motioning him over, he decided to remind his staff and the Ship's Captain what was about to happen. Before he could begin, the Chief of Staff announced to him, "Sir, the Morton is on station off to our starboard, and we're set on course 185 degrees."

The Admiral nodded his head and then pointed to the chart, "Thank you, Captain. Right now, we're going to maneuver in this area and, in about 15 minutes, I want you to set us up for a race track pattern that runs the formation in the 20-mile box that sets us up near the middle of the straits. Tell the Morton Escort Group to maintain position to our west."

Again, pointing to the chart, the Admiral wanted to make it quite clear that this was going to be their home through the night, and that he wanted the fleet maintained in this specifically prescribed patrol area. Turning back to his Chief of Staff, he continued, "Signal the Iowa, and have her take station directly astern of us. Then confirm that the submarines have set up their picket line along the east coast of Iceland, and along the line running parallel with the west coast. I want all the early warning we can get. Now then, do we have contact with USS Wisconsin and USS North Carolina battle group to our south?"

"Yes, sir. They are still about 100 miles south and west of us, and we still have a full screen of Gomer bubble destroyers."

"Excellent. Tell the Captain I want the hole in the water routine to commence one hour before sundown and, just for giggles, remind our ASW screen to keep their ears to the water. Once the ground operations hit at twilight, I think we're likely to see some company coming our way."

"Aye, aye, sir."

Settling back in his chair, and without thinking, the Admiral leaned back and lit his cigar. Now it was going to be about how this would fall into place. He knew his role was to slow down anything that might disrupt the airborne operations to his west, and while he wasn't sure he could stop a determined attempt by the Gomers to reinforce Greenland, he knew he could probably make a dent in them. Assuming there was no company or surprises from a dissident submarine. For some reason, that idea kept creeping into his mind. Finally, the gut feeling won.

"Chief of Staff?"

"Sir?"

"When is the last time you checked with our submarines?"

"Sir, about 5 minutes ago."

"Do we have any of them in an escort position, or are we relying solely on surface ASW?"

"Sir, all the submarines are out on picket duty, to watch for Gomers."

"Shit, we don't have anyone in position to cover us?"

"Well, sir, we might have one, but she is a bit out of position. Do you want me to move her?"

"Hell, yes! And tell the outer screen to get their aircraft up. We're about two hours out from twilight, and I'll feel a lot better once we get some verification that we don't have a dissident running around in a nuke tracking our every move."

No sooner than the Chief of Staff walked away than he came running back with a report that chilled them to the bone. "Sir, the

USS North Carolina, in the Southern Battlegroup, was just hit by a rocket."

"From where? Submarine?"

"No, sir, a small aircraft at very high altitude that somehow got within their escort ring. Probably flying a known air route. It was low detonation with minimal damage, but it also released a burst of a transmission. Intelligence believes it was a transmitter or homing device to guide in the damn Gomers."

"Well, that's new. Okay, tell the fleet to be on alert accordingly. Oh, and get that information off to SAHQ. Nothing like a new twist to a bad situation. This might mean that we're going to have to keep our sky swept before the Gomers arrive with the twilight line. This also tells me that they're up to something, otherwise they wouldn't have tipped their hand this soon."

"Aye sir. We're on it."

In addition to the Gomers, this time the Chief of Staff left with two more bad things on his plate. Now it wasn't just a submarine problem that could bite them, but there was one that could arise from small aircraft, impressed into service to be the eyes and/or ears for the Gomers. Drawing deeply on the cigar, the Admiral was hoping someone could make sense of what to do about it, and then it hit him. He needed the damn carrier battlegroup to start having a shot. Getting up from his chair, he stepped into CIC, and started drafting the message he hoped would get those Airedales off their asses.

Supreme Allied Headquarters, (SAHQ), Lake Summersville, WV:

The operations in Greenland were well underway, and we were less than two hours away from the initial airborne assaults on the rest of the Gomer's Greenland facilities, when things began to break loose. Within minutes, two pieces of information fell into our laps that were extremely problematic. The first was that the USS North Carolina had been struck from high altitude during daylight by what appeared to be a burst transmission device. There was no yield, minimal detonation, but it did damage one turret of 16" guns aft near the stern. The problem here was twofold. The first, the existence of the device itself was quite new and very Gomer. The second is that it was launched or dropped from an aircraft that shouldn't have been capable of such a payload.

A search was conducted through the veritable mountain of data, both near Earth and surface, to determine where this aircraft came from. The identity of the pilots was simple math, obviously dissident, but where did the plane come from and how could it fly into the middle of Denmark Straits? There should be no dissidents with that capability in that region of the planet. Given the size and range of the type of aircraft used, it become clear rather quickly that it had to come from the very Gomer facility that was now in our sights for the upcoming raid. What drove this point home was that we got another piece of rather interesting information. The device itself came from near Earth when it was fired by a Gomer, and then was targeted in much the same way as our laser guided munitions. In short, a human on board the small airplane lazed the target for the Gomer in near space.

Then we got the final piece of the puzzle, just a mere few minutes before our first forces were to land on the Gomers. An intelligence report trickled in from ASOC that human bodies were found onboard among the dead Gomers on both the Battleship and Mountain Class ships. In short, we had to worry about humans being the eyes and ears for the Gomers as they transited ocean areas. Now we had a new problem which was going to cause the Navy some serious headaches. Through two wars, and now most of this war, the "hole in the water" tactics were infallible for our large ships. Now there was about to be yet another paradigm shift.

Fortunately, Admirals Lynch and Steadman had a plan for just such a contingency. Unfortunately, it was probably too late to put into action for the current operations. For them, they could only hope that the deployed assets could make things happen to preserve themselves in the meantime, especially given the import of the goal of what was coming. The good news was that, while the USS North Carolina and probably the USS Wisconsin had been spotted, the USS Montana and USS Iowa were still un-noticed. At least we hoped that was the case. Immediate orders were sent out. The Southern Battlegroup was now headed away from the area into a new position to their east closer to the coast, while their submarine group was maintaining position to spot Gomer traffic and to guide any offensive weapons they could into that area.

Denmark Straits on the USS Montana:

Reading the message from SAHQ, the Admiral was not exactly thrilled. Now he knew what the situation was, but he found little comfort in knowing that he was going to be on his own. He did get two P-8 aircraft out of Iceland who would patrol around him until the twilight was on top of him, and then there was a fighter escort out of Iceland that would then refuel in midair, and continue into Nova Scotia or Thule ahead of the twilight line. Sadly, it was the best they could do for air cover, since sending an Aircraft Carrier into that mess would have been suicide. While you might be able to hide the battleship along the coast line, a carrier with that flat deck that runs forever? It would be like trying to hide an elephant in an envelope.

Turning to his Chief of Staff, the Admiral passed off the message and added, "Well, Barney, we're on our own and, according to Admiral Lynch, the only tactical change they can give us is that we should get our licks in first, and hard, and then run like hell."

"Shit, that isn't a plan, that is wishful thinking."

"Yeah, I know. One thing we can do is send our small boys well to the east of us, and let them cook the bubble off as soon as the bastards start launching. That might keep the little stuff off us long enough to take out the big stuff."

"I don't like it, Admiral. Granted it is a plan, but I would just point out that even that is premised on wishful thinking."

"I agree, Captain, but it isn't like I've got a damn choice." Looking at his watch, he added, "In about 10 minutes, the sky about 100 miles west of us is going to be full of C-17 aircraft and thousands of men. So, I guess our only real option is to make it work with what we've got."

50 miles to the west of the Gomer Maintenance and Supply Facility, Greenland:

Under observation by our Inuit ASOC personnel for weeks, the plan and drop locations were well mapped out. General Larkin knew that the preparation was as complete as it could be, and he also knew damn well that it was now or never. It was right before they reached the initial point, or IP, to turn for the drop zones, when the General was snapped from his thoughts by the young airman handing him an intelligence message that had just been sent out from SAHQ.

IMMEDIATE FLASH

TO: Commander First Allied Army
FROM: Supreme Allied Commander, G-2

Be advised. Dissidents believed to be operating as visual observers for the Gomers, and have been integrated into Gomer flight crews. We have direct evidence that dissidents were present and on board recently Destroyed Gomer craft, and are recently responsible for damage to major naval unit by lazing the target for a strike from space. Act and be on alert accordingly. All such dissidents in company of Gomers are to be handled with the same, say again, same Rules of Engagement as in place for Gomer personnel. Finally, be prepared for possible counter artillery fire, air, or possibly other support through the same lazing process as used on naval unit.

General Larkin was about to stuff the message form into his pocket, and then decided to show it to his aide. Captain Patrick read it, and handed it back. Looking around in the loud aircraft, the General spotted his G-2 and G-3 sitting down the row, motioning them over, they read the message. Knowing that they were limited in communications and not wanting to be overheard, they all nodded their understand. This was definitely a new wrinkle, but it didn't upset the primary focus of his plan at all. They would get in fast, hit hard, and take no prisoners.

Chapter XVII

※

Supreme Allied Headquarters, (SAHQ), Lake Summersville, WV:

Watching a clock and waiting was the hardest thing to do, but here they were, doing it. As the clock ticked over, where things had been silent just second before, all were in a manic scurry of activity. The messages were beginning to come in all at once, and watching the staff react was like watching a large hive of bees being kicked over. The first information was that the Airborne operation was now officially underway. It was only a few moments later that the next critical information rolled in. The picket submarines nearest the UK were picking up a large flight of Gomer ships leaving the North Sea areas. Meanwhile, General McDaniel was on the phone with the news that a large formation had left the Siberian area, and was also entering space to follow the twilight line. We were also getting a number of other reports from our command in the Pacific. No question, things were starting to unfold, and it was about to get very interesting.

Gomer Maintenance Facility, Greenland:

The first C-17s were over their assigned drop zones like clockwork. As the ramps came down, the Exo-suit-A troopers were moving off the ramp at record speeds. These were followed a few minutes later with more conventional Exo-suit forces equipped with the old-fashioned parachute. The assault itself was swift and relentless. The Gomers on the ground, who'd been anxiously awaiting reinforcements from their own forces, were largely out-gunned and overwhelmed within the first thirty minutes. As full twilight finally descended on the scene, the situation was well in hand, and General Larkin was quite pleased with the progress of the operation. He was equally pleased to learn that the covering forces were already in position, and that the limited facilities were already being controlled completely by our own personnel. Now it was a matter of waiting for the bad guys to show up.

In the interim, the plane load of technicians, cyber warriors, and ASOC personnel showed up, along with all the equipment they needed to try and secure one more large Gomer ship. The pickings on the ground were slim, but there was a Carrier Class that was on the ground with a great deal of damage. It didn't take long for them to realize that this wasn't going to be something they could get off the ground anytime soon. Taking their cue from their back up plan, they took up positions near the docking area, in hopes that someone like a really stupid Gomer might deliver them one in one piece. In the meantime, the few dissidents and their conventional equipment on the ground were also rounded up or destroyed. So far, this was a text book operation, and our casualties were very minimal. Fortunately for our ground forces, the Gomers weren't as concerned about losing their base by ground or air attack, but instead seemed to be far more focused completely on trying to find and destroy the Navy.

USS Montana Battle Group, now located in the Denmark Straits:

The USS Montana was being followed in trail by the USS Iowa, and both had their large guns trained out towards the advance of the Gomers. Their escorts were arrayed around them as part of the ASW screen, but each was prepared and equipped to fire their Gomer Bubbles at a moment's notice. Almost 35 miles to their east was the USS Morton and her destroyer flotilla, while scattered even further east were the seven attack submarines, USS Dallas, USS Rickover, USS Oklahoma City, USS Newport News, USS Charlotte, USS Hampton, and USS Toledo. Overhead was a flight of F/A 18 aircraft, while off to the south and west, were two P-8 aircraft maintaining an ASW patrol. Further to the west, over Greenland, was an AWACS from the Air Force, along with her fighter escort.

As the Gomers continued to advance, it was clear that they were heading towards the former location of the USS North Carolina and the USS Wisconsin Battlegroup. As in earlier battles, those ships were now trying to get clear the area, while their submarine counterparts were still making sufficient noise to lead the Gomers into believing that maybe they were still near where the dissident spotted them earlier. The fighter aircraft in support of this Battlegroup were already starting to pick up radar images of the approaching force, and as targets appeared in range, they released their X-51A missiles at the larger targets the moment they were locked into their firing systems. Once their weapons were expended, they turned for their mid-air refueling points, then headed for Thule, Greenland. Once there, they would either refuel for the flight into Canada, or rearm as necessary for the defense of the base.

The main formation of Gomer Ships continued along their course, and it appeared that they were searching for the chance to hit the North Carolina and the Wisconsin Battlegroup. This was a fortunate break for all involved, since this bought the USS Montana Battlegroup some valuable time to reset her defensive posture in light of the latest intelligence. Aircraft from the west of the twilight line were also able to get their licks in on the lead Gomer ships, while the USS Morton and her destroyer flotilla were able to expand their distance from the Montana. Their plan was simple; they hoped to create a kill box through which the Gomer Fleet must enter. In the coming hours, this just might make the difference if they had to release their Gomer bubbles and main armament. In the interim, the aircraft flying cover over the Montana Battlegroup started picking up targets from the advancing Gomers. As before, when the Gomers came within range to the south and east of their position, the aircraft began their aerial assault with the X-51A missile system.

The Admiral in command of the Montana Battlegroup noticed that while Gomer losses were starting to mount significantly in the air, it still wasn't sufficient to forestall the onslaught that everyone knew was coming directly towards them. As everyone on the USS Montana watched, the twilight line was now moving overhead, and their radar indicated that the Gomers were starting to turn northwest in their direction. The Admiral, knowing that the Gomers had human eyes onboard their ships, could only sigh when the information was passed to him. Then information came in which seemed ominous at first. The Admiral learned that the entire Gomer Fleet formation was making a sudden right turn that was going to take them almost due north! Some of the Gomer Fleet was now going to transit to the east of the USS Morton and the rest of her flotilla, taking both the Montana Battlegroup and his best escorts out of the game.

Re-captured Air Base, Thule, Greenland:

The first squadron of naval aircraft was on short final to land for refuel and rearming, just as the twilight line started to reach Thule. It was then they noticed that two large Gomer ships were starting to lift off the ground. One was of the Mountain Class while the other was a Battleship Class. During the briefing, and then later in flight, the Air/Ground Controllers warned them not to react to anything unusual on the ground at Thule. The instructions had been most specific. After arrival, they were to taxi to the east side of the runway clear of all other traffic, and move directly to what should be the rearming point. Still, despite the warnings of "unusual activity on the ground," it was a particularly scary sight to see the two behemoths lifting from the ground and heading west with the twilight line. It was so unnerving that the first few aviators that spotted them in the lift-off mode were taken aback to the point that one of them did a complete go-around of the field. After getting his ass chewed by the lead Controller, the young aviator re-entered the pattern, and landed without further incident.

As each of the Gomer ships left to the west, they were seen on radar until they lifted clear of the atmosphere, and departed outward into space. From here, General McDaniel's personnel took over the observation of the craft. Shortly thereafter, two of the specially outfitted Fighter Class ships took up escort positions, and together they turned towards the outbound course that would take them to Neptune and Triton. Operation Troy was now underway, and it was with many fingers crossed that they would be allowed to complete their mission unmolested by any Gomers along the way. For one thing, both of these monsters appeared to be damaged, which was the intention, and for another, the drone versions of the Fighter Class ships were fully prepared to take whatever steps were necessary to protect their charges. Now we could only watch and wait on that part of the plan to come to fruition. It would be up to General McDaniel to track the trojan horses and to ride herd on the rest of Operation Troy. Meanwhile, the rest of us still had the war to fight.

Supreme Allied Headquarters, (SAHQ), Lake Summersville, WV:

The largest challenge for a centrally located command, in what is truly a global war, is the simple timing of it all. When it is dawn or twilight depends on where you are on the planet, and as the twilight line dictated much of our planning throughout these Gomer wars, sometimes you just had to roll the dice to make things work. Now was just such a time. It was dawn in the Pacific Theater Operating Area, and this meant that the offensive use of certain key weapons on the Eastern Gomer Enclaves were all launched from the daylight into areas that were just experiencing dawn. The timing of this assault was critical to the actions taking place in Greenland, and it was the first use of the "Gomer Bubble" Phoenix based weapons system on the ground. We opted for this part of the world, simply because of the sparseness of any civilian populations that might be in harm's way. It was not optimal, but it was hoped that it would give the Gomers something to ponder, and maybe take some of the heat off the folks in the Denmark Strait and in Greenland.

While monitoring the battle to our North, both in Greenland and in the Denmark Straits, we were also now starting a major offensive in the Pacific, which was all timed to coincide with the launching of Operation Troy. At the very instant we were being advised that the captured Gomer ships were departing the airspace near Thule, on their way to Neptune and Triton, the first Phoenix ever used on earth was unleashed. We also detonated a smaller, but higher yield, nuclear weapon, one of our Sulphur isotope-based devices, over the eastern most Gomer enclave. To say the very least, the impacts of both these weapons systems were devastating to both the Gomers and the dissidents who were foolish enough to be at or near their Gomer hosts.

While we knew that the "gomer bubble" could be a killer for anyone out in the open, we had no idea that the devastation would be this complete. The reports coming in from our forces, who were all in a position to observe, made it quite clear that all resistance in and around the eastern Gomer Enclaves had ceased completely. Adding insult to the Gomers' injury, the small yield nuclear Sulphur weapon took out the Gomer's series of dish and weapon devices that were constructed in that area. Now there was nothing there, much less anything pointed back to their home base on Neptune. The Phoenix had done such a complete cleansing of the area that some initial reports were about destruction so complete, that it appeared to take out the dissidents and Gomers alike, on almost the cellular level.

It can now be admitted that the success of those weapons was so overwhelming and unexpected on both sides, that the impact on the Gomers and their tactics elsewhere was almost instantaneous. The ships moving towards the Denmark Straits immediately moved first due north, and then into near Earth orbit well clear of any shipping we had in the Denmark Straits. Thereafter, they moved into a much higher orbit that took them virtually back to the inner edges of our space mine field, that was sown between Earth and the Moon. At the same time, the Gomers and their dissident forces in the western and central Enclaves also withdrew from most of their advance positions, and took steps to tighten their perimeters under much deeper shelter.

Within hours, almost all of the Gomer ships began to restrict their flight paths to the more northern polar region to avoid any contact with humans. At this point their tactics appeared to be in the process of being modified to compensate for the new threat. At least for the moment, they would only drop down to attack some of our leading units that were still surrounding the Gomer Enclaves, but even then, only if they advanced too close to the newly established perimeters set in place after the initial reduction of the eastern Enclaves. With almost a trench mentality, so prevalent during the First World War, both sides were now starting to dig in hard and deep.

While part of me wanted to keep the advance going with the momentum we'd built up from the first attack on the Far Eastern Enclave, I knew that I was going to need to wrap up the Greenland battle first, and get my assault forces ready to move again. In the meantime, President Dubronin wasn't sitting on his thumbs. He, too, was making plans for an offensive of a different type. His goal was the elimination of the dissident forces, while mine was the elimination of all our enemies. I think he was seeing things a little more personally, and while this troubled me, it wasn't something I could do much about at the moment. At least we were now on the offensive and, with an ever-watchful eye, General McDaniel kept our delivery on course and monitored all traffic headed our way from Neptune.

Then there was the question of the damage done by the original Phoenix II Missile strike. Our resident scientists, Drs. Clarkson and Abramson and their staffs, were rather surprised at the extent of damage, and a very real concern developed about any continued use in the more populated and built-up areas surrounding the more western Enclaves. There was no question that Phoenix and the Gomer Bubble worked, but perhaps too well, since we couldn't be sure of the long-term impacts on its use. Blasting snow and ice in a remote part of Russia was one thing, but when we thought about what it would do to more built-up areas, we had to do some serious evaluation of whether it would be appropriate to continue using such a weapon here on Earth.

It took two days before someone suggested the modification of the Naval version of the Gomer Bubble for possible use by armored forces, and from this the process we began to develop the project further. Unfortunately, we didn't have time to see this to fruition. As always, the enemy wasn't working from our timetable, and as might be expected, they had learned from their mistakes and altered their tactics accordingly.

Command Post #1, Vandenberg Air Force Base, California:

The midnight watch, or midwatch, personnel normally were fighting sleep, but since the launch of Operation Troy, they were working with far more adrenalin than usual. Buried several hundred feet below the earth, this was the headquarters that fought the space part of the War. As a result, they had a lot on their plate at the moment. The monitoring of airspace, coupled with their drone work using the captured Fighter Class ships, was enough to keep anyone busy. Then there were their normal duties of monitoring the near-Earth space, for both strategic and tactical purposes for the forces deployed around the world. They also maintained control and replenishment of all the mine fields between Earth and the Moon, and they were responsible for the launching and monitoring of all offensive nuclear/conventional missile activity, headed into space.

Throughout the first two Gomer Wars, the facility itself, or at least the launching portion of the facility, had been seriously threatened one time. Thanks to the sacrifice of several naval units, the attack that would eventually have caused serious damages to the local launchers was thwarted. This time there were no guarding naval task forces in the area. This time they were all on their own. This time General McDaniel had a surprise or two for the Gomers, but then again, they had one or two of their own for him.

"Officer of the Watch? NE6 Terminal, we have something, sir."

Stopping in the middle of his conversation with a young airman, the Colonel in charge of the Watch immediately moved behind the terminal of a Master Sergeant manning the Near Earth Terminal that was assigned Sector 6. "Okay, Sergeant. Whatcha got?"

"Sir, it looks as though we have a massing of Gomers, and damned if it doesn't look like they're overhead of us here."

Without hesitation, the Colonel said, "Shit. Hit the Alarm, go to Red, and contact the General." Then turning back to the terminal, he asked, "How long have they been building up, and how long do you think we might have?"

"Sir, if they operate like normal, then we should have about three minutes."

As the Klaxon was sounding there was much scurrying around the room and throughout the entire facility. The Colonel's concern wasn't that they would be hit with sufficient force to destroy their command post, but he knew that any air attack would sure play hob with their outside launchers. As he turned back to contact the General on the direct line to his bunker located 15 miles away under the desert, the lights went out.

Command Post #3, Vandenberg Air Force Base, California:

Command Post #3 was a brand-new facility, and one that was made to withstand even the hit from a Mountain Class ship. State of the Art, it was equipped with even better equipment than Command Post #1. General McDaniel's foresight was what made this happen and, despite having dodged a large bullet in the last wars, he wasn't about to sit back and wait for what he knew was inevitable. After the hit on Diamond Head in the first Gomer War, then the destruction of both Dutch Harbor in the last war, and Tiger Island in this one, the General could see how the Gomers' tactics were going to eventually lead to this day. He wasn't surprised. Pissed off maybe, but definitely not surprised.

Within seconds after the Alert was sounded by Command Post #1, the General was headed to Command Post #3. Skidding through the door into the main control room, he arrived in time to see the demise of both Command Post #1, as well as the local launchers in that vicinity. From this vantage point, he also witnessed the destruction of Command Post#2, as a Mountain Class Ship released a blast over that location and reduced the entire area to complete rubble. The entire strike on his beloved missilemen lasted less than 4 minutes from the initial report of the Gomers massing in space until the complete destruction of both Command Posts #1 and #2.

There was no question, the Gomers had tracked the missiles used on the Eastern Enclave back to General McDaniel's two other locations at Vandenberg. Wasting little time to ponder the dead, General McDaniel was contacting SAHQ to get them up to speed on what just happened.

"Get me General Patrick." The voice on the other end appeared to be alert, but confused... "Yes sir, and you would be?"

"Goddamit, this is McDaniel! Now get me Patrick!"

"Sir? General McDaniel? Can you authenticate?"

"Authenticate my ass, get me Patrick on the FUCKING PHONE or I will personally drive my ass to West by-God Virginia, and neuter you and your damn daddy!"

"Yes, sir." With that, there was a moment's silence, then the line got live again, "Mac?"

"Dammit, Sir, what's with all this bull shit about authenticate? I just had my ass handed to me by the bad guys, and this shithead wants my access code?"

"Yeah, well that is probably because we thought your ass was dead. I just got rousted to watch you guys get nailed. Now how bad is it, and where are we with ongoing operations?"

"Sir, first of all, we're still operational. Local launchers are a total loss, except for a few tucked away at a third location. The new command post is operational, but we're still working out a few bugs. The ongoing operation you're most worried about was being controlled elsewhere, so that is fine. Right about now, I can tell you that I've got 100% loss on my two other command nodes, which limits my vision somewhat."

"Okay, what can we do to help?"

"Right now, nothing, sir, unless you can get some of your boys on the air staff to assist in the monitoring from either your location, or over at Greene's location."

"I can do both. Now what else can we do?"

"Sir, give me a Red Dragon authorization, and I will give those bastards an enema they won't forget."

"Oh? What do you have in mind besides vengeance?"

"I want to bait the bastards, and then blast their asses when they mass."

"Okay, I'll bite, Mac. How are you going to bait them, and what are you going to use as bait?"

"I'm going to let them get a look at my last batch of launchers in this area, by stuffing another Sulphur Isotope up their asses in the Eastern area."

"Give me 12 hours, and you can do it over their most eastern Enclave in the Central area. That way you're not completely wasting the shot."

"Done, Sir. Now about the Red Dragon?"

"You've got it, but let me confirm with the boss first. That is the biggest reason for needing the 12 hours. Well, that, and the fact that Troy should be a lot closer to the target by then."

"I assume you want to hit them about the same time as Troy, or maybe just a little before?"

"That's right, Mac."

"Sir, I'll set it up on this end. Just get me permission to use the Red Dragon."

"I'll work on it. Still, I'm very sorry about your losses, Mac, and if you need personnel, just let me know and I'll get someone off their asses and on their way to you ASAP." Hanging up the phone, there was no question in McDaniel's mind. It was time to give the bastards a very nasty surprise.

Supreme Allied Headquarters, (SAHQ), Lake Summersville, WV:

General Whitney and the rest of the staff weren't completely comfortable about our loss of vision out of Vandenberg. While

General McDaniel's remaining Command Post was operational, there was some concern about the lack of redundancy from his location. There was also a great deal of concern over the Gomers' change in tactics in tracking back the source of our missile launches. Fortunately, my concerns were lessened when both Admiral Lynch and Admiral Steadman reminded me of our submarine capabilities for providing on-target support that could not be tracked back to the source. I also knew that we could pick up the slack for General McDaniel's people, if necessary, out of our other facilities at Site X.

After getting off the phone with McDaniel, I immediately got on the line to brief the President. After relating the change of tactics, I sought permission to bait the hook and then see if we couldn't disrupt things for the bad guys. After some discussion, it was finally approved as an additional part of Operation Sparta, and as a precursor to the execution of Operation Troy. This gave us a smaller window for making it come about, but with some brilliant staff work between General McDaniel and General Whitney the timetable was finally developed. Now if only the Gomers cooperated.

While Generals McDaniel and Whitney were working on their timetable, a very fortuitous message arrived from General Larkin.

FLASH IMMEDIATE

CLASSIFIED: TOP SECRET - EYES ONLY ADDRESSEE

TO: CDR, SAHQ
FROM: CDR, FIRST ALLIED ABN ARMY

1. GIANT HAS SECURED ADDITIONAL GROUP OF FULLY OPERATIONAL ENEMY CRAFT, TYPES AND NUMBERS AS FOLLOWS:

    1 MOUNTAIN CLASS
    4 BATTLESHIP CLASS

   5 CARRIER CLASS
   18 FIGHTER CLASS

2. **GIANT HAS FURTHER SECURED NUMEROUS PARTS AND MATERIAL USED IN SUPPORT OF ABOVE.**

3. **BELIEVED THAT ADDITIONAL ASSETS CAN BE DERIVED FROM THE PARTS, ETC., REFERENCED IN PARAGRAPH 2.**

4. **POTENTIAL FLYABLE AND/OR REPAIRABLE ASSETS ARE AS FOLLOWS:**

   3 MOUNTAIN CLASS
   10 BATTLESHIP CLASS
   24 CARRIER CLASS
   214 FIGHTER CLASS
   35 SMALLER TRANSPORT CLASS
   24 SERVICE CLASS

5. **GIANT REQUESTS INSTRUCTIONS FOR IMMEDIATE DISPOSITION FROM MOUSE.**

Reading the decrypted message, I got General Greene on the line at his Headquarters underneath Lake Moomaw. "Daniel?"

"Yes, General? What can I do for you?"

"Have you heard about Giant's haul up north?"

"Yes, sir, but no real details."

"Okay, let me keep this short then. You need to get a full assessment team up there ASAP, and get me a read out on what is usable in the immediate term. I'll also need to know what isn't usable in the near term, and what you can do to get any of them in the air with a real crew."

"Excuse me?"

"You heard me. Can we fly any of them with a real crew?"

"Yessir, I know we can. I've got several teams training to do just that even as we speak."

"How soon before they're ready then?"

"That depends a lot on Doctor Patrick. She is the one handling the training."

"Okay, find out and get back to me. Oh, and let me make one thing perfectly clear..."

Cutting me off before I could complete my sentence, General Greene responded, "General, I already know what you're going to say... Let me guess, you don't want her to be flying one of the damn things."

"Well, smart ass, it just so happens that what I was GOING to say was that she could fly one, but only as a last resort. You know what is at stake, and honestly, I need her skills for later, but then again, if she is the only one that can get one of the damn things off the ground, then so be it."

"Yessir. Well, you'll be happy to know that this time around, we've got someone who can fly it quite well. Seems that Colonel Basham has taken to it like a duck to water."

"Excellent! Get me the read out on how many teams you can put into the air, and then get with Giant to see how many of his boys you can cram into one of those damn things."

"Yessir. Consider it done."

Hanging up the line, I knew we finally had our real Trojan horse for more local use. Now the hard part was going to be getting all of these things to finally hit at the right time. A feat I wasn't holding my breath over by any stretch of the imagination. Turning to the Communications section, I said, "Get me General McDaniel on the line, and make it a conference call with Admiral Steadman." Then turning to General Whitney, I told him to "have General Larkin and my theater commander's liaison persons report to me here in 30 minutes. It seems that it is time for one serious prayer meeting..."

Chapter XVIII

The Captured Gomer Maintenance and Supply facility, Greenland:

The waiting to go is always the hardest part, and Captain Robert Patrick was feeling that very emotion. His boss, General Larkin, was ramming things in forty directions but, as an Aide, he was feeling wholly inadequate in his attempts to keep up with the "old man." One thing he was happy about was that General Larkin insisted on joining the mission onboard one of the three Gomer Battleships that were tasked with this mission. Their ASOC flight crew had just arrived, and were going through the software that was provided to them by his own sister, Doctor Patrick. It took almost two full hours, but then the General gave the green light for the assault contingents to begin loading. As he watched, almost a division of Exo-suited troopers were bounding into the first Battleship with all their equipment. Then looking over at the Battleship parked next to them, he saw that there was another major upload taking place of about the same numbers and compositions as the first one. The General was rather clear on the point that, while they were carrying reserve forces, under no circumstances were the Command Staff to exit their craft. They were going to observe and report, and basically were there only to lead from the front. Still, Robbie couldn't help but notice that another contingent of Exo-troopers were loading on board their own ship that was equal in size to everyone else.

Command Post #3, Vandenberg, Air Force Base, California:

General McDaniel's personnel were making final preparations for their own mission. They were about to launch a major strike on the Central and most Western Gomer Enclaves. This time they couldn't use their Phoenix II system for a ground bubble, but they sure could use the old tactical nuclear Sulphur Isotope weapons. Using their last local launching systems, they were doing the final calculations for the massive launching that was a mere hour away. Noting that the global plan had to hit certain phase lines prior to launch, they were naturally maintaining a constant scan of both the sky and their teletype information about other theaters and their operations.

While everything else was moving forward with the missile launch preparation, a report came to General McDaniel directly from the "HIGH Sky Watch" section of his headquarters. This group was dedicated to maintaining a 24/7 vigil on both Neptune and Triton, and in watching the course of the two ships dispatched on Operation Troy. The word from there was pretty straight forward. They had observed a significant launching of a number of Gomer Ships within the last hour, and this armada was seen lifting clear of both Triton and Neptune. Noting the time, course, and speed, the High Sky section estimated the arrival of a significant alien force within the next 4 to 5 days. The launch was a mixed bag of news, and General McDaniel wasted no time in grabbing the direct line to SAHQ.

"General Patrick available? We have a little problem."

Taking the line, I knew that we were only looking at our first glitch of the day. "Okay, Mac, what is it?"

"General, the bad news is that we've got an armada of the bastards headed our way."

"Define armada, Mac?"

"Sir, from what I can tell there are two Moon Class, four Mountain Class, and around a dozen of their Battleship Class ships headed this way."

"That it, Mac?"

"Well, no. There are at least another 40 plus of the Carrier Class, and your boys can do the math on the rest of the fleet."

"Shit! Okay, you said that was the bad news, is there any good news?"

"Actually, there is, Sir. The points of departure are completely consistent with our other observations, which means that our own Operation in their direction should be right on the money."

"Well, at least that's something. Anything else?"

"Maybe? I'm not sure yet, but since we've sent something their way earlier, we might be able to detonate it when this new fleet gets closer? At least that is one idea."

"Seriously, give it some thought, grab your slide rule, and get back to me. If that is an option, I need to know it for the President's consideration."

"Roger that, sir. In the meantime, everything else is set in the green, and we are prepared to launch on command."

"Excellent. I'll let you know when our delivery boys are airborne." With that, McDaniel hung up the line.

Supreme Allied Headquarters, (SAHQ), Lake Summersville, WV:

After hanging up with Vandenberg, I directed General Whitney to start the countdown for the assault to launch from Greenland.

Our window of opportunity was closing and, new fleet of Gomers or not, we needed to run with what we already had ready to launch. Then I did the only thing I could do for the moment. I lit a smoke, and leaned back trying hard not to pace the room like a nervous expectant father. Unlike my son in Greenland, I had long known that one of the worst parts of going into combat might be the waiting. For me it was always a toss-up between the waiting or the feelings that would envelope you once it was over. The adrenalin as it is draining from you afterwards is almost like someone opened the drain on your soul.

The word came in via VLF message that General Larkin's assault was ready to launch from Greenland, and as the ASOC personnel were starting to lift off on their flights from Greenland, I advised General McDaniel to launch his operation to hit the Enclaves. Within minutes two things were happening. The Battleship Class ships with General Larkin and his men were lifting from Greenland, and heading out into a wider near-Earth orbit above the North Pole, with the plan to eventually circle back towards Russia. Simultaneously, four high yield nuclear missiles of the Sulphur Isotope variety were winging their way from Vandenberg towards the Western and Central Gomer Enclaves in Russia. Within about 35 minutes, the missiles struck their targets, and did what General McDaniel anticipated. The hornet's nest was stirred.

Command Post #3, Vandenberg, Air Force Base, California:

General McDaniel was drinking coffee like a fiend and, as his staff looked on, he was literally eating his cigars. When his Chief of Staff advised that the missiles had found their targets, he couldn't help but stride over to the NE6 monitoring station. Leaning over the Sergeant seated there, he asked, "Anything yet?"

"No, sir. Nothing as of ye..." before he could finish his sentence two things happened. The first was that two Gomer ships slid into position on the monitor. The second was that the General was already moving away at high speed towards the command launch station. As the Sergeant continued to watch, he saw that within mere seconds, there were now four Gomer ships, with another really large one pulling into position. Without turning around, he announced on his microphone, "Status Hot. We have a Mountain Class ship, along with at least four Carrier Class at center line alpha."

No sooner than the Sergeant's brief announcement, General McDaniel was hitting the VLF scrambler with the command to Launch. Without any delay, the Chief of Staff himself was typing in the pre-registered coordinates for that point in space designated as "center line alpha." Now timing was critical, since they had to get their licks in with the Red Dragon before the big Mountain Class Ship took the shot from 125 miles out. The entire process took less than a minute, but when you're staring down the barrel of a Mountain Class ship, that is still an eternity. Once the Red Dragon left the launching tubes of the Virginia Class submarine, the wait was unbearable.

General McDaniel strode back to the NE6 console, and put his hand on the Sergeant's shoulder as he leaned in to see the unfolding events. It was clear that the little attack fleet was now assembled and starting to get in the range of 125 miles for firing their main weapons. Watching the track of the outbound Red Dragon, as it began to converge with the Gomer's firing point, was absolutely nerve-wracking, yet not a soul in the Command Center moved a muscle. More to the point, if you'd found anyone that wasn't holding their breath, you'd have found someone that was in a coma. The tracking information on the big board was now clicking in increments that seemed to be in slow motion. Glancing back at the NE6 monitor, General McDaniel saw the flash of something on screen, and then the screen went dark.

Attack Force, onboard General Larkin's Gomer Battleship:

The ASOC liaison to General Larkin's staff approached and smiled, "General? Sir, we got the 'shot out' from Vandenberg about 36 minutes ago, and now we've got confirmation of some good hits from the boys in Russia. It seems the Gomers are scrambling a force to hit Vandenberg."

"Thank you, Colonel." Turning to his Aide, General Larkin continued, "Head up front and monitor the outbound traffic from the two major Targets. We're going to wait and then head in after their counter strike. Make the SOBs more likely to think we're returning from the raid."

"Yes, sir." Scurrying off, the General was lost in his own thoughts, until it hit him of his best opportunity yet. Looking up at the ASOC Colonel, he said, "Colonel? What kind of weapons does this damn thing have, and can you use them?"

"Sir, we're packing the standard Gomer systems, but they're not modified for our use, and they don't have our beefed-up package to make them more efficient."

"Darn, I was hoping to hit anyone that might return to their base."

"Well, in that case, Sir, I think we might have at least a shot at slowing them down, and if not, we do have one other ace in the hole."

"What's that, Colonel?"

"Sir, we've got a handful of Fighter Class ships onboard, and they ARE equipped with our modifications."

"Good, get them ready."

"Sir, with all due respect, we'd already thought about that one, and General Greene has given the crew orders to launch those on short final to the assault."

"Bastard always plays it close to the vest, doesn't he?"

The young ASOC Colonel simply smiled and gave General Larkin a thumbs up.

As he was headed back towards the flight deck, Captain Patrick sat back down next to his boss. "Sir? The Gomers took the bait. Seems they're launching their strike out of our target area against the launchers at Vandenberg."

"Okay, Captain, get the boys up and send the execute signal. We're going in."

"Yessir. Flight crew advises that we're about three minutes from the insertion at both Enclaves."

"Excellent. Go to radio silence. No emissions!"

Most Western Gomer Enclave:

It can only be guessed what the Gomers thought, not that anyone was particularly interested in asking the question, as the attacking Gomer Battleship entered the airspace above their position. Flaring, and then setting down in the obvious berth for such a craft, the few Gomers who were present for the landing didn't live long enough to venture an opinion as to their surprise. As the hatches opened, the Exo-suited troopers poured out, with their own version of the Gomer hand-held weapons. The attack was swift and brutal with the viciousness that accompanies any surprise assault. The Trojan horse was open, and the battle on the surface was over almost as quickly as it began. Thanks to the missiles from Vandenberg, the above ground structures were degrading rapidly. While the outer guards were being quickly overwhelmed, the bulk of the airborne forces were blasting their way into each of the tunnels.

Within minutes of the initial assault, the first of many flights of forty C-17 aircraft appeared overhead, and more Exo-suited troopers from the 11th Airborne Division, the 1st Airborne Division (UK), the 6th Airborne Division (UK), and elements from the Russian Airborne forces, were appearing as they left the aircraft under the blossoming of their parachute canopies. Once on the ground, they assembled and then took their stations to head down the tunnels in support of the assault forces already in place and moving downward. The battle was joined, and the air was now full of more aircraft and parachutes, all converging on the main Enclave positions. These new forces were entering the Gomer tunnels as follow-on forces and, as they continued to work underground, the fighting became more intense. Casualties were mounting, but not in numbers that would in any way approach the numbers that were feared from such an attack.

Headquarters, 21st Allied Army Group:

General Crouse was tasked with the outer perimeters, and here the attack was far more conventional. Bowing to pressure from President Dubronin, the lead assault forces all came from the 9th Russian Army. Loyal and staunchly opposed to the dissident forces, they moved forward at almost the same instant as the follow-on airborne forces at the Western Enclave. Their assault began with the overwhelming application of both artillery and armor in the classic style of advancing under the cover of the artillery fire. As each blast from a barrage of heavy 155 mm guns was applied and walked forward, the mounted infantry and Armor units advanced to take advantage of their stunned enemies. Supplementing this attack of the 21st Allied Army Group were the aircraft from a number of allied air forces.

This portion of the attack was highly reminiscent of the tactics employed in France during 1940, or with the Russian advance into Germany in 1945. These combined arms type attacks are designed to overwhelm the enemy's senses and, if executed properly, can be devastating to the average defender. Against a dissident, who at best was equipped with a few Gomer hand held weapons, the tactics were largely quite successful. Once a position or strong point was overrun, then any survivors were turned over to the following allied forces. Of this group, the number of prisoners were relatively few. In fact, the few they had were all humans with absolutely no Gomers among their numbers. This isn't to say that Gomers weren't present in the forward areas, since there were a number of them who were recovered later among the dead.

Gomer Central Enclave, located near the Arctic Circle on the Central Siberian Plateau:

General Larkin was far more concerned about the attack on this Gomer Enclave, and his reasons were more than justified. This was by far the largest of the three main Gomer Enclaves located at or near the Arctic Circle in Russia and, as a result, it was the most heavily defended. The intelligence from the area was slight, since there were a number of Gomer and Dissident outposts to preclude any real close observation. More to the point, a number of ASOC personnel, from throughout the allied world, lost their lives in the attempts to get critical information out of this region. Another problem was the availability of a substantial ground force to attack the outer perimeters. In the West, the 21st Allied Army Group could force the outer perimeters back, and maintain pressure to prevent them from just collapsing back deeper into the Enclave during an attack. The Eastern Gomer Enclave also had a large force, in the guise of General Davis and the 42d Allied Army Group, that could have served the same purpose. Now, thanks to the near total destruction of the Eastern Enclave, this Army Group was too far away and otherwise engaged in mopping up the Gomers in their main area. Underemployed to be sure, it was still a necessary task to clear the area of any "bad guys" that would otherwise be left in the rear.

Given the limitation on resources, this left a much smaller follow-on force that, while it belonged to the 42d Allied Army, was mainly comprised of an allied composite force (China, Russia, with some forces from the UK), that didn't always play well together. As a result of these limitations, this force was designed more to contain and defend the area, as opposed to engaging in a concerted assault. Even their equipment was more defensive in nature, and while they had a number of Gomer Gun Batteries, they were lighter in Armor and conventional Artillery assets. Not an ideal force for the attack, and we knew that we'd have to change the strategy for this area.

Because the lack of available assets was very disconcerting to all of us, it was well understood that any attack here was mainly along the lines of a raid or reconnaissance in force. If gains could be made, then we would do our best to exploit them; however, we were equally prepared to pull out what we could, and then utilize another Phoenix II if necessary. The key here was to evaluate what was actually there, and then to take those steps necessary to keep the Gomers' heads down, while we finally eliminated all Gomer resistance at the other Gomer Enclaves. It was our stated tactical goal to get our forces into position for a better assault once we knew the disposition of the Gomers and their Dissident friends. We could then eliminate any threat to our rear, close the lines with both the 21st and 42d Allied Army Groups, and completely encircle and contain this remaining Enclave.

Against this backdrop, the Raid was now underway, and General Larkin and his Battleship Class Ship were heading into harm's way, along with the Assault force loaded onboard the other Battleship Class Ship. The plan of attack was similar to the one about to begin in the Western Enclave. The Battleship would land, dock, and release the initial assault of forces from two Regiments of the 82d Airborne, along with 1st Battalion, 75th Ranger Regiment. General Larkin's Battleship would then exploit with a follow-on force, or be prepared to assist with covering fire for the extraction of the raiding party. Consequently, General Larkin had another Regiment from the 82d Airborne Division, along with two battalions from the 75th Ranger

Regiment, on board his craft to act as a reserve or covering force if it were to become necessary.

General Larkin also had the option of calling for a diversion of assets from the Airborne Operation that was about to begin over the Western Enclave, if it should become necessary, or if the opportunity arose to exploit any gains on the ground. As always, this was about timing, since the Forces to the West were about to land, as were the forces here on the Central Siberian Plateau.

Standing on the bridge of the Gomer Ship, General Larkin observed the flight of both ships as they were coming in for a landing at the Enclave. For the last three minutes, they maintained radio silence as they approached. Opting instead to merely monitor the events taking place to their west at the other Gomer Enclave, General Larkin had entrusted the "easier' assault to his Deputy Commander. It was probably a mistake to allow himself to believe that his presence was necessary, but he also wasn't about to let the more serious calls be made by someone else. Like his old friend, General Patrick, he wasn't about to sit the damn thing out on his backside in a command post if he could help it. Laughing to himself, General Larkin thought to himself *"poor bastard must be going nuts back there."*

"Sir?" Captain Patrick only heard a mumble, but he knew his boss was saying something.

"Nothing, Captain. I was just thinking about your Dad is all."

"Hate to ask now, but what about him, Sir?"

"Nothing dammit. Keep focused. I need you to monitor the skies, and let me know if we need to launch those fighter class bastards."

"Yes, sir!"

Irritated at both his aide and himself, General Larkin watched as the ramps opened on the other Battleship Class ship, and the assault began with a rush of Exo-suited troopers advancing on the Gomers that were still above ground. Here the earlier missile strike wasn't degrading the facilities quite as badly, and General Larkin filed that away for his future use. Tapping his pilots on the shoulder, he gave a thumbs up, and told them to "Stand by to get us airborne again on my command."

Within seconds, the radio was erupting with tactical messages that were meant mainly to draw out Gomers. They also served to keep General Larkin up to speed on the battle that was raging around them. Here, the surface force of Gomers was more concentrated and, compared to the ease with which the attackers were gaining access in the Western Enclave, this was a pure slugfest. It was clear that this was not going to be a pushover by any stretch of the imagination, and General Larkin was now convinced that they might be lucky to get out of this one alive. The more serious firing appeared to be targeted on the other Battleship, while General Larkins craft was not drawing any attention. Taking this as his cue, he issued the next series of Orders.

"Chief of Staff, get over here!"

"Sir?"

"Okay, here we go. Once we're airborne, have them launch the Fighter Class ships. Then I want you to issue the recall Order for the other guys. If they can't get airborne again, then we'll come back for them. Got it?"

"Sir, yessir!" Turning on his heel, the Chief of Staff ran back to his comlink, while General Larkin reached up and tapped the pilots. "Okay, Son, get this bitch back in the air!"

The General's Battleship Class shot from the docking mounts and entered an orbit around the main portion of the Enclave. At this point, no firing was taking place towards them, since it appeared as if he were as surprised at the attack as were the Gomers on the ground. Once the Fighter Class ships launched, the Gomers seemed even more convinced that his ship was a friend who was here to help out. Still monitoring the radio traffic, it was apparent that his ground forces had run into a real hornet's nest and that they would be lucky to be extracted without major loss. As the fighting grew to a crescendo, the Fighter Class ships began to dive on various targets around the Enclave. It still took the Gomers a few minutes to realize that they weren't being hit by friendly fire, as the Fighters began to turn the tide back towards the advantage of the attackers.

General Larkin was never a timid soul, but something stayed his hand from immediately landing, and inserting his additional forces. He wasn't sure why, but something told him to hold pat and get the ground force extracted. Fortunately, his gut feeling was right on the money, the timing was just not right at this point. At the height of the extraction, Captain Patrick reappeared by his side out of breath, "Sir! We have inbound Gomers! Some of the bastards that attacked Vandenberg are now coming home, and they are about 5 minutes out from our location."

"Son of a bitch! Okay, tell the Chief of Staff to get me a count of what we've got coming! OH, and flash SAHQ, and let them know we've got inbound."

"Yessir." Rushing back to the Communications area with the Chief of Staff, there was much scurrying as directions were issued get a better handle on what they would be seeing within the next few minutes. Now that the other Battleship Class was hit, there was no telling how much assistance she could give, or even if she could get off the ground. General Larkin wasn't the least bit pleased with how this was going, and he sure as hell didn't want to lose this many men in the air, where they wouldn't be able to fight back at all. Still, there were damn few other options. He had to save these troops, while at the same time, he hated running away.

Turning, he issued one more order to everyone.

Supreme Allied Headquarters, (SAHQ), Lake Summersville, WV:

The Flash from General Larkin hit like a ton of bricks, yet both General Roberts and General Whitney were remaining stoic about it. Their rare display of stoicism was only because, like General McDaniel, they had a contingency plan to the original contingency plan. Once they heard the news, General Roberts wasted no time in contacting the 42d Allied Army Group. General Davis had a Supporting Tactical Air Force for his Allied Army Group, so it was a simple matter to get online to him for the execution of their plan. In fact, it only took a code word, and things fell immediately into place. Within two minutes, help was on the way.

As the Fighter Class ships piloted by some of ASOC's personnel were making their attack and slowing the Gomers down, three squadrons of F-35 fighters were approaching from below and behind the two approaching Carrier Class ships. Once identified as being Carrier Class, this information was flashed to General Larkin and back to our headquarters. This aerial battle was as short as it was effective. Within moments the F-35s rendered both Carrier Class ships completely unflyable. As they crashed to the Earth, the only thing left were the Fighter Class ships that launched right before they crashed. The ASOC-piloted craft could see that they were likely to become targets given their serious lack of IFF (Identification Friend or Foe), so they immediately turned from the area to return to their work at the Central Enclave. Fortunately, they were not hit, but the dozen Gomer-crewed Fighter Class ships, which had launched earlier by their Carriers, were soon engaged in a fight for their lives with the F-35 crews. Hopefully, none of these Gomer-crewed Fighter Class ships would survive the battle.

Once the ASOC Fighter Class Ships returned to the airspace over the Central Enclave, they could see that quite a bit had changed in their relatively short absence. The destruction was clear to them, when they flew low over the site, and what they were seeing wasn't very comforting. The first Battleship Class ship appeared to be burning, and a very large number of our forces were actively engaged in some hard fighting in and around the wreck. Outward from this scene were a number of hard and deep depressions in the ground that appeared to come from something quite large firing its main weapon system. Searching the skies, they saw it coming back over the Enclave, and after a few moments of panic, they realized it was the other Battleship Class ship.

Gomer Central Enclave, located near the Arctic Circle on the Central Siberian Plateau:

General Larkin was delighted to hear that it was just two Carrier Class ships, but it meant little now. He'd already committed to a course of action that was as gutsy as anything he'd ever done. As the ASOC Gomer Fighters rushed off to engage, he'd already decided that he wasn't about to lose a Division of Airborne Troopers and a Regiment of Rangers, all while they were fricking passengers. He'd made his decision. They were to land the follow-on forces, and then go for broke. They would use the Battleship Class Ship to pound strong points around the Enclave with their own weapons, and then hope for either a breakthrough, or help from above. As the fight continued, he got a little of one, and a lot of the other.

Supreme Allied Headquarters, (SAHQ), Lake Summersville, WV:

The Battle for the Eastern Enclave was virtually wrapped up, with very few survivors from either the Gomer or the Dissident camp still in evidence. In fact, there were zero Gomer prisoners, and it wasn't from our lack of searching. Instead, it was simply that the

Phoenix II had been that devastating to their physiology. Similarly, the Dissidents that were operating in that part of the world were equally devastated. As was suspected, and then later confirmed, the damage that was done to both Gomers and humans was at the cellular level. As the Terahertz blasts were released, Gomers began to disintegrate and humans to cease all muscular functions. Within minutes, the more sheltered humans were no longer breathing, while anyone in the open had their hearts stopped and brain function cease instantaneously.

While the Battle for the Central Enclave was raging, much the 42d Allied Army Group was engaged in patrol and cleanup activities. It became clear rather quickly that massive advances towards the Central Enclave could be made, and even though ground forces would still take time to get into position. Air and Missile assets could be brought to bear almost immediately on our Order. Naturally, these assets were applied to the eastern side of the Siberian Central Plateau region as efficiently as possible, with the logistics catching up to support these operations.

Similarly, the Battle for the Western Enclave was starting to enter the end stage. The 21st Allied Army Group had pushed most of the Dissident Force into a headlong retreat headed to the northern end of the Ural Mountains and the main portion of the Enclave itself. The Airborne attack with follow-on airborne forces was shaping up very nicely, with the combatants now engaged in tunnel to tunnel fighting. While this somewhat favored the Gomers, the use of the Exo-suits was paying great dividends in providing protection and added strength to the individual soldier. From here, we diverted a number of additional Airborne Units from General Larkin's forces to his location. It was obvious to us at SAHQ that the real fight was in the Central Enclave and, while we'd hoped to have a mere raid, this was shaping rather quickly into something much larger. As one might argue, we were in too big to fail, and it was about to get ugly.

Chapter XIX

Command Post #3, Vandenberg, Air Force Base, California:

The dust was still falling when the power was restored and the lights came back. It took about another two minutes to start getting the computers and observation terminals back online, and, as luck would have it for General McDaniel, the last one back online was NE6. This had taken almost a full eight minutes and General McDaniel wasn't the least bit happy about it. As his wife would have gladly pointed out, patience was not his long suit, and being blind at this particular moment was anything but calming for him. Not trusting what was going to fall out of his mouth, the General did what he did best. He remained silent while chewing the end off of his cigar. While the NE6 terminal was still offline, he moved from the other terminals to see what might be discerned from the views they offered. For example, they spotted the two Carrier Class ships limping back towards Russia but, at this point, they had no way of getting the warning out to anyone. His Chief of Staff announced that the "Comms are all down." To which General McDaniel could only grunt.

Finally, as NE6 slowly flickered back to life, the view was spectacular. There was nothing but debris. The Red Dragon had done the job on the Mountain Class and everything around it.

The space surrounding where the Mountain Class had been was now a floating pile of space junk, and General McDaniel couldn't help but pat himself on the back. At least for a few minutes, he was on top of his world, then it hit him. It was a slow realization to be sure, but it was clear he'd done a very ill-conceived thing. When the Red Dragon went off, it fried his entire Command Post. The damage that was done, and the few casualties among the guard force topside above the Command Post, were all because of the Red Dragon having been detonated so close to the Earth above their heads. General McDaniel's idea did accomplish his goal, since it destroyed what we'd hoped was the last Mountain Class Ship still on the planet. As for the casualties, none were fatal, and fortunately, the electronics mess was to be repaired in only a few hours. Still, General McDaniel wasn't really pleased with himself.

Disgusted at his error, General McDaniel only started to snap out of his funk when contact was resumed with the two Gomer ships headed to Neptune and Triton. Thankfully, the computer guidance information, onboard both the Mountain and Battleship Class ships hurtling towards their targets, was in a closed system that wasn't impacted by the power outages at his Command Post. Once his full satellite coverage was reestablished, the surveillance of the large incoming fleet was his next major priority. Now it was a matter of calculations, and it didn't take long before he realized that the outbound Phoenix IV was not going to be in a position to take out this new threat. Instead, he would need to give them a dose of Phoenix III or IV with another launch, and this time perhaps with a Red Dragon or two to go with it. Still, he couldn't do that until they got a little closer which would be at least another two days. Then again, this could be a problem, too, since Operation Troy was only a day and a half away from detonation.

Gomer Central Enclave, located near the Arctic Circle on the Central Siberian Plateau:

General Larkin was finally seeing daylight at the end of the tunnel. His forces were clearing the outside portions of the main Enclave, while elements of the 42d Army Group were engaged in keeping the Dissidents occupied along their eastern perimeter. Tactical Air support was on station almost constantly to strike strong points outside the underground complex. The ASOC Fighter Class ships were now expanding their reach from the Main Enclave into the more serious pockets of Dissidents making up the next layer of their defenses towards the west. It had been a hard slog to this point, but they were only now reaching the point that the forces in the Western Enclave had reached in the first 15 minutes of their assault. The good news was that there were forces streaming in from the 42d Allied Army Group that could help in the tunnel-clearing that was about to begin.

The other good news came in the form of the intelligence he was now receiving again from SAHQ and Vandenberg. Their operation was a great success so far as he was concerned, since the only thing Gomer that was left flyable was either in our hands or part of that Gomer Fleet that was days away. In fact, he also knew that ASOC personnel were doing their best to get these captured craft usable as quickly as possible and, from his rear Headquarters in Greenland, he was aware that they were working hard to get at least one Carrier Class ship in the air. He had no idea if they'd make it or not, but decided that he had enough on his plate. He would let General Patrick and General Greene figure that one out. For now, he was more about getting the right assets into the right holes to kill Gomers. Finally, after almost 30 hours on his feet, General Larkin gathered his staff, and they headed to the Western Enclave to assess the status of that part of the operation.

Supreme Allied Headquarters, (SAHQ), Lake Summersville, WV:

When it became obvious that our outbound Phoenix IV wasn't going to be in the right place to help us with the incoming fleet, the decision was made to stuff a Carrier Class ship with as much Phoenix IV material as it could possibly hold. It was a long shot but, if we were lucky, it might slow down that fleet if we could make a large enough bang. General Greene was working this issue and, by all accounts, he was going to make it a real reception for the Gomers. Dr. Clarkson, Dr. Abramson, and my daughter were already on the way to Greenland to get the right software fixes to put it together.

All of the other news that was coming in to our headquarters was excellent. The Eastern Enclave was definitely in our hands, with a completely clean bill of health. To quote General Davis, "There are no more critters living in these holes." On that report, General Davis began moving the rest of his Army Group to support General Larkin's Allied Airborne Army at the Central Enclave. Meanwhile, we finally got the word that the Western Enclave was now virtually in our hands, with only a few Gomers and a couple of their Dissident friends still holding out in the lower tunnels. It was good news that we weren't met with any nasty surprises, since I halfway suspected that they would draw us in completely, and then detonate something nuclear to take us all out in their complex. As of this point, no such thing had happened, which was great news to the boys who were fighting from hole to hole several miles underground.

I was just walking back into Operations after having a rare meal when the next major piece of news rolled into our Communications Center. "General?"

I turned to General Whitney, who handed me a message form, and then the receiver to the phone. "Yeah, General McDaniel, you back up and running?"

"Yes, sir, and I was just advised that General Greene was about to launch a Carrier Class ship, and that it will be for me to monitor it. I just wanted to confirm it."

"Well, I'm reading his message now, and, yes, I can confirm. Can you make sure it gets delivered to the right address?"

"Absolutely, sir. I've got the codes for the final steering, and I'm also supposed to have Dr. Patrick on hand to make any final adjustments."

"Great! What is her ETA to your location?"

"Sir, she is to arrive in about 12 hours, which should give her about another 8 hours to make adjustments as needed."

"Sounds good, Mac. Oh, and do me a favor."

"Sir?"

"Make sure you sit on her when it is done. She is NOT, say again, NOT to leave your place without my Orders, at least until we get into the final stages of this damn thing."

"I understand completely."

"Yeah, I'm tired of having to read classified mail to figure out where the hell she is at any given moment. Besides, she has a much larger job coming up, and I'm going to want to know where to find her quickly."

Laughing, General McDaniel replied with a hearty "Yes, Sir!" I knew, and so did he, that if things went the way we hoped, her skills would be vital for the next stage of our defense of the planet.

Command Post #3, Vandenberg, Air Force Base, California:

After hanging up the phone with General Patrick, General McDaniel started the process of getting his people lined up to plug in this latest part of the operation. In the meantime, they were starting their official countdown for the impact of Operation Troy. They were into the last stages, and the latest calculations showed that impacts should take place in precisely 5 hours, 15 minutes on Neptune, and 5 Hours and 14 minutes on Triton.

Meanwhile, he had this new project and, regardless of the arrival of Dr. Patrick, the newest impromptu Trojan Horse was already airborne and headed out rapidly towards the incoming fleet. Sitting down with his number crunchers, they worked out the yields, directions, and best place for detonation to wipe out the incoming fleet. They also started to crunch on their time to target, based on the speeds plugged in by the ASOC personnel and Dr. Patrick. It was finally decided, based on their best guesses and calculations (guesstimates), that the Moon Class ship that was positioned in the middle of the formation was the best place to send their Carrier Class ship. They just hoped they could sneak it in close enough without drawing attention to her, and for that they would need a huge diversion. It was a minor irony to their work that, being so engrossed in what they were doing, they almost missed what was to be their perfect diversion.

Planet Neptune and the Moon Triton:

It simply isn't within our ability to know exactly what happened on the surface of the planet or on Triton, but from the telemetry, and observations made by the two escorting remotely operated Fighter Class Ships, we do have at least some idea. The landing areas designated for returning and damaged ships were very near to what appeared to be the central areas occupied by the Gomers. It was observed that the initial blast radiated in a complete 360-degree blue arc that rose to the level of the outer atmosphere, and then expanded virtually around the entire planet. Triton's 360-degree blue arc was equally expansive, and at the height of the explosive spread, the arc from Triton almost seemed to touch the one that rose from Neptune. The observers were stunned at the sheer magnitude of the events, and the initial reports were more along the lines of sheer disbelief that the plan was so effective.

Prior to the arrival of the Trojan Horse ships, several fly-by reconnaissance missions were flown by the Fighter Class ships both on the planet and Triton, and we were quite fortunate that the Gomers were never suspicious of this activity. Perhaps out of hubris or sheer disbelief, they did not seem to be the least bit threatened by the notion that we'd have the reach to sneak one of their own back at them. Still, we did, and from where we were sitting, it not only worked, but it worked with a truly devastating effect.

The original plan for Operation Troy was quite simple. We were going to put our Phoenix IV weapon system on a different, much quicker, means of delivery, one of their own ships. ASOC performed the needed recon of Neptune and Triton to determine the best location to send our surprise packages and to refine the targeting date. When that Mountain Class ship landed on Neptune, and the Battleship Class landed on Triton, it was not a complete matter of luck, since these locations were pinpointed by some very adept scientists. The breakthrough for the entire mission came when Dr. Clarkson and my daughter Holly wrote the program to allow for the ship to be flown without a human presence via a preset computer program. There was no need to have anyone on board either ship, and the notion that this would not be a suicide mission made it quite plausible to all of the planners. We had a need for a large enough delivery system to take down Neptune and Triton, and the combination of Gomer Technology, as refined by our own scientists, made this a very real possibility.

After the blasts, the reports came pouring into our Headquarters from several observers. On one thing they all agreed, the explosions when they came were quite a show to watch. It was an even larger show than the one that took place on our Moon in the First Gomer War. Granted you couldn't see it with the naked eye, but those in position to monitor it through telescopic means, or with the cameras on the Fighter Class ships, got a spectacular fireworks display. When I finally saw the video feeds coming in from the Fighter Class ships, what I saw was that the expanding mass of the weapon system was completely effective in taking out every living thing on the surface of the planet, as well as anything that was flying between Triton and Neptune. I personally know this because within hours of this blast the Fighter Class Ships were flown into the known areas of Gomer activity. It was from this video that I saw that there was nothing left on the surface, except wreckage and pure destruction, while out in the space between the planet and Triton, there was nothing but large bits of debris.

Command Post #3, Vandenberg, Air Force Base, California:

The staff at Vandenberg were beside themselves in celebration, but it was suppressed since they still were quite concerned about the remaining air threat. The Gomer fleet had slowed after the blasts on Neptune and Triton, but otherwise, they had not deviated in course. When Doctor Holly Patrick arrived in the Command Post, she was given star treatment by everyone but General McDaniel. He didn't say much while she was being acclimated to her computer station but, once she was settled, he leaned down and said, "Okay, Kid, you have to make this one really count. How can we do this without them getting suspicious, at least long enough to get the beast right up next to that middle Moon Class ship?"

"Sir, maybe we can sell it the same way as we did the main operation?"

"You don't honestly think they'll bite twice on the same thing, do you?"

"Yes, sir I do. Mainly because they probably don't have a clue what happened on Neptune or on Triton. Which is why, by the way, I think they've slowed down, but haven't changed course."

"So, you don't think anything got out in the way of communications before the blasts?"

"I know it didn't, sir. I wrote most of our interception software, and I specifically asked the guys using it if anything was ever heard. They all responded with a negative." Continuing on, Holly opined that "I recall that the Moon ships carried a lot of things to include some Mountain, Battleship, and a lot of Carrier class ships, right?"

"Yes, that is correct."

"Good, then maybe we can sell them on the idea that this is one of their own coming home from the wars, basically looking for a place to hide."

"Well, it is worth a shot, and keep your fingers crossed, too, since if it doesn't work, I've only got one more Phoenix IV left to send at them."

Grinning at the General, Holly replied, "My fingers are crossed, General, but before this all blows up, where is the rest room?"

Standing up laughing, General McDaniel pointed her down the hallway, and then strode back into his office for a stiff drink and cigar. He wasn't worried about this kid. She had the same ice water in her veins as the rest of those damn Patricks. Thank God!

Supreme Allied Headquarters, (SAHQ), Lake Summersville, WV:

Unlike my daughter Holly, I wasn't so sure that the Gomers would buy the lame duck routine for our latest Carrier Class Trojan Horse. I did agree with her assessment that there was a very low likelihood that they knew exactly what had happened to their bases on Neptune or Triton. I also figured that they slowed down to figure out their own next move. What was a surety was that the news they were getting from the ground wasn't good, and surely the Gomers had to be assessing their chances of influencing the battle. The Western and Eastern Enclaves were either destroyed or virtually under our control. Only the Central Siberian Plateau Enclave was holding out, but even there we were likely to have it under control in fairly short order. If all assessments were any indication, along with the last ace we still had up our sleeve, then we felt that all calls from the ground would cease before their Fleet could arrive to take station at our own Moon.

The ongoing battle at the Central Siberian Plateau Enclave was taking the same shape as the earlier one at the Western Enclave. It was hoped all along that once Operation Troy were completed on Neptune and Triton, the conventional forces would continue their advance towards the Airborne Strike Force. In this case, it meant the combined strength of elements from both the 42d Allied Army Group and General Davis, as well as the 21st Allied Army Group and General Crouse. The plan was simple, once the Allied Airborne Army forces completed the destruction of Gomers (no quarter expected or given), then the entire outer and inner perimeters of resistance from the dissidents would collapse. If they didn't immediately collapse, then the Airborne Forces, in their enhanced Exo-suit configurations, would switch their focus to the dissidents. The idea here was to attack the dissidents from both directions, and to force them to capitulate. Once that was accomplished, we'd have our planet back, and the dissidents that were captured would be repatriated to their respective government (e.g., Russian Federation).

Gomer Central Enclave, located near the Arctic Circle on the Central Siberian Plateau:

General Larkin was exhausted, but feeling a lot better about things. Word had filtered in about Operation Troy, and this seemed to bolster his strength, and that of his staff. Still, despite good news, there were still those damn Gomers in their holes. The fighting was going slow, and while there was about 90% control in the Western Enclave, this one was another story. They were, by all accounts, only about 15% of the way into it. Feeling somewhat stretched, it was with trepidation that he greeted his latest visitor into his Command Post.

"So, General Greene, to what do I owe this unexpected honor?"

"Sir, I've brought you a present from Dr. Clarkson."

"Oh?"

"Yessir. With your permission I'd like to test it out in the Western Enclave, and if it works, I'll be happy to bring you a couple just like them."

"Okay, so what the hell is it?"

General Greene motioned General Larkin closer, and they conferred for about 10 minutes. Captain Patrick was just out of ear shot, and missed the gist of the conversation, but when it concluded, General Larkin was smiling, and General Greene was sprinting out of the area and back to his now garishly painted Fighter Class ship. Captain Patrick understood the paint job, since everyone was briefed not to shoot at the bright red Fighter Class ships that might be showing up here and there. Within a minute, the red Fighter Class was airborne and out of sight.

Turning back to his boss, Robbie smiled and asked, "May I ask what that was about, sir?"

General Larkin looked at him, and said, "Well, son, if Daniel is right, he may have just shortened our part of the war. In the meantime, get me the Corps Commanders on the line, but first let me speak to the XVIII Airborne Corps Commander."

Western Gomer Enclave, near the Ural Mountains:

The bright red Fighter Class settled to the ground, where it was met immediately by the XVIII Airborne Corps Commander and a security team. As the Corps Commander watched, General Greene, along with a dozen or so ASOC Operators, began unloading what appeared to be a number of boxes that looked the world and all like toy remote-control trucks. They weren't, but were instead the ground drones that were being used when the Army only had to worry about things like terrorists and explosives. The Corps Commander couldn't help but notice that the ASOC Operators were unpacking these things, and then fitting them with a large sealed container on top.

Stepping up to greet the ASOC Commander himself, the Corps Commander snapped off a welcome, "General? What can we do for you?"

"Well, for starters, you can assign someone to take each of these guys to the opening of the tunnels you haven't cleared yet."

"Yes sir. May I ask..." General Greene cut him off with a smile, and replied, "I'd love to tell you, but right now, let's hurry and see if this shit works. If you watch close, I'll explain as we go."

Nodding, the Corps Commander fell into step with General Greene, and they walked in step towards the entrance to the Main Enclave itself. Within 20 minutes, General Greene got the go-ahead from his men. Turning to the Corps Commander, he said, "Now, all your guys are out of the hole, right?"

"Yes, they are, but I don't know why, and I sure don't like the idea that they may have let the bastards off the hook by leaving their positions."

"I think you're going to love it. Now watch this." Picking up the VHF radio, he advised all the ASOC personnel to move them into final position. Three minutes later, the last ASOC operator reported that his package was ready. Smiling at the Corps Commander, General Greene turned back to his radio and simply said, "Fire in the hole."

Supreme Allied Headquarters, (SAHQ), Lake Summersville, WV:

General Whitney rushed into Operations with a hand full of messages, all from the Western Enclave. It would seem that our "ace in the hole" worked perfectly. He was grinning from ear to ear when he handed me the official ASOC message from General Greene. Reading through it, there was no question that we'd finally found a way to clear out the Central Enclave, and stop the loss of Allied lives. Smiling, I told General Whitney to issue the Order to the folks with General Larkin, and then to make sure that our packages were being delivered as quickly as possible. Then I asked for a line to General Larkin.

"General? Patrick here."

"Yessir. Larkin here, and I understand that the packages worked very well over to our west. Is that correct?"

"Yep. I've got Daniel and his team headed your way. In the meantime, hold what you have, and just keep the bastards bottled up. Whatever you do, you have to keep them at bay and locked in before we cook off our new bug bombs."

"Yes, sir. I had no idea we could make something this size, but I guess that it must be working. I mean all that talk back in the day about a suitcase nuke, well, it just seemed far-fetched."

"Well, first of all, it wasn't far-fetched back in the day but, more to the point, the Low Yield, Sulphur Isotope Nuke, you know, the one with the shortest amount of hang time, miniaturizes quite well. Dr. Clarkson figured that one out in the last war, but we just never had a reason to make or use it, until now. Fortunately, someone on his team remembered the idea. I just wish he'd remembered it sooner."

"Who remembered?"

"It was my own son-in-law, John. Even Dr. Clarkson didn't remember it, nor did anyone else, until John was talking to Chris about our current hole clearing operations."

"I'll be damned. Okay, well how long do I have to wait? Oh, wow, I see Greene's Red bird coming in now."

"Excellent. Now remember, fight back to a position to keep them boxed in, but do NOT keep your boys too close. These things do make a slight mess, even if the radioactivity clears in short order. Just listen to Greene's people on when to let your guys back in to finish anything."

"I don't expect it will be much, General, since my guys to the West have told me that it cleared out the entire lower sections of the Gomer Tunnels very effectively."

"I know. Oh, and Jerry? Be careful!"

"Yes, sir. I'll keep you posted."

Breaking contact, I had to do a quick assessment of our situation. Triton and Neptune were no longer a threat to us; two out of three Gomer Enclaves on Earth were now cleared completely; the third Gomer Enclave was about to get the bug bomb from hell; Greenland and a veritable fleet of Gomer ships were in our possession; their Mars Base was destroyed; the Moon was clear for now; and, there was absolutely no Gomer Air traffic over the planet that wasn't operated by us. This left us to finish the Gomer clearing on the Central Siberian Plateau, and the destruction of the Gomer Fleet that was headed our way from what used to be their bases on Neptune and Triton. In short, the only thing wrong, was that there was nothing wrong.

Gomer Central Enclave, located near the Arctic Circle on the Central Siberian Plateau:

The blasts were more felt than heard. General Larkin was standing next to General Greene as the series of explosions took place under their very feet. Captain Patrick watched closely the expression on his boss's face, as it went from surprise to almost pure satisfaction. General Greene was the first to say anything as the rumbling ceased. "General Larkin, with my compliments, give it about an hour and you can send your troopers back in to the holes. I would recommend though, that you limit it to Exo-suited troopers only, and make sure they keep the dynamic over-pressure features going."

"Okay, I'll pass the word to the Corps Commanders. I think that will give us enough forces to finish the job."

General Greene smirked and said, "General. If this works half as well as it did in the last location, then your troopers will need dust pans, as opposed to weapons."

"Still, if you don't mind, I'll keep my guard up."

"Yessir. I would expect nothing less." Taking his cue that his role was finished, General Greene saluted and then left towards his Fighter Class ship. There was no question that he was getting used to having his own faster than hell transport. He also knew that, thanks to his pilots, he would be back at ASOC Headquarters, near Lake Moomaw, Virginia, before the first airborne trooper stepped into what used to be a Gomer hole.

Watching the youthful General stride away, Captain Patrick turned to General Larkin and asked, "Sir, do you think all this show and boom worked?"

"I know it worked, because while your Dad's buddy General Greene was doing his thing, I verified that the transmissions were no longer coming out of there in the Terahertz bands."

"Wow, you mean that there no live Gomers down there?"

"Well, none that are using their communications gear to talk to the guys in the sky. Of course, from what I hear about their Neptune and Triton bases, there wouldn't be anyone to talk to about it."

"Sir, does this mean the war is over?"

"Well, son, we've still got to clear these holes, round up all their crap, get it secured and away from where dissidents can get their hands on it, and then we're going to have to deal with them. So, what do you think?"

"I think that we're going to be busy as hell then, aren't we, sir."

"Yep, Captain. We are going to be busy as hell. Speaking of which, get me some coffee, and grab us a hot meal, will you? I have a feeling we've got one helluva long few days ahead of us." Captain Robert "Robbie" Patrick snapped off his best parade ground salute, and then set about making the General happy. It would be a while before he could find that hot coffee, but he did eventually find it.

Chapter XX

Command Post #3, Vandenberg, Air Force Base, California:

Doctor Holly Patrick was now seated and concentrating on her computer terminal. Seated next to her, at another console, was General McDaniel's best missileman, Lieutenant Colonel Braithwaite. Together, they would confer, and observe the course of the Carrier Class ship as it approached the incoming Gomer Fleet. Over the past several hours, the fleet had slowed considerably, which increased the expected flight time for the Carrier Class to reach the target. Noting that, if they hurried, it might alert the Gomers that all wasn't right with it, the missileman was instructed by Dr. Patrick to maintain speed and heading. The idea was to look wounded, and if they were to hasten the pace, then the Gomers might have a clue that this wasn't as it appeared.

What Doctor Patrick didn't know, or General McDaniel for that matter, was that all Gomer transmissions ceased to flow from the Gomer Enclaves on Earth. With the explosions witnessed by her brother, and ordered by her Dad, the Gomer presence on Earth was now just a memory. Right now, the only Gomer threat left in our Universe was coming towards her on the video screen that was mounted just above her terminal. It was about 15 minutes later when General McDaniel found out that all alien resistance on Earth was now virtually over. Stepping behind Dr. Patrick, General McDaniel peered closely at the video, and then at the telemetry information that was dashing over her screen, and the screen of Lieutenant Colonel Braithwaite. Pausing only briefly, he said, "Doctor, I've got some news you'll want to hear."

Not wanting to miss anything, she didn't turn towards the General, but instead motioned him to continue, and then said, "Sir? We're kind of busy..."

"I know, Doctor, but you should know that they've slowed for a reason."

This captured her attention and she now turned and asked, "What reason?"

"Seems that all the Gomers on Earth have met their makers, and are now like the ones on Neptune or on Triton. By all accounts, we've cleared all the Enclaves in Russia, and in Greenland, of any live Gomers."

Wide-eyed, she turned fully to the General and asked, "No wonder they slowed down, and now it makes sense."

"What makes sense?"

"Sir, the Gomer Fleet is starting to slowly turn away. The only things still coming are the Moon Class ships. The rest of their fleet appears to be starting to change course."

Only momentarily puzzled, General McDaniel immediately recognized trouble. "Shit! How long before the Moons get here, and how much time before the turn is completed?"

The Missileman, Lieutenant Colonel Braithwaite responded, "General, the Moons will be here sometime later tomorrow night, since it appears that they are now picking up a little speed."

Turning back to Holly, General McDaniel asked, "Doctor?"

"Yessir, that about covers it. The Moon Class ships are still on their way, while the rest of the smaller stuff appears to be regrouping and headed in a different direction."

"Dammit. Okay, how far out is your Carrier Class, and how long till you can steer it into the Middle Moon Class?"

"Uh, well, General, if we maintain speed on the Carrier Class, we should intercept the Moon Class ship in about three hours."

"Okay, Doctor, let me ask it another way. The Moon Class ships are about to come and bust our asses with something big, while their other ships are going to either escape or wait to take over the wreckage of what used to be us. Meanwhile, I have to know how fast can you get that damned ship to hit their Moon class, while it can still take out most of the Gomer Fleet?"

"OH! Damn! Uh...! If we, ... no that won't work. But maybe, well... Shit. Will a best guess work?" Doctor Patrick was scrambling around with her terminal, trying her best to rework her calculations, and consulting her calculator. Turning away, General McDaniel said, "Get me General Patrick on the horn!" General McDaniel knew exactly what had Doctor Patrick confused, because he'd played this game before, when the fleet was coming from the Moon in the last war. One thing you can't teach a scientist is that fine art of Kentucky windage. Now he was going to get the boss on the horn, and let him know that it was time to roll dice.

Supreme Allied Headquarters, (SAHQ), Lake Summersville, WV:

I hesitate to call it a celebration, but when General McDaniel contacted our Headquarters, he did so while the staff was at their most relaxed in months. There were definitely a lot of cigars and pats on the back going around the room, because ridding the planet of Gomers was something we'd not done since the end of the first Gomer War. These moments of revelry were very short lived, and General McDaniel's news was the basis for that immediate change. When I was summoned to the line by General Roberts, you could sense the instant change back to "serious business" as it permeated the Operations Center. The moment our Air Force staff heard who was on the line, they immediately began more closely following the NE and deeper space telemetry on their back up terminals.

"General McDaniel, what can I do for you?"

"Sir, we've got a situation. The Gomer Fleet is turning onto a new heading that will take them behind Saturn, while the Moon Ships are picking up speed and heading our way."

"Yikes! That ain't good. What's your plan or recommendation, Mac?"

"Sir, I want to risk tipping our hand on the Carrier Class, and try to get it in position to take out the Moon Ships, before their fleet gets out of range."

"So, do it, why are you asking me? You've got full authority."

"Sir, we do not have a good lock on the best place to hit them since their scattering of their fleet. I can't guarantee that we'll get them all, or that we'll even make a dent in them. I do think we can take out the Moon Class Ships though, at least I'm about 90% sure of it."

"Not great odds when we don't have that many of these things to put out there at this point."

"I know, sir, which is why I'm calling."

"Okay, General, I'm going to tell you to give it your best shot, and make the call. You've done pretty well by us through three wars and, what the hell, if your plan fails, we'll get our heads together to see what we can do about the rest of the problem."

"Sir, so you'll know, our loss of the local launchers will limit the hell out of our ability to deal with some of those problems if they get closer. We can't replenish our mine fields at the moment, so you can bet that whatever survives will get through to here."

"Then I would say take out their Moon Class Ships, even if you have to spit at them, since they have what we believe to be planet killer weapons on board."

"Shit, I somehow knew you'd say that."

"Just give it your best shot, Mac. In the meantime, let me get ASOC on the line, and maybe we can reseed the minefield using the Gomers stuff to get it out there."

"Great idea, sir. Let me go, since I have a feeling my hands are going to be pretty full here in just a very short time."

"Go! And good luck, General!"

"Yessir." The line went dead, and I turned to Generals Roberts and Whitney. "Get General Greene on the line immediately, and if you can, make it a conference call with the President."

Planning "on the fly" is what some would call it, others would say it was wishful thinking, while others would simply say you 'pulled it from your ass, in the wild hope that something would work.' I think the latter was closer to our reality, but it wasn't like we had a choice. If the Moon Class Ships were successful, then they could still win this fight, simply by knocking us out of the game. Not really something we like to think would be a good option for us. After briefing the President, and planning on the fly with General Greene, we had a plan. It wasn't a good one, but it was at least a plan. Once he hung up, General Greene instructed his staff to get two Battleship Class Gomer Ships ready for what would be a true suicide mission. It wasn't a happy time but, oddly enough, once they understood the reasons for it, there was no shortage of volunteers to try and make it happen.

Command Post #3, Vandenberg, Air Force Base, California:

General McDaniel was polite, but insistent. Doctor Patrick was moved from her console, and General McDaniel took her place. Watching the numbers, he started giving explicit instructions to Lieutenant Colonel Braithwaite. The Carrier Class began to pick up speed, and without making too many other adjustments to the course, within seconds it was racing towards the Moon Class Ships at full speed. Combined with the change in speed by the Moon Ships, they were all hurtling towards one another at a tremendous rate. Whether this succeeded in taking out the balance of the fleet or not, it was agreed that destruction of the Moon Class Ships was mandatory and clearly their top priority.

Doctor Patrick saw it first, and standing on her tip toes and pointing at the video feed, she screamed, "THERE! They are launching something that is coming towards us."

Lieutenant Colonel Braithwaite simply grunted, "Yeah."

"General, you need to dive under it!"

General McDaniel was doing his best to figure out his Kentucky windage, and Holly's exclamation almost lifted him from his seat. Without looking, he followed her advice, and began the process of sending the Carrier Class ship underneath the oncoming craft. As they held their breath, the smaller Transport Class passed directly over their ship, and started a high-speed turn back towards the Carrier Class. General McDaniel immediately recognized that this was a boarding party for their ship, and he did his best to coax a little more speed from the Carrier Class. No matter how much he grunted, he couldn't make it go any faster than it was already going. As they watched, it was clear that the Transport Class was slowly gaining on them. Now it was a race as to whether they could get to their target before they were intercepted.

Lieutenant Colonel Braithwaite broke the silence, "General? I've got an idea!"

"Great, I could use one about now."

"Sir, what if we continue on this course and drive hard to the center of their formation while on a different plane?"

"Huh?"

"Stay beneath them General, don't act like a threat, but act like someone that is running like hell to catch up with the folks that are leaving."

"Okay, but what does that get us?"

"Then once you're under the center of the Moon Class Ships, change your plane and drive straight up into them as hard as you can."

"Well, Colonel, one helluva idea, but once we turn straight up, then we give the Transport Class a shot at us as we bleed off inertia, and start slowing as we ascend."

"WAIT!" Holly interrupted them both, "I've been crunching these numbers, and I think the Colonel's plan might work to a point. Dive under, and maintain that until you're just short of the first Moon Ship, then begin your ascent in front of the first one."

"Okay, how is that going to help?"

"Once you start up, then do the unthinkable. Stop! I've been calculating their speed, and if you just stop, the middle one will be directly over you in about 20 seconds. At their present speed, the inertia of them passing will continue their forward momentum, even if they try to stop. It will also throw off the aim of the Transport Class."

"Okay, now that might work. So, detonate when?"

"The millisecond the one in the middle is over head, or given signal time, you might even want to hit it a hair earlier, say at 13 seconds after you stop."

"Doctor Patrick? You sound like you've been hunting before." Continuing on to the missileman, "Colonel. You heard the lady, now let's make it happen. You drive, and I'll detonate."

"Okay, Sir. I have the controls! Doctor? Do you have the stop watch?"

"Yes, Colonel. I'll tap you when to turn, and when to stop. Okay?"

"Go for it, Doc."

Holly then looked at General McDaniel and said, "If you'd like, General, I'll tap you when you are to detonate."

"Okay, but don't be surprised if I fire when I am ready."

"Yessir." Holly was already back on the count, and watching the timing and the video monitor. As the transport was almost on top of them, she tapped Braithwaite on the shoulder, and the Carrier Class shot straight up. It took a moment to adjust, but the Transport Class turned to follow and, in the process, lost a little position, until it ramped up the speed. It was then that Holly tapped Lieutenant Colonel Braithwaite again. In the process of stopping, the forward momentum carried the Carrier Class upward, but at such a slowed pace that the Transport Class Ship overshot them and was now traveling at an extremely high rate of speed upwards towards the middle of the oncoming Moon Ship formation. While they watched, a burst of something from the middle-positioned Moon Class Ship took place, and the Transport Class disintegrated before their eyes.

General McDaniel was now starting to see that there was a great deal of luck involved here. The mere fact that they had to adjust their original plan was now quite fortuitous. There was no question that the Carrier Class might well have met the same fate as the Transport Class, had they continued with the initial flight plan, and such an early detonation of the ship might well have kept any part of the Phoenix IV from working. At least now they still had a shot at it. Watching the monitor, he was starting to get antsy. Just at the moment he would have fired, he was still waiting on a tap from Holly, that came a second later. Not wasting time, General McDaniel hit the button that sent the signal to the Carrier Class Ship. It was now or never.

Supreme Allied Headquarters, (SAHQ), Lake Summersville, WV:

There is an old expression that would best describe the Operations Center at this point. Civilians would say "it was so quiet you could hear a pin drop," while the military personnel would say, "it was so quiet you could hear a mouse fart." Regardless of your preferred version, there was no question that everyone was holding their collective breath, and completely glued to the same pictures as were being flashed on the screen in front of General McDaniel and his personnel. We didn't have the discussion between the players out west, or the commentary of what was happening. Instead, we had nothing but silence and more silence, as the various actions took place. There was almost a collective sigh when the Carrier Class turned straight up, and a gasp, when it stopped. The old fighter pilots in the room had a clue, but several of our staff members weren't privy at all to this tactic. When the Transport was blown from the sky, another gasp rose from everyone in the room. Like General McDaniel, I realized immediately that the Transport Class was a lucky break.

Then it came, when many were afraid it wouldn't, with a huge and growing flash of light that expanded until it completely blinded our monitor. We knew then that General McDaniel and his people had cooked off the Phoenix, but we still had no way to assess the damage to the Gomers. Switching to various positions and other monitors, it took almost three minutes to find a craft or station that was still sending us a signal. What we finally got from a near-Earth Stealth Satellite wasn't very detailed, but it did show a huge amount of wreckage in and around the point where the Moon Class Ships were intercepted. We had no other telemetry indicating that the Moon Class Ships were still headed our way. There was no way to know for sure whether that was because they were destroyed, or that we just had all our sensors knocked out. Then there was still the question of where did the rest of the Gomer fleet go?

General Roberts, after almost 10 minutes, turned to me and shrugged his shoulders. Turning in my seat, I saw General Whitney frantically working the lines to any observer stations that could have seen something. Universally, we had little information other than a strong belief that we'd taken out the largest threat, and that was finally the information I passed onto the President and then to the representatives of the United Nations. As for much else, we were as blind as bats, and about as informed as mushrooms. Early on, even before contacting the President, I contacted General Greene at ASOC, and had him stand down the potential suicide mission. Instead, I ordered him to disable the weapons for the moment, and send out a reconnaissance in strength. Now it was time to try and get some eyes out there to find the Gomers, if they were still around, and to report back to us. In the meantime, we could not stand down any of our conventional or special airborne forces. As the minutes turned to hours, and then days, we still had to continue working on contingency plans in case the Gomers were still on the way.

As history teaches, wars seldom, if ever, end cleanly. The prior World Wars of the Twentieth Century certainly didn't end that way, and this one wasn't going to be any different. In some ways, perhaps these Gomer Wars were worse, since these were wars where the entire Globe was fighting to exist. This was our third time down this road, and we'd sincerely hoped that some of us had learned something from it all. We had no real geopolitical end game, since survival was our only end game, and there were no real politics involved. Sure, Russia and President Dubronin had a dissident issue, and there were collaborators in other countries as well, to include ours.

For example, our own Mr. Adams and Mr. Lombardi were eventually dealt with through the American Justice system as domestic terrorists. Dusting off the old Patriot Act provisions, these individuals were tried, convicted, and eventually executed for their crimes of treason. I guess what struck me the most was that these people weren't just traitors to their country, but to their entire species. I will admit to insisting that the civilian, as opposed to the military, justice system handle their cases, but it was mainly because I did not want to be accused of influencing the process. I provided testimony, but it was a jury that decided their fate.

In Russia and other parts of the world, the dissident survivors, who did not have large numbers after the last attacks on the Enclaves, were dealt with by their governments. Some were more harshly treated than others, but at the end of the day, this was a decision to be made by their peers and, unlike after World War II, we stayed out of those decisions. The International War Crimes Commission was left by the wayside, since these traitors to the human race were dealt with as criminals within their own countries. As with us, they were tried under their own civil justice systems and, as you can imagine, very few would ever be allowed to rejoin the human race.

During this same time frame, ASOC ships were fanned out in a constant search for the Gomers that might be lurking somewhere in our Solar System. The rest of us were engaged in rebuilding, but we all still remained ever watchful and on alert. It would take almost three months to verify that Neptune and Triton were no longer bases for the Gomers, and that there were no more Moon Class Ships hiding anywhere in our Solar System. Unfortunately, we did not have the same level of confidence about the location of the balance of the now-missing Gomer fleet. We could only content ourselves that wherever the rest of those Gomers went, it wasn't here, which is hardly comforting to a planet that was as ravaged as we were after three wars with them.

It would be several more years before things even remotely appeared to be returning to any semblance of normal. The President, Martin Blanchard, was now out of office, but there was no question that he was still working as the elder statesman in keeping things together among the world's nations. Other leaders, such a President Dubronin, were now completely on board with maintaining a truly global defense capability and, under their leadership, some of their executive powers over their own militaries were delegated to the Global Defense Forces. Thanks to the Gomers, we were now building a force for the future, and were doing it by piggy backing on the equipment and technology that the Gomers had left behind. What we could repair, we did repair, and what we could improve, we improved. We also maintained the ground, naval, and air forces as an Allied Effort in case the outer defenses failed.

Oddly enough, this wasn't always easy, since neighbors have disputes, but for the first time in recorded history, the world's individual nations seemed to be pulling together. I guess it took the near-extinction of the human race to achieve this, but every time a nation felt as though it was going to have a war like dispute with a neighbor, we would encourage our ASOC Personnel to put on a display of technology as a reminder of what was, and what could have been, had we not all worked together.

As you might imagine, this story is far from over. The birth of the Global Defense Forces arose from the ashes of this third war and, while there is a new generation to lead it to the outer edges of our Solar System, it is a generation that learned the hard way. It is a generation that was forged in the fires of the most epic conflict in recorded human history. At least we hoped it was the most epic, since it is the job of every soldier, sailor, and airman to keep these things from happening. With fingers crossed, what comes next will be driven by them, or defended by them. For me, it was now about spending time with my lovely bride, my children, and my grandson. I was more than happy to consult and help where I could, but I really wanted to enjoy my time left as just an old guy with a family. At least that was my genuine hope, but I'd held that hope before, and you see where that got me.

APPENDICES

APPENDIX I

Order of Battle

US NAVAL FORCES
PACIFIC FLEET

3rd Fleet, Battle Groups
    TF-31.1
BB   USS Alabama
CG   USS Mobile Bay
DDG USS Howard
USS Spruance

    TF-31.2
BB   USS New Jersey
CG   USS Port Royal
DDG USS Fitzgerald
USS Higgins

7th Fleet, Battle Groups
    TF-71.1
BB   USS Missouri
CG   USS Vincennes
DDG USS O'Brien
USS O'Kane

    TF-71.2
BB   USS Alaska
CG   USS Antietam
DDG USS McCampbell
USS Stethem

    TF-74
CVN USS Ronald Reagan
USS George Washington
LHD USS Boxer
USS Makin Island
CG   USS Princeton
USS Chosin
USS Valley Forge

TF-38	TF-78
	DDG USS Russell
	USS Benfold
	USS Cushing

TF-38	TF-78
CVN USS Nimitz	CVN USS John C. Stennis
USS Carl Vinson	USS Kitty Hawk
CG USS Shiloh	CG USS Lake Erie
DDG USS Shoup	DDG USS John Paul Jones
USS Hopper	USS Decatur
USS Briscoe	

ATTACK SUBMARINES ASSIGNED TO THE PACIFIC FLEET:

SSN 688 Los Angeles
SSN 698 Bremerton
SSN 701 La Jolla
SSN 705 City of Corpus Christi
SSN 707 Portsmouth
SSN 711 San Francisco
SSN 713 Houston
SSN 715 Buffalo
SSN 716 Salt Lake City
SSN 717 Olympia
SSN 718 Honolulu
SSN 721 Chicago
SSN 722 Key West
SSN 724 Louisville
SSN 725 Helena
SSN 752 Pasadena
SSN 754 Topeka
SSN 758 Asheville
SSN 759 Jefferson City
SSN 762 Columbus
SSN 763 Santa Fe

SSN 770 Tucson
SSN 771 Columbia
SSN 772 Greeneville
SSN 773 Cheyenne

ATLANTIC FLEET

2nd Fleet Battle Groups,
    TF - 20.1
BB   USS Montana
CG   USS San Jacinto
DDG USS Morton DDG
USS Gregg
USS Inoye

    TF - 20.2
BB   USS Wisconsin
CG   USS Vicksburg CG
DDG USS Oscar Austin
USS Ignatius

    TF-25
BB   USS North Carolina
CVN USS Abraham Lincoln
LHD USS Wasp
USS Bataan
USS Iwo Jima
CG   USS Gettysburg
USS Vella Gulf
USS Thomas S. Gates
DDG USS Bulkeley
USS Laboon
USS The Sullivans
USS Porter

4th Fleet Battle Groups
    TF-40.1
BB   USS Massachusetts
CG   USS Monterey
USS Stout
USS O'Bannon

    TF-40.2
BB   USS Iowa
USS Cape St. George
DDG USS Winston Churchill
USS Mitscher

TF-27
CVN USS Harry Truman
USS Dwight D. Eisenhower
CG   USS Hue City
USS Ticonderoga
DDG USS Arleigh Burke
USS Ramage
USS Ross
USS Thorn

TF-47
CVN USS Theodore Roosevelt
USS G. H. W. Bush
CG   USS Anzio
USS Yorktown
DDG USS Barry
USS Carney
USS Mahan

ATTACK SUBMARINES ASSIGNED TO THE ATLANTIC FLEET:

SSN 690 Philadelphia
SSN 699 Jacksonville
SSN 700 Dallas
SSN 706 Albuquerque
SSN 708 Minneapolis-Saint Paul
SSN 709 Hyman G. Rickover
SSN 710 Augusta
SSN 714 Norfolk
SSN 719 Providence
SSN 720 Pittsburgh
SSN 723 Oklahoma City
SSN 750 Newport News
SSN 751 San Juan
SSN 753 Albany
SSN 755 Miami
SSN 756 Scranton
SSN 757 Alexandria
SSN 760 Annapolis
SSN 761 Springfield
SSN 764 Boise
SSN 765 Montpelier
SSN 766 Charlotte

SSN 767 Hampton
SSN 768 Hartford
SSN 769 Toledo

ALLIED GROUND FORCES
General Edward Whitney, USA (Atlantic Command)

1st Allied Airborne Army - General Jerry Larkin, US
    XVIII Airborne Corps. - Major General James Sturdivant
        17th Airborne Division
        82nd Airborne Division
        101st Airborne (Airmobile) Division
    IX Airborne Corps. - Major General John J. Powers
        11th Airborne Division
        13th Airborne Division
        108th Airborne (Airmobile) Division
    Russian Airborne Forces - General Igor Sevitch (6 numbered divisions)
    UK Airborne - General Peter Farley, UK
        1st Airborne Division (UK)
        6th Airborne Division (UK)
    XXXII Corps. Lieutenant General Harmon Clarkson, US
        145th Airborne Division
        15th Air Defense Brigade (Gmr)
        18th ADA Brigade (Conventional)

21ST ALLIED ARMY GROUP - General Jerry Larkin, US
(Left to command Abn Army)
    General Walter G. Crouse, US

<u>FIRST ARMY - Lieutenant General Daniel Mickelson</u>
    II Corps. - Major General Clyde Stubben
        5th Infantry Division
        36th Infantry Division
        4th Armored Division
    V Corps. - Major General Marvin Russell
        6th Infantry Division
        42nd Infantry Division
        7th Armored Division

XXI Corps. - Major General Michael Decatur
    10th Mountain Division
    102nd Infantry Division
    9th Armored Division

THIRD ARMY - Lieutenant General S. L. Simpson
    VII Corps. - Major General William H. Prosser
        99th Infantry Division
        106th Infantry Division
        1st Armored Division
    VIII Corps. - Major General Alvin Simpkins
        8th Infantry Division
        18th Infantry Division
        8th Armored Division

SEVENTH ARMY (Allied composite Army)- Lieutenant General Karl Kessler, Germany
    I French Corps. - Lieutenant General Henri Reneau
    I German Corps. - Major General Hermann Smetzler
    II German Corps. - Major General Rudolph Heinz
    I Spanish Corps. - Major General Francisco Carlos

EIGHTH BRITISH ARMY (UK) - General Sir. Edward Fitzhugh Mallory
    X Corps. - Lieutenant General David Thatcher, Royal Army
    XX Corps. - Lieutenant General William Houser, Royal Army
    XXX Corps. - Lieutenant General Stephen Wintergable, Royal Canadian Forces

PACIFIC THEATER
42nd ALLIED ARMY GROUP - General Richard Davis, USA

SIXTH ARMY - Lieutenant General Manuel "Manny" Ortiz, USA
    III Amphibious Corps. - Major General D. E. James, USMC
        1st Marine Division
        2nd Marine Division

3rd Marine Division
15th Marine Expeditionary Unit (MEU)
XIVth Corps. - Major General David Chandler
    2nd Cavalry Division
    2nd Armored Division
    25th Infantry Division

EIGHTH ARMY (US) - General Winfield David Smith
    I Corps. - Major General John Montgomery
        4th Infantry Division
        7th Infantry Division
        3rd Armored Division
    X Corps. - Major General Thomas Westerman
        28th Infantry Division
        29th Infantry Division
        5th Armored Division
    XXIV Corps. - Major General George Foster
        1st Cavalry Division
        24th Infantry Division
        77th Infantry Division

TENTH ARMY - General Roberto Guzeman, USA
    XX Corps. - Major General Mark Scutarski, USA
        21st Infantry Division
        12th Infantry Division
        14th Infantry Division
        10th Armored Division
    I Australian/New Zealand Corps. - Lieutenant General Edmond Hurt, Australian Army
    I Japanese Corps. - Lieutenant General Hideki Tochihara

CHINESE ARMY GROUP- General Xi Jintao, PLAGF

Composed of 18 Group Armies, One through Eighteenth Army Groups. Each Group is approximately the same composition and strength as a US Corps. These Sixteen Corps sized elements are the equivalent of Six Armies, and are all under the command of the Chinese Forces. Relations with the PLAGF and the PLAN, are excellent under the current conditions, and both forces have had no difficulty in working with the Allied Command as a semi autonomous grouping of forces.

RUSSIAN ARMY GROUP - General Vladimir Petrofsky, Russian Federation

Composed of 10 Field Armies, the Field Armies were each were organized into Four Corps, with Four Divisions assigned to each Corps. The strengths of each element was about 75% the strength of a comparable United States Army Force.

ALLIED NAVAL FORCES

CHINESE NAVAL GROUP - Admiral Zao Tse Hue, PLAN, is providing a number of diesel submarines, and frigate/corvette size surface escorts. All operating in conjunction with the US 7th Fleet, during the Anti-Gomer operations.

RUSSIAN NAVAL GROUPS - Admiral Viktor Suchkov, Russian Federation, Consisted of the Black Sea, Baltic Sea, and Pacific fleets. While there were a few surviving surface combatants, most were of the destroyer or frigate types. The largest surviving surface ship was a single Missile Cruiser, the Varyag, in the Russian Pacific Fleet. The majority of naval assets were 15 nuclear powered submarines, and 20 diesel/electric submarines. These assets were relied on heavily in their respective areas to assist in the escort of transports in conjunction with the applicable US Fleet for that theater of operations.

JAPANESE NAVY - Admiral Tanaka Sato, JPNDF. Japan contributed 15 additional Destroyer class escorts, mostly US Arleigh Burke Class, which operated in conjunction with both the US Navy's 7th and 3rd Fleets.

ROYAL AUSTRALIAN NAVY - Admiral David Hugh McDermott, RAN. Australian naval forces, were comprised of a number of submarine and surface vessels, to include sealift and escort type ships. These forces also were operating as part of the US Navy's 3rd and 7th Fleets, providing both escorts and active participation in all seaborne operations.

US AIR FORCES

First Air Force	Lieutenant General L. L. West
Second Air Force	Lieutenant General G. Foster
Eighth Air Force	Lieutenant General T. J. Lilly
Tenth Air Force	Lieutenant General A. Brooks
Eleventh Air Force	Lieutenant General C. C. Nowak
Twelfth Air Force	Lieutenant General S. Kaminski (trsfr'd)
	Lieutenant General D. F. Stout
Eighteenth Air Force	Lieutenant General R. S. Young
United States Air Forces Southern Command	Lieutenant General F. R. Casner

ALLIED AIR FORCES

RAF -	General Sir. Harold Manning
RCAF -	General David Horn
RAAF -	General Donald Taviner
Danish AF -	General Bjorg Christian
Norwegian AF -	General Lars Hanson
Finland AF -	General Svork Sevotstock
France AF -	General Robert Marcel Delamey
German AF-	General Heinrich Hoefer

PLAAF-   General Tsi Xi Woo
Russian Fed. AF-   General Pyotr Nemerov
Russian Strategic Missile Forces - General Mikail Tuporovski

STRATEGIC RESERVE US FORCES

Naval Forces: (Adm. Charles Steadman)
    Atlantic: SSBN USS West Virginia
                            USS Louisiana
                            USS Florida
                            USS Georgia
    Pacific: SSBN USS Pennsylvania
                            USS Kentucky
                            USS Ohio
                            USS Michigan
    10th Fleet (Attack)
              SSN   USS Virginia
                      USS Texas
                      USS Hawaii
                      USS North Carolina

Air Forces: (General Quentin J. Thayer, Jr.)
    14th Air Force, Vandenberg, CA, General Randolph McDaniel

Allied Special Operations Command - General Daniel Greene, US
USSOCOM
    JSOC
        1st SFOD-D
        2nd SFOD-D
        75th Ranger Regiment (3 Battalions)
        95th Ranger Regiment (3 Battalions)
        160th SOAR
        USAF Special Operations Wing
        Seal Teams, USN
            Seal Team 2
            Seal Team 6
            Seal Team 8

SAS
> RC SAS/Armed Forces
> Australian SAS
> Danish/Finland/Sweden/Norway Special Operators to operate in the Arctic Regions, in conjunction with indigenous recruited personnel.

US Special Forces
> 1st SF Group
> 3rd SF Group
> 5th SF Group
> 7th SF Group
> 10th SF Group
> 19th SF Group
> 20th SF Group

US Artillery/Gomer Batteries (ASOC) +
> 101st Gmr Arty Brigade *
> 202nd Gmr Arty Brigade
> 303rd Gmr Arty Brigade
> 110th Gmr Arty Brigade
> 120th Gmr Arty Brigade
> 121st Gmr Arty Brigade
> 145th Gmr Arty Brigade
> 173rd Gmr Arty Brigade
> 181st Gmr Arty Brigade
> 210th Gmr Arty Brigade
> 804th Gmr Arty Brigade
> 903rd Gmr Arty Brigade
> 1101st Gmr Arty Brigade
> (Each Gmr Arty Brigade is comprised of three battalion of three Batteries apiece. Each Battery is comprised of 1 Main Gmr Gun and 3 ADA Gmr Guns; a Battalion is 4 Main Guns with 12 ADA pieces; while the Brigade is 12 Main Guns with 36 ADA pieces.)

+ Additional Gmr Arty Brigades were assigned to various key locations, and are NOT listed here, but were instead base forces for New Washington, SAHQ, various key ports around CONUS, and the New Pentagon. There were, at the conclusion of the war, an additional 40 such additional Brigade sized units, which were apportioned to deploying units as follows: One Brigade assigned to each US Army Group HQ, one Brigade assigned to each US Army HQ, and an additional Brigade assigned to each Corps HQ. (Ultimately this was roughly one Battalion for each Operational Combat Division.)

FOURTH ARMY (US) (CONUS)(Deployable) **General Walter G. Crouse, USA left to command 21st Army Group. Replaced by General James E. Fien.**

    IV Corps.   Lieutenant General Howard Masters (CONUS Reserve)
        45th Infantry Division (Conus Security) (Security Reserve)
        50th Infantry Division (Conus Security) (East Coast Port Security)
        98th Infantry Division (Conus Security) (New Washington Area)
    XXII Corps.   Lieutenant General Phillip Travis (Strategic Reserve)(Infantry)
        63rd Infantry Division (Conus Security) (Allied Hq area)
        68th Infantry Division (Conus Security) (New Pentagon area)
        51st Infantry Division (West Coast Port Security)
    XV Corps.   Lieutenant General Larry Waxman (Strategic Reserve)(Armor)
        20th Armored Division
        21st Armored Division
        23rd Armored Division

SECOND ARMY (US) (CONUS)(Training) - General Willard Washington
    XXXI Corps. Lieutenant General James E. Fien (Advanced Unit Training/USAR/NG Training) Promoted and assumed Command of Fourth Army. Replaced by Lieutenant General Harvard A. Katz.

        107th Infantry Division (Tng)
        59th Infantry Division (Tng)
        14th Armored Division (Tng)
        73rd Aviation Brigade (Tng)
        121st Artillery Brigade (Tng)
        339th Engineer Brigade (Tng)
        1st OPFOR/GOMER Group
        293rd Artillery Brigade/School (Gmr)
        803rd Artillery Brigade/School (Conventional/S&P)
        170th Special Tactics/Research Detachment/School
        JFK Warfare Center and School

    XXXIII Corps. Lieutenant General April S. Freeman (f/k/a TRADOC)

        Armored Center and School
        Infantry Center and School
        Engineer Center and School
        Artillery Center and School
        Aviation Center and School
        Logistics Center and School
        Medical Center and School
        ADA Center and School
        C&GSC
        War College,
        Center for Strategic Studies

APPENDIX II

Key Personnel

❦

NATIONAL COMMAND AUTHORITY

President Martin "Marty" Blanchard
National Science Advisors: Dr. Anthony Abramson, Dr. Walter J. Clarkson, and Dr. George Marvin; Dr. Holly Patrick
Secretary of State   The Honorable Timothy Case
Secretary of Defense   The Honorable Richard Todd
National Security Advisor: Dr. Henrich Khelm (KIA)

SUPREME ALLIED COMMAND

Commander: General of the Army, Michael "Mighty Mouse" Patrick, USA
Deputy Commander: General Edward "Whit" Whitney, USA

Aides: Lieutenant Colonel T. G. Fellers, USAF; Captain Alexander Dubronin, Russian Federation;

Chief of the Allied Staff: Lieutenant General T. James "T-J" Roberts, USA

Chief of Allied Air Ops: General Samuel Kaminski, USAF
Chief of Allied Logistics: General David Marvin Clark, USA (also Rear Detachment Commander, SAHQ).

Chief of Allied Naval Ops:	Admiral Carl Lynch, USN
Chief of Allied Intelligence:	General David Campbell, AUS Army
Chief of Pacific Planning:	Rear Admiral Li Dejiang, PLAN, China
Chief of Atlantic Planning:	Vice Admiral Klaus Blucher, German Navy.
Chief of Allied Spec. Ops:	General Daniel Greene, Jr., USA
Deputy:	Major General James Anawak, Canadian Forces
Deputy:	Major General Sir. Martin Talbot, SAS, UK
Deputy:	Brigadier General Bjorg Christenson, Norway
Deputy:	Brigadier General Deacon Jones, USA, (Liaison, SAHQ).
Russian Liaison Officer:	Colonel General Gregor Motilkov, Russian Army

US - JOINT CHIEFS OF STAFF

CHAIRMAN:	General of the Army, Michael Patrick, USA
Vice Chairman:	General William C. Mahan, USAF
ARMY:	General Edward "Whit" Whitney, USA
NAVY:	Admiral Charles "Chuck" Steadman, USN
AIR FORCE:	General Quentin Thayer, USAF
MARINE Corps:	General Albert C. Durham, USMC
Director of the Joint Staff:	Lieutenant General Stephen C. Carpenter, USMC

J-1	Major General Drew Sullivan, USMC
J-2	Rear Admiral Albert H. King, USN
J-3	Major General Alan E. Townsend, USA
J-4	Major General Thomas Jackson, USA
J-5	Major General Stephen Hickman, USAF
J-6	Major General R. E. Caughman, USAF
J-7	Major General Thomas Moss, USMC
J-8	Rear Admiral Anthony Brinkman, USN
J-9	Major General Hank Carter, USAR

CPSIA information can be obtained
at www.ICGtesting.com
Printed in the USA
BVHW072325050721
611166BV00006B/158

9 781637 672532